LET THE BONES BE CHARRED

A STELLA COLE THRILLER

ANDY MASLEN

TYTON PRESS

For the cops:
Andy, Jen, Ross, Sean, Simon and Trevor.

So heap on the wood and kindle the fire. Cook the meat well, mixing in the spices; and let the bones be charred.
Ezekiel, 24:10 (New International Version)

'All that I am, or hope to be, I owe to my angel mother.'
Abraham Lincoln

1

THEN

Malachi awoke and knew immediately that trouble lay ahead.

The sheet beneath him was wet and he could smell the tang of urine. Before he could even think how to escape his punishment, Mother appeared by his bedside. She grabbed him by his skinny bicep and dragged him from the narrow bed.

'You dirty little boy!' she shouted. 'Lying in your own filth. Not even trying to be good. As God is my witness, I will teach you to behave yourself like a decent human being. You are five years old. You should have stopped this disgusting behaviour years ago.'

She dragged him down the hallway. He stumbled and cried out in pain as his arm twisted in its socket.

'Don't, Mother!' he screamed.

She clouted him on the side of the head.

'How dare you shout at me! Remember the fifth commandment. What is it?'

'Honour thy mother and thy father.'

'Well do it, then.'

She pushed open the door to the spare bedroom. The room was

devoid of furniture. Not even a carpet softened the hard-edged cube, although thick, plum-red velvet curtains kept the outside world where it belonged. Outside.

In the centre of the bare boards stood a six-foot-tall wooden post, eight inches in diameter. It had been mounted on a sturdy platform which was screwed down through the floorboards and into the joists. To stabilise the post, a braided steel wire ran through a neat hole drilled through it, three inches from the top. The wire was secured to eyebolts in opposite walls and strung to a humming tension with heavy-duty galvanised turnbuckles.

The boy struggled half-heartedly. He knew it was pointless. Mother was so much stronger than him. For now. And the punishments weren't usually painful. More uncomfortable, he supposed. Though he hated the feeling of powerlessness they imposed upon him.

'Put your hands behind you,' his mother said.

He complied, interlacing his fingers around the pole. He felt her rough hands tying the knots that bound his wrists. Swore to himself, once again, that there would come a reckoning. A Judgement Day.

When she'd finished, she came round to stand in front of him. Bent closer so he could smell the alcohol on her breath, see the fine hairs on her cheeks where the grains of powder had caught.

'The Christian saints endured so much suffering for their faith. Yet you cannot even live like a civilised human being amongst all this luxury we provide for you.'

She turned and left him there, although she didn't close the door.

When she returned, she was carrying a kitchen knife. And she had the strange twist to her lips that he'd christened 'the danger smile'.

There were other times after that. Mother was determined to instil in the boy the correct attitude to faith. Obedience. Self-discipline. Chastity.

The first time she touched him while he was lashed to the post he recoiled, earning himself an extra three hours in the room on his own. He passed the time by going into his head, an increasingly troubled place but one where he could escape Mother's endless sermons, strictures and alcohol-fuelled fits of weeping self-pity.

Once, he walked into the bathroom to wash his hands before tea and stumbled on his mother, naked, one foot up on the edge of the bath. Her breasts were white and flabby. She was looking down at herself. Holding something in her right hand and sort of scraping it against the hair on her – *fanny!* He said the word in his head. The other boys said it out loud at school, down the field, far from the buildings, where the teachers wouldn't hear. And worse words, too.

She looked up at him and her eyes blazed so it looked as if they would burst from her face. She snatched a towel from the rail and covered herself up.

Red in the face, she didn't scream as he'd expected her to. She just pointed to the door across the hall.

'Go and wait for me,' she said, in a voice all the more terrifying for being so quiet.

She tied his hands behind the post, then fetched the kitchen shears she used to cut up chickens. She dragged his trousers and underpants all the way down round his ankles, then pulled his penis out with her thumb and forefinger, so hard he thought it might actually come away. He didn't cry out. He knew better. Mother opened the jaws of the shears and placed them around the pathetically stretched length of tissue.

She looked him in the eye.

'You are filth. Don't you know it is a sin to do what you just did? Would you lie with your own mother? Fornicate with her?'

He tried to answer in a way that would placate her, but it was so hard to know which words and phrases would achieve the desired effect and which would only enrage her. Her eyes were glistening and her cheeks flushed.

'No, Mother,' he said, finally, in a whisper, feeling sick with the anxiety of losing his 'thing'.

'No, Mother,' she repeated.

3

She drew the tip of her tongue over her top lip, then straightened suddenly and withdrew the shears.

'What you saw, you must unsee. What you thought, you must unthink. Lust is a deadly sin, as well you know.'

Then she left, towel clumsily wrapped around her.

A little while later, just as he was wondering whether he'd be able to control his bladder any longer, and fearing what would happen if he couldn't, the door opened. She was standing there. Slowly, she came towards him, her eyes full of pity. She moved behind him and began untying the knots.

2

NOW

MONDAY 13TH AUGUST 12.05 P.M.

Detective Chief Inspector Stella Cole watched, frowning, as bloody foetuses were shoved into the women's clenched faces. The TV news showed them pushing the horribly realistic dolls aside and hurrying into the clinic.

A female reporter's voice spoke over the footage.

'LoveLife's pickets have been on duty at The Sackville Centre for the past week. The centre claims on its website that it offers advice on sexual health and contraception, but the protesters I spoke to earlier have a different take on it.'

The picture cut to a woman wearing a cream blouse and an angry expression on an unmade-up face, helmeted by coarse-looking iron-grey hair.

'We are sure in our hearts of one thing. That place,' she jerked a thumb over her shoulder, 'is an abortion clinic. Pure and simple. A murder factory!'

The director cut back to the unfolding events.

'Look at it closely,' Niamh Connolly, the charity's glamorous chief executive said, speaking through a megaphone. 'Beyond those walls, unborn babies are being slaughtered. It is nothing more than a whited sepulchre. But no amount of modern design or pristine paint can mask the stench of death within.'

Stella had seen Niamh Connolly on TV before. It seemed to her that the CEO knew her swept-back blonde hair and well-maintained good looks made her a magnet for the TV cameras.

'Mrs Connolly, aren't you actually restricting these women's rights to have what is, after all, a perfectly legal procedure?' the TV reporter asked.

Niamh smiled as if to say, *it's OK that you're stupid*. She waved her left hand at the protesters who at the time were offering leaflets to a hunched young woman walking up the path to the clinic's solid-looking front door.

'Nobody's restricting anyone's rights, Janine, except the doctors and nurses inside that building, who are denying unborn children their right to life. Because let's remind ourselves of something. The overarching document that enshrines people's rights is called the Universal Declaration of Human Rights.

"Now the two words that really matter in that title are 'Universal' and 'Human'. Its drafters didn't call it the *Partial* Declaration of Human Rights. Nor did they call it the Universal Declaration of *Women's* Rights.

"So unless you are going to deny that a foetus is human, in which case I would invite you to tell your viewers which species you believe a foetus belongs to. Or you're going to say that although a human foetus is *indeed* human, it is not part of the universality of the human race. Then I think you have to agree with me that a child, even an unborn child, has the same rights as every other human being. And first of all of these is the right to life.'

The young reporter sounded flustered. Stella felt a degree of sympathy. She was just doing her job, after all.

'But your people are—'

'I'm sorry, I must interrupt you there, Janine. Those people are not "my people",' – she made air quotes – 'they have volunteered their time and their prayers to speak up for those who have no voice of their own. I do not employ them.'

'But you organise them. You encourage them.'

'No. I offer them my help, my support, my prayers, and the resources of LoveLife. They have chosen to exercise their right to free speech. As have those misguided souls.' Niamh pointed at a crowd of about thirty counter-protesters who were waving placards asserting a woman's right to choose. 'I take it, as a journalist, you're not in favour of restricting freedom of expression?'

'Of course not. But they are harassing women who may not even be thinking of having an abortion.'

'And good for those women if that's true. Good for them! But as everybody who lives in Mitcham knows, The Sackville Centre is one of the biggest abortion clinics in South London. Legally, since you are fond of quoting the law, a baby has been defined in case law as a gift from God. As a devout Christian who draws her inspiration from God, I believe it is not just wrong but evil to take that gift and treat it as a tumour. Something to be cut out of a woman's body and dropped into a bloody bucket to die.'

At that point, and presumably fearing a tongue-lashing from her producer, as she was reporting for a lunchtime show, Janine Everly ended the interview with a hurried thank-you.

Stella switched the TV off and changed into her running gear. She'd worked the last ten days straight and was enjoying the prospect of two days off.

As she entered that blissful, flowing state of mind that arrived when her heart and lungs had adjusted to the new demands she placed on them, she thought back to the news item. She wasn't opposed to abortion. Not exactly. She knew plenty of women who'd had them. But she also carried around with her the grief of losing her own baby daughter. For her, 'getting rid' of unwanted babies carried a devastating emotional charge.

Even though Stella had killed the people responsible for Lola's murder, and that of her daddy, the pain still lodged in her heart like

7

a thorn. She'd grown a strong, protective sheath around it, but it was still there. Once she had thought it would kill her. Her colleagues thought it had.

———

Stella would never forget the day she came back from the dead. On March 5th 2012, her boss, Callie McDonald, had convened the Murder Investigation Command on the fifth floor of Paddington Green Police Station at 8.00 a.m. with a promise of 'some very good news indeed'.

The whole team, upwards of fifty detectives, crime analysts, forensics officers and civilian employees, were gathered in the CID office. Most were sitting on tables or standing. A few of the older detectives leaned back in their chairs as if to say, 'go on, then, show me something I haven't seen before'.

Callie had told Stella to come in at 8.05 precisely: they'd synchronised their watches. She'd followed orders, walking quickly but not fast, through the civilian-staffed reception area, before swiping her Metropolitan Police ID at the access-controlled doors leading to the rest of the station. The goggle-eyed stares and dropped jaws her passage through the ground floor occasioned made her stomach flip.

But it was the reaction from her former colleagues that was the real concern. Would they go into shock? Cry? Shout at her? Laugh? Scream? She had to admit to herself, she had absolutely no idea. After all, it wasn't every day you got to meet a colleague the new boss had told you had been run over and killed while escaping from a secure psychiatric unit.

She elected to take the stairs rather than the lift, reasoning that she'd be less likely to meet someone on her way up to the fifth floor and, even if she did, it would be orders of magnitude less uncomfortable – *Uncomfortable, Stel? How about unbelievable?* – than being trapped in a toilet-cubicle-sized stainless-steel box.

She arrived on the fifth-floor landing breathing easily: in the previous few months she'd walked almost six hundred miles from the US-Canadian border to Duluth, Minnesota.

Wishing she'd not had anything to eat for breakfast, she walked along the corridor towards the double doors at the far end. Stella peered in through the left-hand square of wire-reinforced glass positioned at head-height in the plain wooden door. Everyone bar Callie had their backs to her. Callie was speaking, making expressive gestures with her hands. Stella felt a sharp pang of grief as she saw that a new detective was sitting at her old DS's desk. Frankie O'Meara and Stella had been a team. Then their boss, the now-dead Detective Chief Superintendent Adam Collier, had murdered her. He'd shot her with a police-issue Glock 17 at the house of a former gangster, then staged the scene to look like an arrest gone wrong.

She leaned closer to the crack between the two doors and heard Callie clear her throat.

'Now, in setting up the Special Investigations Unit, I realised I would need to call on the very best detectives I could find. And... and there is one officer in particular whom I just couldn't do without. She'll be my right-hand woman as well as heading a team of her own as DCI.'

Stella looked around the room and saw, with a sinking feeling, that a few of the detectives were looking round at DI Roisin Griffin, who was struggling to keep a smile off her face. Stella's heart was bumping in her chest and she suddenly realised Callie would have to change her plan. *There's no way she'll be able to keep order once I go in.*

Callie resumed her speech.

'Now, some of you attended the memorial service for Stella last year.'

Eyes that had been on her a moment earlier were now downcast.

'And I know you thought you were doing right by her.'

People looked up and frowned at her.

Stella caught her eye again and thought, *This isn't going well at all. Abandon ship! Women and children first.*

'Oh, shit!' Callie said with a sigh. 'Look, there's no easy way to say this. I, we – no – *I* lied to you. About Stella, I mean. She's not dead.'

The room erupted. People were shouting, launching questions at Callie. The cynics had pulled their feet off the desks and were leaning forwards, mouths open. Callie simply looked over at Stella and beckoned her in. Stella inhaled deeply, plastered on a smile she wasn't feeling and stepped back into her old life.

The noise hit her like a wave. A collective gasp immediately segued into laughs, shrieks and, from one or two of the younger women in the room, sobs. Everyone leaped out of their chairs, pushed away from walls or jumped down from desks and rushed towards her. Feeling she might be trampled to death before saying as much as 'did you miss me?', she did the only thing she could think of and held her hands out in front of her, palms outstretched like Moses parting the Red Sea.

The noise decreased a little, but everyone was still talking at once. She was relieved to see that they were smiling or, in a couple of cases, laughing. Suddenly tongue-tied, despite having been awake half the night rehearsing possible openers, she said the first thing that came into her head.

'If anyone's been using my coffee mug, I'll kill them!'

Stella accepted hugs and kisses from every member of the MIC. They were firing questions at her and she gave them the answers she and Callie had cooked up between them the previous night.

'Where were you, then, if you weren't dead?'

'It was a joint operation with Lothian and Borders Police. I couldn't tell anyone for operational reasons.'

– I was in the US, killing your and my former boss for his part in the murder of my husband and baby daughter.

'When did you get back?'

'Only last week.'

– Three months ago, but I was undergoing intensive psychiatric care and psychotherapy to make sure I was sane.

'Do you know what happened to The Model?'

'Adam enjoyed his sabbatical with the FBI so much he asked them to make it permanent.'

 – He was trapped in his SUV as it sank beneath the freezing waters of a lake in Minnesota and I made sure he was dead by shooting him between the eyes.

 Shaking her head to free it of the vision of Collier with that obscene crater in the centre of his forehead, Stella ran on.

3

After answering questions from a few more reporters, Niamh drove herself back to her house on Wimbledon Parkside. She arrived at 'Valencia' at five past twelve and parked her white convertible Mini on the gravel drive beside her husband Jerry's dark-green Jaguar XJ saloon. He ran an insurance brokerage in the City of London and cycled down to the station every morning to catch the 7.38 to Waterloo.

They'd bought the house in the nineties with the proceeds of a spectacular insurance deal Jerry had closed as a new partner in the firm. A tall yew hedge shielded the occupants from passing traffic, wide entrance and exit gates the only clue that a substantial house lurked behind the evergreen foliage. While she waited for the cloth roof to lock into place with its satisfyingly muted clicks, she checked her makeup in the rear-view mirror. *Not bad for fifty-two, Niamh. Not bad at all.*

She ran LoveLife from a converted stable block that abutted the house. No secretary, no assistant, no marketing executive. She had people to organise her schedule, coordinate her social media campaigns, book meeting rooms or negotiate speaking fees, but they all worked from home, as did she. 'Just as long as I have my iPhone, I'm fine,' she liked to say to people who questioned her lack of in-house staff.

She checked it now. One meeting scheduled for 1.00 p.m. with MJ Fox, CEO, GodsGyft. Then nothing until dinner with Father Reid from The Sacred Heart at 7.30 p.m. Plenty of time for a shower and a change of clothes, then a light lunch before her visitor arrived at the house.

Even in the few steps it took her to reach the ornate oak front door from the car, the heat boiling off the pea shingle drive brought a light sheen of sweat to her top lip. Cream hydrangeas in rust-red glazed pots each side of the door were watered automatically by a computerised system Jerry controlled from an app on his phone, but even so, the flowers looked unhappy. Brown edges scarred a couple of the blossoms, and as she pulled a few dead leaves free they crackled between her fingers.

She pressed her thumb to the pad to the right of the door and waited for it to open automatically on its silent, German-engineered mechanism.

'Come on, come on, you stupid thing,' she muttered, cursing Jerry and his obsession with automating everything in the house, 'I'm getting heatstroke out here.'

As soon as the door had swung open far enough to admit her, she stepped through into the deliciously air-conditioned interior of the house and practically ran up the thickly carpeted stairs, so eager was she to cool down under the stinging jets of her wet room shower.

In her dressing room she stepped out of her skirt and hung it and the matching jacket on a hanger on the airing rail. The cream silk blouse went into the laundry hamper. Bra, knickers and tights she laid out on a second airer. The 'Niamh Connolly look' as she thought of it, and as one or two social media commentators had noticed, was part of her brand image, but in a summer like this one, extraordinarily uncomfortable. Freed from 'the look', she pirouetted clumsily in front of the full-length mirror, her arms stretched overhead to lift her breasts, before walking out of the room and into the en suite bathroom.

A noise from downstairs stopped her in mid-stride. But as the house was empty, and Niamh Connolly was not an easily scared woman, she put it down to the air-conditioning system and turned on the shower. As she paddled around on the slate floor tiles, letting the temperature-controlled water jets sluice the heat of the day from her skin, she missed a second sound, this time from the stairs. A riser creaking as the summer heat dried the wood, perhaps.

———

Twenty-five minutes later, she applied fresh daytime makeup, rather more subtle than her 'TV slap' as she called the matte foundation, eye-catching red lipstick and full-go eyes. She dressed in a pale-green linen blouse, a white skirt and soft loafers that matched her blouse, and misted her wrists, throat and cleavage with perfume. With the light fragrance of orange blossom coiling its way into her nose, she slipped on a pair of discreet emerald earrings and her beloved rose-gold Patek Philippe watch, a wedding present from her parents, and went downstairs.

She sat at the kitchen table, a glass of sauvignon blanc to her left, scrolling through her messages as she forked tuna salad into her mouth, careful to avoid catching even a morsel of the food on her lips. Mostly they were emails asking her to speak, agree to an interview, or contribute to other pro-life charities. A death threat from some loony-left, women's rights type that she moved to a folder headed 'Crazies'. And a note from her lawyer about the charity's funds.

Yes, well, that little problem should all be sorted once I've met the lovely MJ Fox, she thought, finishing the salad.

A soft click from the hall made her turn round in her chair. It sounded like the latch on the front door engaging. But that wasn't possible. She'd heard it close behind her on the way in, hadn't she?

She rose from her chair, dabbing her lips on the white napkin by her plate.

'Jerry?' she called, turning towards the kitchen door. 'Is that you, darling?'

She left the kitchen, feeling ridiculous as her eyes fell on a white marble rolling pin on the countertop and she briefly considered picking it up.

The front door was closed. Of course it was. *Silly fool, Niamh. You're getting menopausal. Now, relax. You've ten minutes before MJ gets here.*

Someone tapped her shoulder.

4

TRANSCRIPT FROM METROPOLITAN POLICE DIGITAL, VOICE-ACTIVATED RECORDER, EXHIBIT NUMBER FF/97683/SC6 1/4

Isn't this funny? Who'd have thought I'd have you of all people in my little cabin? Are you sitting comfortably? Well, lying comfortably? Then I'll begin.

Niamh screamed when I touched her shoulder. I thought she was going to faint. That or wet herself. She whirled round. I kept my wide social smile plastered across my face and extended my hand. 'Niamh?' I asked. 'I'm MJ. MJ Fox?'

She took my hand – she had to. It's like a bit of programming. Only the strongest-minded person can reject the offer of a hand to shake. 'How did you get in?' she asked me. 'Our meeting's not until one.'

I went for a sort of 'silly-me' embarrassed look. 'I know, and I'm sorry for startling you,' I said. 'The door was open, so I thought you were trying to get a through-breeze. I was just looking for your reception area when you appeared.'

Niamh smiled. She was relaxed now. It doesn't take much, believe me. She said we could talk in her office.

'Lead the way,' I said.

She took me out through the French doors to a sort of converted stable block. I became all business. I said, 'Listen, Niamh. It's too hot to make small talk. Let's cut to the chase.' Then I told her this story about how I'd made a pile when I sold my Christian app company. I said I wanted to find a way to share my good fortune. We did a bit of dancing around each other – well, you have to make it feel real, don't you? She looked as though she wanted to lean across the table and kiss me. Instead, she limited herself to a demure smile, looking up at me from beneath lowered eyelids, like Princess Diana used to do in her TV interviews.

'That is more than generous, MJ,' she said. 'I hope I can find an appropriate way to thank you.'

I said, 'Oh, I'm sure something will come up. But really, you must think of it purely as a donation from one God-fearing individual to another.'

Something about the way I said 'God-fearing' must have got to her: she frowned. Then it was gone. She dismissed the sensation that Mother Nature bestowed upon prey animals to give them a fighting chance against predators. I couldn't really blame her. Niamh, I mean, not Mother Nature. After all, it isn't every day an angel flies down and solves all your financial worries with a stroke of a pen. And who wants to think that the angel might be Lucifer and not Michael?

When I judged the moment was right, I glanced over her shoulder, and put a frown on my own face. I said, 'Is that someone in your garden? I thought I saw a man.'

She twisted round in her chair to look. I'd read in the local rag that there'd been a rumour Irish travellers were on their way from Richmond, planning to set up their caravans on the common. Then I got out of my chair and stuck her.

She cried out as the needle went in.

'Ohh.'

Like that, as if a wasp had stung her, or one of those big ones, you know, hornets. She made a feeble attempt to grab my wrist. But it was too late by then. 'What have you done?' she cried out. 'Why are you hurting me?'

I stood, keeping the pressure on the side of her neck. I came round the table and pushed down hard on her left shoulder. I pulled out the syringe and held it in front of her face where she could see it. She tried to stand, but I wasn't going to allow that. Not yet. I confess I was grinning as I pushed her back into the chair.

'Wha—' It was really funny. You know, like she'd forgotten how to speak. She tried again. 'Why you did, did do it me?' It was worse than before.

Now I was really smiling. I had her where I wanted her and I could afford to relax.

I said, 'I saw you on the TV again today. You say you draw your inspiration from God. Well, I am God's messenger. He told me to tell you he really doesn't care about you, or your cause. He told me to tell you it was time for you to learn something very, very important. He told me to tell you that he doesn't exist.' Then I led her back into the kitchen, where I dumped her in a chair.

My special cocktail of Temazepam and Ketamine made her biddable but it hadn't knocked her out. I spent ages researching the different tranquilising and anaesthetic drugs before I found the particular combination of effects I wanted. Then I stole some Temazepam from the university medical centre's pharmacy. I laughed at the thought of all those panicky, screw-loose students they have to cope with. The Special K I bought on the street round the back of the yard.

She watched me pull a carving knife from the stainless-steel block on the countertop. Then I started cutting her shirt off her. I leaned over her and she whimpered as I unsnapped the catch on her bra.

I put my briefcase on the table. She watched me lift the lid and reach inside. When my hand reappeared with my chosen instrument for her punishment, she managed to squeeze out a pathetic little whimper. As I began, her bladder let go, but that was OK. The smell doesn't bother me. Never has.

5

MONDAY 13TH AUGUST 8.00 P.M.
WIMBLEDON

Jerry Connolly returned from another successful day in the City at 8.00 p.m. He'd been out for a few cocktails with a couple of the partners and was feeling more than a little drunk. He didn't bother calling out as he entered the hall. Niamh was very good at keeping him apprised of her many and varied social engagements. He expected she'd be deep in conversation with that sanctimonious old alkie Father Reid over a decent bottle of claret that Jerry'd no doubt be paying for.

Hope you get your fair share, darling, he thought, grinning lopsidedly as he made his unsteady way into the kitchen, thinking of opening a bottle of something cold from the wine fridge. As he entered the room, he staggered a little. Then he stopped. His wife was leaning back in one of the chairs wearing what appeared to be a scarlet fringed bikini top above her skirt, which was white with a splotchy scarlet pattern of poppies

'Oh, hello, darling. I thought you were having dinner with Father Reid. Why are you dressed for the beach?'

Then reality asserted itself, in the most violent, horrifying way imaginable. The rough red ovals on her chest weren't the top half of a bikini at all. The poppies weren't flowers. And the floor and walls were spattered, streaked and puddled with red.

Jerry finally saw the plate on the table. He made a sound halfway between a groan and a cry. A hoarse, cracked sound in the still of the house that made the wine glasses ring on the dresser shelves.

He staggered back against the wall, his eyes roving all over the kitchen, anywhere but the grotesque tableau in front of him. He sat down heavily on the floor, his legs sliding out in front of him until his heels clicked on the limestone. He dragged his phone out.

'Emergency: which service do you require: police, fire, ambulance or coastguard?'

'It's my wife,' he answered in a croak. 'My wife. She's, someone has...'

'What about your wife, sir? Do you need emergency assistance?'

'Yes, yes, of course I do! She's dead, Goddammit!'

'Forgive me, sir. You sound as if you've been drinking. Are you sure she's dead? Could she be asleep?'

Collecting himself, and drawing on all his mental strength as a former Guards officer, Connolly tried one final time, articulating each word as if teaching English to a foreigner.

'Someone has removed my wife's breasts and put them on a plate on the kitchen table. So I am fairly sure she is not sleeping. Now, could you please send an ambulance and the police?'

He swept his free hand over his face, which was wet with cold, greasy sweat. He gave his name and location and after agreeing that he would wait for the police to 'attend', he ended the call and closed his eyes.

Silently, he began to cry.

6

Sweating from her run round Regent's Park, Stella stuck her front door key in the lock and once again was delighted with the smooth action as the internal mechanism rolled over, the pins lifted and the door opened. Not a crunch, not a squawk, not a refusal to move: it just opened. Unlike the crappy old five-lever mortise on her house in West Hampstead. That had been an exercise in Zen meditation every time she wanted to go out or come in. A jiggle, a lift, a fraction of a twist to the left before a firm turn clockwise and a muttered prayer.

The old house, she'd realised soon after moving in, had been nothing more than a bolthole. A refuge from the crushing grief she'd felt after Richard and Lola had been murdered. The fact that she'd been practically psychotic with grief hadn't helped. First, she'd conjured her dead baby daughter back to life again and imagined she'd hired a nanny to look after her. Then her hyper-violent, vengeful alter ego 'Other Stella' had emerged from the mirrored door of her wardrobe to point out the truth: Lola was dead and the 'baby' she was cuddling was nothing more than Lola's teddy bear, Mister Jenkins.

With the money she'd made from the sale, she'd bought a two-bedroom flat in a 1930s block on Lisson Grove. Her new place was just ten minutes' walk from Paddington Green nick, or a three-minute burn if she took her bike. Not even enough time to warm up the Triumph's engine.

From her balcony, she could actually see the top of the station, though she preferred to ignore that part of the view and let her eyes rove over the cityscape beyond.

Unlike the West Hampstead house, this, she felt, was home. Somewhere she was happy. She could be alone there. Not with her ghosts, but with her memories. She let herself into the flat, stripped off her running gear and wadded the whole lot into a ball before tossing it into the laundry basket in her bedroom. She switched on the shower and when the blue light had stopped flashing, stepped under the powerful jets and let the water ease her aching muscles.

She'd put on some weight since she'd been living in the flat. In a good way, she felt. Her boobs had returned to their post-pregnancy B-cups after almost disappearing during the months she became addicted to running to blot out her grief. And there was a bit more flesh on her hips and bum.

She'd turned thirty-nine the previous September and had reached a stage in her life where she liked the way she looked and didn't care what other people thought. She looked down. Yes, the belly was curved outwards again after the Spartan era in her early thirties when she'd actually created a rippled six-pack like a member of Team GB at the Olympics. And that, too, was OK. Good, in fact. The mini cobblestones of her abs had receded into a smooth curve, though a few crunches were all it took for her to be able to feel them again.

She dried herself and swiped a hand over the mirror above the sink. Next, she applied mascara and a little dark-brown eyeliner, a new lippy she'd bought on her way home on Saturday evening – Chanel Téméraire, a deep plum red – then got dressed for her day off. Faded skinny Gap 1969 jeans, a white T-shirt from Swedish brand Arket and black ankle boots with silver buckles.

She slotted a latte pod into the coffee machine and while it huffed and puffed, made herself two slices of toast and peanut butter. She took her second breakfast out onto the balcony and sat at the small round table to enjoy it. Below her, through the leaves of the plane trees, she watched the pedestrians, cyclists and drivers jostle for their own little piece of territory. Up here, she felt free of the competition. She could just *be*.

And now, on this fine summer's morning, she had nothing to do. A precious day off.

She looked at her watch. Nine-thirty. The high spot in her otherwise unplanned day was lunch with her best friend, Vicky Riley, a freelance journalist. Vicky had helped Stella nail the bastards who'd killed Richard and Lola, though she'd not emerged unscathed. She'd suffered the loss of her godparents in the murderous conflict between Stella and the Pro Patria Mori conspirators.

Stella finished her latte, a reasonable approximation of what she'd get from the independent coffee shop she favoured on the Edgware Road, and set the glass in its chrome cage back on the table with a little *plink*. She smiled.

Stella enjoyed being able to smile again. Even though the dreadful events of 2012 lay in the past, not a day went by when she didn't find herself thinking about the trail of destruction she, and Other Stella, had left in their wake. The bodies. Of the guilty, yes, but also the innocent. Bystanders who'd got caught in the crossfire between her and the people who'd torn her family from her.

Innocent, Stel? she wondered. *Innocent in the matter of Cole vs. PPM*, she replied. Yes, Ronnie and Marilyn Wilks were gangsters. And so was Marilyn's father, Freddie McTiernan. But they were the type of traditional criminals that the police, or the old-school coppers anyway, respected. The 'never kill women or children', 'always look after your family', 'beat up a nonce' type of villain.

And then there was Frankie. Dear, sweet Frankie O'Meara,

Stella's right hand and a friend who she could always rely on whether she'd run out of cigarettes or needed a shoulder to cry on. Until that fateful day when Frankie joined the mounting roll call of PPM victims. Not because she had escaped justice and therefore deserved to be punished, but because she'd discovered that her own detective chief superintendent, Adam Collier, was in charge of the vigilantes. He'd shot her dead to silence her.

Out of all the deaths, and there had been plenty, including that of Collier's wife, Lynne, Frankie's was the only one to really trouble Stella. She had been acting out of a sense of duty, a sense Stella shared with her and had discussed in their frequent chats over drinks, coffees or on car journeys.

It was unfashionable to talk about such things publicly nowadays: that was Stella's impression. A belief in the rule of law, in doing the right thing even at personal cost; a belief in one's country and its institutions and the need to defend them: these were mocked as being out of touch. It wasn't what you believed in that mattered so much as what you *identified* as.

The previous week, Stella, like all the coppers at Paddington Green, had received an email from the HR department. Never popular at the best of times, it was apparently soon to be renamed Organisational Competencies and Culture (OCC). Much to the delight of the older coppers, who had immediately coined a new version of the acronym to explain their reluctance to attend the many and varied workshops and 'lunch and learn' sessions: Out Catching Criminals. The email announced a new workshop, not, as yet, compulsory, on 'Trans Sensitivity and Awareness'.

'I used to know a tranny, worked as a tom down in Greenwich five years back,' DI Arran 'Jumper' Cox said, as a few of the SIU detectives were relaxing over drinks in The Green Man. They'd discovered a few years earlier during a particularly violent protest march that the pub was, literally, a stone's throw from the station. Arran was a seasoned detective with, by common consent, the best contacts book in the team.

'Oh, God, here we go,' DS Garry Haynes said, setting his pint of lager on the crisp-strewn table, a smile spreading over his dark-brown face. 'Another tale of the unexpected from Paddington Green's very own Roald Dahl.'

Over much good-natured jeering, Arran carried on, patting the air for silence.

'Toni, she used to call herself. Real name Anthony Stevens, a former Barclays Bank assistant manager until he was nicked for fraud. Made a nice little living satisfying the difficult-to-meet needs of her former colleagues. They're all pervs, you know. Bankers, accountants, solicitors—'

'Don't forget the judges!'

This from DS Stephanie Fish, known from day one in CID as 'Definitely Fit' by her male colleagues, and, as time went on, 'Def', at which point her female colleagues had adopted the moniker too. It was hard not agree. Def was twenty-five and on a fast-track programme, just as Stella had been in her own twenties. Five foot six tall, slender as a willow wand and with bright-blue eyes that dominated a heart-shaped face framed by streaky-blonde hair, she had a grace to her that belied her ferocious attitude to catching villains. More than one suspect had been lulled by her innocent-sounding enquiries into revealing more than they should have done about this blag or that kidnap plot.

'Yeah, they're the worst,' Garry said to laughter. 'They get so used to being around briefs wearing wigs and gowns, they can't get it up unless they're with a bloke in a dress!'

'You do know trans people aren't transvestites, don't you, Jumper?' Stella asked him, before finishing her glass of pinot grigio.

His eyes widened. He put his finger to the point of his stubbled chin, and grinned.

'Aren't they? You better enlighten us, then, Guv.'

'Don't be a dick, Jumper,' Def said with a smile. 'You know perfectly well what they are.'

'Yeah, well, that's not the point, is it?' Arran said, suddenly serious. 'The point is, why are we being forced to sit in some bloody conference room learning about preferred pronouns when there are rapists and terrorists driving vans into crowded pavements and psychos and bloody child killers roaming about London doing God knows what? You don't think they bother finding out what pronouns their victims prefer before gutting them and stringing them up in their basements, do you?'

Everyone knew what Arran was talking about. The previous year, the team had caught a man who had abducted, tortured and killed three teenage boys in Brixton. The victims had all been black and one had been a transsexual, which had drawn the sort of media attention commonly known within SIU as a Force-Ten Shitstorm.

'Well, that killed the mood,' Stella said, drily. 'What you need, Jumper, is another pint. Anyone else?'

It was a feature of Chief Superintendent Callie McDonald's Special Investigations Unit: the banter. All cops indulged in it. They were, in this respect, no different from doctors, nurses, firefighters and, for all they knew, quality-control managers and school crossing assistants. What did they used to call them in the pre-PC days? Lollypop ladies? But the SIU banter sometimes ran off the rails. One minute you could be telling off-colour jokes about death and destruction, the next picking the scabs off old cases where there really was nothing, not even a glimmer, of anything to laugh about.

———

Reflecting that at least the serial killer Robert Mabondebe was no longer a danger to young boys, having been sent down for life without possibility of parole, Stella idly flicked through her Facebook feed. The photos of her friends' children no longer caused a physical pain in her chest. She could read about cello exams passed or cricket cups won without wanting to scream and fling her phone against the wall. But still she wondered, as her eyes skittered across the series of posts, why people felt this compulsion to share everything that was happening in their lives. *Come on, Stel, you're getting old. You sound like Mum used to.*

The thought made her smile. Then the cheery sound of a vintage dial-phone rang out from the iPhone's little speaker.

It was the end of her day off calling.

7

TUESDAY 14TH AUGUST 10.15 A.M.

Garry. That's what the caller ID on Stella's phone displayed. Her bagman, Detective Sergeant Garry Haynes.

'Shit!' Stella said as she put the phone to her ear.

'Morning to you, too, boss. Sorry about this but we've got a case. The guvnor wants you in, pronto.'

And although part of Stella's brain regretted this intrusion into her lazy morning, another, sharper part rejoiced. Work! A new case.

'It's fine. I didn't have anything planned that I can't change. What's up?'

'Murder. Very weird murder. Happened in Wimbledon yesterday. One of the South Division MITs handed it to SIU first thing this morning.'

Stella's brain immediately started computing the factors that had brought her to work from her day off. If a Murder Investigation Team passed up the chance to investigate a homicide, that meant a number of things.

For a start, it wasn't a domestic, or a pub brawl that got out of hand. Probably not a drug-related killing, either. The Met's

Homicide and Serious Crime Command would usually assign those sorts of killings to an MIT to investigate. Witnesses were usually abundant, and if they weren't, the doer had usually been sufficiently angry, pissed, high or all three to leave his, or more rarely her, DNA and fingerprints all over the place.

It also meant that the MIT had concluded it wasn't some sort of gang hit. Drug-related murders were usually fairly straightforward. Certainly no need to call in the 'Freak Squad' as the SIU was widely known.

Garry was still speaking.

'I reckon the Wandsworth MIT guys worked the angles and realised it was out of their league, so now it's come to SIU before it screws up their metrics.'

Stella liked Garry for lots of things. His attitude to the job, which was serious and dedicated, but leavened with a mischievous streak of humour. His lack of rancour towards his ex-wife, Sandy, with whom he had an eight-year-old son, Zane. His physical courage. But one thing she couldn't abide was his management-speak.

'Please don't say metrics, Garry,' she said now, giving half a grin. 'It makes you sound like a management consultant. And tell me what makes a DCI running a South London MIT kick a juicy murder up to the SIU.'

'The victim had her breasts removed and put on a plate in front of her on her own kitchen table.'

A tremor rippled through Stella's insides. *We've got a bad one.*

'Do we have a name for the victim?'

'Yep. Hold on. Yes, Niamh Connolly. Mrs. She was the—'

'Chief Executive of LoveLife. Oh my God! I was literally watching her on the lunchtime news yesterday. She must have been killed almost straight afterwards. Right, where are you? In the office?'

'Yeah. The guvnor just called me in. Told me to call you, too. You need to get a team together.'

'All right.' She checked her watch. 'I'll be there in ten minutes.'

She stuffed the remaining morsel of toast into her mouth and washed it down with the coffee, scalding her tongue and leaving it feeling dry and furry.

In the hall, she grabbed her favourite item of clothing bar none. Her bike jacket. She'd owned it from new, buying it with money she'd saved over from her summer job the year she left school. Made by Harley Davidson, it was black with a wide horizontal orange stripe and thinner cream stripes above and below. A zip at the front and a round collar that fastened with a press stud. The intervening two decades had been good to the jacket, which had acquired a patina of creases, crinkles and the odd scuff mark.

On the way out she called Vicky.

'Hey, Stella, everything OK?'

'Not really. I have to blow you off for lunch. Something's come up.'

She knew Vicky wouldn't ask. As journalist and cop they were easy-going about sudden changes to their social arrangements.

'OK. I'll miss you but tell me all about it next time, OK?'

'OK. Gotta go.'

Jogging down Lisson Grove, Stella turned right onto Bell Street and followed it west until it joined the Edgware Road. Fried chicken aromas mingled with exhaust fumes while she waited for a gap in the traffic, which clearly would be a long time coming.

Swearing, she took her life in her hands and sprinted in front of an onrushing white transit van, earning herself an extended blast on the horn from the driver. She reached the narrow central reservation, then repeated her Olympic performance, before taking the steps two at a time up to the front doors of Paddington Green Police Station.

This had been her workplace for more years than she cared to remember. She'd been posted there the year before Richard and Lola were killed. What did that make it? Eight years? Nine? As well as the usual CID and traffic, uniforms and firearms commands, Paddington Green also held Britain's most dangerous terrorism suspects.

It wasn't unusual to be walking into the office and find yourself face to face with some bearded Muslim youth being frogmarched to the holding cells between two uniforms, yelling about Allah and infidels and the usual crap.

Either that, or one of the remaining hardcore Irish republicans with flint chips for eyes. Or, more and more these days, a shaven-headed, extreme-right nutjob ranting about immigrants and English independence, having just thrown acid into the face of a hijab-wearing mum walking her kids to school. Fuckwits, the lot of them.

She nodded to the civilian receptionists and touched her ID card to the reader pad on the side of the glass security gate.

———

SIU had the whole of the eighth floor of 'The Tower' – the multi-storey office block at the centre of the half-acre plot of land sandwiched between the Edgware Road and the Westway. The lift lady announced in her unruffled, Home Counties voice that they had reached the eighth floor.

Stella stepped into the midst of the hum and chatter of a major crimes unit in full swing. Not just the new case: Callie's unit was working on a handful of cases. Detectives, civilian database collators working on HOLMES, the second version of the Home Office Large Major Enquiry System, forensics officers and Crown Prosecution Service lawyers were buzzing around the hive.

As in every other station she'd worked in as a copper, the SIU office was a functional place, and that was being diplomatic. Basically, a rectangular, open-plan space crammed with utilitarian desks and swivel chairs, filing cabinets, walled-off conference rooms, a couple of private offices, a tea and coffee station and a few storage cupboards.

Stella had her name on the door of one of the offices, but she preferred to work in the open area and had a second desk out there.

She'd often wished that the powers-that-be had watched a few more cop shows on the telly. Then they might have housed SIU in a converted print factory or tobacco warehouse. All stripped wooden floors, Victorian ironwork and brick-arched windows giving out onto the Regent's Canal, or an atmospheric landscape of post-industrial developments.

They'd all tap their reports into gleaming, brushed-silver Macs and gather for meetings in frosted-glass meeting rooms painted in inspiring-yet-serious shades of sage-green and petrol blue.

Instead, SIU had to make do, like every other command in Paddington Green with a broad swathe of grey nylon carpet that generated enough static electricity to power the lights after dark. Ageing desktop PCs that took longer to boot up than the average bail hearing.

No original sash windows. Instead, smeary, steel-framed windows that you had to keep shut unless you enjoyed working to the roar and stink of the traffic heading into, or escaping from, the Smoke.

And for the walls, a delightfully inspiring shade of grey that, everyone agreed, Facilities had picked up cheap at an army surplus depot.

Each of the teams, which were fluid and hand-picked by the Senior Investigating Officer, based itself at one of the clusters of desks, pulling them around until they found a configuration that suited them. Floor-to-ceiling whiteboards acted as a focal point for each investigative team.

As Stella made her way to Callie's office she glanced at the boards. Each one, in its own way, painted a depressing picture of people's inability to leave each other alone.

Here, a row of photographs of young men, some taken from school photos, others from holiday pictures or corporate websites, interspersed with their blackened, greenish-yellow or bloodied faces post mortem. There, photos of terror suspects, their faces bearded or clean-shaven, white or brown, but all with the fanatical stare of a zealot.

Among the photos, crime scene reports, scribbled questions in red, blue and black dry-wipe markers, Post-its and all the assorted paraphernalia of an ongoing criminal investigation, Garry sat at his desk, reading documents enclosed in a brown folder. He looked up as Stella approached.

'Hey, boss. Sorry to put the kibosh on your day off. Lovely day for it.'

'Yeah, well. I was only going out for lunch with my best friend and then maybe a swim and some shopping and a nice evening in with a takeaway and a film on Netflix, so it's not as if I had anything planned.'

He grinned.

'Lucky I saved you. You'd have been slitting your wrists by tea-time.'

Stella looked over at Callie's glassed-in office. The boss was pacing up and down, phone clamped to her ear, nodding and waving her free hand around. She had the look her team had learned meant her normal good humour had, temporarily, deserted her. Lips pressed together, eyebrows arching even more sharply than usual. Pale cheeks. 'The wee lassie's pure ragin',' the office wags liked to say, in a passable imitation of Callie's Edinburgh accent. Though always well out of the wee lassie's earshot.

She spotted Stella and waved her in.

Stella looked at Garry, who was standing next to her, straightening his tie.

'Ready?'

Stella knocked and entered: standard protocol, established years earlier when Callie had set up the SIU. 'If my door's open, come in. If it's closed, knock,' she'd said at the first team briefing. 'If I can't help you, you'll know soon enough.'

Callie mouthed a 'sorry' and waved Stella and Garry to the chairs pushed under a round wooden table in the corner of the office. They sat and listened to Callie's end of the conversation.

'Yes, commander, I do see, which is why—'

...

'No, commander, that's—'

...

'No, sir, but with all due respect, I—'

…

'I'm putting my best people on it, so—'

…

'Yes, sir.'

…

'Yes, sir.'

…

'No, sir.'

…

'Thank you, sir.'

Two alarming spots of colour had appeared high on Callie's cheekbones. If she'd been overweight and a smoker, Stella would have been prepping to administer CPR. As it was, she merely readied herself for what was coming next.

The call ended. In the ensuing moment of quiet, Stella could hear Garry breathing beside her. Finally, Callie spoke.

'That bloody tadger will be the death of me. Commander Nick Bloody Hallwood wants this one clearing up toot de bloody sweet if you don't mind. "Especially with the mayoral elections going on, Callie,"' she added in a rough approximation of Hallwood's voice.

'Tadger, guv,' Garry asked, winking at Stella. 'Would that be any relation to todger?'

Callie looked down at Garry, frowning, though Stella was relieved to see the 'ragin'' look was fading.

'It means, prick, Detective Sergeant Haynes, as I'm sure you deduced. Low Edinburgh slang, if you must know. Now, forget Tadger Hallwood for a wee minute. Stella, you're the last one in so here's what we have.' She sat at the table and looked at each of them in turn. 'Niamh Connolly. Fifty-two. Chief executive of LoveLife, an anti-abortion group, though she liked to call it a children's rights charity. She was found dead and mutilated in her home on Wimbledon Parkside, last Friday. Wandsworth divisional CID did some basic legwork then kicked it up to a South London

MIT under a,' she consulted a note in front of her, 'DI Mark Hellworthy. He took one look at the crime scene report and handed the case to us.'

'Garry said the killer removed her breasts and left them on the table,' Stella said.

'Yes. On a Royal Crown Derby dinner plate, if ye please.'

Callie opened a slim cardboard folder and pushed a stack of 10 x 8 colour photos across the table.

Stella and Garry leaned together the better to look at the topmost image. Stella inwardly steeled herself. Although she'd seen countless dead bodies, and had hardened herself to a degree, she'd always tried to retain that part of herself that was horrified by death. It helped her think of the victims as people and not just cases: vics, DBs, crispy critters or any of the other euphemisms cops used to anaesthetise themselves from the horrors they so regularly had to confront in the line of duty.

The woman in the photograph was slumped in a chair at a scrubbed pine kitchen table. The killer had crudely removed Niamh Connolly's breasts and placed them on a large dinner plate. The wounds had bled copiously, streaking her ribcage red.

'Is that what killed her?' Garry asked, wincing. 'The mutilation? Blood loss?'

Callie shrugged. She tapped the photo.

'There's a dark-red mark on her neck, look. Could be a ligature mark.'

'Post mortem?' Stella asked.

'When DI Hellworthy passed it to us, he also halted the PM. Thought you might want to be there for it in person. He sent the preparatory photos their snapper took at the mortuary, though. Have a look.'

Stella and Garry spread out the rest of the photos. Under the harsh, blue-white mortuary lighting, Niamh Connolly's ravaged body looked almost as if a sculptor had created it, albeit a very sick sculptor.

8

TUESDAY 14TH AUGUST 10.30 A.M.

'Is anyone else thinking what I'm thinking?' Garry asked. 'We've got a weirdo on the loose.'

'Well, let's not jump to conclusions,' Callie said. 'It might not be a weirdo. Although if it's not then for the life of me, I can't think what else it could be. But if it *is* some sadistic psycho then I want him caught and in irons before he does it again.'

Stella glanced sideways at Garry, then down at the photos again. Then up at Callie.

'It does *look* as though we've got a sexually-motivated murder.'

She paused. Callie obviously caught the hesitation.

'But?'

'But, it doesn't *feel* like a rapist taking a step up. Not to me, anyway. There's something ritualistic about the way he's placed her breasts on a plate like that.'

Callie looked at Garry.

'DS Haynes?'

Garry ran a hand over the back of his neck. Stella could tell he was torn between loyalty to his guvnor and the desire to put his version across to the chief.

'It's OK, Garry,' she said with a wry smile. 'Say what you think, I won't be sad.'

'I'm not so sure. Stella's insights into killers' minds are off the scale, but I just think we should start at the obvious place. Start with the husband. Pull in any known violent sex offenders for a chat, put the word out with our snouts, ask Vice maybe if any of the toms have been having more than the usual amount of trouble from perverts wanting the rough stuff.'

All three officers knew that the Vice Squad was one of many departments renamed in the Met's furious drive to present a more PC face to the world. Sadly, for the committee animals who dreamed up Human Exploitation and Organised Crime Command, everyone still called it Vice.

Callie nodded.

'I think you're both right. Look, set the investigation up the way you want to, Stel, you know I trust you. I'm going to get onto the press office. Something like this we're going to be getting a shitload of media attention and we need to get out in front of it. I'll want you there with me. She was a high-profile victim and while we all know here that every victim counts, the media and the general public are going to be more,' she paused, '*exercised* about Niamh Connolly than a dead tom or a smackhead single mum from a council estate. It's just the way it is.'

———

Back in the SIU incident room, which was humming with activity as various teams worked their cases, Stella turned to Garry.

'Coffee?'

'Yeah, go on, cheers,' he said.

While she waited for the kettle to boil, Stella folded her arms across her chest and turned to him.

'What do you think?'

He shrugged.

'Like I said in there. We've got a sex killer. A bloke that does that to a woman has got a screw loose. No, make that a whole box of screws. Economy size. He hates women. Might have form for rape or sexual assaults. Might have started flashing his dick at schoolgirls and graduated to worse. Could be a knicker fetishist who got bored of stealing undies off washing lines.'

Stella wrinkled her nose. She'd run through the same thought processes as Garry, but something was bothering her.

'Could be. I mean, obviously there's the sex angle. And he did kill her, but don't you think there was just something, I don't know, off about the whole thing?'

Garry frowned.

'What, you mean apart from leaving her tits on the table like a main course in a fancy restaurant? How much more "off" do you need, boss?'

She shook her head. She knew she was struggling to articulate the feeling she had, deep down, probably what an old-school copper would call a hunch, that this was far from a straightforward sexually-motivated murder.

'I know, I know. That's not what I meant. Let me try again.' The kettle clicked off as she said this and she made them both mugs of coffee, beckoning Garry back to her office. 'Come on.'

When they got there, Garry sat facing her.

'Go on, then. Have another crack at it. I'm all ears.'

She drew in a deep breath and sighed it out again.

'OK. One, he did it at her place. Not in some deserted farmhouse out in the woods. Or a disused factory. This wasn't a killing ground. So he found a way to get in. No signs of a struggle, either at the house or on the dead woman's body. Either she knew him, or she was expecting him, or when he turned up unannounced he was sufficiently convincing that she let him in. Two, he took his time. He tortured her, strangled her, readjusted her clothes and posed her together with her breasts on the table. So either he's the Lord Mayor of Don't-Give-A-Fuck-Town or he knew she'd be alone long enough for him to do what he came to do. Three, the lack of a struggle, 'cos I'm sure you noticed there were no defensive wounds, means he probably drugged her. And four, there was something about the way he displayed her breasts.'

Garry nodded.

'It'll be a new London Ripper for the media to get all excited about.'

Stella scrunched up her face and tilted her head on one side.

'It's more than that, though. He butchered her all right, but why the plate?'

Garry shrugged again.

'Who knows? They're all nutters, aren't they? Otherwise they'd be doing normal shit like the rest of us and not cutting women to pieces.'

Stella conceded the point with a nod. But she was thinking. *When I was a nutter, I wasn't doing normal shit. I took a CPS lawyer to pieces with an electric carving knife for God's sake. Post mortem admittedly, but still. But that was for convenience: I needed to get her into the freezer. This guy, he* displayed *what he'd done.*

———

Stella spent the next twenty minutes sorting out a corner of the SIU office as her team's operations area. The usual whiteboards dominated and she kicked off the 'murder wall', as it was known, with two photos of Niamh Connolly: one a LoveLife colour publicity photo of its diminutive yet charismatic CEO in one of her trademark power suits, the other an altogether more gruesome shot, taken by the police photographer at her house.

She sat at her desk to compile a list of the people she wanted on her inner team.

Arran first. That rarest of creatures, a happily-married cop. Fifteen years with the same woman, his childhood sweetheart at that. Kath Cox never seemed to mind his erratic hours. Despite the fact that those of inspector rank and above didn't have to work shifts, Arran, like everyone else, Roisin and Stella included, and quite often Callie, could often be found burning the midnight oil at Paddington Green, whatever their contracts of employment might stipulate. Arran and Kath had two mid-teenaged boys as well, Fergus and Ewan, and Arran doted on them. Not as computer-literate as Roisin, Arran more than made up for it with formidable copper's instincts honed over ten years' service in the Met and an ability to cajole, caress and occasionally coerce people into going the extra mile for the sake of an investigation.

Roisin – 'It's Rosh-EEN not ROY-sin' – was the SIU's longest-serving DI. No shortage of ambition from the thirty-seven-year-old, but with a backbone of dogged policework and a flair for the IT side of things, which was often where investigations ended up. Stella knew that when Callie had brought her back from the dead and into the number two spot, Roisin had had her nose put out of joint, but there didn't seem to be any lingering ill feelings. The detective sergeants. Def, Barendra 'Baz' Khan and Garry. Where Def was all butter-wouldn't-melt, Garry was more gung-ho than she was, always ready to rush into the middle of the action. Not as a fool while angels held back, more like someone who didn't believe in backing down from a fight, either physical or intellectual, and had the integrity to go with it.

Baz, the team's intelligence specialist, was more cerebral. He managed the HOLMES team of collators. These were the people, police staff mostly, though a few uniformed officers, too, who entered the SIU's data into the latest version of the Home Office Large Major Enquiry System. Just as painstakingly, they interrogated the vast national database for the answers to the detectives' questions, or for background information that might support, or sink, a line of enquiry, a hunch, or a wild 3.00 a.m. flash of insight.

Rounding out the squad were the three 'babies': ambitious, talented and hardworking detective constables who'd been seconded to the SIU for six-month rotations to see whether they had what it took to go up against, and catch, Britain's most dangerous criminals. DC Camille Wilde, a street-smart white girl from the black-dominated enclave of Brixton in South London. DC Will Dunlop, a psychology graduate from Surrey who'd arrived at the Met with a posh accent he'd worked hard to lose. And DC Becky Hu: her parents had left Shanghai for London in the 1980s and raised a family there. She spoke fluent Cantonese and Mandarin.

Finally, the non-warranted police staff. Lucian Young, the chief forensic officer and a good friend; plus Alec Stringer, the crime scene manager, and a couple of former detectives, now freelancing as investigators.

They'd have support from other commands as needed, but these were the ten key members of the crew she hoped would put Niamh Connolly's killer behind bars. *Before he kills again.* Because that's what was really niggling at her subconscious. What she didn't, yet, want to say out loud to Callie. *This looks like the work of someone who's not going to stop at one.*

9

TUESDAY 14TH AUGUST 11.00 A.M.

With the detectives and investigators gathered around her, Stella took a moment to make sure she had their full and undivided attention. Then she made brief eye contact with each one of them.

Show time.

Stella slid forwards off the desk and went to stand centre-stage in front of the whiteboard, just to the right of the two photos of Niamh Connolly.

'I've been in touch with the SIO who caught the case. A DI Mark Hellworthy—'

'Apt,' Roisin muttered from her place directly in front of Stella.

'Yeah, well, I'm going over there later to have a chat. But he's happy that we're going to go back to square one on this. Roisin, can you and Will go over to Wimbledon and start interviewing the immediate neighbours? And get one of our POLSAs over there to sort out an extended search. The initial perimeter was only fifty metres and I want it doubling. I've noted that in my policy book. Reason being: I considered that in a sparsely populated road like

Parkside, the killer may have gone further before finding somewhere to dump a weapon or something he used in the attack.'

The POLSA – police search adviser – was a highly skilled officer who knew the best way to work outwards from the epicentre of a crime scene. Stella continued.

'I'm sure the Wandsworth CSIs did a decent job but I want one of our teams going back to the house and—'

'Doing it properly,' Roisin finished for her.

'Double-checking,' Stella said, trying to smooth out a frown of irritation at Roisin's second interruption. 'Garry? Can you get hold of Lucian Young for me? I want him on standby.'

Garry nodded and made a note.

'Yes, boss.'

'Thanks.'

'OK, next up. Jumper, I want you and Def to look at LoveLife. For those of you who don't already know, that's the anti-abortion charity that Niamh Connolly set up. Finances, employee records, the usual. Maybe she pissed off someone badly enough they came after her. It's not like it's exactly an uncontroversial subject.'

'How about her opponents? You know, the pro-choice lot or whatever they call themselves?'

'Good idea. I know it looks like a sex killing but we can't afford to make any assumptions. Baz, Camille and Becky: you're our intelligence team on this one, for now anyway. Can you get the HOLMES team looking for unsolved sexually motivated attacks in the Greater London area over the last however many years you think we should go back – five?' Baz nodded. 'OK, for five years. Especially if there were mutilations. Plus, can you put together a list of known sex offenders – not the nonces, not at this stage, anyway – who've done time and are currently at liberty? Let's say, their victims were twenty or older.'

Baz nodded.

'That leaves me and Garry. I want to talk to the husband. He discovered her body, after all.'

'Boss?'

Camille had all but stuck her hand in the air.

46

'What is it, Camille?'

'Any news on the initial pathologist's report?'

'I received it about twenty minutes ago. Nothing we haven't already figured out for ourselves. Basically, Mrs Connolly was subdued somehow, possibly by being drugged, then mutilated by having her breasts cut off, and then she was strangled.'

'Jesus!' came the low mutter from Will Dunlop, 'we've got a real nutcase on our hands.'

'Or not,' Roisin said. 'This could still be a common-or-garden domestic dressed up as something weird to throw us off the scent. You know that most murders are either a domestic, a drunken brawl that went sideways or a side-effect of some other criminal activity, don't you?'

Way to motivate the new guys, Roisin, Stella thought. She stayed silent, wondering how Will would handle the implied criticism from the senior detective. Admirably, it turned out.

'Of course I do. But I can't see a woman like Niamh Connolly being involved in the sort of criminal activity that would get her killed. And anyway, villains don't usually go in for anything quite as baroque as what happened to her, do they? And a pub fight? I don't think so. Which just leaves the husband. I'll go out on a limb here, but even the most royally pissed-off husband who's been cheated on or otherwise shafted is hardly likely to turn his wife into that, is he?'

He pointed at the crime scene photo of Niamh Connolly on the whiteboard.

'Baroque? What's that then, some kind of new grunge music?'

This was Arran, gamely trying to defuse the incipient spat between Roisin and Will.

Will put his hands up in mock surrender.

'OK, OK, I know. I lost the accent but not the vocabulary. Guilty as charged, officer. Arrest me!'

He held his hands out to Arran, wrists together, palms uppermost.

'If I may, ladies and gentlemen?' Stella said, just loud and sharp enough to cut through the banter. 'There's a dead woman in one of the stainless-steel capsule hotel rooms over at Westminster mortuary, so let's get a move on, shall we?'

———

Back in her office, Stella called Jerry Connolly's mobile number. He answered almost before the first burring ring tone had started.

'Jerry Connolly.'

'Mr Connolly? I'm Detective Chief Inspector Stella Cole. I work in the Metropolitan Police's Special Investigations Unit. We are the team responsible for catching the person who murdered your wife.'

Over the years, Stella had found that plain speaking was her friend more often than her enemy. Trying to find appropriate euphemisms for the worst atrocities one human being could inflict on another rarely did anything beyond adding embarrassment to the grief, shock and horror the victim's family were already having to cope with.

'I thought the Wandsworth people were doing that.'

'They did begin the investigation but, for crimes of this nature, the Met's policy is to have a specialist unit handle the case. We are part of what's called the Homicide and Major Crime Command. What I would like to do is come and talk to you, if that's OK?'

Connolly sighed. He sounded drained, as if even expelling the air from his lungs took some sort of monumental effort.

'Very well. If it will help catch the man who did that to Niamh. When?'

'As soon as possible. I don't know if you're working or…?'

Connolly's voice hardened.

'You know, detective chief inspector, although the City has a reputation of profits before people, when one's wife is brutally murdered, one does, actually, take a few days off for compassionate leave.'

'I'm sorry. Of course.'

'I'm staying with friends in Wimbledon. My house is still off limits. Come whenever you like. The address is 71 Edge Hill. Geoff and Sue are both out at work,' he added. 'Will you want to talk to them?'

'It's possible, but we can arrange that separately. For now, we'd like to talk to you. We're based in Paddington. Would an hour from now be OK? Say, midday?'

'Fine. Goodbye.'

Stella pocketed her phone and shook her head.

'Great! First conversation with the husband and I've already put his back up,' she said to the four walls.

Grabbing her bag and checking she had a notebook and pen as well as a digital recorder, she headed for the door.

'Ready, Garry?' she called across the squad room.

Garry had just returned from the kitchen with two aluminium travel mugs with what she hoped was coffee.

'All good, boss,' he said with a smile.

The drive from Paddington Green took fifty minutes. Although the Westway was running freely and they made it through Shepherd's Bush and Hammersmith in good time, things choked up as they approached Putney Bridge.

This meant Stella had plenty of time as they crawled their way along Putney High Street to remember. The High Court judge, Mister Justice Sir Leonard Ramage, had driven along this route in his purple Bentley on the way to murdering Richard and Lola. Ramage had paid for his crime with his life and she experienced a dull ache of grief now, rather than the homicidal rage that had driven her to find and execute the men and women responsible.

The traffic freed up as they hit Putney Hill and then they were driving along the eastern edge of Putney Heath and onto the southeastern edge of Wimbledon Common.

'It's down here on the left,' Stella said five minutes later, after consulting her phone.

10

TUESDAY 14TH AUGUST NOON

Stella knew the look well. The man who opened the door wore it like a sad overcoat of the most threadbare construction.

Jerry Connolly was around the six foot mark, she estimated, but his stoop had reduced him by a few inches. His face seemed devoid of animation. His red-rimmed eyes were likely the result of drinking or weeping or a combination of the two. And his thick blonde hair, though cut short, was a mess, sticking up at odd angles as if he'd showered then slept on it.

The interview Wandsworth CID had conducted had furnished her with the bare bones of the couple's life. Jerry Connolly was fifty-eight, a successful insurance broker. He and Niamh, his second wife, had been more or less happily married for eight years. He'd been a Guards officer before going into finance.

His first wife, Clarissa, had died of breast cancer in 1998. Their son, Giles, was now twenty-six and working in South Korea as an estate agent. Niamh Connolly and her first husband, Niall, had divorced in 2001. Their son, Cormac, was twenty-one, two years into an Archaeology degree at Reading university.

'Mister Connolly? DCI Stella Cole and DS Garry Haynes.'

'Come in,' Jerry Connolly said, in a voice even wearier than it had sounded on the phone an hour earlier.

He turned and shambled into a brightly lit sitting room at the front of the house. Stella took a seat on an immaculate dove-grey suede sofa, and Garry sat beside her. Connolly sank into a matching armchair and seemed to almost blend into its upholstery. His grey needlecord trousers and white polo shirt did nothing to lift the unnatural pallor of his complexion.

Stella began with the usual formula, although she tried as best as she was able to inject a note of genuine sympathy. She knew first-hand how grief could rob you of everything, even your sanity.

'First of all, Mr Connolly—'

'Jerry, please.'

She nodded and continued speaking in a quiet but firm voice.

'Jerry. We are very sorry for your loss. I want you to know that we are going to do everything in our power to find the person who murdered your wife.'

'I hope you do,' he said. 'I don't think he's going to stop at Niamh.'

'Why do you say that?'

He rubbed a hand over his unshaven cheeks. In the quiet of the cool, immaculately tidy room, the sound of his palm against the bristles was clearly audible.

Stella scanned the shelf behind him and saw a row of typical family photos. Some were clearly casual holiday snaps, others more likely studio shots, husband and wife with two grownup daughters, attractive young women both. A type of photo Jerry Connolly would never, ever pose for again.

'It's pretty bloody obvious, don't you think? A man does that to a woman, well, I can tell you it wasn't someone settling a personal grudge, although believe me there are plenty of those. I don't know if Niamh was his first or not, but it's clearly a serial killer.'

He uttered the last two words as flatly as if he were describing the colour of his shirt.

Stella was caught in two minds. Part of her agreed with

Connolly's assessment. It was the thought that had been running laps inside her brain since she'd seen the crime scene photographs. But another part screamed, 'Take care!' If word got out that there was a sexually sadistic serial killer stalking London's streets – its wealthiest streets – there'd be a media shitstorm, quickly followed by the political version.

'I know how distressing the circumstances of Mrs Connolly's death were, but it's far too early to start jumping to conclusions.'

Connolly flapped a hand, almost languidly, as if to say, *whatever, I don't really care.*

'Fine,' is what he actually said. 'You're the experts. So, what do you want to ask me?'

'Actually, the first thing I want to ask you is where your family liaison officer is? Didn't the officer who spoke to you on Friday appoint somebody to stay with you?'

'He did, yes,' Connolly replied in clipped tones. 'A Detective Constable Lewis. Very capable young woman. I told her I could handle my grief in my own way without her jumping up to make a pot of tea every five minutes. She's back at Wandsworth police station, I believe, though she said she would keep me posted on developments.'

Far from the FLO being the sympathetic tea-maker of TV dramas, Stella knew they played a crucial investigative role. No sense in pushing the point with Jerry Connolly. Not yet, anyway.

'And would you like her to stay as your FLO? I can appoint a new officer if you would like, now that the case has been transferred to us.'

Connolly heaved a deep sigh.

'Do you know, I really don't care. DC Lewis, one of yours, whatever you think best.'

Stella made a note. She raised her head and looked Connolly in the eye.

'Did your wife have any enemies? People who'd want to do her harm?'

Connolly sat a little straighter in his chair.

'You do know what Niamh did for a living, detective chief

inspector?' he said, sounding incredulous, which Stella knew he had a right to be.

'Of course.'

'Then you'll know she picked a job, a *calling*, to use her words, where making enemies was pretty much a condition of employment. You only have to look at the emails and letters she received on a daily basis to see that. The comments on her Facebook page were just as bad. Hate-filled people sending death threats, saying the most—' He passed a hand over his face again and Stella could see the pain it was causing him to talk about his wife, '—the most, obscene, disgusting things you can imagine.'

'Did she keep the hate mail?'

'Yes, in a filing cabinet in her office. It's in the converted stable block in our back garden. I think they took it all away, the first lot of police who came out.'

'How about the emails and online messages?'

'Oh, yes. Niamh kept them all. Had a folder she named "Crazies".'

Stella made another note. Something to pick up on with Mark Hellworthy.

'And from those you saw, or the things your wife discussed with you, did anybody in particular stand out? Anyone who went further than messaging her and writing?'

He shook his head.

'Not really. They're only brave when they're hiding behind a keyboard. People like that run a mile if you confront them personally.'

'And did you ever have to do that? Confront someone personally? At your house, for example?'

'Never. Niamh used a PO Box as the charity's address. The house is in my name and there are far too many J Connollys for anyone to make the link to Niamh.'

'How about in public? I know that Niamh,' Stella paused, 'is it OK if I use her first name?'

'Yes, of course.'

'I know Niamh went along to the LoveLife protests. I've seen her on TV. Did she ever mention any of the rival protesters getting physical, threatening her to her face?'

'Not to me. One thing you have to understand about Niamh, she wasn't afraid of anything. This was everything to her, part of who she was. She didn't back down from anything. If one of those bloody women's rights people had threatened her, she would have dealt with it there and then. I used to ask in the early days but she just told me not to worry.'

'OK, well, we'll follow that up anyway. It's what we call a line of enquiry. As SIO, sorry, Senior Investigating Officer, it's one of my jobs to develop a working theory as to how we go about catching Niamh's killer. Lines of enquiry are the different hypotheses we follow through. So people violently opposed to her views would be on our radar. What about in her personal life?'

'What about it?'

'Was there anyone with whom she had fallen out? Anyone from her past who might wish her harm?'

Connolly frowned and Stella could see from the way his lips tightened that he didn't think her questions were relevant. She agreed with him, but that didn't mean she could afford not to ask them.

Every copper has a simple formula drilled into them from day one on the job. ABC: Assume nothing, Believe nothing, Consider (and check) everything. That's what she was doing now. Even though she was pretty sure Mark Hellworthy would have already gone over the same ground.

'Nobody,' he eventually replied. 'Outside of her work, Niamh had only friends. And to save you the trouble of asking, our marriage was fine, too. No infidelities on either side. We loved each other very much.'

'Thank you. I understand that these questions may seem irrelevant to you, or even insulting, but we have to go through every possibility in order to make sure we don't miss something. And that's why we also need to ask you one last question today, Jerry.'

'What?'

Garry spoke for the first time. He and Stella had agreed that he'd be the one to ask the most risky question of all. The one that could provide a valuable lead or righteously piss off the most important witness.

'Can you tell us where you were between 11.00 a.m. and 4.00 p.m. last Friday?'

As though he'd been expecting the question, Connolly answered simply and straightforwardly. No emotion. No flaring temper. Mark Hellworthy would have asked him the same question on the day his wife had died.

'I was at work. In my firm's offices all day. We had a board meeting first thing, which lasted until lunchtime. I took lunch at my desk and then was in a series of meetings until six. You said that was your last question?'

'Yes,' Stella said.

'Then here's something I want to tell you. I was in the army before the insurance business. Scots Guards. I served in the Balkans, Afghanistan and Iraq. I've seen what men will do to women in war. Rape, mutilation, torture. It's used to terrify and demoralise local populations. To exact revenge sometimes. Or just to satisfy an individual's bloodlust. But it's chaotic, the way it's done, I mean. Frenzied. What happened in my house was cold. Clinical. I've seen evil in my life, as I'm sure you have. And on Friday, I believe I saw it again. Tread carefully when you go after this man, DCI Cole. Tread very carefully.'

———

After thanking Connolly, and promising once again that she would not rest until his wife's murderer was arrested, charged and convicted, she and Garry let themselves out of the house and climbed back into his silver Ford Mondeo.

'What d'you make of him, boss?' Garry asked as they headed for the main crime scene, or, rather, group of scenes: Valencia, on Wimbledon Parkside.

'I think he's in shock. I think he's falling back on his military training to prevent himself screaming.'

'You like him for it?'

Stella turned in her seat to look directly at Garry, who kept his eyes glued to the road ahead.

'Seriously?'

Garry shrugged. 'Nine times out of ten it's the husband.'

'You saw the photos, right?'

'Yeah. But what if you wanted to get rid of your wife? You'd know the stats. You read the books, watch the shows on TV. So you do it like a serial killer and send the cops off on a wild goose chase. Stranger things have happened.'

'OK, well, let's say, for the sake of argument, I do like him for it. He has an alibi—'

'Unchecked.'

'An unchecked alibi, but he'd have to be mad to provide one as detailed as that if he couldn't back it up with witnesses. And can you really see a guy like that hacking his wife's breasts off while she was still alive?'

'Yeah, it's a long shot. But you always say Occam's Razor when one of the babies starts flinging wild theories about.'

'Yes, I do. But the idea that you look for a solution to a problem involving the fewest assumptions doesn't mean throwing everything else out of the window.'

'He did sound kind of sarcastic when he talked about her "calling", you remember? I made a note. Hey, arsehole, learn to drive!' he barked suddenly, as a beige Fiat 500 in front of them suddenly slammed its brakes on to dive into a parking space beside a meter.

'I heard that, too. But that was about all I heard that wasn't one hundred per cent what any grieving husband would say. You want to know what I think? What my gut instinct is telling me?'

'Go on.'

'Jerry Connolly knows. He said it.'

'A serial?'

'Yep. The hallmarks are all there. We've got a sex killer on our hands. The media are going to go mental.'

11

The sign for the house – a small slab of engraved slate – was discreet to the point of invisibility and Stella wondered why the Connollys had bothered.

Garry parked on the side of the road and together he and Stella walked to the uniformed constable logging visitors in and out of the outer cordon. She looked hot in her uniform, stab vest, and heavy equipment belt, cheeks pink and forehead shining beneath her bowler cap. Stella introduced herself and Garry and both showed their Met IDs.

The loggist noted names, collar numbers and the time on her clipboard, then lifted the blue-and-white POLICE tape to let them onto the drive.

'At least the hedge means there's not too much trouble with gawkers,' Garry said as they approached the next cordon, more blue-and-white tape, this time printed CRIME SCENE – DO NOT CROSS. Another uniformed officer stood guard, a male PC this time, bulked out by his equipment belt and clearly as uncomfortable in the heat as his colleague at the end of the drive.

Stella held out her ID.

'Morning, ma'am,' he said. 'Taking over, are you?'

Wanting as many cooperative officers around her as possible, Stella chose her words carefully.

'Your DI Hellworthy invited us to take it on. We're working closely with him and his team.'

The PC gave her a look she translated easily. *Whatever you say*.

Stella lifted the tape and she and Garry stepped inside the inner cordon.

'Noddy suit time,' Stella said.

Garry grinned and nodded.

'Gonna be sweating like pigs,' he said.

'Like we aren't already.'

She put her murder bag down and unzipped it. She pulled out the white suit and struggled into it, then the matching nylon booties, nitrile gloves and, finally, her face mask. The hood went up last of all. Garry was beside her doing the same.

The Wandsworth CSIs had laid down a common approach path using clear plastic treading plates. Useful for seeing potential evidence beneath them, not so useful if you were on the heavy side.

Stella had seen at least one overweight detective crack one of the plastic plates in their haste to get into a crime scene. The front door was only latched closed. She noted the high-tech security pad to the right of the door and winced. *Didn't do you any good, did it, Niamh?*

The CSIs hadn't done a bad job of cleaning up after themselves, but Stella still noticed a few smudges of aluminium fingerprint powder on door jambs and dado rails.

'We'll look at the kitchen first,' she said.

Garry nodded as they entered the principal crime scene.

———

Any experienced investigator knows that there's no such thing as the smell of blood. It's like the Inuit and words for snow.

So, there's the coppery tang of freshly spilled blood. The sweet aroma if the victim was a heavy drinker and the ethyl alcohol in their bloodstream percolates out into the air around the corpse. The butcher-shop smell when the claret's been splashed around liberally. And the unmistakable charnel-house stink when not only has it been spilled in quantity but been given time to start drying out and decaying.

Through her mask, Stella drew in the last of the signature smells of violent death. A heavy, meaty, organic stench that wormed its way into the mucus membranes of her nose and mouth and then stubbornly refused to leave.

The source wasn't difficult to identify.

At the far end of the rectangular scrubbed-pine kitchen table, one of the matching chairs had been pushed back. Niamh Connolly's. The table top at that end was spattered and streaked with blood. *From dozens of minor arteries letting go*, Stella concluded.

But the real source of the smell was the archipelago of small pools surrounding the chair. Flies buzzed lazily over the blood, now dried to the colour of damson jam and with about the same consistency, landing at the periphery now and again to feed or lay eggs.

Stella crouched beside the chair. She pointed to the floor just in front of it, beneath the edge of the table. Two long oval shapes cut into the otherwise smooth-edged curve of the largest patch of blood.

'I think that's where her feet were,' she said.

Garry straightened up.

'Where next?'

'Jerry Connolly said they had a summer house or whatever, a converted stable block, where she had her office.'

Navigating the route on the treading plates, they made their way down the hall and out into the back garden. On their right, they found what they were looking for.

The Connollys, though they had modernised everything else, had kept the original Elizabethan structure of the stable block more or less intact. Gnarled and blackened oak beams infilled with red bricks in a herringbone pattern. A densely perfumed white wisteria clambering up one wall. Double doors painted a soft shade of blue that reminded Stella of the hens' eggs she used to collect on family farm holidays on the Welsh coast.

A couple of CSIs in white suits were working inside. Stella knocked lightly on the glass before entering.

'Hi, guys,' she said. 'DCI Cole and DS Haynes from SIU, Paddington Green.'

They nodded, but neither spoke, clearly preferring to carry on lifting tapes from the various surfaces inside the immaculate office and flicking fingerprint dust from a magnetic wand onto the coffee table.

The narrow slats of the Venetian blinds were closed against the sun, but the space was still overwarm. Stella and Garry stood against the wall to the right of the double doors.

'According to Jerry, Niamh had an appointment at the house on Friday lunchtime. A potential donor apparently. He couldn't remember much more, probably the shock. Said Niamh kept her whole life on her phone.'

'How are we doing with that? Have they unlocked it, yet?'

Stella shook her head.

'Jerry said she used the fingerprint-lock on it.'

'Touch ID. So we should be able to get it open at the PM.'

'Yup. In fact, make a note. I want that phone. What with the case coming from Wandsworth to us I hope someone didn't misfile the thing or we'll never find it.'

Stella inhaled deeply, thankful that the worst of the blood-stink had left her nose, though she could still register its presence somewhere in her brain. Then she let it out in a controlled exhalation and closed her eyes.

What happened here, Niamh? You met him here? He dangled a big donation in front of you, charmed you into letting your defences down? Then what? How did he get you from here to the kitchen? Rohypnol in your drink? Bashed you over the head and carried you? What does it mean to him to cut your breasts off you? Sex, obviously, but why? Is he inspired by Jack the Ripper? You weren't a tom, like the Ripper's victims. Anything but. Respectable, upper middle class. Did you die for your stance on abortion? I thought the fanatics were all on your side of the debate. Was I wrong?

She tried again, assuming the killer's persona, something she was far, far better at than any of her colleagues, with the exception of Callie, could ever imagine.

I hate you. I hate you with a passion. I'm going to make you suffer, and I'm going to enjoy myself. I've tricked you already and here we sit in your summerhouse. You think you're about to score a major cash injection. But I know it's not cash I'm going to be injecting. Once I've subdued you I'm going to tell you why I hate you so much. Then I'm going to take you back into the kitchen. And I'm going to cut your breasts off and display them for your husband to find. But I'm not going to rape you. Or bite you. Or leave a turd on your bed. I'm not into any of the perverted shit. I'm above all that.

————

Over the years they'd been working together, Garry had learned to wait while Stella 'did her thing', as he called it. She'd stressed the very first time that she wasn't some kind of amateur profiler, drunk on improbably prescient TV behavioural analysts. The way she'd explained it, without going into detail, was that she sometimes had a sense of why people killed.

Now he took time to look around the smartly converted stable block. He took in the lurid posters mounted in sleek black frames. In unsparing detail, they depicted late-stage foetuses above headlines reading, 'Some women pray for these: you KILL them!' and 'Don't they have human rights too?'

He had some sympathy with the questioner's stance. Growing up in a fervently religious household dominated by his churchgoing mother, and augmented by older sisters, aunties and his paternal grandmother, he'd absorbed plenty of their fierce arguments for the sanctity of life. Although even as a kid he hadn't been immune to the irony when they'd also prayed loudly for paedophiles and child-killers to be hanged, 'like the animals they are, Lord'.

But there was politics, or ethics, or whatever you wanted to call it, and then there was murder. And the big lesson he'd absorbed at his mother's floral-dress-clad knee, Sunday School and church was the sixth commandment: Thou shalt not kill.

As an adult, and then a police officer, he'd learned that there were subtleties. *If thou art a soldier and acting within the Law of War then thou canst kill if thou has to.* Half the guys in SCO19 were ex-military and they'd all killed. *And if thou act in self-defence, and believe* at the time *that the force thou employest is proportionate to the perceived threat, then thou canst use lethal force.* Subtleties, yes. But not many.

Garry knew to keep his lip buttoned when the conversation at the station or in the Green Man turned to the abortion debate. The squad was fairly evenly divided between men and women and the latter were vociferous in their assertion of a woman's right to choose. He'd weighed in once with what he thought was a mild and reasonable point about the child's right to choose, or even the man's, but been assailed by a barrage of counter-arguments that had left him nose-deep in his pint glass as he weathered the storm.

Stella nudged him, bringing him back to the present.

———

'I don't see this as a pro-abortion thing,' she said, clear now in her own mind that they were looking at an unknown-motive murder. 'I think her views were secondary. She'd never have let one of her opponents into her home. I think it's clear that the donor Jerry mentioned was her killer. Want to talk me out of it?'

Garry shook his head. 'I was only throwing ideas out before. We've got ourselves a serial. Question is, was she his first or are there others?'

'Let's save that until we've got a bit more information to go on. In the meantime, we need to get over to Wandsworth. I called Mark Hellworthy before we left the station. He's expecting us at two-thirty.'

They left the house, nodding an acknowledgement to the PC on duty before struggling out of their crime scene gear and stuffing it all back into their bags.

12

TUESDAY 14TH AUGUST 2.15 P.M.

While Stella and Garry were making their way to the CID office at Wandsworth, a meeting was drawing to a close at City Hall, on the south bank of the Thames, hard by Tower Bridge.

'Is there any other business? No? Good. Then I declare the July meeting of the London Assembly Police and Crime Committee closed at two fifteen p.m. As scheduled. We meet again in a month's time. Thank you, colleagues,' the chairman said.

Having endured the committee's toothless questioning of his new anti-knife crime strategy, the thirty five-year-old Deputy Mayor for Policing and Crime stood, nodded at the room as a whole, while being careful not to make eye contact with anyone in particular, gathered his papers and left.

His phone buzzed. He lifted it free from the inside pocket of his suit jacket, enjoying the way the movement made the Armani label flip outwards for a second.

'Craig Morgan,' he said in a clipped voice.

'Hi, Craig, it's Melissa. Roly Fletcher's secretary? Just wanted to remind you of your meeting at three.'

'Yes, thank you, Melissa. I'm well aware of my meeting with Roly. Excuse me, I have to go.'

He hung up, frowning. *Bloody secretaries, always bossing us around.* He launched Uber and sorted out a ride. *Man of the people, that's me. No chauffeur-driven limos for your future mayor.*

He walked through Potters Fields Park, a quirky little expanse of manicured grass – currently burnt to a crisp by the unrelenting sun – and picked up his Uber where Duchess Walk met Queen Elizabeth Street

On the journey to the Labour Party headquarters in Victoria, he rehearsed his answers, or the appropriate attitudes underlying them, to the questions he imagined Roland Fletcher would be asking him.

– How would you deal with the bankers in the City?

– I'd acknowledge the contribution they make to London's economy and that of the country as a whole, but remind them that financial capitalism was a failed experiment, and that they need to address the real investment needs of the country and, especially, the needs of the many not the few.

– What would be your stance on a visit to Parliament by the prime minister of Israel?

– As mayor, I'd make it clear I would ensure the safety of any foreign dignitary, but that I would not engage either politically or socially with the leader of an apartheid state during his visit.

– London will always be a magnet for immigrants. What's your stance?

– I'd want to maintain London's vibrant, multicultural atmosphere, and celebrate the massive contribution immigrants have made, while recognising that we need to strike a balance and protect jobs, especially where low-skilled migrants from Eastern Europe are concerned.

With each answer, Morgan felt his confidence growing. He was going to nail it.

———

The car jerked to a halt.

'We are here, sir.'

'Thank you,' he said in over-enthusiastic tones to the driver, who, Morgan judged, had recently arrived in Britain from

Afghanistan or Iraq. *Another victim of Blair's illegal war,* he thought. 'Five-star service.'

'Thank you, sir,' the man said in a bored voice. Or maybe it was lack of confidence. *Completely understandable,* Morgan thought as he slammed the black Prius's door behind him. *Just make sure you give me a decent review.*

He pushed his way into the building through the revolving door and sighed with relief as the cool air of the interior chilled the sweat on the back of his neck.

He approached the receptionist sitting behind the shiny marble slab that constituted the front desk. *Pretty. Nice tits. Let's hope she doesn't have one of those accents that sound like a crow cawing.*

'Good afternoon, sir. Welcome to Southside.'

Aaand she does.

'Yes, I'm here for a meeting at the Labour Party headquarters.'

'Have you been here before, sir?'

'Yes, of course I have! I'm Craig Morgan.'

She smiled, raising her oddly squared-off eyebrows just a fraction.

'Sorry, Mister Morgan. I'm new. How are you spelling your name? I'll see if you're on our database.'

'I'm *spelling my name,* as you put it, C-R-A-I-G, and Morgan like Captain Morgan. You know. Rum?'

She tapped on the keyboard in a rapid tattoo.

'Sorry, sir, I don't drink. Here we are!' she said triumphantly, pointing a long, aubergine-painted fingernail on the screen. 'Craig Morgan. Wait while I print your ID, please.'

Morgan stood at the desk, quietly fuming at the young woman in front of him. *What are you, twenty-seven, twenty-eight? Fucking Millennials. No respect.*

She folded the ID, from which Morgan's face glared out of a postage-stamp-sized picture, and slid it into a plastic holder on a red lanyard.

'Second floor,' she said, already tapping her computer screen to feed another call into her headset.

Morgan slid the ID across the sensor panel beside the nearest glass security gate, the one reserved for visitors, stepped through and walked to the bank of lifts. The two flights of stairs weren't the problem. He wanted to check his appearance.

Ensconced, alone, in the lift, he glanced at himself in the polished-steel wall. Dark-brown hair neatly in place. *Suit jacket unbuttoned. Smart yet casual. Not overawed. If only my eyes were a little further apart.*

Almost before it had jerked into motion, the lift stopped and the doors opened. Morgan turned for the reception and, after repeating the same rigmarole with the Party functionary behind the pale-wooden desk, took a seat in the waiting area.

He picked up that day's *Guardian*. Relations with Europe. A planned far-right march against illegal immigration. Another stabbing on London's streets. *What a mess. We'll certainly have our work cut out.*

He looked up at the wall clock. Five to. He tugged his shirt cuffs clear of his sleeves and adjusted them. Half an inch of white showing. The red silk tie was straight, retied that morning seven times until the point just kissed the top of his shiny belt buckle.

'Honestly, you look fine,' Fiona had said as she kissed him on the cheek in the hallway of their Islington house. 'Now go or you'll be late for work and you don't want that.'

And what, precisely, do you know about what I want? What I really want? Frigid bitch. Well, you'll find out soon enough.

The sound of footsteps made him look up, a smile already jacked into position.

'Craig, good to see you,' the woman said. Kendra Fawcett's official title was Fletcher's political private secretary. Morgan always thought of her as The Rottweiler. Blonde hair cut so short she could pass for a man if it weren't for her figure. Acne scars disfiguring her cheeks and a visible pinprick in her right nostril. *Keep the nose ring for the weekends, do you, Kendra?*

'We're just down the hall, in Bevin, if you'd like to come with me. Good day so far?'

'Oh, you know, the usual. Committee meetings, staff meetings. Meetings with local people. Meeting with LGBTQ campaigners angry about attacks on trans people. Basically, committees and meetings. You?'

She smiled, a tight-lipped expression he didn't think signalled a great deal of humour.

'Oh, you know, the usual. Keeping Roly out of trouble. Fighting off the right.'

'You mean those fascists in the English Defence League?'

'Don't be daft. I mean *our* right. The bloody crypto-Tories in the Party.'

'Oh, yeah. Totally. Backsliders.'

They arrived at the white-painted door to a committee room labelled on an aluminium plaque, 'Bevin'.

Fawcett pushed the door open and stepped inside. Morgan followed. Sitting at the end of the long white-surfaced table was Roland 'Roly' Fletcher. The new Labour leader.He looked more corporate than his predecessor. Clean-shaven, dark business suit, mid-brown hair cut short and parted on the left. But Morgan knew it was all a disguise to reassure the City and the right-wing media. Fletcher was a proper leftist with a radical agenda.

Fletcher stood and extended his hand. The two men shook and Morgan noted how dry Fletcher's hand was. Resented the fact, since his own was hot and slick with sweat. He also noticed the flicker of disgust that passed across Fletcher's face, though it was gone in a split-second. *Bast– No. Smile. Be cool.*

'Thanks for making the time to see me, Roland.'

Fletcher smiled for the first time.

'Please, call me Roly.'

'Roly,' Morgan said, sitting.

'I've asked Kendra to take a few informal notes. Not minutes, by any means. Just to help me remember what we talk about.'

Morgan forced himself to smile at Fawcett.

'Of course. No problem.'

'Right. Let's cut to the chase, shall we? You've been selected as official Labour candidate for mayor. The election's not for a couple of years, so we do still have a little bit of time in hand,' he said, then paused.

Morgan realised it was for him to acknowledge the witticism. He smiled, dutifully. Fletcher continued speaking, in his measured way, not stressing any particular words, as if his vaunted passion for radical equality even extended to his own speech patterns.

'I need to know that you're one hundred per cent loyal to Party ideals and policies.'

'Of course. That goes without saying.'

'Actually, it doesn't,' Fawcett said, 'But it's sweet you think that.'

Struggling to bite back a smart rejoinder, Morgan turned away from Fawcett so he was facing Fletcher directly.

'As I said, I am cut from the same cloth as you, Roly. Your ideals are mine.'

'Good. Good. Now, how about the backstory?'

'Pardon?'

'You! Your history.'

'What about it?'

'Obviously, we've had a good poke around in your CV and haven't found anything untoward. Not that I would have expected to, of course, but this is a sensitive appointment, and a crucial one, so we have to be careful. No, what I want to know is whether there are any skeletons in your closet that will come tumbling out once the media circus and the Tories' dirty tricks department start ferreting around.'

Morgan locked his gaze onto Fletcher's. And saw, reflected back to him in those pale-blue eyes, the women. Crystal. Shanisse. Roxy. Dannii. Mindy. And the most recent one. Arianna. So many women. So much young, springy, compliant flesh. So much pain.

'They can shake the closet as hard as they like. The only thing that might fall out is an old copy of the Little Red Book. But I'm happy to defend that.'

'Yes, well, let's hope it doesn't come to that. Tell me, what do you think about Remi Fewings?'

Shit! The killer question. How do we fight a mixed-race Tory?

'That's a very good question. With her…background…it's hard to play our usual cards. I mean it's not exactly a feat of investigative journalism to point out that our front bench is whiter than theirs.

And I'm white myself, obviously,' he added, as if it wasn't blindingly obvious to Roly and Kendra.

'So the race card is out, at least as a lead. But don't forget, Craig, that whatever the colour of her skin, Remi Fewings can hardly claim to be in touch with the daily concerns of people of colour living and working in London.'

Morgan thought of the most recent social media spat involving his opponent, the incumbent mayor. She'd been called out for speaking dismissively of black Londoners after she'd been recorded at a private dinner saying 'they' needed to 'get off their arses and start working hard, like the Asians. Bettering themselves'.

'I'm thinking we play the law and order card,' he said. 'Never mind the colour of Remi's skin, look at knife crime. Look at hate crimes. Look at the murder statistics, for God's sake! You saw the reports in the media from February. London had more murders than New York. We should crucify her over it. After all, if there's one thing the Tories have always been able to claim as their natural territory, it's law and order.'

Fletcher pursed his lips. He looked sideways at Fawcett. Morgan watched the interplay of facial expressions between them. Tried to decode them. What the hell were they saying to each other with their raised eyebrows and pinched lips?

'What do you think, Kendra?' Fletcher asked, finally.

She nodded.

'I think Craig has a point. It's time we went beyond race as a vote-winner. Let's hit them where it hurts.'

13

Garry turned into the rear entrance to Wandsworth Police Station. He parked in one of the marked bays and followed his boss out of the car. Detective Inspector Mark Hellworthy met Stella and Garry on the station's ground floor and showed them up to the incident room they'd hastily thrown together after discovering Niamh Connolly's body the previous Friday.

Nice-looking bloke, Stella thought as he introduced himself. Early forties, blond hair cut short and parted haphazardly on the left. Deep-set blue eyes and a mouth that appeared to be permanently on the verge of a smile. No signs of over-fondness for the booze, either, the perennial risk of working in CID. His eyes were clear, his cheeks unflushed, his gut well under control beneath a white shirt open at the neck.

The Wandsworth CID office smelled like every other detectives' haunt Stella had ever been in. Fast food and coffee, a heady mixture of aftershave and perfume and, underneath, the faint aroma of bodies owned by people working too hard and too long to get to a shower as often as they'd have liked to.

73

The searing heat outside didn't help; without air conditioning the open-plan space had become heated to the temperature of a sauna. All the open windows did was admit pre-heated air.

'Thanks for referring it to us,' Stella said, when they were seated at Hellworthy's desk. 'I know it's hard to let a juicy case go.'

Hellworthy pulled his mouth to one side and shrugged.

'We get our fair share of murders and, to be honest, if it was a straightforward domestic, or maybe a street fight, we'd have dealt with it here no problem. But you saw the crime scene pictures. Well, it was hardly your common-or-garden kill, was it? No. On balance I think I'd sooner see you guys take the heat from the media.'

Stella smiled. 'Jesus! If I take any more heat I'm going to melt.'

Hellworthy returned the smile, with interest. 'I'm sure you're used to keeping your cool with the media.'

'Oh, you know. I just flutter my eyelashes and tell them we're doing all we can and they clap and throw flowers.'

'Can't blame them there. I would.'

Suddenly aware of Hellworthy's intense blue eyes staring into hers, Stella nodded and took out her notebook. *To business.*

'What were your first impressions? When you went in.'

Hellworthy looked up and to the left, accessing his memory. It didn't take long.

He looked back at Stella, then at Garry.

'D'you ever see the crime scene photos they took of Jack the Ripper's victims?'

Both nodded. Stella doubted there was a copper on the planet who hadn't gazed at the set of smudgy black and white photos at some point in their life. If it came to that, she'd include just about every officer of the court and probably half the teenagers and adults with access to the Internet.

'The last victim: Mary Kelly. The worst one. Turned her into a pile of meat. He cut her breasts off. Didn't put them on a plate like our killer, but that was my first thought. Basically, oh shit, we've got Jack the Second.'

'No other mutilations, though,' Garry said. 'Jack the Ripper went to town on Mary Kelly. Gutted her, took her face off, the thighs, everything. Mrs Connolly was basically intact apart from her tits.'

'They start off with a try-out though, don't they? Get a feel for what they're doing. He'll escalate, you can bet on it,' Hellworthy said.

'We're all thinking the same, then? A serial?' Stella asked, a sinking feeling in her gut.

'I think so,' Hellworthy said.

'Uh-huh,' Garry echoed.

'Shit!'

'What about forensics?' Stella asked.

'OK, so you have the crime scene photos and the video. I'll get all the physical evidence sent over to you after this. I started a policy book. I've got a copy you can take away with you.'

'Any witnesses?'

Hellworthy shook his head.

'We had uniforms and DCs on a house-to-house Friday night and through the weekend. You saw those houses. The owners love their privacy so they're all behind bloody great hedges, fences and walls. We put out an appeal for passers-by who may have seen anything but, to be honest, I'm not hopeful. The chances of some dog walker bumping into a blood-spattered maniac waving a carving knife are worse than zero. I'd sooner bet on Wimbledon winning the FA Cup.'

'What about the husband?'

'What about him?'

'He says he has an alibi. Did you guys get a chance to check it out?'

'Not yet. It's on the action list. But if it's him, I'll buy you a lifetime supply of Scotch.'

'He said Niamh kept a list of the cranks who sent death threats and hate mail. Have you got that?'

'I'll have it sent over. Someone's going to have a lovely time reading it: there's hundreds of the things. Death threats are the mild ones.'

The rest of the conversation took ten minutes. Mostly

speculations on the kind of sicko who got his rocks off cutting up women and the budget cuts that made even getting a working force-issue mobile a work of Zen-level patience.

With promises on both sides to keep in touch should anything significant crop up, Stella and Garry shook hands with Hellworthy and saw themselves out.

———

'He seemed nice,' Garry said in a light voice, keeping his eyes fixed on the road ahead as they wove their way back to Paddington Green.

Stella snapped her head round to see whether he was grinning. He was.

'Meaning?'

'Nothing. Just making conversation. Lovely eyes, too. So blue!'

'Oi, you!'

Garry laughed.

'So you weren't giving him the glad eye, then?'

'No! Just making sure the local MIT are onside seeing as we're nicking their investigation off them.'

'He didn't seem too bothered. He was more interested in your charms, if you ask me.'

'What do you mean?'

'Shirt button, boss.'

Stella looked down. An extra shirt button had popped open, exposing a little bit of cleavage and the edge of her bra. She refastened it.

'Bollocks! I must've caught it when I was getting out of my Noddy suit. Why didn't you say something?'

'Me?' Garry asked, now in full pantomime mode, holding his hand flat across his chest. 'And risk you reporting me for inappropriate behaviour? I don't think so.'

'You total git! You were enjoying it, weren't you?'

'Maybe,' he said, grinning. 'You like taking the piss about my love life, I thought I'd return the favour.'

'And how is the lovely, who is it this week, Mel? Or was she last week's conquest?'

'You know perfectly well it's Mel. We've been going out for five weeks and three days.'

'Wow!' Stella said, her voice dripping fake admiration. 'Are you talking about a mortgage, kids? I mean, five weeks and three days, that's got to be a record of some kind, hasn't it? I'll tell the boss. She'll want to organise a party. You know, for the two of you. An anniversary party. We could have cake!'

Garry threw his head back and laughed.

'All right, all right. You win. Stel one, Garry nil. So how's *your* love life, then? Are you going to see if DI Hellworthy wants to go over some evidence over a nice steak dinner one night? I didn't see a wedding ring.'

Stella shook her head. Her grin was genuine, more or less, but somewhere inside she could feel the effort she was still having to make whenever the subject of relationships came up.

'Not my type.'

'No?'

'Too—'

'Too what?'

'Too detective-y.'

This garnered another guffaw from Garry, a rich, warm sound that filled the Mondeo's cabin.

'Too...oh, boss, you're wasted in the job. You should be doing stand-up.'

'Thank you for that ringing endorsement of my professional skills, Detective Sergeant Haynes. Now, please overtake this idiot in front of us so we can get back to the station before nightfall. I've got a report to write, and no doubt a press conference to go to.'

14

Stella was sitting at her computer, bashing out a report of her visit to the crime scene and conversations with Jerry Connolly and Mark Hellworthy.

Around her, the members of her team were hitting the phones, searching the Police National Computer, reading action notes or speaking to other officers drafted in to cover the ground at the labour-intensive early stages of the investigation.

In the background, Radio 1 was playing. Someone had brought in a bag full of Thai takeaway and the smell was making her mouth water. She realised she hadn't eaten since breakfast time and it was now 5.00 p.m. Coffee would have to do instead.

For a time, she'd been able to get through the whole day on caffeine and nicotine, stuffing her face with pizza, Chinese or Indian takeaways at the end of a very long day. She'd managed to kick the fags, but the coffee and fast-food addictions were still in play.

One windowsill in the SIU incident room was lined with jars of coffee, boxes of tea bags and an assortment of herbal teas, chamomile, rosehip, ginger and the like, that were referred to by the squad's older officers as 'the gay tea'. The decaf jar was almost full, but when Stella picked up its caffeinated counterpart she saw to her dismay that it was empty, barring about a quarter of a teaspoonful of sticky-looking grains.

Brandishing it like a hand grenade, she turned and addressed the room in general.

'Who's been playing coffee-chicken again? Leaving just enough behind so they didn't have to buy a replacement?'

Much shaking of heads and muttered 'not me, guv's from the assembled detectives.

'Really? Nobody? OK, then you leave me no choice. I'm going to turn my back and I want the guilty person to put a fiver on the desk behind me. Ten seconds.'

She turned her back.

The noise of scuffling behind her made her smile. She whirled round after a count of five.

Def and Camille were holding Will Dunlop by the elbows, and Stella could see they'd both got their fingers deep into the soft spot just above the joint. A little extra pressure here and you could bring even the most obdurate prisoner into meek submission.

'We've got him, boss,' Def said above the laughter. 'The SIU caf-head bang to rights. Go on, Dunlop, fork over the cash or it's the cells for you!'

'It weren't me!' Will shrieked in a decent approximation of the average teenage numpty caught nicking cars or dealing weed on a Saturday night. 'I never!'

Stella marched over to the trio. She stood in front of Will, hands on hips, legs apart in the classic 'power pose'. She thrust her chin out and went nose-to-nose with him. In her best old-school, Cockney copper growl, she said:

'Don't come that old nonsense with me, you slag. We got you bang to rights. Your dabs were all over the jar and we've heard from your dear old mum that you're a bit too fond of the old brown stuff. So, you going to cop to the nickin' or am I gonna 'ave ter beat it out of yer?'

Playing his part to perfection, Will stared defiantly back at Stella.

'I know my rights. I want me phone call. I want a brief.'

Stella was readying her comeback line when Callie stuck her immaculately coiffured head out of her office door.

'Stel! Can I have a word?'

Hilarity over for now, Stella poked Will in the chest.

'Go and get another jar, would you? I'll give you the cash when you get back.' She winked. 'Nice acting job, by the way.'

————

'So, where are we?' Callie said, when Stella was sitting opposite her across a desk mounded with folders, computer printouts and what looked like half a forest's worth of admin: forms, leave rotas, budget spreadsheets, reports, memos from HR, all the usual crap designed to keep the most experienced detectives chained to their desks.

'I've assigned roles and everyone's working. As to Mrs Connolly, it's all as described in the report from Wandsworth. She was drugged, then mutilated and strangled to death.'

Callie pursed her lips.

'Lovely. I've arranged with the media office to hold a press conference at five-thirty. That way we'll catch the six o'clock TV news. I'll want you there.'

'OK, boss. Any line you think we should be taking?'

'Och, you know. The usual. Terrible crime, hearts go out to family. Doing all in our power to find and arrest the killer. Ask anyone who saw something or knows something to come forward or call Crimestoppers. So what did you find out over in Wimbledon?'

Stella blew out her cheeks.

'Not a lot, really. Jerry Connolly seems genuinely devastated by his wife's murder. Garry and I kicked around the idea that he might have done it and made it look like a serial to cover himself, but it's not really a goer in terms of a hypothesis. Plus I'm certain his alibi will check out. We spoke to DI Hellworthy over at Wandsworth nick, too. He came to the same conclusion, I think as soon as he saw the body. We need to try and stop the media turning this into Jack the Ripper: the Sequel, but it's going to be bloody hard.'

Callie pursed her lips, coloured today, as always, a shade of dark red that emphasised her pale complexion.

'Any mileage in emphasising Mrs Connolly's respectability? Maybe they'll think twice before painting her in the same light as the toms the Ripper did. London or Yorkshire,' she added, almost as an afterthought.

'Maybe, but then we run the risk of some right-on journalist accusing us of caring more about middle-class victims than poor ones.'

'Brilliant. So we're buggered either way, is that what you're telling me?'

Stella smiled. Her boss's Edinburgh accent grew stronger when she was under pressure, as did the general saltiness of her language.

'I think we just lay it out the way it is. Niamh Connolly was murdered by an intruder. She wasn't raped or sexually assaulted. We're keeping an open mind.'

'Oh, and obviously, we should hold back the details of her mutilation,' Callie said.

'Agreed. Simple enough to screen out the cranks and the serial confessors that way. Plus copycats.'

Callie scowled.

'Although, how likely d'ye think it is that someone doesn't tip off a journalist for a few quid, no questions asked and "I never reveal my sources"?'

In her heart of hearts, Stella knew the answer to that question. *Not very*. But she had an idea.

'Could you come out in a minute and give a quick pep talk? Mention it then. That we're holding back details of the mutilations to use against genuine suspects. It'll carry more weight than if I do it, which I will anyway.'

'OK. Let's say in five minutes. One last thing. You know I've already had the brass on the phone, bending my ear about the need to get a quick result on this one. And despite what we say about all victims getting the same treatment, you and I also know that's one hundred per cent, weapons-grade horseshit. Niamh Connolly was a high-profile, media-savvy CEO of a charity with some very influential donors, married to an extremely rich and successful City insurance broker. Whatever you may or may not think of LoveLife and its aims, and personally I think they should stick them up their Bible-bashing arses, there's going to be enough heat on this squad to fire a bloody hog roast. And I for one,' she jabbed a red-varnished fingernail at Stella, 'am not going to be the little piggy going round and bloody round with a bloody apple in my mouth!'

Having delivered herself of this speech, Callie slumped back in her padded leather chair and ran a hand across her face.

'Don't worry,' Stella said, sounding more confident than she felt. 'We'll get him, boss.'

'Well, I bloody hope so, Stel. I really, really do. Because if he does it again it's going to get a bit hot around here. We'll have the whole bloody lot of them with their boots on our necks, up to and including that arrogant wee twat, Craig Morgan.'

———

Stella had just finished her report and added it to the policy book, as well as emailing it to Callie when the Chief Super herself left her office and stood beside the 'Murder Board' as they called the main whiteboard for the case.

Not being the tallest of women, Callie couldn't be seen by many of the officers. Although those closest to her fell silent at once, there were plenty at the back of the room who were still attacking their keyboards, making calls or just bantering.

Callie caught Stella's eye and winked. Then, in the Leith docker's accent she'd learned to imitate as a girl, rough enough to cut sheet steel, she spoke.

'Excuse me! If ye wouldn't mind buttoning your bloody lips for a couple of minutes, I'd like to say a few words.'

Apart from the plasticky click as a Biro rolled off a desk, the room was silent. Stella waited. Callie's party piece had a second act. She counted silently in her head. *One…two…three…* The tension in the room was as tight as a guitar string as everyone waited for the overboss to speak. Finally, Callie plucked the string.

'Thank you,' she said, at conversational volume, her genteel Morningside accent now firmly back in place. 'DCI Cole and I have to go and feed the hyenas in a wee while.' There was a murmur of appreciative laughter at this. 'For obvious reasons, we're holding back the details of Mrs Connolly's injuries. I know I can trust you lot. You wouldn't have been selected for this team if I couldn't. Which means the media won't be running any lurid stories about a sexual serial killer on the loose. As far as they and the general public are concerned, this is a stranger-murder. Full stop. So please keep your knowledge about the case private and exclusive to this team. OK?'

'Ma'am?' Baz had raised his hand.

'Yes, Baz, what is it?'

'What if he does it again? I mean if he kills another one and mutilates her the same way, or worse, won't we have to give some details at that point? And then we risk being accused of holding back intel that could have protected the public at the start?'

A few other officers mumbled agreement. Stella had been running the two strategies through her head, too, and still wasn't sure they'd picked the better option. In the endless mental tussle between public anxiety versus public safety, public safety always came first. She waited to hear what Callie would say.

'It's a good question. The answer is, we do risk that but, right now, I'd rather not start a panic. Apart from anything else, he'll be pulling his tiny wee tadger in expectation of all the gory coverage. So we're going to deny him the satisfaction of having his work discussed in the media. It's exactly what his type get off on. But if he *does* do it again before we catch him, which, by the way, is what I hope and expect we will do, then we'll have a rethink. I'll take the heat if it comes. You lot concentrate on finding him before he does it again. Any other questions?' Silence. 'No? Good. So you go back to finding our killer, and DCI Cole and I will go and change into our chain-mail knickers.'

15

Callie touched Stella on the shoulder as they made their way to Paddington Green's first-floor media centre.

'Quick chat?' she asked, nodding at the door to the ladies toilets.

Stella nodded.

Inside, the two senior detectives stood elbow to elbow at adjoining sinks, checking hair and makeup. Stella always thought it was unfair that male cops could put their suit jackets on and be ready. But that was life. A female detective with a wonky fringe or panda eyes would make the front pages but for all the wrong reasons.

'As it's a Cat A+ murder we've got a dedicated media manager. Tim Llewelyn, you know him?' Callie said without preamble.

'Yeah, he's OK. Doesn't push too hard for stories when there's nothing to say.'

'He'll introduce the conference and then hand over to me. I'll give them the big picture and then I want you to make a short statement about what we're doing, like we discussed. But there's one more thing.'

'Yes?'

'I'm sure you're keeping an open mind, but something in my waters tells me this one's going to be a runner. And if we're still working on it a month or a year from now, I'm going to want to shield you from the media. As SIO you'll know everything and I don't want to put you in the position of having to lie to the media. You know, all that, "Do you deny that it's a member of the House of Lords" rubbish. Damned if you do, damned if you don't. That's OK with you, eh?'

'Fine by me. Less time I spend in press conferences the better, as far as I'm concerned.'

Callie bared her teeth at herself in the mirror and rubbed her finger across her incisors. No lipstick on her teeth for the hyenas to snap.

'Good! Let's go then.'

Tim Llewelyn met them outside the media centre. His thinning hair had recently reached the point where he'd adopted the shaved head favoured by many of the blokes at Paddington Green, from the firearms officers, who saw it as a badge of office, to the detectives and police staff who probably went with it because it was easy. Only a few of the older guys bothered trying to disguise it with a comb-over these days. Which was, in Stella's opinion, A Very Good Thing.

He smiled as he straightened the knot of his navy-blue tie.

'Evening, ma'ams,' he said.

'Knock it off, Tim,' Stella said, smiling back.

'We've got a full house this evening. Standing room only. Must be a slow news day. Oh, and—' He glanced down.

'What?' Callie asked.

'We have a special guest. On the top table.'

Callie's eyes widened and her lips compressed into a thin line. Stella knew the expression well.

'And just who might that be?' Callie asked in a voice that could freeze boiling water.

'The Deputy Mayor for Policing and Crime.'

Stella's heart sank. Though Callie's response lifted it momentarily.

'Craig bloody Morgan? The officious wee prick! Trust him to muscle in on our show. You know he wants to be the next mayor, don't you?'

Tim looked crestfallen.

'His press secretary is on our list. I'm sorry.'

Callie patted his arm.

'Not your fault, Tim. Ah, well, let's get it on and get it over with, eh?'

So saying, she gestured at the door. Tim pushed through and then stood aside to hold it open so Callie and Stella could make their way to the table, draped in a dark-blue tablecloth and dressed with a Met-branded vinyl frontage.

Sitting in the seat to the left of the centre chair was Craig Morgan, immaculate in a sharply tailored suit, crisp white shirt and an expensive-looking red tie. To Stella's eye, the Labour *wunderkind* looked like an identikit politician on the way up, the make, or both. Trim figure. Close-set brown eyes. And neat brown hair cut short like a forties' movie star.

Stella looked out across the ranks of expectant faces and saw one she recognised. Vicky Riley was there, in the middle of the third row. Vicky smiled and nodded at Stella, who dropped her eyelids in a minute gesture of acknowledgement.

Morgan stood as Callie and Stella mounted the low podium and took their own chairs at the table, which was groaning with mics. Face a picture of concern, he leaned across to shake hands, first with Callie, then Stella.

Already irritated by his presence, Stella felt her emotions tick up a notch as the photographers' digital cameras whirred and hissed like a chorus of vultures. *So it begins.* She plastered a professionally grim expression on her face. No expressions the media could capture and then mischievously title, 'Cop smiles while murderer still at large'.

'Ladies,' he said. 'Craig Morgan, Deputy Mayor for Policing and Crime. Welcome. Ready when you are.'

He sat, leaving Stella fuming. Beside her, occupying the centre chair, Callie stared out across the forty or fifty journalists seated in tightly packed rows. As usual, the camera operators were at the back, with their tripods. A handful of sound operators stood each side of the stage, wielding their long grey fluffy mics like furry cudgels.

Stella had no need to glance to her right. She knew what would be going on beneath Callie's immaculate black and silver dress uniform. On the one hand, rage that she had been outfoxed by a politician. On the other, a professional desire to use the media to help her SIO catch the killer.

Perhaps sensing what could happen at any moment, Tim wisely brought the press conference to order. Standing to one side of the table, he spoke without a mic, patting the air for silence.

'Good evening, ladies and gentlemen. Thank you for coming. As usual, with briefings of this nature, we will have a short statement from the police officers in charge of this new case and then there will be time for questions.'

Morgan leaned forward and flicked the switch to activate the Met's own mic, on a slender black wand.

'If I may, Tim,' he said.

Callie and Stella's heads both snapped rightwards as if they'd been slapped.

'Ladies and gentlemen, as you may know, I am Craig Morgan, Deputy Mayor for Policing and Crime. My role here is purely supervisory, but afterwards I shall be available for statements and interviews.'

As the reporters made notes and a few more cameras clicked, Stella heard the slow hiss of air being expelled under control from between Callie's lips.

'Thank you, deputy mayor,' Tim said. 'Detective Chief Superintendent McDonald?'

Callie straightened in her chair and performed her three-seconds-of-silence trick on the media waiting for the story that might lead the six o'clock news.

'Last Friday, a woman was brutally attacked and killed in her home in South-west London. We are treating her death as murder. We are devoting considerable resources to solving this terrible crime.

Murder is always horrific and frightening, but I want to reassure the public that London is still a very safe city and that there is no cause for undue alarm. Now I will hand over to the Senior Investigating Officer on the case, Detective Chief Inspector Stella Cole.'

Heart thumping all of a sudden, Stella inhaled and leaned forwards. The mic was sensitive enough to pick up her words clearly if she stayed sitting upright, but she felt it lent her words an extra edge of urgency, authority and sincerity if she appeared to the TV viewers to be speaking directly to them.

'On Friday July twentieth, the body of Niamh Connolly was discovered by her husband at their house in Wimbledon. She had been subjected to a violent attack that left her dead. As SIO on the case I have a team of over one hundred officers working on discovering the identity of Mrs Connolly's killer and bringing them to justice.

'At this point we are asking members of the public for any help they can give us. If they saw anything unusual on Wimbledon Parkside between midday and 8.00 p.m., or any kind of suspicious activity, please get in touch with one of my officers at Paddington Green Police Station. The number should be visible on your screens. You can also call Crimestoppers on 0800 555 111 or via their website.

'We are working flat-out round the clock in these vital early days and—' She paused. *Never promise, Stel. Never! It'll come back to bite you in the arse.* She opened her mouth to say she and her team wouldn't rest until the case was brought to a satisfactory conclusion, but the voice she heard belonged to Morgan.

'— and I have full confidence that the Met will catch the killer. They have my full support. Thank you.'

Stella closed her mouth with a clack of her back teeth. *What did you say that for?*

Tim sprang to his feet.

'Questions?'

The room erupted. It sounded as though every single journalist was shouting at once. Tim pointed to a notebook-wielding reporter in the back row, speaking over the heads of the others and leading the room to crane their necks to see who'd been picked. In a voice that carried surprising authority, he called to her.

'Yes. Rosie.'

'Rosie Booker, *Telegraph*. DCI Cole, Mrs Connolly was a well-known anti-abortion campaigner. Was this some sort of political killing? Sending a message?'

'It's very early days. We're keeping an open mind. At this stage we are trying to determine a motive. I can't comment further, I'm afraid.'

As Tim stage-managed the media pack, the questions came thick and fast.

'James Tabor, *Times*. Was there anything unusual about the murder, DCI Cole? If it wasn't political, was it a sexual motive?'

'Again, it's far too early to be speculating.'

'Gary Collinson, *Daily Mail*. Was it a stranger?'

At last, an intelligent question, and one she felt she could answer a little more fully. Although the term 'stranger' meant different things to the public, the media and the police.

'Although we are still checking alibis, I believe on the basis of the available evidence that, yes, Mrs Connolly was murdered by a stranger. It appears she may have inadvertently admitted her attacker into her home, but if she did have any prior acquaintance it would have been because her killer used a false identity.'

Stella glanced at Callie and signalled with her eyes that that was enough. There was nothing else to put out and any more answers to the media's fishing expedition would only compromise the investigation, possibly by alerting the killer to their lines of enquiry.

Callie stood.

'That's all, ladies and gentlemen. Thank you.'

Over a renewed chorus of shouted questions, she and Stella left the podium to Morgan.

As they turned the corner, the last view of Morgan Stella had was of him giving an interview to the BBC.

16

'I'd like to murder him,' Callie said. 'Grandstanding like that. And what was all that "I have full confidence in the Met" business? Before he got appointed deputy mayor he was at us like some flag-waving student protester.'

Callie had retrieved a bottle of Scotch from a drinks cabinet in her spacious office and was busy pouring two decent measures into cut-glass tumblers. She handed one to Stella, clinked rims and then took a hefty slug.

'I don't know. But I had a burning desire to take one of the boom mikes and shove it up Craig Morgan's arse.'

Stella drank, enjoying the slow burn of the whisky as it coursed down her throat.

'It'll be political. He wants the mayor's job in a couple of years. You just watch. Even though he's been on our case about efficiency savings and all the other budgetary bullshit, I bet you he'll be making waves in the press about how he always wanted to give us more money but his hands were tied by the mayor or the Home Office.'

'Aye, or bloody little green men from Mars!' Callie said, finishing her drink and pouring another. She dropped the neck of the bottle towards Stella's glass, raising her eyebrows at the same time.

'Go on, then. But I really need to get some food inside me before long. It's going to be a long night.'

Callie nodded.

'We'll get someone to run out for a takeaway. So come on. You visited the site this morning. You met the Wandsworth SIO. What are you thinking?'

Stella looked past her boss at a framed commendation on the wall, one of many, while she arranged her thoughts into a succinct pattern.

'I'm telling the team to keep an open mind and not get carried away while they do the basics. We need to check the husband's alibi and see if she had any disgruntled lovers in the background...'

'But?'

'But my gut is telling me it's a serial killer. The mutilation. The way she was displayed.'

'Not somebody trying to throw us off the scent, then?'

Stella shook her head then ran her fingers over her ponytail.

'I can't see it. I want to. I just can't.'

'OK. So what's your next move? What're your urgent lines of enquiry?'

'One, get her phone and get it unlocked. See if she made any record of meeting someone on Friday afternoon. Two, budget permitting, I want to call in Jamie Hooke. He's the best forensic psychiatrist I've ever worked with and I'd like to get his take on it. See what he thinks is going on in our boy's head.'

Callie nodded, sipping her whisky.

'Budget-wise —' she winced immediately '— Sorry, Stel, I know how much ye hate jargon. I tell you it infects your bloody head while you're not looking. Well, the budget's as tight as a duck's arse, as I think you know. Another year of austerity and I swear we'll be writing our policy books on the backs of Cornflakes packets. Which means outside consultants, especially expensive ones like Mister thousand-pounds-a-day Hooke will have to wait for now.'

Stella frowned. It was the answer she'd been expecting. But she felt she needed to push back before giving in. Just once.

'A day of Jamie's time might help us stop the killer in his tracks. Is a second life worth so little?'

Callie shook her head.

'Ah, Stel, you would have to pull the moral blackmail on me, wouldn't you? You know if it were up to me –' she held up a hand to stifle Stella's onrushing riposte ' – and I know it is, in the end, well, I'd give you a trolley-dash round the forensic expert supermarket. But I've got at least two dozen serious crimes being investigated out of this station, including terrorism offences, rapes and a handful of murders. If I said yes to every DCI who wanted to hire a consultant, I'd be pawning my uniform to pay for my morning latte. Just hold off for now, OK? You might catch a break with good old-fashioned coppering. And if anyone can round here, it's you.'

Stella smiled tiredly and sighed.

'OK, your flattery trumps my moral blackmail. On my cost-free list I have number three, get a request into SCAS' – Stella pronounced the acronym for the Serious Crime Analysis Section 'scaz' – 'for any similar murders on the National Homicide Database. And four, I'm going to put in a Heads of Crime request through the Intelligence Bureau. Shake the tree and see if anything weird falls out.'

Callie smiled.

'Good. We've got forty-three forces plus one in Scotland. I'll keep everybody sweet if any Chief Constables start getting arsey. Ah, Jesus, Stel, why do they have to be such twisted little shits?'

'What, Chief Constables?' Stella asked, face neutral.

'No, ye silly mare! Serial killers.'

'Honestly? I have no idea. Maybe they caught their parents shagging. Maybe they have unresolved mummy issues. Maybe they were born with it.'

'Aye. And maybe it's fucking Maybelline.'

Stella snorted, propelling whisky into her nose and unleashing a violent coughing fit.

Eyes streaming, she held out her hand for a tissue.

93

'We'll catch him, Callie,' she said, finally.

'Aye, well, I hope you're right, Stel. And the sooner the bloody better. If that wanker Morgan turns up at one of my press conferences again I'll make good on my promise. So listen, parking the shop talk just for a minute, how are things? With you, I mean.'

'Oh, you know, they're all right. A little romance wouldn't go amiss, but I'm OK.'

'Still seeing your shrink?'

'Once a month. He says I'm fine and I don't need to keep going but I just want to know it's all as it should be up here,' she said, tapping the side of her head. 'I still have the odd nightmare where she's back.'

'Other Stella, you mean?'

'Uh-huh.'

'You're not really worried, are you? That shaman guy in Canada cured you, didn't he? And our psychiatric team confirmed it. She's gone, Stel. It's OK. You're just you.'

Stella sighed.

'Yeah, yeah. But you know what I did when she was in control. I just… It's not a part of my history I'm particularly proud of.'

'None of us are. Gordon Wade and I burned a lot of midnight oil and sank a few bottles of his finest single malt agonising over that little business, believe me. But in the end, you know what? You did this country a service. A messy, bloody, violent service, but a service nonetheless. If she helped then I think you can make your peace with her over that. Or her memory, at any rate. She's gone, Stel. Trust me. Trust yourself, for God's sake. Now,' she said, clapping her hands together. 'I have calls to make to smooth your path with my oppos around the country. But I can't do it on an empty stomach. What do you fancy? Thai, Indian, pizza, Chinese?'

―――――

While they were eating, Garry put his head round the door of Callie's office.

''Scuse me, ma'am,' he said, then looked at Stella. 'Niamh

Connolly's iPhone just arrived from Wandsworth along with the rest of the physical evidence they gathered. Locked.'

It was only what Stella had been expecting, but it was a small obstacle to add to the pile nonetheless.

'Well, we have three options. We can find some tame IT company, which will cost money. We can email Apple, which will cost time, and my patience. Or we can wait for the post mortem and do it the old-fashioned way.'

17

Stella rounded up the people she wanted present at the post mortem. As well as the three obvious picks, Garry, Lucian Young and Alec Stringer, she pointed at the three DCs.

'Will, Cam, Becky. Take a car and meet us at Westminster mortuary, OK?'

'Yes, boss,' they chorused.

Was that a flash of anxiety that crossed Cam's face? Stella hoped it wouldn't presage a fainting fit. It was hard enough getting respect as a female DC, despite having a woman in the Commissioner's office.

—

The on-call forensic pathologist was Doctor Roy Craven. He spread his arms wide in greeting as Stella, Garry and the rest of her team entered the post mortem room at Westminster Public Mortuary in Horseferry Road. He was gowned in an oversized pair of pea-green scrubs, with a black plastic apron over the top. His hair was gathered under a surgical cap printed with characters from *The Simpsons*.

Stella had never minded Dr Craven's eccentricities: she knew that beneath his occasional departures from what some of the brass regarded as 'protocol', he cared as much as any of them for the people whose soul-emptied husks he had to take apart on his tables. Before transforming Niamh Connolly from a human being into a piece in the judicial jigsaw puzzle that would hopefully lead, one day, to her killer, he would mutter a quiet prayer.

Three stainless-steel tables occupied the centre of the twenty by twenty foot space. The table furthest from the door was vacant, a gleaming stainless-steel bed with room for one.

The centre table held the mortal remains of Niamh Connolly. At the moment, her body was shrouded in a green drape, beneath which the contours of her limbs, torso and head were clearly demarcated. And on the closest table, another green cloth lay across a low mound that, with a jolt, Stella realised must be the murdered woman's breasts.

The room smelled of antiseptic and the unmistakable stink of recent death, which to Stella always put her in mind of her grandad's butcher's shop in the small Berkshire town where she'd grown up. 'Cole's High-Class Family Butcher – All Meat Home-Killed' the blue-and-white glazed tiling had declaimed above the door and display window. *High-Class. Home-Killed*, Stella thought. *One out of two, I suppose.*

Flanking Craven were two people in green scrubs and white rubber boots: a slender young woman, wisps of blonde hair escaping her green scrub cap, and an older man, grey stubble on his cheeks, a digital SLR camera slung round his neck. With a purple nitrile-gloved hand, Craven pulled his surgical mask under his chin so he could speak to the detectives.

'Good morning DCI Cole, DS Haynes,' Doctor Craven said, offering a small glass vial of oil of camphor. 'And good morning to you all,' he continued, beaming at the other five members of Stella's team.

They took turns tipping the bottle against the pads of their index fingers, and smearing the aromatic waxy substance along their top lips, the better to dispel the stench of decay emanating from the body.

'Ready when you are,' Stella said.

Craven nodded and, almost ceremonially, Stella thought, withdrew the draped cloth from Niamh Connolly. He pulled the green cloth down to her waist, then, with a flourish, all the way to her feet, from where he swirled it like a bullfighter's cape before spinning it into a corner.

Stella heard Garry's indrawn hiss of breath as he took in the horrendous wounds to Niamh Connolly's chest. Though they had both seen the photographs, the reality was infinitely worse.

'Behold!' Craven said, theatrically. 'The latest testament to man's inhumanity to man, or, as is so depressingly common, woman.'

From behind her, Stella heard a moan and then a crash. She spun round to see Will crumpled on the floor.

'Probably the smell,' Craven said. 'That's what gets them ninety-nine times out of a hundred. The smell.'

Lucian and Garry hauled Will over to a chair and got him sitting, head dangling between his knees until he came round. Stella noticed Cam and Becky exchange a glance. It wasn't hard to read. *Thank Christ it wasn't one of us!*

As Stella had known he would, Craven bowed his head and spoke briefly, and quietly. She caught the odd muttered word – enough to make the gist clear.

'... struggles ... over ... pain, likewise... allow us ... bring her killer to justice ... Amen.'

Taking a pair of dressmaking scissors from a stainless-steel tray, Craven cut through the fabric of Niamh Connolly's skirt on the right-hand side. He signalled for the mortuary technician to pull the skirt away and seal it in a paper evidence sack.

'Thank you, Verity,' he said, after she'd placed the rustling paper bag on a bench.

He repeated the process with the plain white cotton knickers and the shoes. The blouse and bra had been recovered by the Wandsworth CSIs and were on their way to Paddington Green.

While Craven worked, the photographer moved around him, in a series of moves that looked choreographed not to get in his boss's way, taking pictures of the body at every stage of undress. These would be added to the Murder Book and kept on file when, hopefully, they closed the case.

Delicately, as though the dead woman might still be capable of feeling pain, Craven removed an emerald stud from each earlobe, refastened the butterflies on the posts, and placed them in an evidence bag Verity held out to him. The watch followed.

'Nice timepiece,' Craven remarked, turning it so that it caught the light. 'Mrs Connolly was a stylish lady.'

Stella looked down at the body.

She saw a woman in her middle years who had kept herself in good shape. Curvaceous but definitely not overweight. Still some muscular definition beneath the subcutaneous fat that was only natural in a woman of her age. Fine, silvery stretch marks across her lower abdomen, little more than strokes of a pen.

A maroon bruise, a finger's width, encircled her neck. And there, dominating her abused torso, the mutilations that Stella had flinched at when Callie had shown her and Garry the photograph sent in by Wandsworth's Crime Scene Manager. Irregular ovals chopped out of her flesh so that the torn pectoral muscles were visible with their marbling of whitish-yellow fat. Her pubis was a stubbly triangle.

'Oh, shit!' Garry said. 'I can see the headlines already. London Ripper on the loose.'

Stella wanted to silence him. Wanted to deny what was staring her in the face. The very worst kind of murderer was active on her patch. A psychopath with a paraphilia – a sexual deviancy that drove him to commit this sort of desecration on a woman's body. A sex killer.

'Maybe we should let Doctor Craven do his stuff before we jump to any conclusions, eh?' she managed to mutter.

'A very wise sentiment, DCI Cole, if I may say so,' Craven interjected. 'Let's start with what our eyes tell us, shall we?'

He reached up and pressed a button on the mic dangling above the body on a shiny coiled black plastic cable. From another ceiling mount, the red light of a digital camcorder indicated the process was also being filmed.

'For the record, I am Doctor Roy Craven. I'm a senior forensic pathologist based at the Iain West Forensic Suite, at Westminster Public Mortuary. The date is fifteenth of August, two thousand and eighteen. The time is oh-nine-oh-five a.m. Present are Detective Chief Inspector Stella Cole, Detective Sergeant Garry Haynes and, ah…' He paused.

'Senior Forensic Officer Lucian Young,' Lucian said, then nodded at Alec.

'Crime Scene Manager Alec Stringer.'

The babies followed suit.

'Detective Constable Will Dunlop.'

'Detective Constable Becky Hu.'

'Detective Constable Camille Wilde.'

Craven continued after nodding his thanks and smiling at the three DCs.

'I am conducting the post mortem of Mrs Niamh Andrea Wilhemina Connolly, fifty-two, of Valencia, Wimbledon Parkside, London, SW19 5TR.'

Craven began a verbal description of the condition of the body. Stella half-listened while following his words on the actual terrain of the dead woman's flesh, observing closely, trying to imagine what had led her killer to contemplate, and then inflict, these particular wounds.

The days when she had been shocked at the methods one human being could – and would – choose to end another's life were a fading memory. And a faint whisper deep inside her head echoed the sentiment. *After all, Stel, you got quite creative with PPM, didn't you? At least Niamh's in one piece. OK, three pieces. Not like poor old Debra Fieldsend.*

18

After his preliminary remarks concerning the effects of *livor mortis* – the pooling of blood in the downward-facing portions of the dead woman's anatomy, giving them a distinctive dark-red, bruised appearance – Craven moved on to the chest.

'Both breasts have been entirely removed. Judging from the blood loss evident in the corpse, it seems clear that the excision was performed *ante mortem*.' He turned to the babies and opened his mouth.

'That means—'

'Before death, Doc,' Cam said, grinning. 'I speak enough path-lab Latin to understand that.'

'Forgive me, DC Wilde. Old habits.'

'It's fine. Sorry,' she said, 'we're here to learn, after all.'

'Very well,' he said, winking at Stella. 'Perhaps you'd like to take a look at my little toolkit here and give me a run-through.'

Cam rounded the table and came to stand by Craven's right side. She looked down at the array of instruments, mostly stainless-steel, and pointed at them in turn.

'Scalpel,' she said. 'Is that right, Doc?'

'Bravo!'

'Used for making incisions. The big curved blade is 'cos you're not doing anything massively delicate.'

'And the long handle?'

Cam wrinkled her nose, making the camphor oil shine as the light caught it.

'Um.'

'Is it to get deeper into the body cavity?' Will asked.

'Very good.'

One by one, Cam itemised the tools on Craven's work-tray, from hammer to bone saw, rib-cutters to the T-shaped chisel he'd use to pry off the dead woman's cranium. Only the bread knife stumped her.

'Sandwich break?' she asked, eyes wide, all innocence.

He smiled and shook his head.

'Anyone else?'

'They're for slicing off organ samples for histology,' Becky pronounced.

'Excellent! My goodness, DCI Cole, you have a whole squad of budding pathologists here. Now, let's continue. Skin, fatty and glandular tissue have all been removed, along with irregular sections of the *pectoralis major* muscle.'

Stella observed the ragged muscles and couldn't help thinking of a side of beef.

''Pause the recording for me, would you, Verity? Tell me what you see, detectives,' Craven said.

Out of the corner of her eye, Stella saw Garry lean closer. The slick of oil of camphor glistened in his moustache under the bright blue-white light of the halogen spots above the table. The three DCs, now fully engaged with the proceedings, leaned in behind her. Thankfully, Will's faint seemed to have been a one-off.

'I know it's usual to say, like, Oh, wow, he clearly has some rudimentary knowledge of surgical procedures,' Garry said.

'Go on,' Craven said with a smile.

'But this looks like butchery. The edges of the wounds are

ragged.' He poked a white-gloved finger into the space where Niamh's left breast would have rested. 'Bits of the muscle are, sort of, lifted. Like they were chopped at and not cut cleanly.'

'Very good, DS Haynes,' Craven said. 'If this was the work of someone with medical training, or even a tangential connection to the profession, I will eat my hat. No,' he said, with authority, 'we are looking at the work of a killer whose reach exceeded his grasp.'

Stella let her eyes travel down the body, from the chest to the belly which, she noted, was marked at its lower curve with a faint pink, crescent scar.

'It looks as if she had a caesarean at some point.'

'It does indeed,' Craven said, pulling the belly skin upwards a little to stretch it taut. 'Although there are other procedures that could account for a scar like that. If she ever donated a kidney, the latest surgical techniques could very easily leave that sort of scar.' He looked up at the three DCs. 'A manual laparoscopic nephrectomy, for example. Keyhole surgery to remove a kidney. Her medical records will confirm it once they arrive.'

Stella pointed to the dead woman's pubis.

'He shaved her.'

Garry interrupted.

'Really, boss? I mean, not telling tales out of school or anything, but I can definitely state that most girls do that these days. It's something to do with porn, apparently.'

'That's just the point, though, Garry. She's not a girl, is she? Yes, if she was in her thirties or younger, I'd say it wouldn't tell us anything. But she's in her early fifties. That generation tend to favour the natural look.'

She peered a little closer. Several small nicks had crusted over with blood. *Clumsy*, she thought, then, *why blood?* She turned to Craven.

'I'm right, aren't I? She didn't do it herself, did she?'

Craven inclined his head as though conceding a point to a bright student.

'Obviously, we can't be certain, but those cuts appear to be more than just shaving nicks. And if they'd happened during the regular course of Mrs Connolly's personal care regime, I wouldn't expect to see any blood at all.'

Stella looked again. A thought crossed her mind.

'Even if a woman of fifty-two did want to remove her body hair, she wouldn't shave. I saw Niamh Connolly on the telly. She always looked immaculate.'

She turned to Cam and Becky.

'If anything, she'd get a wax, wouldn't you say, ladies?'

They both nodded.

'So the killer did it, then,' Garry said.

'That would be my guess, yes,' Craven said.

'Before or after he killed her?'

Craven sniffed.

'There's very little blood. I would say the depilation happened after Mrs Connolly was dead.'

Stella looked back at the purplish-red mark around Niamh Connolly's throat. She pointed.

'Is that the cause of death, Doc?' she asked. 'She was strangled? Or was it the blood loss that killed her and he either subdued her by choking her or did it later?'

Craven held up his hands, smiling.

'Slow down, DCI Cole. Too many questions! First of all, as you know,' he paused, 'I should be drummed out of the Royal and Ancient Order of Grouchy Forensic Pathologists if I were to offer you my opinion on COD before conducting my post mortem. But...' He held up a hand as Stella opened her mouth to protest,

'– but, from the preliminary report from the onsite pathologist and the forensic report the Wandsworth crime scene manager sent over, it doesn't appear as though blood loss was sufficient to kill her. She would have been in extreme, and I mean excruciating, pain, and probably in shock, but people have been known to survive mutilations of this,' he sighed, 'egregious severity.

'I volunteered in Rwanda in the aftermath of the genocide. We were able to save people who had had hands, feet, breasts or genitals cut off by machetes. So, I don't think that exsanguination or shock were the cause of death. I can't go further than that.'

'Thanks, Doc. I can live with that.'

'Unlike Mrs Connolly,' Garry said, to groans. 'Sorry,' he added. 'Couldn't resist.'

Cop humour. Better than a drink sometimes.

Stella could see Craven was itching to get his hands on the body and start the PM proper. But she had one final question.

'Doc. The breasts. Are they...?' She pointed at the table behind her.

'Yes. Shall we take a look?'

'Would you mind?'

'Not at all.'

19

Without the theatrics this time, Craven lifted the green drape aside to reveal the severed breasts.

'Oh, Jesus!' somebody said behind her.

Stella bent closer to examine the flattened mounds of flesh with their dark-brown nipples and ragged red edges. No cuts on the skin, no bite marks, either, but each breast was imprinted with five small, roughly oval bruises, four above the nipple, one below.

'So, he holds the breast and clamps his fingers onto it hard to pull it out so he can cut it off,' she said. 'Which is which?'

'I'll need to examine the musculature and match the wounds to the torso to give you a definitive answer. But from a cursory examination, we have determined,' he glanced back at Verity, who smiled at him, before pointing, 'that this is the left, and that the right.'

Stella put out her left hand, laying her fingertips gently on the pattern of bruises on the right breast.

'Would he be right-handed, d'you think?'

'A very good question. Again, further analysis of the cut

direction will give us more to go on, but it's certainly a strong possibility, over and above the statistics.'

'Thanks, Doc.'

Craven reached for the mask below his chin.

'My pleasure. Now, unless you want to stay here for the PM, rather than watch on the CCTV next door, I'll simply say that my report will be with you by the end of today.'

'Actually, there is one last thing I need, Doc,' Stella said, producing Niamh Connolly's iPhone still sealed in a transparent evidence bag with its yellow chain of custody tag. 'We think she used Touch ID to lock it.'

She handed the bag over and watched as Craven deftly slit the seal with a scalpel. He retrieved the iPhone and then picked up Niamh Connolly's right hand.

'Around nine in ten of the UK population are right-handed. So let's try the right thumb first.'

'That's what I use,' Garry said, watching closely as the doctor gently pressed the dead woman's right thumb pad onto the circle of plastic.

The phone unlocked. No drama, no trying every finger in turn.

'Thank God for predictable human behaviour,' Stella said, taking the phone from Craven.

'Indeed. I am led to believe that many people still use "password" as their password.'

Stella tapped the Settings button and disabled the phone's touch ID and password, leaving it unlocked permanently. She resealed it in the evidence bag and, together with Garry and the others, left the room for the comfort and stink-free air of the viewing room.

―――――

With the dissection room cleared, Dr Craven settled his mask over his mouth and beckoned to his mortuary technician to come over from her work station and help him.

Verity had been with him for a year and a month, and he appreciated her quiet and careful way of working. At times she struck him as being too young to be spending her days unloading torsos of their contents, measuring the length and depth of incisions made in human flesh, and sieving stomach contents.

At twenty-six, she was the same age as his daughter, Gemma, who was an accountant. But then, as Verity had said when he'd asked her the question at interview, 'All my friends wanted to do after school was be famous. I wanted a career where I could help make things better.' Then she'd smiled, showing crooked teeth. 'Plus it would make it easy to get rid of creeps in pubs when I tell them what I do for a living.'

And now she stood beside him, watching as he selected a long-handled scalpel from the tray of instruments by his right elbow.

He touched the tip of the blade to the raw red wound on the left side of the chest.

'What do you make of that?' he asked.

She brought a large, plastic-handled magnifying glass from the pocket of her apron and bent over the body, adjusting distances between wound and lens, lens and eye. She took her time, another facet of her working method Craven appreciated, moving over the whole of the surface of the wound before peering even closer at the edges.

'He didn't use a knife,' she said, finally, without turning away from her examination.

'And you say this why?' Craven asked, meaning to prompt not criticise, as he knew Verity would understand.

'Well, if I was going to cut off a woman's breast, I would use something like a carving knife. You know, one with a long flexible blade. Maybe nine inches.'

'And?'

'And in that case, I would use a long-stroke, sawing action. That would leave a series of clean, longitudinal cuts, layered upon each other. You'd see a distinctive shallow, zig-zag pattern progressing across the remaining tissue.'

'So, what are you seeing instead?'

Verity bent over the ravaged flesh again with the magnifying glass.

'I'm seeing a mixture of marks. There are shallow, triangular punctures. There are marks where the muscles appear to have been almost crimped as well as cut. And the skin around the wounds has little peaks at the end of the separate cuts. May I have some tweezers, please, Doctor Craven?'

He handed her a pair of tweezers and watched closely as she picked at the darkening red flesh on the left-hand wound. He held out a petri dish ready as she turned and tapped the tweezers against its side. A small dark fragment of what could have been dried blood fell into the glass dish.

'I'm not sure,' she said, 'but I think there's rust in the wound.'

'So what do we have here, in terms of a weapon?' Craven asked her.

He had already formulated an initial hypothesis, but he wanted his protégée to arrive at her own answer, albeit with a little guidance from him. Verity straightened, without the groan or grunt of the middle-aged man feeling his lower back protesting, Craven noticed somewhat enviously.

She turned to face him. Spoke decisively.

'Some sort of two-bladed implement. With a scissoring action. But the cuts weren't clean or neat, so I'm not thinking anything even remotely designed for the job. Not kitchen scissors, for example.'

Craven smiled. She was good, this young woman with the cast-iron stomach and curiously matter-of-fact attitude to the grislier tasks of her chosen profession.

'So what, then? If you had to hazard a guess?'

She smiled back.

'If I had to hazard a guess?' She looked up and to the right and touched her chin with a purple-gloved index finger. 'Hmm. I would have to say, given the fragments of what I will assume, just for the moment, is rust, and the unusual wound signature, that the killer used some short of shears. Old ones at that.'

Craven nodded. Verity was going to go a long way. He saw a future pathologist standing beside him.

'We should advise the police to get a tool marks specialist to have a look, of course, but I agree with you. That's very good work, Verity.'

She looked down for a second, then back at him. No blush, just the steady gaze of someone totally in her element.

'Thank you, Doctor Craven. And before we get to the internal examination, I just want to say I agree with DCI Cole about the pubic area. My friends and I are all bare down there,' she pointed at the patch of stubble on the body's pubic area. 'But nobody goes at their lady garden with a razor blunt enough to do that. And nobody would want to, either. You do waxing, sugaring or you use a special shaver. That's the killer's handiwork. And look.' She lifted the thighs apart on the table, exposing the labia and the cleft where the buttocks met. 'Only the front's been done. No woman would leave herself looking like that, razor or not.'

Not for the first time Craven felt amazement at his assistant's utterly unflappable attitude to, and openness about, intimate subjects. *If I didn't know you came from North London, I'd swear you were Swedish*, he'd thought in her first week, when they'd discussed the sex toy he'd found inside a male cadaver. Now, he could only smile and agree.

'My feeling, too. Now, how about the wound on the throat?'

20

Verity moved around the steel table and looked down at the purple circlet around the dead woman's neck. She crouched before gently tipping the head to one side, lifting up the hair and peering at the nape of the neck.

'Not manual strangulation,' she said immediately.

'Why?'

'We have one continuous ligature mark: even width, even colour, therefore even pressure. No separate bruises that would indicate the killer used his hands. When you open her up I doubt you'll find that the hyoid bone is broken, as would be the case if the killer's thumbs or fingers were clamped over her throat.'

Craven nodded his appreciation again. *Let's test you a little further.*

'Any thoughts on the ligature itself?'

She placed the magnifying glass close to the bruised neck. The mortuary was silent as she examined the marks. Silent, apart from the whirr of the air extractor and the occasional gurgle from the drain beneath the table.

'There are faint diagonal marks where the bruising is less pronounced. That makes me think of something plaited or twisted, not smooth. So not a modern cable like a clothes line or electrical wire and more like a rope. Hold on, there's something sticking to the skin. May I have the tweezers again, Doctor?'

Moments later she was holding the clamped, needle-pointed tweezers up to the light. Craven looked closer.

'Is that a thread, Verity?'

'Yes, I think so. It's golden.'

She went to the bench and trapped the minuscule fibre in a petri dish. When she returned to the examination table, Craven was extracting a second fibre, which she captured in a new dish.

Craven picked up the left forearm, turning it over so the paler inside was uppermost.

'What do you see?' he asked.

'No defensive wounds. No cuts or bruising.' She flexed the fingers then looked at the palm. 'None here, either.' She looked at the other arm and hand. 'Or here.'

She fetched a small, narrow-ended tool like a clockmaker's screwdriver and deftly ran it beneath each of the ten fingernails in turn, placing the meagre scrapings in a dish.

'Whatever we find, I'm not hopeful there'll be any epithelials from the killer,' she said, once she'd placed a lid over the dish.

'And she wasn't subdued physically, we can see that. No head wound, no ligature or handcuff marks on her wrists.'

Verity frowned.

'I know this isn't our job, Doctor, but that suggests to me that she knew her killer.'

'Possibly so, possibly so. But even if she did, he would still have had to render her immobile while he tortured her.'

'He drugged her.'

'Or knocked her out by briefly stopping the blood supply to the brain. I suggest we stop hypothesising here and let her body tell us its story.'

Craven reached up to switch the mic back on.

'Well,' he said, 'shall we get going? We'll start with a rape kit, I think.'

He watched while Verity combed through what was left of the pubic hair, took separate swabs from the mouth, anus and vagina, labelled each sample, and sealed them in evidence bags.

When she'd finished, Craven took the largest of the scalpels and, starting at the point where the right collar bone met the shoulder, drew the blade towards the sternum. The wounds to Niamh Connolly's chest meant that he had to modify the traditional Y incision, directing his blade beneath the site where her right breast had been removed to a point on her solar plexus. He repeated the process on the other side, then drew the blade smoothly through the cold, pale skin and yellow fat to the pubic bone.

Verity helped him peel the two large sheets of skin and subcutaneous fat away from the muscles wrapped in their silvery shrouds of fascia and lay them folded to each side. The triangle of skin from throat to sternum that sat in the valley of the Y they lifted up and laid carefully over the dead woman's face. The abdominal wall went next.

Using the rib-cutters, Craven cut through the costal cartilage attaching the ribs to the shield-shaped breastbone and opened up the ribcage with a series of sharp cracks. And then began the business of removing, weighing and sampling the internal organs.

Craven worked steadily, handing each glistening organ to Verity who would carry it, almost reverently, to the large stainless-steel pan of the scales, note its weight, then remove a small piece for further examination before finally depositing it in a large Tupperware container.

'DCI Cole was right,' Craven said, after examining the dead woman's uterus. 'Mrs Connolly had at least one child delivered by caesarean section.'

Carefully, he handed her the soft bag of the stomach. She made a long incision on one side and ladled the contents into a cylindrical plastic container. At once, the sharp tang of stomach acid filled the space between them, overlaid with the sweet smell of partially digested alcohol.

With the particulars of gross anatomy out of the way, and the organs returned to the body cavity, Craven invited Verity to sew up the Y incision. He watched her work, noting with approval the care she took.

More than one mortuary technician he'd worked with had treated the dead as though they were working with leather, bashing in stitches any old how and cinching them tight with so much force that the re-joined edges of the wound puckered.

When she'd finished, tying a knot and snipping the final length of black thread short, Craven began on the cut known as a modified sagittal-temporal incision. Maintaining firm pressure on the scalpel blade, he opened a semi-circular cut from ear-to-ear round the back of the head. Then he tugged the scalp and the face forward and back on themselves, exposing the pinkish bone of the skull.

He leaned in to examine the revealed flesh beneath the scalp then paused as he spotted something on the right side of the neck, just below the ear, framed by the red flaps of skin that met just above it.

'Could I have that magnifying glass, please?'

He adjusted the glass until the skin on Niamh Connolly's neck came into pin-sharp clarity. And there, in the soft space behind the angle of her jaw, was a tiny red mark.

He straightened, rueing the way his crackling spine sent pops echoing off the hard surfaces of the autopsy room.

'What do you make of that?' he said, pointing at the mark.

Verity took the glass and repeated the sequence of movements Craven had just made.

'That looks like a needle prick.'

'It does, doesn't it?'

'So she *was*,' Verity paused, 'sorry, Doctor Craven, she *may* have been drugged.'

Craven waved away the apology. Someone who made as few mistakes as Verity did was entitled to the occasional lapse into certainty before the evidence.

'Toxicology will tell us what we need to know on that score. Pass me the Stryker saw, please. Let's see what Mrs Connolly's brain can tell us.'

The room filled with the buzz of the electric saw, which changed to a high-pitched whine as its finely engineered teeth bit into bone.

21

THURSDAY 16TH AUGUST 08.00 A.M.

The briefing room was thrumming with energy. Stella knew it was vital they achieve some quick results in the case: what started off as a restless enthusiasm to get things done could change all too quickly to dispirited lethargy as cases dragged on and leads failed to pan out.

She looked round at the thirteen faces. The warranted officers, Rosh, Jumper, Garry, Def, Baz, Will, Becks and Cam. And the police staff: Alec, Lucian, and Martin Brabey and Shirley Trott, two ex-detectives now contracted as civilian investigators. All held her gaze. All had coffees, teas or Cokes in front of them. Garry was munching on a ham roll, Stacey was eating fruit salad out of a M&S pot.

'Morning,' Stella said. 'Let's go through team reports first, then I'll update you on what I know. Then we'll figure out which lines of enquiry we're going ahead with. OK, Roisin and Will, you're up.'

Roisin spoke.

'The neighbours were useless. We didn't even get the usual "lovely couple" stuff. "Parkside people like to keep themselves to themselves",' she said in a cut-glass accent that had the others sniggering. 'But,' she said, as Stella opened her mouth, 'after we extended the search to a hundred metres, guess what?'

'Please tell me they found something!' Stella said, feeling a buzz of excitement in her stomach.

'They did.'

Stella noticed Will squirming in his chair like a small boy in class who needed the toilet.

'Will, do you want to tell us something, or do you just need a wee?'

More laughter.

'It's OK, boss. I can hold it,' he said with a grin. 'They found some rope. It was stuffed down inside a skip in a front garden, which, incidentally, was about the size of a tennis court. Obviously the householders were having building work done. It was full of old shower units, a toilet, shelving units, you know, shit they'd grown tired of.'

'What kind of rope?' Camille asked.

'I don't know. I mean, not specifically. There was about a metre. It wasn't very thick.' He held up his finger. 'Like that, maybe? It's in the exhibits room.'

'That's fantastic!' Stella said. 'Lucian, can you prioritise that, please. Sounds like we've got the murder weapon. OK, anything else?'

Roisin and Will shook their heads.

'Jumper, Def, how are you getting on with LoveLife?'

Arran looked at Def.

'Do you want to kick off?'

She smiled, and Stella couldn't help thinking Def had chosen the wrong career, since she could be earning about a thousand times more as a model than as a DS.

'So, the charity itself is squeaky-clean. I spoke to their board of trustees, six of the most upstanding and morally unbending people you could ever hope to meet. Apart from the fact that they nearly choked us with their self-righteousness, and their mediaeval attitude to women's rights, I couldn't see anything out of place.'

Arran waited for Def to finish then leaned forwards, looking around the table before speaking.

'Their finances are clean, but they are a bit strapped for cash. Probably like most charities these days, what with austerity and everything. But no loans, no dodgy investments, no gifts from paedo bishops, nothing.'

'Jerry Connolly said she was meeting a potential donor the day she was murdered,' Garry said. 'Anyone looking to get inside her defences, that would be a smart ploy.'

'Yeah. And that's where I think we should be looking, boss,' Arran said. 'Not the charity people, but the other lot. What the trustees called, I kid you not, "the Devil's disciples".'

Stella blinked.

'That's a bit strong, isn't it? I thought it was all *Guardian* readers and card-carrying feminists, professors of Women's Studies, that lot.'

'It is,' Arran continued. 'Plus the usual rent-a-mob from the Socialist Workers' Party and a few of the more hardcore lefties in the Labour Party. But that's not the way the LoveLifers see them.'

He consulted his notebook.

'According to Mister Frederick Galley, seventy-two, one of the trustees, the pro-abortion lot, and I quote, "slake their unquenchable thirst for blood on the tiny corpses of the unborn, so enslaved are they to Satan".'

He looked around the room, took a beat and delivered the punchline:

'Makes the Arsenal-Spurs rivalry look a bit tame, doesn't it?'

Once Stella had restored order, she pointed at Def.

'Mark Hellworthy at Wandsworth CID sent over Niamh Connolly's files on the nutters who sent her threatening letters and emails. Can you start working through them? Maybe our killer's hiding in plain sight.'

'Yes, boss. What about her phone? Are there more on there?'

'It's unlocked and in the Exhibits Room.'

'Boss?' Becky asked.

'What is it, Becks?'

'They usually film the demos. Maybe one of the camera crews caught someone, you know, off.'

Feeling justified at another of her picks, Stella smiled.

'Great idea! Can you call round the TV companies and, I don't know, Buzzfeed News or HuffPost or whoever the web companies are who do any filming? See what footage they've got and get them to send us copies.'

'Yes, boss,' Becky said, looking like a head girl being praised by the headmistress.

'OK, this is great, guys. Really good. Baz, what did you guys pull up from the databases?'

'We've got a lovely long list of the country's dregs to talk to. Couple of hundred violent sex offenders. Plus about a dozen unsolveds where the victim was stabbed or slashed across the breasts. We're putting together teams to do the interviews, attackers and victims, both. And Cam had a brilliant idea. Tell them, Cam.'

Camille sat straighter in her chair, blue eyes narrowed.

'Maybe it's not about all the abortion stuff *or* sex. Maybe it's about her being a Catholic. What I mean is, look at all the nonce priests who keep crawling out of the woodwork. And all along, the bishops have been protecting them. I've got a mate works in Melbourne on their Child Protection squad. He was one of the ones who arrested that bishop last year. What was his name, McClaren, MacAdam? Anyway, he said there're a lot of really angry people over there who are practically setting up lynch mobs. So maybe our killer was abused as a kid. He was, like, an altar boy or in the Scouts, and he keeps reading all the media coverage and, finally, he just snaps. You know, gets triggered or whatever the shrinks call it. So he kills a high-profile Catholic.'

'What, sort of an anti-hypocrisy thing?' Will asked. 'She's setting herself up as a champion of the rights of the unborn child while all along her church is trampling over the rights of children who've already been born.'

Camille nodded.

'Could be, which ties it back to the abortion angle.'

'He could have been stalking her at the events,' Becky chipped in.

Stella could feel it: that indefinable sense of the motor running at peak efficiency. People were still getting enough sleep, food and fresh air to think straight and work together.

'Right,' she said. 'That's worth following up. Which just leaves me and Garry. We spoke to Jerry Connolly. He's got a watertight alibi so even if we did like him for it, which we didn't, did we, Garry—'

'Tried it on for size, didn't fit,' he said laconically.

'– he couldn't have done it. All right, here's where we go next. Becks, you're onto the news teams for footage of the crowds at the last two or three rallies. Def, you're going through the crazies files. Rosh, can you look at the mystery donor? The timings, the fact he was going to meet her at her home – this looks like our strongest lead so far. Jumper, can you manage the interview teams working the sex offenders and victims, please? And, actually, take Def with you.'

She turned to the blonde DS.

'You're our best interviewer, Def. If anyone can get any details out of the victims, it's going to be you. So instead, let's have Will on the crazies file. Baz, keep on hammering the databases. And I put in a form one hundred to SCAS yesterday, so can you coordinate that, too, please? Cam, I want you to put together a list of the most outspoken critics of the whole Catholic Church-slash-paedo thing. Especially online: Twitter, Facebook, blogs, whatever. Anyone suggesting direct action, or violence, or—'

'Taste of their own medicine?'

'Exactly!'

'On it, boss.'

Stella's phone pinged. The alert in the top-right corner of the email icon told her it was Dr Craven's post mortem report.

'That's the PM report. OK, everyone know what they're doing?'

There was a chorus of agreement as people pushed chairs back and made their way back to their desks or out of the room.

'Right. I'm going to read this, see what Dr Craven discovered. Lucian, can I have a word before you go?'

Once the room was emptied, Lucian moved to the chair next to Stella's.

'You wanted to see me, ma'am,' he said, winking.

She punched him affectionately on the upper arm. Apart from Callie, Lucian was the only person at Paddington Green who knew the torturous path Stella had travelled only a handful of years earlier. Only half-jokingly, she referred to him as a member of her 'sanity team'.

'How's it going on the forensic side?'

'We've had all the evidence the Wandsworth CSIs collected. We're reviewing it now. But I can tell you this, our killer was forensically aware. No fingerprints around the victim, none in the office. There was a glass with traces of lemonade in it but it had been wiped clean. The rope sounds interesting, though. I'm going down to the Exhibits Room after this.'

Stella grunted.

'Send my regards to Reg the Veg, won't you?'

Reg 'the Veg' Willings had been managing the Exhibits Room at Paddington Green since, according to received wisdom, the early part of the reign of Henry the Eighth. His passions were his allotment, hence the soubriquet, ballroom dancing and trotting out platitudes in a variety of what he clearly considered to be amusing regional accents.

Lucian let his eyelids droop to cover his deep-brown eyes for a second as he nodded.

'You'd have thought he'd have retired by now. He must have his thirty in.'

'Twenty-nine's what I heard. Counting the days, eh? So, how are things otherwise? Domestically, I mean? You and Gareth doing OK?'

'It's our three-year anniversary this year,' Lucian said with a smile. 'In fact, we're having a dinner party in a couple of weeks. We'd love you to come.'

'And I'd love to be there, work permitting. Send me the details.

And if you've got a nice single, straight male friend with no hang-ups, a steady job and a respectful attitude to working women, please invite him!' she said, raising her voice at the end of this request and clutching the front of Lucian's shirt, her eyes pleading.

He laughed as he gently dislodged her hands.

'That would be Stefan. And yes, we are inviting him.'

'Wait. You mean you actually *know* someone like that?'

'Uh-huh. He's forty-five, divorced, two kids who live with his ex. He's a landscape gardener, runs his own business and, as far as I know, thinks women should be free to do pretty much whatever they want. And because I know you're not shallow enough to ask, I'll tell you that he's not bad-looking. Full head of hair, nice eyes. Gareth said he was a great loss to the gay community.'

'Sounds perfect. So why's he divorced?'

'His ex is a finance CEO. She couldn't take his irregular hours. Thought he should be there cooking her tea every evening.'

'Right. I am definitely coming. Can I wear heels?'

Lucian smiled.

'He's over six foot, so heels are no problem.'

'Thanks,' Stella said, smiling. *Maybe there's hope for me yet.* 'In return, do you want to read the PM report with me?'

Lucian clapped his hand to his chest.

'Oh, Stella! You really know how to make a boy feel special!'

A minute later they were sitting side by side at her desk, reading the opening lines of Niamh Connolly's post mortem report.

Craven gave cause of death as strangulation by ligature (probably rope). The manner of death, he felt, was homicide. *God, you're so cautious, Roy,* she thought. *What else could it be?* He gave time of death, as indicated by digestive process markers and the anal temperature as taken by the on-call police surgeon, as somewhere between 12.30 p.m. and 6.00 p.m. His next note, highlighted, caught her eye.

NOTE: two fibres found in ligature mark, one gold-coloured, one cream. RECOMMENDATION: send for forensic analysis. Identification of fibre could lead to type of rope.

In his precise, unemotional prose, Craven reported that:

Mrs Connolly was tortured before being killed, by having her breasts cut off. Her killer employed some form of double-bladed implement that performed a scissoring action on her living tissue. Particles of rust were found in the wounds.

RECOMMENDATION: consult tool marks expert.

The breasts themselves are otherwise intact. No semen. No bite marks. No other damage.

The mons veneris was denuded of pubic hair, by shaving with a safety razor, probably disposable, although the depilation did not extend to the perineum or anus. This action was, in all probability performed post mortem.

A rape kit has been performed and has come back negative. No semen in the mouth, vagina or anus, on the belly, buttocks or breasts, or in the wounds. No evidence of penetration, either by a penis or object. No damage to the external genitalia or anus. No bite marks. No defensive wounds to hands or forearms.

Awaiting DNA results on epithelial cells and loose pubic hairs trapped by combing.

Fingernail scrapings revealed nothing but household dust and minute fragments of tuna (cooked).
The stomach contents have been analysed: the victim's last meal consisted of a tuna salad and, in all likelihood, a single glass of white wine (sauvignon blanc).

Stella raised her eyebrows at Craven's apparent ability to detect grape varieties even when confronted with the sour, acidic overlay of stomach acid and half-digested food.

The victim had no external or internal bruising or haemorrhaging, apart from the gross injuries to the upper thorax and small bruises consistent with a firm manual grip on both breasts.

NOTE: needle mark detected on the victim's neck, just below the right ear. HYPOTHESIS: the killer injected some form of incapacitating drug. Toxicology will confirm/deny.

The rest of the report consisted of what Stella thought of as 'housekeeping'. Not exactly boring, but routine data on weight and condition of all organs including the brain, evidence of past illnesses and surgical procedures, and miscellaneous observations on the body's general condition.

In short, apart from the fact that she had been tortured and then strangled to death, Niamh Connolly, was in excellent physical shape and would probably have lived a long and healthy life, unless one of the big, random bullets – cancer, heart disease, stroke – had felled her first.

The lack of sexual assault was interesting. In Stella's experience, mutilation of a woman's breasts or vagina was always accompanied by rape, whether directly or through use of a dildo, a bottle or whatever object came to the attacker's hand. But this guy hadn't touched her that way.

According to the CSIs, who'd been over the whole house with alternative light sources, the only semen to be found was in the marital bed and on a pair of pyjama trousers in the laundry basket, and DNA tests would likely confirm it came from Jerry Connolly. Whose alibi had checked out. She had a team looking at the possibility of a spurned lover but, in her heart, she knew they wouldn't find one.

She turned to Lucian.

'Do you do tool marks?'

'I may have a little database, yes. And I have a friend over in West End Central who has a tame expert at Imperial College who's a forensic engineering consultant. Between us, we'll pin it down.'

22

THURSDAY 16TH AUGUST 9.30 A.M.

Becky's trawl through the media companies' news departments hit paydirt on her ninth call, the first eight all having been met with either vague agreements to 'check what we shot' or even vaguer references to 'getting clearance from Legal'. *Don't you know women are being murdered?* she wanted to shout down the phone at them. *You ought to, you're covering them!* But no, that would be counter-productive, and Becky was all about efficiency.

The BBC News producer she spoke to said he had footage of the LoveLife picketing of The Sackville Centre in Mitcham. He listened while Becky explained what she wanted and then told her he had some footage of the crowd of onlookers and the counter protesters. What he called, 'the B-Roll. Stuff we cut away to when we want to vary the viewpoint.' He promised to burn it onto a DVD and courier it over and he'd been as good as his word. An hour later a bike messenger dropped off a padded envelope marked:

DS B. HU
PADDINGTON GREEN POLICE STATION

LONDON W2

A uniformed PC brought up the envelope and Becky ripped the flap open, in her hurry shedding fluffy grey padding all over her keyboard.

'Shit!' she said. Then again in Cantonese: '*Lā shǐ!*', which felt more satisfying.

Having blown the soft grey fluff off her desk, she inserted the DVD into the PC and waited for it to load. A simple viewing program launched itself automatically and she clicked the play button.

Almost immediately, a crowd of protesters filled the rectangular pane on her screen. These were the ones in favour of women's reproductive rights. Niamh Connolly's supporters could be seen off to one side, some praying, others hurling abuse back at the yelling women who carried a variety of placards. The closest to the camera read, 'A woman's right to choose comes first!'

The footage lasted for twenty minutes. She nodded her thanks as someone placed a mug of coffee at her elbow, though as she didn't look away from the screen she didn't know which of her colleagues was feeling generous this morning.

Eventually, the video froze on a woman screaming directly into the camera. Becky finished her coffee then took the video back to the start and watched it again, this time at half speed.

When she saw him, she paused the video, wound back a few seconds then noted the time stamp from the top-right corner: 5'17'.

She hit PLAY and watched the young man who'd caught her eye for the three seconds he was in view.

He was the kind of man eye-witnesses usually described as tall/short, skinny/well-built, blond/mousey/brown hair, beige windcheater/green jumper/grey hoodie. Mr Average, in other words.

In fact, Becky put his height at about five foot eight. His lower half was obscured by other protesters, but his torso, Becky could see, was well-muscled. Wide shoulders and a broad chest beneath a dark-grey sweatshirt, no hood. And his hair was best described as dirty blond. None of which interested Becky greatly, though it would help when they came to tracking him down. No, what had caught her eye was a placard he was holding.

**DEATH TO
NIAMH CONNOLLY!
YOU CAN'T KILL
WHAT DOESN'T LIVE!**

She printed a copy of the frozen video image and went looking for one of the DIs.

————

Roisin saw Becky approaching her desk and signalled with an upraised finger for her to hold on.

When she finished the call, she turned to Becky.

'What've you got?'

Becky showed her the blurry black and white printout.

'It's from the BBC's news footage of the last LoveLife demo. The one Niamh Connolly got killed after. Look at his placard.'

Roisin peered at the image for a few seconds. *Really? You interrupted me with this?*

'Just another crank, Becks,' she said finally. 'Our guy's hardly likely to advertise his intentions on a bloody placard, is he?'

Becky clearly hadn't expected a putdown. *Well, that'll teach you to be a bit more discerning, won't it?*

'But, look at his expression. It's like there's nothing there. The others are all yelling, screaming. They look like they'd like to throw stuff. He's so calm.'

It was true, Roisin had to admit. The guy looked oddly relaxed. Though there was something around the eyes that made her uncomfortable. Where had she seen it before? She closed her eyes, willing herself to flip through the dozens of cases she'd worked since joining SIU.

All the killers, rapists, terrorists and paedophiles that had marched into her working life, and sometimes her dreams, before being arrested, charged and convicted. She mentally reviewed her internal mugshot book now. Then she had it.

Of them all, there was only one who'd really frightened her. Arthur Gregory Chater. He'd abducted, raped and then strangled five-year-old female twins from a housing estate in Camden. When they'd finally caught him, he'd seemed almost surprised. He couldn't really understand why they would be so concerned. 'They were only kids,' he'd said to her calmly, in the sort of middle-class accent she associated with doctors and teachers. 'Hardly worth all this fuss, surely? There are so many more running about all over the city.'

Chater had had the same look as the unnamed guy in the grainy still in front of her. As if he were looking at sheep, or even something inanimate, like packing cases, rather than living, breathing, feeling human beings.

She opened her eyes to see Becky standing there, watching her closely, perhaps hoping some of her investigative powers would rub off on her. *Not today, sweetie.*

'Look, it's a long shot, but leave it with me, OK? I'll have a think, but honestly? Like I said, killers don't tend to go around holding up signboards that say, "I'm your man!", do they?'

'No, I guess not,' Becky answered, eyes downcast before turning away and retreating to her desk.

Roisin knew she had a solid lead. But she wasn't about to run off to Stella with it. This was her lead and it would be her collar. She'd bring him in on her own and make sure everyone, right up to Callie, knew that it was she, Roisin Mary Griffin, who'd found him, and not the golden girl, Ms Back-From-The-Dead Cole.

Now, how to track you down, sunshine, hmm?

Her first call was to the organisers of the counter-protest outside The Sackville Centre. The main body of them had been carrying placards with a pink and grey logo reading WAGSARR. A quick search revealed that the acronym stood for Women and Girls' Sexual and Reproductive Rights. The group's website claimed on its homepage that WAGSARR was 'standing up to the Patriarchy and its gender-traitor accomplices in the fight for abortion and sex education on demand'.

She read a few blog posts and watched a couple of videos and formed the impression that these were women (and a few men) who were more than happy to get physical with 'the enemy' as their overheated prose referred to anyone opposed to abortion, from Catholics to conservative intellectuals.

Roisin had had an abortion herself as a seventeen-year-old, travelling alone from Belfast to Liverpool after being raped by an uncle. She'd never told a living soul about either the rape or the abortion. But despite this, she began to tire of the strident rhetoric that permeated each page on the WAGSARR site.

'Jesus Christ! All right, we get it!' she said, exasperated at yet another impassioned attack on anyone who might wonder whether a foetus was indeed a human being and not just a vestigial organ on a par with a woman's appendix.

She picked up the phone.

'WAGSARR,' a young woman announced. She sounded like she was issuing a challenge, not welcoming an enquiry.

'Hi. This is Detective Inspector Roisin Griffin, from the Metropolitan Police. I need to speak to someone about the LoveLife event you guys were picketing last Friday.'

Instead of meekly complying and putting her through to the CEO or events director, the young woman went on the offensive.

'Roisin. That's an Irish name, isn't it? You sure you're not with the Catholic Church, doing a bit of digging?'

Roisin's eyes widened at the cheek of it. A few choice replies fizzed through her mind and one almost made it past her lips, but if she was going to get anywhere then tact would have to take precedence.

'Here's the front desk number for Paddington Green Police Station: 020 7321 8517. Call me back.'

She hung up, staring at the desk phone malevolently.

Two minutes passed, then it rang.

'DI Griffin.'

'It's the front desk here. I've got a Nancy Blakeney from, I didn't quite catch the company. It sounded like, wagser?'

'Thanks, put her through,' Roisin said, already warming up one of the responses she'd toyed with a few minutes earlier.

'DI Griffin.'

The young woman's tone was completely different. The spikiness had gone from her voice, leaving a much younger-sounding person altogether.

'Oh, er, hi. It's Nancy from WAGSARR? We were just speaking?'

She had the annoying habit, now spreading even into the Met, of making every simple sentence sound like a question. Roisin decided to play on it.

'Are you asking me or telling me, Nancy?'

'Oh. Telling? I mean, you, like, know that, right?'

'Yes, Nancy, I do. Now if you've finished wasting my time, I want you to put me through to –' she nearly said, 'a grown-up' but swerved at the last second, '– someone in charge.'

'Yes, of course. Sure. I'll, like, find Eleni? She's our boss?'

The line clicked. But the silly girl hadn't put her on hold, just put the receiver down on her desk. Roisin could hear the ensuing conversation clearly.

'Shit! I've got the cops on the phone? They want to speak to Eleni?'

'What do the pigs want with Eleni?'

'I don't know! She, like, went all official on me? Maybe they know about, you know, the rally? Maybe they're going to, like, film it or whatever?'

'Tell her to piss off and come back with a lawyer.'

'I can't! They've, like, probably got a file on me? You know I got fined for possession last year? Where is she?'

'Eleni's in her office. I wouldn't bother her if I were you. Tell the pig she's out at a meeting.'

Roisin heard a rustle of papers then the muffled sound of the receiver being held against Nancy's cheek.

'Er, hi. Yeah, I checked but Eleni is, like, out at a meeting? So I can take a message?'

Roisin had had enough of being jerked around by this bunch of clowns.

'I heard everything you just said, Nancy. So put me through to Eleni right now,' she raised her voice, 'or, *like*, this pig is going to come down there right now and arrest you for obstruction of justice. Three seconds.'

She heard a swift gasp, then silence as the line was cut.

Swearing, she was reaching for her bag when the phone crackled.

'This is Eleni Booth. To whom am I speaking, please?'

'DI Griffin, Metropolitan Police. I'm investigating the murder of Niamh Connolly. I want to show you something. If you've got any meetings – real ones, that is – please either cancel them or be prepared to take a break. I'll be with you in half an hour.'

'I'm not sure I care for your tone, DI Griffin,' Booth calmly replied. 'I may well have to go out shortly. Can't this wait?'

So much for sisterhood, Roisin thought. *Guess it doesn't cut across ideological lines.*

'I'm sorry if my *tone* offended you Ms Booth. But I have just been lied to by one your staff and called a "pig" by another. So you'll have to forgive me for being a little impatient. As I said, I am investigating a murder.'

'Very well,' Booth sighed. 'Do I need a lawyer?'

What you need is someone to teach you some manners, Roisin thought.

'I can't advise you on that.'

Fearing she'd explode if she had to listen to any more of the woman's casually patronising questions, Roisin ended the call, grabbed her bag and car keys and headed out.

'Where're you off to in such a hurry?' Baz asked as she marched past him.

'Interviewing a potential witness. Probably turn out to be a waste of time.'

And she was gone.

By the time she arrived at the offices of WAGSARR, her earlier anger had dissipated, to be replaced with a determination not to let Eleni Booth get under her skin again.

The group had their offices in Bow on the fifth floor of a narrow office building sandwiched between a pub and a boarded-up shop. A grubby aluminium intercom to the right of the plate-glass door had six names on slips of paper beneath plastic covers. Roisin jabbed a finger at the button beside the WAGSARR logo and held it for a count of three.

'Hello?' a tinny, suspicious voice squawked from the grille.

Roisin rolled her eyes. *Very professional.*

'DI Griffin to see Eleni Booth.'

The latch buzzed and Roisin pushed her way in. She looked around for the lift and was dismayed to see only a plain concrete staircase.

'Oh, you have to be joking,' she groaned.

Adjusting the shoulder strap on her bag, she started climbing. She could feel her determination to stay calm growing more fragile with every half-landing.

Sweating after the climb, and hating whoever had designed the building on the cheap without leaving any money for a lift, she pushed through the door labelled with the WAGSARR logo and looked around for a reception desk.

In that, she was disappointed. No seating area for visitors, no obvious receptionist, just half a dozen women of various ages between twenty-five and sixty clicking away on keyboards or talking on the phone. She was just about to tap the nearest twenty-something on the shoulder, hoping it was the suddenly-helpful Nancy, when a door at the far end of the room opened.

Out strode a woman of striking Mediterranean appearance – large dark eyes and a mane of luxuriant, glossy black hair. Her black dress was severe yet sexy and Roisin found herself wondering, inappropriately, what such a beautiful woman was doing in such a scuzzy office block.

The woman, Eleni Booth, she assumed, came towards her. No smile. No outstretched hand. *OK, so this is how you want to play it? Fine. I can do formal.*

Not giving Booth time to speak, Roisin hit her with her best officialese, making sure her voice carried to every corner of the room. She was gratified to see that all heads had turned towards her.

'Ms Booth? I'm Detective Inspector Roisin Griffin, Special Investigations Unit, Metropolitan Police. I'm investigating the murder of Mrs Niamh Connolly, former CEO of LoveLife. Do you have somewhere private we can talk?'

There! Suck on that, you snotty cow!

'Er, yes. Of course. My office, I think.'

Booth's office was a small, square, glass-walled cubicle about eight feet to a side. Books and magazines lined the walls, crammed onto white metal shelves. In contrast, her desk was an exercise in minimalism. All it held was a silver MacBook, a desk phone and a lamp, a thin, angular affair with an oval head housing a bright LED bulb.

Without waiting to be asked, Roisin sat down in the white plastic chair in front of the desk and waited for Booth to make her way past boxes of papers that sat on the grey carpet between her and her own chair.

23

WEDNESDAY 15TH AUGUST 10.45 A.M.

Lucian sat at his workstation with the length of rope in front of him, still in its evidence bag. He wanted to get going but he needed to set wheels in motion on the tool marks first. Doctor Craven had emailed him high-resolution photographs of the wounds to Niamh Connolly's breasts and rib cage.

Seen in extreme close-up, the flesh resembled a hellish landscape of reds, purples, blacks and yellows. As he moved the image around on his screen, enlarging one section, adjusting the brightness and contrast on another, different topographical features swam into focus. Here, a sharp-pointed mountain peak, there a valley with creased sides. A serrated ridge, a flat plain, a gouge as if a meteorite had ploughed into soft red earth.

Then he found it. A distinctive pattern where the blades had sheared through a muscle and clipped a bone. He magnified the section and altered a control to render the image in black and white. His iMac screen was almost three feet across, and the resolution of Doctor Craven's camera meant Lucian could zoom in until even the landscape disappeared and all that was left was a vast abstract image: straight lines, curves, patches of light and shade.

The section of the image that interested him was a series of parallel lines – cut marks – scored into the anterior surface of a rib. He counted them: a closely spaced group of seven plus a further three a little way out. The edges of the cuts were rough and pockmarked.

He switched the display back to colour. Scattered along the cuts, like autumn leaves, were dark-brown particles. He'd read Craven's comment about the presence of rust particles. Now he could confirm it: the crystalline structure of the iron oxide was unmistakable. He made a note to request a sample for testing.

Next, he zoomed out in small increments, watching the shape of the lines change. After five clicks of the mouse, he found himself looking at a slight change to the pattern. The lines were still parallel but now they exhibited a distinct if shallow curve. The curves meant the tool was hinged. A small, but significant breakthrough.

Holding a key down, Lucian clicked the cursor on one end of the longest cut then on the other end. He selected the line, copied it, and pasted it into a geometric analyser program he'd written himself.

He repeated the process on the other six lines. He'd specialised in coding at university, developing a piece of software with a couple of friends that had netted each of them enough money to buy flats, start businesses or, in one of their cases, bid for and win a rare 1970s Ferrari, which the proud new owner had wrecked two weeks after taking delivery.

GeomAlyser could perform a number of useful functions that would be possible to do manually, except it did them in a fraction of a second and didn't require pencils, tracing paper, protractors, a pair of compasses and a calculator.

The relatively shallow depth of the cuts as revealed in the PM report indicated that the murderer had used a hand-held tool, and not some industrial bolt- or cable-cutter. A few keystrokes later, and the programme told him what he wanted to know: the radius of the blades was 38 centimetres plus-or-minus 3 millimetres.

That's secateurs out, for a start, he thought, smiling with satisfaction as a piece of the puzzle fell into place.

What did it leave? He ran through the options as they came to mind, rather than in any order of likelihood. Ceremonial ribbon-cutting scissors. Professional garden shears. Maybe some sort of agricultural implement.

He launched the toolmarks database, marvelling once again at the Met's ability to torture the English language into coughing up 'appropriate' acronyms. STABS stood for Signatures of Tools And Bladed weaponS. Lucian felt the terminal S was a cheat, but the database was a goldmine, so he forgave its creators.

In billions of ones and zeroes it encoded the wound signatures of tens of thousands of bladed, pointed and blunt weapons that had been used in crimes across the Metropolitan Police Service's jurisdiction over the previous three and a half decades.

A notch on the side of a machete, an imperfection on the blade of a pair of hairdressing scissors, a maker's stamp on a hammer head. All had been enough to convict those who'd wielded them in the heat of passion or the cold of a premeditated murder, and all now gave up their secrets willingly to the person who knew which keywords to enter into the search box.

Lucian's first search was for the type of weapon used on Niamh Connolly to such devastating effect.

In a few seconds the database returned three hits based on a cut radius of 38 centimetres. The first, as he'd already surmised, was a pair of oversized scissors as used by dignitaries or, these days, celebrities, to cut the ribbon on a new shopping centre, playpark or hospital ward.

He wrinkled his nose. Although the blade length was right, the handles added almost as much again in length, which would make them very unwieldy and hard to conceal. The fact they'd been used by one factory worker on another at the place they were made reinforced Lucian's gut feel that this wasn't the weapon.

The next hit was a vintage pair of garden shears. But these had the same problem as the scissors in terms of overall length, although the rusting blades ticked a second box.

He clicked on the third line of text:

Sheep-shears, manual, 141/2' length.
Mfr: Burgon & Ball.

The forensic photographer had shot the shears against a standard white background with a chequered, black-and-white, L-shaped ruler for scale. Lucian did a rapid mental calculation: 141/2 inches equated to around 37 centimetres. He tapped the numbers into a desk calculator: 36.83. Bingo!

The shears in the photo were rusted and bloodstained, the colours of the two contaminants almost matching. They resembled the blades and long, thin tangs of a pair of handleless butcher's knives, facing each other and riveted at their ends into a heart-shaped spring of flat sprung steel. The blades would slide over each other to clip the sheep's fleece free, springing apart after each cut.

He printed out a colour copy, making a note in the printer use file and shaking his head at just how far budgeting had crept in the justice system. He was sure criminals didn't have to keep receipts for every packet of staples or duct tape.

'Now for the big one,' he breathed. 'Are you in our database?'

For this operation, Lucian needed a schematic diagram of the cut marks: the groups of seven and three parallel lines. Twenty minutes later, he had a cleaned-up black-and-white image reorientated so the lines were vertical. He imported the schematic into STABS and asked for a comparison, using the database identifier SS/m for 'sheep shears manual'.

The little hourglass spun jerkily for ten seconds. Lucian sat calmly, waiting for it to finish, thinking now about the rope sitting before him inside the paper evidence bag.

The chances of a weapon's already being in the database weren't high, but they weren't zero, either. It was more usually employed when a suspect's property had been searched and a weapon matching that used on a victim of crime had been found there. A characteristic pattern found on a murder weapon and suspect's tool would be enough for an arrest and often a conviction.

The hourglass came to rest.

No hits.

Lucian frowned. Then he shrugged. If only a lone, brilliant CSI could sit at his desk and solve major crimes by tapping a computer keyboard! Pulling on a pair of gloves, he slit the tape closing the evidence bag and removed the rope, holding it between thumb and forefinger.

He stretched it out on a green rubber cutting mat marked with a yellow grid of centimetres and millimetres, each tenth centimetre demarcated with a thicker line.

He noted the length: 95 cm. And the diameter: 12 mm.

The colour to the naked eye was off-white. At one end, and again roughly in the centre, the rope was stained with what appeared to be blood. Small patches of red, rather than a soaking.

He dabbed a forensic swab on one of the red stains and sealed it in a plastic tube. It would be the work of moments to ascertain if it were indeed blood. Now for the rope itself. First, a simple magnifying glass. Some of the younger CSIs and technicians always wanted to rush for the 'big toys' as they were known, the scanning and backscatter electron microscopes.

Lucian preferred to start as low-tech as possible and work up. He reckoned you caught more that way and, in any case, you could usually tell more about a broken-off acrylic fingernail or shell casing by inspecting it visually than blowing it up to the size of a continent.

Under the magnifying glass, an antique with a brass frame and mahogany handle he'd bought on eBay, Lucian examined the surface of the rope. Sticking out at random intervals were short crinkly fibres in black and gold.

'Hmm,' he muttered. 'What are you, then? Wool? Silk? Cotton?'

Time to delve a little deeper. Using needle-pointed tweezers, he eased one each of the gold-and- black fibres away from the rope fibres, and trapped them between two glass microscope slides.

Five minutes later, he had an answer he was ninety-nine per cent sure of: the black and gold fibres were wool. The scaly pattern, like the bark on a monkey-puzzle tree, confirmed it. He ran them through the gas chromatograph to be sure, and the result, when it arrived, gave him the missing one per cent.

He repeated the process with the white fibres themselves: the distinctive appearance, like bamboo sticks, gave him his answer: flax.

Two hours later, after running the rest of his tests and writing up his findings, he called Stella.

'What've you got for me, Lucian? Please say it's good news.'

'It *is* good news. Here's what I can give you right now. The rope they turned up in the search is flax: the same stuff they use to make linen. And it's got black and gold wool fibres in it.'

'Do the wool fibres match the fibre Verity pulled from the ligature mark in Niamh's neck?'

'They do, but only as far as saying they're wool, and they're the same colour. Evidentially, it's not bad, but a decent defence brief could pull it apart in seconds.'

'OK, but it's still a really strong link,' Stella said, her relief evident. 'And the tool mark analysis is fantastic. There can't be many of those sitting around. Any DNA?'

'I found blood and skin cells. We can test them in-house but that'll take about a week. Or I can send them to an external lab, put a rush-notice on them. That'll give you results in either twenty-four or forty-eight hours depending on how much you want to pay. Until we get a match to Niamh's DNA, all we really have is a bit of rope someone used while bleeding.'

'Shit! Why does everything come down to money? Fine. Leave it with me. I'll talk to Callie about the budget. My parents would be so proud. They always wanted me to be an accountant.'

Lucian laughed.

'I'm sure that's not true.'

'OK, it's not. But I may as well be the amount of bloody time I spend looking at spreadsheets. So, what about the weapon he used to mutilate her?'

'I can tell you that for nothing. Sheep shears. Vintage. They use a scissoring action. The blade radius, cut marks, they're all consistent. They found what appeared to be rust in the wounds at the PM. I ran it through the mass-spectrometer, which confirmed it.'

'You can't see me, but I am kneeling before you. Thanks, Lucian, you're a star. Gotta go. I need to ask Callie to increase my pocket money.'

24

THURSDAY 16TH AUGUST 11.15 A.M.

Eleni Booth interlaced her bony fingers on the desk in front of her and, finally, smiled. The expression changed her face completely, animating it with a liveliness that was completely disarming.

'So, detective inspector. You said you had something you wanted to show me? As you can see, I decided I could manage alone. We're a small charity and our funds don't really stretch to lawyers.'

Roisin extracted the photo from her messenger bag and placed it front and centre, facing Booth. She tapped the young man's face.

'Do you know that man?'

Booth pulled open a drawer and brought out a slim silver spectacles case, from which she extracted a pair of rimless reading glasses.

She peered at the image.

'It's not very clear, is it?'

'Not very, no. Do you know him?'

Booth shrugged.

'His face looks familiar, but we get a lot of people turning up when we're protesting. He doesn't work for WAGSARR, if that's what you're asking.'

'It's not what I'm asking, as I think you heard. What I *am* asking, Eleni, is whether you know him?'

Booth sighed.

'Let me get Nancy in here. She was at The Sackville Centre last Friday. Actually, as you're closer to the door, would you mind?'

Ha! Not at all.

Roisin stood and opened the office door.

'Nancy?' she barked. 'You're wanted.'

A young woman dressed in a black leather biker jacket, tie-dyed T-shirt and black jeans ripped across both knees stood and made her way over to the office door, which Roisin held wide for her. A wisp of perfume trailed along in her wake, something light and floral. She wore her hair in bunches, which gave her the look of a schoolgirl bunking off for the day.

She sat in the only other chair in the cramped space, a folding wooden seat she had to retrieve from its position leaning against a fling cabinet. She looked at Roisin guiltily, her lower lip trembling, and the DI took pity.

'Look, it's nothing to worry about, OK? I just want you to look at the bloke with the placard in that photo and tell me if you recognise him.'

Know him would be better, but I'll settle for anything at this point.

Nancy took the photo from Booth's fingers and spun it round to face her.

Without hesitation, she turned to Roisin.

'That's Isaac Holt?'

Feeling the first flutter of excitement she'd had on this case, Roisin pressed a little harder.

'And that's just your way of telling me, yes? You're sure you recognise him?'

'Yeah. Hundred per cent? He's like, a regular?'

'So do you know Isaac?'

'Oh, we all know him? Kim gives him a lift to all our demos? They live a few streets away from each other?'

Roisin felt like punching the air. She forced herself to speak in a conversational tone of voice.

'So, what's he like then, Isaac? That's a fairly ferocious placard he's holding up.'

Nancy laughed, revealing a black stud in her tongue.

'I know, right? He does take things to extremes? You should hear the things he says down the pub afterwards?'

Then her hand flew to her mouth and her eyes, as blue as cornflowers, widened above her clamping fingers.

'Oh, my God,' she said, bringing her hand down. 'You don't, like, think he did it, do you? Murdered Niamh Connolly, I mean? Cos, he's like, so gentle? I mean, he's into animal rights? He's, like, a vegan?'

In Roisin's experience, animal rights fanatics were capable of the most extraordinary acts of violence. She didn't bother opening that particular can of worms.

'I'm not thinking anything at this point, apart from that I'd *like* to talk to Isaac. This colleague of yours, Kim. Is she here today?'

Nancy nodded.

'Over there, by the window?'

'Could you go and get her for me, please?'

While Nancy was fetching her colleague, Roisin looked at Eleni, who'd watched the exchange with Nancy without moving.

'You don't approve of us, do you?' Eleni said.

'I don't approve or disapprove, it's not my place. I'm here to investigate Niamh Connolly's murder. We're looking at LoveLife as well, if that's any consolation.'

Booth snorted, derisively.

'Huh. They call us murderers. But do you know how many women, especially young women, die after having botched backstreet abortions? It still happens, you know? Right here in the UK, supposedly a civilised country. We have to fight for the woman's right to choose. We have to fight for—'

'Look, spare me the soapbox, OK? Abortion's legal in this country. And so is protesting against it. We don't take sides in any of these debates. We just do our jobs. Keep the peace. Protect the innocent. Arrest the guilty.'

Booth wrinkled her nose.

'Innocent? Ugh. Always the innocent. But what about the girl raped by her father? What about the single mother whose new boyfriend refuses to use a condom? Aren't they innocent? Where's the compassion for them? You sound just like Niamh Connolly and her kind.'

Against her will, Roisin found herself being dragged into the one argument she never wanted to take part in. She tried to wrest control of the conversation away from Booth.

'Niamh Connolly doesn't sound like anything anymore. Because she's dead.'

That silenced the older woman, and any further discussion was forestalled by the arrival of Nancy and Kim at the office door.

'Do you, like, need me anymore?' she asked Roisin. 'Only, I've got a blog post to finish?'

'No, thanks, Nancy. We're good.'

Roisin turned to Kim. Early thirties. Curvaceous where Nancy had been skinny, dressed in black and with bright-pink hair cut into punky tufts.

'Take a seat, please. Kim, isn't it?'

'That's right, what's going on?' she countered.

Her accent was from somewhere in the Northwest. Manchester, Roisin thought. Maybe Salford. Or Blackburn. Who was she kidding? Once she went further north than Tottenham, she really had no idea who was from Yorkshire, who was from Lancashire and who was from the arse-end of who-knew-where?

Once more, Roisin offered the photo, apparently of a pacifist, animal-loving vegan called Isaac Holt.

'Nancy says that's Isaac Holt.'

'Yeah, that's Isaac. Funny bloke.'

Making a mental note to come back on that comment, Roisin pressed ahead.

'Nancy said you live quite close by to Isaac. That you give him a lift sometimes.'

'We both live in Newham. Couple of streets away from each other. Car-sharing's more environmentally friendly.'

'Does he come to you or do you pick him up somewhere?'

Please say you go to his place.

'I normally pick him up outside the King's Head on Barking Road.'

Shit!

'Have you ever collected him from his place?'

Kim shook her head, making the silver hoops in her ears, three to a side, jingle against each other.

'Nope. He's sort of quite private?'

Double-shit! OK, one last try.

'But do you know his address?'

'Yeah. Why didn't you ask me to begin with instead of all this *detective stuff?* He pointed his house out once when we had to take a diversion. He's at 1 Blackbarn Lane.'

Willing herself to stay calm, Roisin made a note of Holt's address.

'Does he work?'

'Not sure. I think he's got some sort of zero-hours contract. Might be an Uber driver.'

Roisin made another note.

'OK, thanks, Kim.'

'Is he in trouble, then, Isaac?'

Roisin smiled.

'Nothing like that. We just want to have a chat with him. He might have seen something helpful, that's all.'

'Good. Cos it's like Nancy told you. He's the nicest guy in the world. Just cos he's, you know, a bit quiet, that doesn't make him a murderer.'

Now, Roisin said to herself.

25

THURSDAY 16TH AUGUST 11.25 A.M.

Roisin fixed Kim with a hard stare.

'A minute ago you said he was a funny bloke. What did you mean by that?'

Kim looked down. Roisin followed her gaze to see that the woman's hands were clamped together, the knuckles white.

She shrugged.

'You know, like I said, he's just a bit quiet.'

'Yes, you did say that. I don't know about you, Kim,' she turned, 'or you, Eleni,' back to face Kim, 'but if I meet a guy, you know, a nice guy, and he's just a bit quiet, shy maybe, I would probably say he doesn't have much to say for himself. Or he's a good listener for a change. But "funny"? That's a word I use when I get a sense something's a bit off about a bloke. Maybe I'd cross the road if I was on my own at night and he was coming towards me. So again, what did you mean when you called him a funny bloke? I'll remind you I'm conducting a murder investigation. I would really value the truth from you right now.'

Kim sighed. She raised her eyes to meet Roisin's stare.

'OK. Look, it's nothing. He just, I mean sometimes, in the car, he points out a woman and makes a remark about her. Like, an inappropriate remark?'

Roisin's pulse quickened. She kept her voice light. Neutral. But she could smell blood.

'Inappropriate, how?'

'You know, about her appearance.'

'What, her makeup? Her hair?'

'No.' Kim was practically squirming in her chair. Roisin suspected she was embarrassed at what she was about to own up to, given that her employer was sitting two feet away. Because Roisin knew that Isaac Holt's comments were about something other than hair and makeup.

'What, then? Kim, please tell me. It's important you tell me the truth right now.'

'Fine! Their tits!' she blurted. 'Their breasts, I mean. He'll say something like, oh, I don't know, "Look at those. Why doesn't she put them away?" Or, "She should get a breast reduction, they're too big for her figure."'

Kim looked across the desk at Eleni, who was staring open-mouthed at her.

'I'm sorry, Eleni. I should have told you. But Isaac's so passionate about our work. I just think he's a bit immature. Emotionally, I mean.'

'We'll talk about Isaac later,' Booth said quietly.

And in her head Roisin could hear the voice of a psychologist she'd once consulted about psychopaths. Doctor Yvette Law had enumerated a number of pointers to a psychopathic personality. 'They're almost always emotionally stunted,' she'd said. 'If they do experience emotions, they're invariably shallow and very immature. Like a toddler screaming with rage because its mother has denied it an ice cream.'

Time to go.

She stood, retrieved the sheet of paper from the desktop and slid it back into her bag.

'Thank you, both. You've been very helpful. Please don't get up.'

Reaching the door, which was only a matter of a couple of sideways steps, she stopped dead, her hand on the doorknob, and turned.

'I'm sure the thought will cross your mind, Kim, but I advise you strongly not to call Isaac. Your number and the time would show up on his phone records, and we really don't want that, do we? Tell Nancy as well.'

In her car again, she set the satnav for 1 Blackbarn Lane, Newham and pulled away from the kerb, heart pounding. As she drove east, she called Will.

'What's up, boss?' he asked, voice chipper.

'I want you to meet me at the northern end of Blackbarn Lane in Newham. I'm going to be there in thirty. Park in a side street and stay in your car. I'll call you when I arrive.'

———

As she drove through the midday traffic, Roisin revolved the problem in her head, looking for the angle she liked best. She had the first solid lead the team had had since Niamh Connolly's body had been found. Holt clearly had issues with women, with their sexuality, specifically. And he'd been carrying a placard with an explicit death threat against Niamh Connolly.

The boss was dead-set on it being a serial killer, but Roisin wasn't buying that. You needed three-plus for a serial, and they were only at one. She'd always thought Stella Cole was a glory-hunter and had never truly forgiven her for getting the DCI job that Roisin felt was rightfully hers.

So, Isaac Holt. She could place him at the last public appearance of the victim, too. And he looked weird. Had that flat stare she'd seen before on the faces of vicious killers. No compassion, no remorse. Serial? No. Psychopath? Almost certainly.

There'd be comeback because she hadn't kept Stella in the loop but she could always fall back on the old standby, 'my radio was on the fritz and I couldn't get a signal for my phone'. It was thin but impossible to disprove. Anyway, bringing in Holt would soon shine a different kind of spotlight on Roisin.

After half an hour's drive, she arrived at Blackbarn Lane. This part of East London had somehow avoided, or simply been passed over by the creeping gentrification that had transformed formerly working-class areas into trendy, bourgeois enclaves where a two-bedroom flat cost half a million quid. Newham had plenty of council houses or, what did they call them nowadays, social housing? Cheaply built flats, miniature terraced houses squashed together like cages in a battery farm.

Holt's street was identical to those either side, mostly pale-sand brick houses interspersed with low-rise sixties blocks. Lots of cars parked nose-to-tail, but from the tattier end of the second-hand market.

Roisin had worked a case the previous year that had involved interviewing the residents of a leafy square in Kensington. On the walk back to her car she'd counted nineteen Porsches, four Aston Martins and three Bentleys. The Mercs, BMWs and Audis were so numerous she hadn't even bothered.

She pulled in at the opposite end of the street from Holt's house and texted Will.

I'm here. Outside 79. U?

The answer came back within a few seconds.

Farthingale Rd. Next 1 over. I come 2 u?

She sent a terse Y then climbed out of the car and into the roasting, humid air. Immediately, she felt a flush of sweat break out all over her body. She breathed in deeply, then regretted it. Someone nearby had obviously left their dustbin out too long. The stink of rotting domestic refuse was unmistakable.

While she waited for Will, she looked around for the source of the stench. There! Piled up outside a house featuring six bell buttons in a metal panel by the front door were a dozen or so bulging black bin liners.

The bag nearest the door had split, or, more likely, been ripped open, and a mess of fast-food containers, chicken bones and some indefinable reddish-brown goop had spread onto the pavement. Foxes, most likely, she thought. Scrawny little bleeders got everywhere these days.

The sound of footsteps made her turn. Will was ambling up to her, hands in pockets, pinstriped navy cotton blazer flapping above a pair of clean but crumpled chinos.

'Still rocking the preppy look, I see,' she said.

Will smiled.

'Glad you like it, boss.'

'I didn't say I liked it.'

'What's the deal, then?'

Down to business. Roisin nodded sideways, towards the low-numbered end of the street.

'Isaac Holt. He was there at the LoveLife protest in Mitcham. On the pro-abortion side. Had a placard saying, "Death to Niamh Connolly". According to a woman at the group who organised the counter-demonstration, he's *funny*. Got a hang-up about women with big boobs or something. I want to bring him in for questioning.'

Will's face betrayed his obvious nervousness. His forehead creased with concern.

'You think he's going to be dangerous? Do we need back-up?'

'You *are* the back-up,' she said. 'Hang on.'

Roisin rounded the car and opened the boot. From behind a small black cargo net attached to the wheel well she withdrew a short, black ribbed-rubber cylinder.

'ESP SH-21 extendo,' she said. Then, keeping her back to the street, she gave the extendible baton a deft flick, and the telescopic black steel sections slid out and locked into place. 'He gives any sign of going for a weapon, let him have it with this.'

She pressed a button on the side of the handle and smacked the baton closed with the heel of her hand. Will took it and slid it into the waistband of his trousers at the side, then arranged his jacket to cover it.

The two detectives, both ambitious in their own way, walked down the street. Apart from a small child outside a house about halfway down, sitting on the kerb and playing with a grubby plastic tea set, the road was devoid of people. Roisin looked up, shading her eyes. The sun hung in the sky like a PI's desk lamp in a pulp-fiction novel, giving Londoners from Newham to Richmond the third degree.

'I wish this heatwave would let up,' she said with feeling. 'I'm melting in this suit.'

'Not much chance of that,' Will said. 'Apparently the Jetstream's stuck over Scandinavia. The only place getting cool weather is Iceland, fittingly enough.'

'Yeah, well, I hope they're enjoying it. God, I could kill for a cold lager right now.'

'Maybe once we get Holt squared away, we could go out and get a couple?'

Roisin cast a sideways glance at Will. He was looking straight ahead. Was that as innocent as it sounded? Or was there something just below the surface? *Later*, she cautioned herself. *Let's deal with Mister Isaac Holt first.*

26

THURSDAY 16TH AUGUST 2.17 P.M.

Standing outside the flimsy-looking red-painted front door of 1 Blackbarn Lane, Roisin felt a familiar sensation in her gut. *I'm close.* That's what the churning, wriggling worms of energy were telling her. She wiped her forehead and straightened the lapels of her jacket. She turned to Will.

'Ready?'

'Yup.'

'OK, follow my lead.'

'OK, boss.'

She watched him as he patted the grip of the baton through the thin material of his own jacket.

Doorbell or knock? she asked herself. *Different levels of authority. Softly, softly, catchee monkey, Roisin.*

She pressed the bell push and heard a reedy electronic ringing on the other side of the door.

She waited for a count of five. Nothing.

'He could be at work,' Will said, unnecessarily in her opinion.

'Yeah, or he could be hiding behind those lovely net curtains,' she answered, jerking her chin in the direction of the rectangular window to the left of the front door.

She raised her right hand and knocked. Not loudly, not an aggressive '3.00 a.m. Special', just a firm, assertive, rat-a-tat-tat on the thin wooden panel above the aluminium letterbox.

'Yeah, yeah, yeah,' a high-pitched male voice called from the other side of the door. 'I 'eard you the first fackin' time. Just 'old your fackin' 'orses, will ya?'

The door swung inwards. Roisin straightened her posture, adding another inch to her height. Beside her she sensed Will adjusting his stance, moving his feet further apart. *Keep it toge*ther, *DC Dunlop,* she thought.

The bleary-looking man framed in the open doorway was Isaac Holt. No question in her mind. His sandy hair was sticking up at odd angles and he had at least a day's growth of beard on his narrow jaw. He was wearing a stained grey T-shirt and a pair of pink-and-white striped pyjama trousers. He rubbed his face, drawing a hand down over his mouth.

Roisin seized the moment.

'Isaac Holt?' she asked him in a pleasant voice, though inside she was as tense as a feral cat ready to pounce on an unsuspecting rat.

'Tha's right. Listen, I had your lot round here last week. I told them, I ain't interested in God, all right?'

Roisin plastered a smile on her face.

'We're not Jehovah's Witnesses, Mr Holt. I am Detective Inspector Roisin Griffin and this is Detective Constable Will Dunlop. Can we come in, please?'

She showed Holt her warrant card and caught Will's in her peripheral vision. Holt didn't bother scrutinising them. That could mean one of two things. Either, like most law-abiding citizens, he assumed people saying they were police officers *were* police officers. Or he knew a Met ID when he saw one and didn't need to check if they were genuine.

'Fine,' he said, rolling his eyes.

He turned and led them into a small sitting room, furnished

with a vinyl-covered sofa, the brown cushions scabbed from much use, a matching armchair, similarly distressed, a huge flat-screen TV with the usual array of slim black boxes underneath it, and an oddly prissy side table with barley-sugar twist legs and an octagonal top featuring a chessboard demarcated in light and dark squares.

A packet of cigarettes, glass ashtray and a half-empty bottle of lemonade sat atop its polished surface. But what caught Roisin's eye was the Samurai sword hanging by its red, twisted-silk sling from a hook on the wall.

Holt flung himself down into the sofa, legs spread, and extracted a cigarette and a disposable lighter from the packet on the little table. He offered it to the two detectives, both of whom refused.

'Yeah, well, gotta die of sumfing, ain't you?' he said before lighting the cigarette and inhaling deeply. 'So, what do you want?'

Roisin gestured for Will to stand by the door, while she sat across from Holt in the armchair. *Now, Isaac. Which way do I play this?*

'We are investigating the murder of Niamh Connolly. She's—'

'I know who she is,' Holt said with a sneer.

'Yes,' Roisin said, pleasantly. 'We saw you on the news. Quite a placard you had with you last Friday. What did it say again, Will?'

'Death to Niamh Connolly. You can't kill what doesn't live,' Will recited in a deadpan voice.

'And now you got your wish, didn't you, Isaac?'

Holt gazed levelly at Roisin. She saw that look again. The look of a man with a burning, deep-seated hatred for women. Hiding in plain sight among a whole gang of them at WAGSARR.

'I never wrote it. They gave it me to carry.'

'Who did?'

'WAGSARR. They get them done up by some printshop over Shoreditch way.'

'Really? Because we took down the wording on all the other placards. Yours really stood out. The others were all about women's right to choose, that sort of thing.'

Holt shrugged and blew out a stream of smoke towards the ceiling before hacking out a cough.

'What d'you want me to say? I told you I didn't write it. They

163

hated her, you know. Used to call her all kinds of names.' He fixed Roisin with a steady glare. 'Traitor. Bitch.' He paused and ran the tip of his tongue over his lower lip. 'Cunt.'

Roisin was too experienced to fall for such a cheap provocation.

'What about you, Isaac? Is that what you thought of Niamh?'

He spread his hands, holding the cigarette between his lips and tilting his head back.

'Me? Not really. I didn't kill 'er if that's what you're finkin'.'

Time to switch track.

'So why do you go to those demos? Bit of an unusual hobby for a bloke like you, I'd have thought. Kim from WAGSARR gives you a lift, doesn't she?'

Holt leaned forward, grinned, the cigarette bouncing on his lip as he spoke.

'Easiest way I've found to meet women, that lot. A man gets all passionate about abortion being a woman's right? They can't wait to shag you. You're safe, see? No threat. Me and Kim? She gives me a lift and I give her a ride, know what I mean?'

Then he winked. And suddenly Roisin felt dirty, just being in the same room as Holt. Dirty and apprehensive, and glad, too, for Will's presence in the house. She was glad the Samurai sword was behind her.

Roisin scratched the back of her head. Acting on the pre-arranged signal, Will spoke.

'Isaac, can I use your toilet, please?'

Holt turned to Will and pointed upwards.

'Top of the stairs, turn left, first door on your right.'

He turned back to Roisin as Will left the room.

'You got any more questions for me, Roisin? Nice name, by the way. You a Catholic like Niamh, are you? I went out with a Catholic girl once. I tell you, she was gaggin' for it. Up the arse, that's how she liked it best. No risk of getting pregnant, eh?'

He leaned back, spreading his arms across the top of the sofa, eyeing her. Roisin could feel the PAVA spray in her jacket pocket digging into her hip. *One move, and you're getting a faceful of liquid chilli, sunshine. One move.*

'Where did you go after you left the demo, Isaac?' she asked, returning the stone-faced look. She made a mental note to question Kim again. The woman had lied to her about her relationship with Holt.

'Home.'

'On your own, were you?'

'No. Kim gave me a lift.'

A girlfriend's alibi isn't worth as much as you seem to think, Holt.

'Really? And then what?'

He leered at her.

'What d'you think?'

'I don't know. Why don't you tell me?'

'We 'ad sex, didn't we? Tell you the truth, I think goin' on them demos gets 'em all worked up. All that yellin' and screamin', plus, obviously, you know, the sex stuff.'

Roisin frowned.

'The sex stuff,' she repeated, flatly.

He seemed to get animated, for the first time since she'd begun questioning him. His eyes widened and he leaned towards her.

'Yeah! You know, the abortion stuff. You know where babies come from, don't you? Even as a Catholic, you must know, right?'

'Yes, Isaac. I do know where babies come from.'

He nodded triumphantly.

'That's what I'm sayin', innit? They come out of a woman's belly. Shoot out between her legs from 'er, you know, and into the big, wide world. Bound to get a woman all hot an' bovvered. Stands to reason.'

Holt was not the first offender Roisin had encountered with distorted ideas about what got women 'all hot and bovvered', but the abortion angle was a first. Time to dial up the pressure.

'What time did Kim leave?'

Another shrug.

'I dunno. Three-thirty. Four, maybe?'

Which would still work. Just. He could have driven across London to Wimbledon, murdered Niamh and got away well before Jerry Connolly returned home from work at eight.

'So after Kim left, what, you were on your own?'

'Yeah. Had some stuff to take care of.'

'Can anyone vouch for your whereabouts between 4.00 p.m. and 8.00 p.m.?'

'Ohhh. You mean an alibi?'

'Yes. An alibi. You know what that means, right? While Niamh Connolly was being tortured and strangled, you prove to me that you were elsewhere. That's what it means, you know. In Latin. Elsewhere.'

Holt sat forward and stubbed his cigarette out. Took his time lighting another while staring, very obviously, at her breasts. He inhaled, then blew out a smoke ring towards Roisin.

'I never did Latin. Nelson Mandela Comprehensive wasn't that kind of school, know what I mean? I bet you did, though, didn't you? What was it, a convent school? All them nuns giving you the cane?' He leered at her. 'Loads of lezzers, too, I bet.'

Before Roisin could answer, Will reappeared. His face was a mask. He nodded, once. That was the signal he'd found something incriminating enough to want to bring Holt in for questioning.

Roisin moved forwards towards Holt.

'Isaac, we'd like to continue this conversation at Paddington Green Police Station. How would you feel about that?'

'Why? Are you arrestin' me?'

'Do I need to?'

Holt jumped to his feet. Roisin reared back, instinctively reaching for the cannister of pepper spray in her jacket pocket. Beside her, Will was going for the extendible baton.

Then Holt smiled. Hands out in front of him, palms facing Roisin, he spoke.

'Whoa! Calm down, all right? You wanna take me down your nick, 's fine with me. I ain't doing anything this arvo. Might be fun to see the inside of a real police station.'

'Go and put some clothes on. Will. Go with him.'

At Paddington Green, Roisin put Holt in an empty interview room and left him there, with an instruction not to smoke. She spoke to Will outside.

'OK, when we go in, I'll kick off. When I lean back and look at you, that's when you hit him with your questions, all right?'

'Got it,' he answered with a grim smile. He was enjoying himself, Roisin could tell. About time you saw a bit of real police work, Will, she thought. Watch and learn.

27

THURSDAY 16TH AUGUST 4.00 P.M.

Roisin led the way into the stuffy interview room and took the chair nearest the door. Will sat next to her.

'Ain't you s'posed to be recordin' this or sumfing?' Holt asked.

'You're not being interviewed under caution, Isaac. This is just for us to sort out a few more details with you. So, no. No recorder.'

Holt fidgeted in his chair, seemingly unable to get into a comfortable position.

Not so cocky now, are you, you pervy little shit! Roisin thought.

'Maybe I should 'ave a lawyer,' he said, looking at the scratched and pitted table top.

'What for?' Roisin asked.

'I dunno. Like, advise me an' that.'

'Innocent people don't usually start asking for a lawyer, Isaac. Is there something you want to own up to?'

He shook his head, still not meeting her gaze. He scratched ferociously at the back of his head, then inspected his fingernails.

'No. Like I said. I never did nothin' to Niamh Connolly.'

'Fine,' Roisin said briskly. 'Let's crack on then, shall we? You said you left the demo with Kim. What time was that. Exactly?'

He picked a bit of loose skin from the side of his right thumb. Then he flicked it onto the carpet.

'One o'clock.'

'And how can you be so sure?' Roisin asked, making a note.

'Checked me watch, didn't I? I wanted to get back to mine for a shag, like I said.'

'And Kim didn't mind leaving the demo early? It said on the news it went on all day.'

He shook his head.

'I said I really wanted her. Said she was drivin' me crazy. The usual shit. Always works.'

Not with me.

Roisin smiled.

'OK, so Kim drove back to yours. How long did that take?'

'An hour. Maybe a bit more?'

'Let's say an hour and fifteen, then, just to be on the safe side. So, you got back to yours at two-fifteen. Did you shag straight away or have a few drinks or something first?'

He smirked, looking straight at her.

'Straight away. She was gaggin' for it, wasn't she?'

'How long did it take? Five minutes? Ten?'

The smirk slid off Holt's face for a moment, then returned, now accompanied by a narrowing of the eyes.

'Funny. We were up there for about an hour.' He folded his arms across his chest.

Defensive body posture. Feeling a bit exposed, are you, Isaac?

'Right. That takes us to three-fifteen. Then what?'

'Then she left. I told you. I 'ad stuff to take care of.'

Keeping her face neutral, Roisin was rejoicing. He'd just cut back his alibi by fifteen minutes.

'Like driving to Wimbledon and killing Niamh Connolly?'

'What? No! I told you at mine. I never touched 'er.'

Roisin sat back and glanced to her right at Will.

Right on cue, he leaned forwards.

'Tell me about the porn, Isaac.'

Holt's eyes slid sideways. His hands went to his pockets.

'What porn?'

'You know. The porn in your bedroom. The magazines. The DVDs.'

Holt's mouth twisted, showing oddly small teeth.

'You ain't allowed. You need a warrant.'

Will spread his hands.

'I took a wrong turn looking for the toilet.'

'You fackin' liar!' Holt shouted, half-rising from his chair.

'Sit down!' Will shouted back, impressing Roisin with his reaction.

Holt complied, but his face was suffused with blood. She hoped Will hadn't overdone it. As if his yell had been delivered by someone else, Will resumed talking in a quieter voice than before.

'The porn, Isaac?'

'What about it?'

'Pretty hardcore stuff. Bondage. S&M. You get off on causing women pain, do you?'

'It's all fake. You know that, right? Your lot see it all and I bet you've had far worse than that in 'ere. It's not like I'm a nonce or nuffin. I bought it all legal, in Soho.'

'Oh, right, yeah, of course. Legal. So, I read one of your little stories while I was up there, too. You fantasise about hurting women, don't you, Isaac? About hurting them with knives. Cutting them up. Cutting their breasts off. Don't you?'

Holt looked as if he was about to argue, then clearly he changed his mind. He sat back in his chair.

'I wanna go. I ain't done nuffin wrong. You can't force me to stay 'ere if I don't want to.'

Roisin checked her watch: 4.15 p.m. Then she stood.

'Actually, I can. Isaac Holt, I am arresting you on suspicion of the murder of Niamh Connolly. You do not have to say anything, but it may harm your defence if you do not mention when questioned something which you later rely on in court. Anything you do say may be given in evidence. Do you understand what I just told you?'

'I s'pose so, yes.'

She turned to Will.

'Cuff the suspect please, DC Dunlop. Let's get him down to the custody sergeant. Then get a move on with the search warrant for his place. The PACE clock starts ticking as soon as he's officially booked in.'

They booked Holt in with the custody sergeant at 4.30 p.m. Roisin smiled at her prisoner as he was led away to the cells with a blanket, a copy of the codes of practice relating to arrest, a pencil and notebook. On being advised he could call someone to let them know he'd been arrested and was at Paddington Green, he'd called his mother.

28

THURSDAY 16ᵀᴴ AUGUST 6.00 P.M.

Holt had, unsurprisingly, not had a solicitor of his own, so Roisin detailed Will to ring round till he found the duty solicitor.

'Which is good for us,' she said. 'Poor sods are underpaid and overworked, unlike those Armani-wearing reptiles from the big firms.'

'When do we go back and interview him again?' Will asked.

'Not yet. We've got twenty-four hours, minimum. We're going back to his place to search it.'

———

Stella had spent the day reading reports, assigning priorities and teams to new lines of enquiry and, in the latter half of the afternoon, interviewing a man named Gregory Johnson. Johnson had served two sentences for aggravated rape in his life. One had started when he was eighteen, the other twenty-seven. She'd identified him as a suspect based on a report at the time of his second conviction that he had cut his victim's breasts with a knife. He was now out on licence.

It had been a waste of time. At the time of Niamh Connolly's murder, Johnson had been in a meeting with his parole officer twenty-three miles away. Frustration, plus a copper's combination of too much caffeine and not enough food had combined to give her a pounding headache behind her right eye.

Arriving at Paddington Green, she nodded a greeting at the custody sergeant. She'd known Rob Blanchard a long time. He'd booked in more than a few of her collars. He nodded back.

'Evening, ma'am. Good to see your team's got someone in the cells for the Connolly murder.'

Stella stopped dead in her tracks.

'Sorry, Rob. What?'

No-one had called her about an arrest. And she hated not knowing what was going on with one of her investigations.

'DI Griffin brought him in, ma'am. Scruffy little shit goes by the name of Isaac Holt. He's in number two.'

Massaging her forehead above her eye, which now felt as if someone were sticking a newly sharpened pencil into it from behind, Stella pushed through the door that led to the cells. She reached the door to cell number two and slid the steel viewing window open.

Sitting on the narrow cot, staring at his hands, a white male, average height, muscular torso, slim hips, turned to the door at the scrape of metal on metal. He jumped to his feet and crossed to the door, going eyeball to eyeball with Stella.

'Oi!' he shouted. 'Where's my lawyer? Why ain't that copper come back? I never done nuffin to Niamh Connolly. I only said I'd come down 'ere 'cos I thought it'd be a laugh.'

Stella slid the window cover shut. Swearing at Roisin under her breath, she retraced her steps and went up to the SIU incident room.

Baz and Def were deep in conversation when she arrived. They looked up at Stella, took in her expression and turned fully round to face her.

'Evening, boss,' Baz said. 'How was your day? Nothing much to report, I'm afraid.'

Stella sighed.

'Oh, you know. Reading a shitload of paperwork. Interviewing a violent rapist who couldn't take his eyes off my tits the entire time and who waited till the very end of the interview to tell me about his alibi. And then I come back and find Roisin's arrested a suspect I knew nothing about. So, you know, just another brilliant day. Plus my right eye feels like it's going to burst.'

'I've got some Nurofen in my desk, boss,' Def said. 'Want a couple?'

'Oh, God, yes please.'

Def scooted off to her desk and returned with a battered silver carton.

'Here you go.'

Stella swallowed the pink tablets gratefully with a mouthful of cold coffee from a mug she'd left on her desk first thing.

'Thanks, Def. So, either of you know anything about Isaac Holt?'

'Who?' Baz asked.

'Isaac Holt. Roisin's collar. Shifty little IC1 in cell two downstairs.'

They shook their heads in unison.

Her head popping up from behind her screen like a meerkat, Becky piped up.

'Boss? I showed DI Griffin a guy on some news footage I was reviewing. Could that have been him?'

'Thanks, Becks. But, honestly? I don't know. You'd better show us this bloke on the video.'

Gathered round Becky's computer, Stella, Baz and Def watched intently as Becky manipulated the onscreen playback controls. After a couple of failed attempts she froze the film at the moment Holt was in full view.

'Yeah,' Stella said. 'That's him. And I can see why Roisin went off to find him.' She stabbed a finger at the placard Holt was holding aloft. 'Not quite a confession. But not bad.'

Inside though, she was far from happy. She'd established her housekeeping rules right at the start of her tenure running the day-to-day operations of the SIU. All intelligence, especially relating to arrestable suspects, came through her. In advance. No one-man, or one-woman shows. No off-books activities. No mavericks.

Anyone knowing even a little of Stella's recent history might have wondered at the last imperative. After all, acting as a one-woman vigilante squad, Stella had shot, stabbed, electrocuted and defenestrated enough people to count as a serial killer several times over.

The fact that they'd been trying to murder her, and been classified as enemies of the state at a top-secret review hadn't changed things. But that was precisely why Stella felt the need to keep her new squad well inside the line demarcating the right – and wrong – sides of the law.

She called Roisin.

Roisin answered almost at once.

'Yes, boss?'

'You arrested a suspect.'

'Yes, boss. I'm over at his gaff now with Will, searching the place.'

'Why the radio silence? Why did I have to find out from Rob Blanchard and not you?'

A pause, during which Stella imagined she could hear cogs whirring in her DI's brain.

'I tried, boss. Couldn't get a mobile signal.'

'And your Airwave?'

'Not working. I did try, boss, honest. Look, I've got to go. We're nearly done here and you're going to like what we're found.'

'OK. But we're going to interview him together when you're back, OK?'

'Whatever you say. You're the boss.'

———

It was after 10.00 p.m. when Roisin and Will arrived back in the incident room. Both were clearly on a high. Stella recognised the signs. The flush in the cheeks, the wide smiles. The strutting body language. You got it when you knew, deep down, you were onto something that would close a case.

Stella intercepted them.

'Coffee, Roisin?'

'Yeah, that would be great. Thanks.'

'Come on then. I heard they've got a Nespresso machine on the third floor. Let's go and get a couple of decent cups.'

Stella stepped into the lift ahead of Roisin. As soon as the doors closed, she spoke.

'What the hell are you playing at, Rosh?'

Roisin's eyes widened.

'What do you mean? I just arrested an absolutely prime candidate for Niamh Connolly's murder.'

'I know. That's not what I mean. Why didn't you let me know?'

'I told you. I tried.'

'Oh please, Roisin, don't give me that old one. You've been out all day, half of it with Will by all accounts, and neither of you had service once?'

Rosin's voice hardened a fraction.

'I wasn't sure it would pan out. I tracked him through a pro-abortion charity. By the time it looked like it was a goer, we didn't have time. It all happened too fast.'

The doors opened on the third floor, halting their tense conversation. At the CID coffee station, they stood awkwardly, waiting for the hissing, plopping, huffing machine to deliver two frothy coffees. Stella motioned for Roisin to follow her into the stairwell.

'Look. I know where this is coming from. You got your nose put out of joint when Callie put me in as her DCI. But that was almost six years ago. It's time to draw a line under it, don't you think?'

Roisin took a sip of her coffee, narrowing her eyes as the steam coiled away from the surface.

'I don't know what you're talking about, Stella. Really I don't. Look, I'm sorry for the radio silence, OK? It won't happen again.'

29

Back in the SIU incident room, Will had brought up all the bagged and tagged evidence they'd retrieved from Holt's house, mainly the bedroom.

Laid out on a table it made a compelling case on its own. A foot-high pile of glossy, luridly colourful hardcore porn magazines, the covers featuring women in what looked like excruciatingly painful positions, their wrists and ankles bound with rope, ball-gags in their mouths and, in one eye-catching photo, ropes tied tightly around the woman's breasts. Beside the magazines, a stack of DVDs revealed more of Isaac Holt's tastes.

A clear plastic Ziploc bag held an A5 notebook with a yellow cover.

Will tapped it.

'That's the killer, no pun intended. His fantasies. In his own hand. The last entry is a story about Niamh Connolly. He, Holt, I mean, rapes her all ways from Sunday and slices her tits off with his samurai sword. Not much in the way of literary merit, but it reads like a report of her murder.'

The sword itself lay on the end of the table in its own evidence bag.

Taken together, the items arrayed before them did make a superficially impressive case. But doubts were already swimming around in Stella's brain. The pain behind her eye had finally eased and she was thinking more clearly.

'At first sight, this is all good stuff. Well done, guys,' she began. 'But there are a few things that don't fit what we know of the killer's MO. Anyone?'

Baz pointed at the topmost porn magazine. The naked woman on the cover lay spread-eagled on a bed, hands and wrists manacled to the bedposts. She was blindfolded. A man with hairy, tattooed shoulders stood to one side holding a carving knife at the same angle as his huge erection.

'She's not shaved, is she? Mostly they are these days.'

Def snorted.

'Made a study have you, Baz?'

'Very funny. It's true, though. You all know it. Liking hairy girls is actually counted as a fetish these days.'

'You really have, haven't you, you dirty devil?'

Garry strolled over.

'Have what?'

'Baz's just giving us the benefit of his extensive knowledge of contemporary hardcore porn,' Stella said.

'Apparently,' Def said, 'not wanting a girl with a shaven haven is a, what did you call it Baz, a specialist interest?'

More laughter, the sound of cops bonding over an emotional coin-toss, tumbling and spinning in the air only to come down hard on a flat surface with a bloody queen's head uppermost.

'Baz's got a point, though, hasn't he?' Stella asked the assembled detectives. 'You've all read the PM report on Niamh Connolly, right? Right? The killer shaved her, post mortem. It might seem like a small thing to you, like, oh, I don't know, toast for breakfast today, cereal tomorrow. But for these guys, it's an article of faith. What else?'

'The rape fantasy, boss,' Camille said.

'Go on,' Stella said.

'We know Niamh Connolly wasn't. Raped, I mean. If that was Holt's thing, and he had Niamh drugged up and helpless, well, he'd have raped her. Wouldn't he?'

'I think you're right, Cam. And then there's the choice of weapon. In Holt's little story he uses a sword, whereas we know from Dr Craven's report that the killer used something that created a scissoring action. It could add up, I'm just saying there are a few areas that don't point to his being our man. I'm sorry, Rosin, but we're out on a limb here.'

Roisin clearly wasn't ready to admit that arresting Holt had been a mistake. She turned to Stella.

'He was carrying a placard with an explicit death threat against Niamh Connolly. He was one of the last people to see her alive. He had violent pornography in his bedroom. He wrote a story where he pretty much described what happened to her. And he hasn't got an alibi.'

This was the hard part. The part of the job Stella hated more than any other. She'd landed this plum role because she was a good detective, a fighter, a sharp operator. Despite, or perhaps because of her unorthodox methods, she had pretty much singlehandedly dismantled – OK, destroyed – a vigilante conspiracy high up in the English legal establishment.

Was she a good manager? A shoulder to cry on? A team leader able to bring out the best in a disparate group of people with conflicting loyalties, ambitions, drives and goals? Sometimes she wasn't sure.

'All of which is true. But it's also true that there is no evidence linking him to the crime scene. No fingerprints. No footprints. No CCTV. Nothing. And the search didn't turn up rope or vintage sheep shears. Did you get him swabbed, yet?'

'Yes. Sample's with Forensics now.'

'OK, good. We got epithelials and blood off the rope we found in the skip near the Connollys' house. If they turn out to match Niamh's DNA then we've got the murder weapon. And if the killer was dumb enough not to use gloves we might even have his DNA as well. So we better pray they match Holt's.'

'When will we get the results?'

'A week.'

'A week? What happened to the golden hour?'

'I think it expired. I'm sorry. I talked to Callie but the budget's under pressure. There are too many other strands we're trying to cover. Get the sword down to Lucian. It doesn't fit the wound signature, but he can check it for blood.'

'He could easily have dumped the shears,' Roisin said. She sounded defeated. Which Stella didn't want. Forget her ambitions, Roisin was a great detective. She wouldn't be working in the SIU otherwise. Stella needed her on top form and she needed everyone to see she was there to support them.

'I'm not trying to rain on your parade, Roisin, but there are probably hundreds of blokes in London who fantasise about committing violent sexual attacks on famous women. At this point, it's all circumstantial. We've got nothing. If Holt had anyone better in his corner than some bleary-eyed duty solicitor, he'd already have walked by now.'

Roisin's pale-blue eyes flashed.

'Then let's get at him.'

30

THURSDAY 16TH AUGUST 10.45 P.M.

Roisin switched on the digital interview recorder, the DIR, in interview room five on the fifth floor of Paddington Green.

'Interview of Isaac Holt, 10.45 p.m. Thursday 16th August 2018. Detective Inspector Roisin Griffin present.'

Stella spoke next.

'Detective Chief Inspector Stella Cole, present.'

Holt's solicitor leaned towards the machine.

'Ibrahim Rahman, solicitor.'

'What about me?' Holt said, from a supine position in his chair, almost horizontal, legs spread wide.

Roisin bestowed an icy smile on him.

'Be my guest. State your name for the record. Please.'

'Isaac Holt. And I never done nuffin!' he added, shouting at the recorder.

Rahman whispered in Holt's ear.

Yeah, Roisin thought. *Go on. Tell him to keep calm. It won't help.* She placed her hands on the table, one on top of the other.

'Isaac? Last Friday lunchtime, you were filmed carrying a

placard calling for Niamh Connolly's death. A couple of hours later, she was. And just like in your story, she'd had her breasts cut off. That was you, wasn't it?'

'No. I was in my flat with Kim from WAGSARR, like I said before.'

Roisin shook her head.

'Until three-fifteen, you were. That's what you told us. Then, who knows?'

'It wasn't me!' he said, almost pleading. 'Why won't you believe me?'

'You like it when women give you what you want, don't you?'

'What do you mean?'

Roisin smiled, a co-conspirator.

'Come on, Isaac, don't be coy. You're a stud, aren't you? Those frigid bitches at WAGSARR are gagging for it, you said so yourself. They just can't admit it to themselves.'

'DI Griffin, are you going to ask my client a question?' Rahman said, looking up from the notebook in which he'd been scribbling frantically.

'Of course. Isaac, did you write a story where you raped Niamh Connolly?'

'You know I did,' he mumbled, looking down.

'I'm sorry, for the DIR, could you repeat your answer a little more clearly?'

'Yes!' he snapped.

'Yes, what?'

'Yes, I wrote a story where I raped Niamh Connolly. Happy now?'

'And in that story, Isaac, apart from raping Niamh Connolly orally, anally and vaginally, did you also cut off her breasts with your samurai sword?'

Holt clamped his lips together, forming a thin line. Rahman whispered again into his ear.

'Isaac?' Roisin prompted. 'Perhaps Mr Rahman is giving you good advice.'

'No comment,' he said, staring defiantly back at Roisin.

'No comment? Really? Because I would have thought, you know, most *normal* guys, if they were asked if they'd written down something like that, which is,' she turned to Stella, 'I don't know about you, guv, but I'd definitely call it *nonce* territory, well, they'd pretty much jump at the chance to deny it.'

'DI Griffin,' Rahman said, 'you asked my client a question, and he gave you an answer. I must insist you move on. It sounds to me like you've embarked on a fishing expedition. If you have any real evidence linking Mr Holt to Mrs Connolly's murder, I think you should go ahead and charge him, otherwise, I respectfully suggest you let Mr Holt go.'

Holt folded his arms across his chest. Stella had seen the move hundreds of times before. *Is that your best shot, then?* She decided to intervene. Not because she believed she was sitting opposite Niamh Connolly's murderer, but because she wanted to tip the scales back in their favour. Even a little would be enough.

Maybe there were other ways of creating the wounds Lucian had identified as having been made by shears. She'd had Becky do a little background research on Holt. She employed the findings now.

'Isaac. Is it OK if I call you Isaac?'

Seemingly startled that the second cop opposite him could speak, Holt straightened convulsively in his chair.

'Whatever. It's my name, ain't it?'

'Of course,' Stella said, smiling sweetly. 'What line of work are you in?'

Holt shrugged.

'This and that. All zero-hours now, ain't it?'

'Yeah, I know. No security, no pension. Must be a real bitch to make a decent living.'

'You said it, not me. Bosses are all in it for what they can get. They don't give a shit about working blokes like me.'

'So, what do you do to pay the rent, then? When you *are* working, I mean?'

'Driving, mostly.'

Stella smiled, as if encouraging a shy person to volunteer

information about themselves at the beginning of a training workshop.

'What, like Uber or something?'

He shook his head.

'No. It's all sewn up with the Afghans and the Pakis and the Somalis or whatever. Immigrants, anyway.'

'What, then?'

He looked at his solicitor, then at the ceiling, then at his hands, which were interlaced on the table top.

'Deliveries.'

'Of?'

'It's a Muslim firm. Newham Market Limited.'

'That's nice. You working for a Muslim-owned company. Very,' she paused, 'diverse of you. Tell us, what do Newham Market Limited trade in? I mean, what's in the van when you're driving for them?'

He muttered a short, one-syllable word into his collar.

'Sorry, I didn't catch that,' Stella said. 'Can you speak up, please. You know, for the recorder.'

'Meat,' Holt said, glaring at her.

'Oh, right. Like halal meat?'

'I guess so. That's what they eat, ain't it?'

'If you mean Muslims, yes, it is. So, do they ever get you to help prepare the meat before you drive it around? They bleed the animals to death, don't they? Are you good at butchering, Isaac? Do you know how to cut up a dead animal? Useful with a blade, are you?'

'Detective Chief Inspector!' Rahman said, wiping a hand over a tired-looking face. Stella wondered if his day had started earlier than hers. *Probably, poor sod*, she thought.

'You're haranguing my client. One question at a time, please.'

'Very well. Have you ever taken a knife to a dead animal, Isaac? I'll remind you, you're being interviewed under caution here. We can check your answers.'

Holt scowled at her. She tried to imagine him mutilating Niamh Connolly. Found it remarkably easy. But then, she reproached herself, the gap between a copper's imaginings and a CPS lawyer's decision to charge could be wider than the Thames between Waterloo and Westminster.

Holt nodded.

Stella spoke clearly while looking directly at Holt.

'For the DIR, the suspect nodded.'

'So you know how to take a body apart using knives, saws, shears, things like that?'

Holt didn't need a whisper in his ear to answer Stella's question. He looked her in the eye, held the glance for a few seconds. Then spoke.

'No. Fackin'. Comment.'

Stella looked sideways at Roisin and dropped her eyelids for a fraction of a second. The meaning was clear.

'Interview suspended at,' Roisin checked the time, '11.07 p.m.'

Then she snapped the recorder off.

Rahman spoke, startling Stella. The little man seemed to have dozed off during the last few minutes of the interview.

'DCI Cole. My client is entitled to an eight-hour rest break. I don't want him questioned again until at least,' he checked his watch, '7.07 a.m. tomorrow.'

Stella nodded.

'Of course, Mr Rahman. We know the law.'

31

Craig Morgan had struck lucky when he married Fiona Weatherley. She was the daughter of a Labour peer, ennobled for his financial generosity to the party, made possible by the hugely profitable industrial plant hire business he'd founded as a young man.

Fiona's widowed father had died the week after they had announced their engagement and, amidst the grief, one shining shaft of light had penetrated the gloom.

He had left the bulk of his two hundred-million-pound estate to his only daughter.

At the time, Morgan had been a Labour councillor in the London Borough of Hackney. With his wife's money and vocal support, he had parlayed that position first into a seat on the Greater London Assembly, and from there to the deputy mayor's position under Remi Fewings.

The couple, childless – 'child-free', Fiona would insist if questioned – lived in urban splendour a few streets away from Labour's former leader, in a four-storey Islington townhouse built during the reign of George III.

Fiona's money was essential to him, and freely given, but Morgan had realised early on in their relationship that he needed more from her in the bedroom than she was prepared to deliver.

Her attitude to sex, while not precisely puritanical, was, he thought, Victorian. Any position as long as it was missionary. A blow job on his birthday. And, if he made enough of a fuss, she'd roll her eyes before rolling a pair of stockings up over her shapely thighs.

But the first time he'd asked her to hurt him, well, he'd known from her wide eyes and open mouth followed by the door to the spare bedroom slamming shut behind her that he'd have to look further afield.

And further afield was precisely where he was on a scorching August evening.

Though the well-heeled residents of Islington could give their counterparts in Chelsea and Hampstead a run for their money, their splendid Georgian residences were only a short drive from the less-salubrious environs of Stoke Newington.

Here, among the council flats, run-down pubs, fried-chicken joints and payday loan shops, a man with money and determination could find what he was looking for. Pleading a late-night meeting with party officials, Morgan left Fiona watching TV and made his way to a flat on the second floor of a sixties tower block that loomed over what passed for 'Stokey's' high street.

Despite the heat, he wore black jeans and a black hoodie, inside which he was sweating profusely. When the young woman he'd called earlier opened the door he pushed past her and frantically pulled the hoodie down, raising his hair into damp spikes.

'Awright, then, Tony?' she asked when he'd smoothed his hair down and thrown himself onto the bed.

He'd used Arianna, if that was her real name, before. It amused him to employ a *nom d'amour* of his own, and choosing that of Labour's most successful prime minister added a certain, undeniable charge to his erotic encounters.

'Fine, thank you, Arianna. How are you?'

She shrugged her bony shoulders, over which black bra straps were looped.

'OK, I s'pose. This wevver's bad for business though. Too hot to fuck, that's what me and the other girls reckon. You want the usual, then?'

Morgan nodded. His penis was hard inside his jeans and he could feel the familiar ache for what she could give him.

He let his eyes travel over her body. Not much in the way of tits, or arse, come to that. But strong, wiry muscles. A few tats here and there, including a crow perching on her right hip, which, for some reason, excited him.

He did notice the scabbed pustules on her inner elbows and forearms, how could he not, but, reasoning that what he paid for wouldn't leave him at risk of HIV, he ignored them.

'Yes, please,' he said.

She grinned as she reached behind her back and unsnapped her bra.

'Well then, you'd better do what you're fuckin' told then, 'adn't you? Now, get undressed, you piece of shit. Then bend over.'

While Morgan gratefully complied, Arianna strapped on an obscenely large black dildo.

As her long red fingernails clawed into his skin, he groaned with pleasure, the sound merging with an exhaled hiss as she shoved a well-lubricated finger into his rectum.

32

FRIDAY 17TH AUGUST 7.45 A.M.

Sarah Sharpe moved closer to the microphone in the BBC Radio 4 studio to deliver the closing lines of her two-minute, forty-five-second, 'Thought for the Day'. It meant she could drop her voice but keep the same level of audibility. She'd used the trick when preaching and it worked superbly.

'So although social media *appears* to offer us salvation, in the form of likes, retweets and followers, from the spiritual emptiness that plagues so many of us in today's world of hollowed-out spirituality, this salvation is *illusory*. Jesus, of course, had his followers. But these were flesh and blood men and women, many of whom ended up laying down their lives for him. They knew the truth: that there are worse kinds of suffering than not being noticed.'

She glanced up at the studio clock. The second hand was just sweeping from 9 to 10: she'd finished at 7.47 a.m. precisely.

Through the glass screen the producer gave her a thumbs-up and a smile. She smiled back as she removed her headphones and laid them on the black, felt-covered desk in front of her. She ran her fingers through her thick mane of silver hair and pushed through the swing door to the outer office.

The producer, an eager-faced woman in her early thirties wearing all black except for a startlingly bright pair of electric-blue loafers on her tiny feet, smiled warmly as she shook her hand.

'Thanks, Sarah, that was fantastic. As usual. We'll be in touch in a few months about another slot, OK?'

'I'd like that. Thanks, Lottie.'

As editor of the *Church Times*, a job she'd landed on her fiftieth birthday ten years earlier, Sarah was often called on to make speeches or contribute to debates on TV and radio. But *Thought for the Day* was her favourite. The chance to preach directly to the country's elite on their favourite morning radio show was, she liked to joke to her friends, 'manna from heaven'.

On the walk back to the tube station, she checked her phone for messages and emails. The subject line from one email, sent by an MJ Fox leapt out at her:

Our US viewers need your help

Curiosity aroused, she tapped the line to open the full message.

Hi Sarah,

We don't know each other, but I am a massive fan of your media work. My name is MJ Fox. I made my money in investment banking in New York, but now I am turning my face from Mammon, and back towards God.

I am about to make a bid for Twelve Saints Broadcasting out of Los Angeles. TSB is one of the top ten Christian media networks in the US.

My vision is to broaden out the network's appeal and get our viewers to think on a more global level about their faith. To do that, I really need a showrunner (that's a term media folk use over here to mean the Big Boss – ha ha!) with international experience and a fresh perspective.

I have listened to all your *Thought for the Day* slots, and believe me when I say, you are the answer to my prayers.

Would you consent to meet me, and hear a proposal that I think will interest you? I am sure that money is not the reason you get up and go to work at the *Church Times* every morning, but I can promise you that, working with me, you would certainly not lack for material wellbeing, alongside the obvious, spiritual fulfilment.

I will be totally frank with you. I took the chance you would agree to see me, and flew over from Memphis yesterday. I am staying at a small hotel in Victoria, which, to be honest, is not the sort of place I would willingly invite a tramp – is that the word? – let alone a respected broadcaster.

You'll understand that this type of situation is extremely sensitive. I need to keep everything 'strictly on the QT', as I believe you Brits say. One sighting of me in a restaurant or commercial premises could set the rumour mill turning. Is there any chance we could meet at your home?

I have no plans to return to the US until I hear back from you, and am at your disposal, time- and date-wise.

Praying for a positive answer!

God bless.

MJ Fox

Somewhere around the second paragraph, Sarah had experienced a sense of profound calm descending. The outside world faded away. The screeching of car tyres beside her as two drivers narrowly avoided a collision barely registered. Her concerns about the rest of the day's appointments dissipated like candle smoke in a side-chapel.

When she reached the part about MJ's need for privacy, what should have been the loud ringing of an alarm bell was reduced to a faint tinkling. She prided herself on having sensitive antennae when it came to weirdos, perverts and all the other species of predators a single woman living alone in London had to learn to avoid. But this just felt right.

Back at the office, she Googled Twelve Saints Broadcasting and there it was. A financially-sound Christian media outfit based in Los Angeles. And yes, there were news reports about a possible bid, although none of the news items were able to confirm the identity of the bidder.

She tried searching for 'MJ Fox, Investment Banker' and drew a blank. But that didn't necessarily mean anything. Maybe this American banker felt the same way about social media as she did.

MJ had probably been listening live to her broadcast this morning. And, she supposed, American investment banks were probably pretty quick to clear their websites of staff who'd left Mammon for God.

She tapped out a brief reply.

Dear MJ,

Thank you for your email. I'm flattered that I should have come to your notice.

Yes. I would love to hear more about your proposal.

I'd be delighted to meet you at my house.

Would this evening be too soon? Say eight? I could probably rustle up supper.

Kind regards,

Sarah

She inhaled deeply, let it out in a sigh, and hit SEND.

The reply from MJ arrived moments later. Almost as if they were actually holding a conversation in real-time. Or as if Someone had been orchestrating the whole thing.

Dear Sarah,

Thank you so much!

I am honoured.

Where shall I present myself?

God bless,

MJ

. . .

She sent her address then, smiling, went to find her news editor.

———

At Paddington Green, Holt had just been released. The initial twenty-four hours were up and Callie had refused Roisin's request for a twelve-hour extension to his custody. She'd listened first to Roisin, then Stella, then, feeling more and more like Solomon, given them her decision.

'He's a skanky wee shite and if there were any way that was an arrestable offence, I'd say lock him up and do what ye like with him. But, sadly for us, it's not. I read his little storybook, well, as much of it as I could stomach. Did you know he's got similar tales in there about the defence secretary, that wee girl off the telly who won the dancing show and Willow Heatley off breakfast TV? I'm sorry, Roisin, but there's nothing concrete. I'm not going to waste more time on *Mister* Holt because, unless he confesses, the CPS will just roll their eyes and tell us to piss right off. Politely, of course. You find some evidence, re-arrest him and I will come down and watch while you book him in.'

———

At 6.00 p.m. Sarah Sharpe tidied her desk, making sure every piece of paper had been initialled, signed, acted upon, passed on to one of her staff, or filed away. She closed every program on her laptop and shut it down. Then she zipped it into its bag, slung it across her chest, picked up her handbag and closed her office door behind her.

'Bye, Georgia, bye, Tom,' she said to a couple of staff members still at their desks.

With the friendly goodbyes hanging in the air, she left the office and took the stairs, practically running down to the ground floor. In her head she was planning a simple but nicely cooked meal that would impress an American investment banker-turned-Christian media network owner.

By the time she'd reached the tube station, she'd decided. Roast cod served with green beans and boiled new potatoes. The fish was a subtle touch, she thought. A nod to MJ's being a fisher of men – and women.

———

The ingredients were all laid out on her kitchen counter, the oven was up to temperature, a bottle of wine was cooling in the fridge and the table was laid by 7.30 p.m. Anxious, despite telling herself she had nothing to be nervous about – MJ had approached her, after all – she poured a glassful of vodka, added ice and downed half of it in a single gulp. As the fiery spirit cooled and then burned her throat, she sighed out a breath.

She went upstairs and changed into a plain navy linen dress and a pair of low-heeled navy pumps. To avoid giving the impression she was a nun, she added a splash of colour: a bright yellow string of beads at her neck that lay neatly across her chest.

She looked at herself in the mirror above the hall table and smiled.

'MJ! How lovely to meet you!' she said to the slender, soberly-dressed woman facing her. 'Come in, please. I hope you're hungry. No, too effusive. Dial it down a bit, Sar.'

She tried again.

'MJ. Please, come in. It's been a hot one, today. Would you like a drink?'

She shook her head.

'Might be a teetotaller.' She smiled at her reflection again. 'Would you like something to drink? Better.'

Her attempt at a third variation was forestalled by the doorbell pealing. Despite the fact she was expecting her visitor, the sound made her jump. She turned to the front door, and, huffing a quick breath into a cupped hand and sniffing, she opened the door.

33

TRANSCRIPT FROM METROPOLITAN POLICE DIGITAL,
VOICE-ACTIVATED RECORDER, EXHIBIT NUMBER
FF/97683/SC6 2/4

I need the toilet.

I don't care. Hold it or piss yourself, it's all the same to me.

Why are you keeping me alive? You'd killed the other ones by now.

You know why. You're my confessor. I'll kill you when I'm good and ready, believe me. Sarah did a double-take when she opened her front door and saw me standing there with my best social smile firmly in place. I can understand why. But that's what I think is so clever about, what would you call it, my MO? I have the element of surprise right from the start. They can't catch up and by the time they realise the trouble they've let themselves in for, it's far too late.

I stepped across the threshold, dragging my wheelie suitcase behind me. I said, 'Sarah Clarke. The editor of the *Church Times* and, soon, I fervently pray, the showrunner for *Faith Across the Globe*, our flagship show.' Talk about slapping it on with a trowel!

She made some stumbling attempt to welcome me and offer me a drink. I had to interrupt her when she started reciting all the different cordials she had. I said, 'I could kill for a glass of white wine.' Then I winked! Can you believe it? I was playing her like a violin. Off-balance from the very first second. 'Of course,' she said, plastering a smile onto her sanctimonious little spinster face. 'I have a very nice Chablis chilling in the fridge.'

So she poured us both a drink and, by the way, I could smell vodka on her breath, so I was fairly sure the old Temazepam/Special K cocktail was going to work beautifully. 'I'm cooking us fish,' she said, turning to the oven. 'I hope that's OK?' I said, 'Fine by me. Just as long as you haven't invited another four thousand, nine hundred and ninety-nine guests.'

It was a lame enough little joke but poor old Sarah laughed as if I was the world's funniest comedian. Then I stuck the needle in. Us being in the kitchen made the whole process remarkably easy. I caught her as her knees sagged and gently manoeuvred her into a chair. We went through the whole, 'what did you just do?' routine then, and when her eyes got that druggy look, I explained.

I said, 'I listened to you on the radio this morning. I liked the point you made about the followers of Jesus. You said that they knew the truth: that there are worse kinds of suffering than not being noticed. And you know what? You're absolutely right. There's the suffering of a small boy being tortured by his mother, for one thing. And then there's the kind of suffering you are about to experience directly.'

It took a while to get her undressed. She'd gone quite floppy so it was the Devil's own job. Eventually I managed. Then I began. Despite my little Mickey Finn and the vodka playing together like good children, she managed a scream after the first bolt. Nothing that would alert her neighbours but I didn't want to take any risks, so I used a strip of her dress to gag her. After that it was plain sailing all the way.

Cleaning myself up took a while, and I was careful to wash and dry my wine glass before replacing it on the shelf in the cupboard.

There wasn't as much blood this time, but I'd still been careful not to stand in it or get my fingers on anything that might leave a print. Then I left. Simple as that.

34

TUESDAY 21ST AUGUST 7.38 P.M.

Gaynor Marzano stood outside her friend's front door, sweating despite being clad in the thinnest of badminton gear: loose black cotton shorts and a dusty-pink vest top over her sports bra. Her racket in its teal-and-black plastic cover lay across her back and she could feel the patch of sweat where the head was resting against her exposed right shoulder blade. She checked her watch: 7.38 p.m.

'Come on, Sarah, we're going to lose our court,' she said to the closed front door, trying not to allow the irritation she was feeling to grow any stronger.

She rang the bell again, listening intently for the sound of badminton shoes slapping on the tiled hallway beyond. Nothing. She pulled out her phone and hit redial but, again, it went straight to voicemail. Gaynor didn't bother leaving a second message.

'Oh, for goodness' sake, Sar, come on! What are you *doing*?'

Exasperated, she knelt at the letterbox and lifted the sprung outer flap of brightly polished brass, intending to yell words of encouragement to her friend, who, she knew, could get side-tracked as easily as Gaynor's teenage daughter. She pushed her index finger against the inner flap and drew in a breath, ready to shout.

The gust of hot, putrid air seemed to enter her nose and mouth simultaneously and lodge there like slime. She reeled backwards, gagging, before turning to vomit into a flower pot beside the front door.

When she'd finished, she pulled a tissue from her shorts pocket and blew her nose before crumpling it and dropping it to the ground. She spat on top of the mess and wiped her lips with the back of her hand.

'What *is* that?' she asked the glossy painted panel of wood facing her. Somewhere, deep down, she realised she knew.

Her walk from Farringdon tube station to work at Bart's Hospital took her through Smithfield meat market. Once or twice that hot summer, she'd had to reverse at high speed after coming across a barrel of offal already starting to rot in the early morning heat. The smell emanating from her friend's letterbox was worse. Much worse. A smell akin to gangrene which, as a nurse in a geriatric ward, she'd come across more than once in her career.

With a deep sense of foreboding gathering in her chest like a lump of undigestible food, she lifted the outer flap once more and placed her eyes to the narrow gap, holding her breath. Index finger trembling, she pushed the inner flap up and held it while she lowered her head until she could see in.

At first she didn't recognise the thing lashed to the bannisters as human, let alone her friend. Blackish-green and swollen to grotesque proportions, it fulfilled none of the criteria Gaynor normally used when she thought, 'human being'.

Then her training kicked in, along with a dawning horror.

She didn't scream. Nurses tended not to, in her experience. She'd been out with a friend when a bus had been blown to pieces on a London street a few years earlier and they'd both rushed to help, not that there was much they could do, while all around them members of the public were screaming. She and Moses kept their heads, and did what they could until the ambulances arrived.

She realised her phone was still clamped in her left hand. She called the emergency services and explained what she needed, where she was and what she could see through her dead friend's letterbox. Then she slumped with her back to the front door and, dry-eyed and shaking, set about waiting for the ambulance. And the police.

———

The first uniformed officer to arrive at 63 Finstock Road was a police constable, fifty-three, cropped greying hair, dark eyes beneath neatly trimmed black eyebrows, more of a gut than his wife was happy with, and the measured pace of a man who knew not to hurry when he didn't have to. He was running now, red-faced and panting as he turned into the front garden path.

Dave Harris had been a uniformed constable all his career, almost twenty years since leaving the Navy. 'I'm not bright enough to be a sergeant,' he'd quip if anyone teased him about his lack of career progress. 'Too much law to learn.' But the truth was, Dave liked walking the streets of Ladbroke Grove and Notting Hill. No, that was a lie. He didn't like it. He *loved* it.

He reckoned he knew a few hundred people personally, by name. The people he could nod to or exchange a few words with in the street ran into the thousands. And he knew Gaynor.

Seeing her white face and her oddly disjointed posture, he crouched before her.

'Hey, Gaynor. What's happened? Is it Sarah?'

She looked into his eyes and, in that split second, he knew he'd be calling in a suspicious death inside of three minutes.

Gaynor nodded.

'She's dead. Has been for a while.'

She got to her feet and stood aside. Dave wasn't a detective, but given his many years of service he reckoned that meant he'd seen more dead bodies than most CID officers.

The Regent's Canal was part of his beat and he'd stumbled upon a handful of floaters over the years, not to mention the stabbing victims dead in a pool of their own blood round the back of one of the rougher pubs in the area, or the domestics – wives and girlfriends, mostly – stabbed, bludgeoned or strangled by their husbands, boyfriends, pimps or, just very occasionally, teenaged sons.

So before he put his eye to the letterbox he pulled out his handkerchief, an old-school cotton square with DH embroidered in the corner in royal-blue thread, folded it into eighths, and clamped it over his nose. Then he looked.

He nodded. Even through the folds of white cotton, ironed to wrinkle-free perfection by his wife, he could detect the sweet-sour top notes of the smell of death. It stung his eyes. He felt a fleeting pang of sorrow for Sarah Sharpe. A nice woman. Living alone, apart from her cat, Gavin. Another murder on his patch. Another set of relatives to be informed, comforted and interviewed. He turned away and spoke into his radio.

'Control from PC 562 Harris. Suspicious death at 63 Finstock Road. Ambulance on its way,' he looked at Gaynor for confirmation: she nodded. 'We're going to need the on-call police surgeon and CID. CSI, too. Over.'

'OK, Dave. Wheels in motion. Out.'

He touched Gaynor on the elbow.

'Can you stand, love? Let's get you down the path, OK?'

'OK,' she said, getting to her feet and preceding Dave down the path to the gate, which swung open on silent hinges.

35

Stella was sleeping when the ring of her force mobile jerked her out of a dream. Instinctively, she checked the time and made a mental note: 8:06 p.m. She'd been asleep for an hour, give or take. Not bad, she reflected, after having been up for twenty-three hours straight. She grabbed the ringing and vibrating phone, which had almost reached the edge of her bedside table.

'DCI Cole.'

'It's Camille, boss. We've got a body in Finstock Road. A weird one. CID put it straight through to us.'

Stella was still groggy from waking. *First rule, get yourself sorted before talking, Stel.*

'OK, Camille. Can you call me back in five minutes?'

She hadn't undressed before flopping onto her bed and falling immediately into an exhausted sleep, so spent the time splashing cold water over her face and grabbing a foil-wrapped sandwich from the fridge and making a flask of coffee. She stuffed them into her murder bag then sat at the kitchen table waiting for Camille.

'A weird one. Is this number two? Are you getting into your stride now?' she asked the empty flat.

She was pulling on her boots when her mobile rang again. She snatched it up.

'Camille?'

'Yeah. It sounds like Niamh Connolly's killer just went for the double.'

'Address?'

'63 Finstock Road. It's—'

'It's OK, I know it. Who else is in the office?'

'Just me, boss. The others are all over the place. I think Garry's down in Wimbledon again.'

'Right. So you're going to get to see the sharp end. Meet me at Finstock Road as soon as you can.'

'You don't want me to come and get you?'

'I'll take the bike, it's quicker. Now go.'

———

Stella's old bike had been totalled by an Albanian hitman. He'd paid for that particular crime with his life. Since then, she'd stuck with Triumph and her current mount was a metallic blue Bonneville.

She'd added leather panniers and a top box to the retro-styled bike, and the police garage, after consulting a protocol manual and pronouncing themselves satisfied it was legal, had fitted a siren and a blue flasher above the big, round headlight. The boys in Traffic had grudgingly admitted it was a nice piece of kit, and even if it wasn't as fast as her old Speedmaster, it got her around faster than any of the cars the other detectives used.

Three minutes after taking Camille's second call she was thumbing the starter and pulling away from her spot in the carpark beneath her apartment block.

Even though the rush hour had, technically, finished, it appeared nobody had told the drivers of the cars, vans and lorries sitting stationary on the Westway between Stella and the crime scene. She flicked on the blues and twos and carved a path between the two lanes of traffic, accelerating up the elevated section and westwards towards Ladbroke Grove. Ten minutes later she was turning left into Finstock Road.

Two marked cars had been parked diagonally at either end of Finstock Road, effectively blocking traffic from entering or leaving. Stella showed her warrant card to the uniformed cop standing next to the chequer-sided Ford Mondeo and he waved her through.

She pulled up just outside the blue-and-white tape marking the outer cordon, heeled out the sidestand and dismounted, pulling her helmet off and hanging it on the handlebar.

A small crowd of onlookers had gathered and were busy filming the activity outside 63.

A white CSI transit van was parked in the middle of the street. Two unmarked cars sat with their doors open, blue lights still flashing on their dashboards and from between the radiator grille bars. And she recognised Camille's bright-blue Honda Civic.

Stella nodded to the burly uniformed PC manning the outer cordon and unbuckled the righthand pannier, from which she extracted her murder bag.

'DCI Cole, Paddington Green,' she said, showing him her warrant card. She waited for him to note down the details on his log. Then he lifted the tape.

'There you go, ma'am.' He nodded at the wide-open front door of number 63. 'Nasty one. Been there a few days, and in this heat, you know, it's pretty smelly.'

'Thanks.'

Camille was talking to a youngish guy – mid-twenties, maybe, ginger hair – wearing a pale-grey suit and a look of irritation on his freckled face. Stella crossed the twenty yards between them at a trot. Camille turned as she arrived and held out a takeaway cup.

Stella slurped some coffee down, wincing at the heat but grateful she could leave her homemade instant in the pannier.

'Thank Christ!' Cam said. 'Can you explain to DC McKay here that this is an SIU case, please? And that just because he's got a dick doesn't give him the right to patronise me?'

The male DC put his hands on his hips and jutted his chin at

Stella, apparently not ready to give up whatever jurisdictional claim he felt he had without a fight.

'And you are?' he said, in an accent she recognised. It was the same, arrogant, well-educated tone Will Dunlop had arrived with, before realising in double-quick time that he ought to lose it.

Stella took a more cautious sip of the scalding coffee. Then she fished out her warrant card. 'Detective Chief Inspector Cole. Special Investigations Unit,' she said sweetly, showing him her warrant card. 'Is there a problem,' she paused, 'Detective Constable?'

He coloured instantly, his pale cheeks turning a furious red. His hands drifted out from his hips, palms outwards.

'No, ma'am. But I was not informed this wasn't a straight CID job. And I don't appreciate being sworn at, either,' he added, glaring at Camille, whose posture had relaxed markedly: one hip cocked, one eyebrow raised as she waited for the inevitable.

'Graduate fast-track?' Stella asked.

'Er, yes.'

'Good university?'

'York. I think that would count.'

'Bath,' Stella said, jabbing a finger at her own chest. 'But here's the thing, DC McKay. I appreciate that you weren't informed *to begin with*. But I'm sure DS Sharpe here did, in fact, inform you. That right, Camille?'

'Yes, boss. That's what I was trying to tell him when you rocked up.'

'Right. Well, believe it or not, even her lack of a penis doesn't make my DC into a liar. And as for the swearing, I don't, actually, care whether you like it or not. Now, as you clearly need some experience working with proper detectives, get yourself suited up and, if you're good, you can come in with me and Camille. All right?'

'Yes, ma'am,' he said, failing to keep the sullenness out of his voice.

'Right!' Stella said. 'Shall we?'

Fully enclosed in protective clothing, with Camille and DC McKay behind her rustling in their own white forensic suits, she walked towards the front of the house. Just as she'd done in Wimbledon, she negotiated the inner crime scene cordon and then entered the house.

Behind her, Stella heard Camille gasp.

McKay uttered a short, 'Hell's teeth!'

Arranged as if for a grotesque religious painting, two white-suited CSIs were on their knees at the feet of the naked corpse, which was suspended by its wrists from the bannister of the narrow staircase.

Inside her Tyvek CSI suit, Stella broke into a sweat that had nothing to do with nerves and everything to do with the sauna-like conditions inside the crowded hallway. The heating in the small terraced house had clearly been turned up to high, which, coupled with the ferocious London summer temperatures, had combined to accelerate the decay of the corpse.

The skin of the distended abdomen was a dark, purplish-green, shading to black in places. The eyes and tongue protruded from the grossly swollen face, itself the same sludgy colour as the rest of the body. In terms of the stages of decay, she put it firmly at putrefaction.

The CSIs both wore rebreathers that covered the lower halves of their faces, the cylindrical twin filters giving them the appearance of scuba divers stranded on dry land. Stella and the two DCs were exposed to the full, awful stink of a rotting human body: the sickly sweet, heady smell of acetone overlaying the fetid stench of rotting meat and raw sewage.

A blackish-red liquid had pooled around the corpse's feet, its shining surface alive with flies and the writhing white bodies of maggots.

Stella reached inside her suit and extracted a small bottle of oil of camphor. Turning away from the body for a moment, she offered it first to Camille and then McKay. Gratefully, the two younger cops smeared the pungent substance on their top lips.

'Thanks, boss,' Camille said.

Camille turned to McKay, whose face had lost its earlier colour and now had a waxy sheen.

'You OK?' she asked.

He nodded, mutely.

'This your first murder?'

He shook his head.

'But your first Sloppy Joe?'

Another nod.

She leaned over and patted him on the shoulder.

'Focus on your training. Try to think yourself into the offender's mind. Look at the door. Was there forced entry?'

Gratefully, it seemed to Stella, McKay turned away from the hideous sight in front of him and went back to examine the front door.

'That was kind, Cam,' Stella said.

Camille shrugged.

'Yeah, well. Even wankers need a little love now and then.'

Stella turned back to the corpse and began a methodical appraisal of what she could see.

36

TUESDAY 21ST AUGUST 8.29 P.M.

Though the abdomen had swollen grotesquely, breasts were still visible above the distended stomach. No cock and balls either, although on its own that single fact would not be conclusive. She'd seen the handiwork of killers who liked to castrate their male victims, *ante-* or *post mortem* as Doctor Craven would probably enjoy saying. Longish silver hair, though beginning to come away from the scalp, was tied into a loose ponytail.

She voiced her thoughts so Camille could hear.

'So, we have a female victim. Correction, a *second* female victim.'

'You reckon this is the same killer who did Niamh Connolly, then?'

'Mm, hmm. No doubt in my mind, Camille. Too weird to be a coincidence.'

'Shit! This is it. It's a serial killer, isn't it?'

'Between you, me and the newel post, yes, I'm sure of it. But three's the standard, so at the next press conference it's going to be a second tragic death. Keeping an open mind. Blah, blah, blahdy-blah.'

Stella had seen corpses in this state of decay, and worse, before: she wasn't immune to the horror, but it was neither the putrid smell nor the viscid appearance of the dead woman's flesh that held her attention now.

She pointed at the left side of the torso, where a small three-pointed star like an orange Mercedes logo sat flush with the taut, glistening, black skin. Protruding from the centre for half an inch or so was a metallic-blue cylinder about the diameter of a pencil.

'Look at that,' she said to Camille. 'Is that the end of an arrow?'

Camille leaned closer, paused for a few seconds, then nodded.

'Shall we put out a wanted marker for Robin Hood, boss?'

One of the CSIs snorted inside their rebreather. Stella grinned.

'Yeah, and tell Control he might be accompanied by a giant with a big stick and a fat bloke in a monk's habit.'

The CSIs shook their heads as they carried on scraping up samples from the pool of blood and liquefying soft tissue.

Stella moved carefully around the body. She counted three more arrows embedded in the torso and one stuck through the right calf. Apart from the one in the lower leg, the arrows were all virtually invisible, as the bloating had pushed the flesh out and around the shafts.

'Has the police surgeon been in yet?' Stella asked the CSI to her left.

'No, ma'am.'

Aha, you're a woman. Couldn't tell behind all the gear.

'If he arrives and I'm not here, give me a shout, OK?'

'Yes, ma'am.'

'DS McKay?'

'Yes, ma'am?' he answered, emerging from the kitchen.

'What did the front door tell you?'

'It's not been forced. I checked the back door, too. Solid as a rock. Windows on the ground floor all secure. Same upstairs.'

'So…?'

'So no forced entry.'

'And that tells us, what?'

'She knew her attacker.'

'You sure about that, are you?'

'Oh, er, OK. No, wait, it means she let him in because she knew him or he convinced her he wasn't a threat. Could have been posing as a market researcher or the gasman or something.'

'Very good, DS McKay. We'll make a decent detective of you yet.'

Stella turned back to the body. She wanted more. And for that she needed a bit more elbow room.

'Camille, can you go and talk to the neighbours on each side? DS McKay—'

'It's Scott, ma'am. If that's OK?'

Stella nodded.

'OK, thanks. Scott, I want you to see if you can find out how long the police surgeon's going to be. Oh, and one more thing,' she shouted after his retreating back.

'Yes, ma'am?'

'OK, two more things. Please stop calling me "ma'am". Boss, guv or DCI Cole are fine. And can you find out where the central heating controls are and turn them off?'

With the two DCs gone, and the CSIs almost invisible, so silently did they work, Stella stood facing the remains of the woman who had until very recently been the owner, or at least the occupier, of 63 Finstock Road.

'I'm so sorry,' she said under her breath. 'But we'll catch him. I promise you.'

Something about the way the woman had been posed caught at Stella's memory, but the stench, and the revolting sight of a body softening to the point it could flow out of the ropes holding it upright, obscured whatever tendril of an idea she was grasping for. She spoke to the killer.

'You took Niamh Connolly's blouse and bra off. But you stripped this one. Why? What are you doing? It's a different MO but you've got a signature. I just have to find it.'

The brief silence was interrupted as two men entered the hall. Both in paper CSI suits, both over six feet tall. One portly, the other altogether a more athletic figure.

'DCI Cole, Paddington Green,' Stella said. 'I'm the SIO. Is one of you the police surgeon?'

'That would be me,' the portly man said, extending his right hand. 'Dr Howard Byatt.'

The other man didn't bother with the handshake.

'DI Hamlyn. I hear you've been offering one of my DCs some on-the-job training?'

Stella couldn't tell if he was amused or angry. There was so little of his face on view behind the protective gear. She decided on diplomacy.

'Yeah. Sorry about that. You know, chaos of the first few minutes on scene. I just grabbed whatever bodies I could find.'

The DI barked out a short laugh.

'Please don't apologise. Arrogant little prick could do with learning a bit more humility to go with his bloody PhD in criminology.'

Relieved that she'd not misread the situation, Stella turned back to Dr Byatt.

'I need you to certify death, Doctor. I want her at Westminster Mortuary as soon as. And a time of death would be good. To the day would be OK at this point.'

Byatt peered at her through narrowed eyelids.

'You know that—'

'You can't give a time of death before a forensic post mortem's been conducted, yes. But please. Just a rough idea. I mean this week? Last week?'

He sighed.

'The heat we've been enduring would have accelerated the process of decay but, even so, I suppose I wouldn't be sticking my neck out too far, not so far as to risk my professional reputation, as it were, if I were to hazard that she may have been dead for three or four days, at least.'

'Thank you, Dr Byatt. So, can you certify death, please, so we can get the body over to the mortuary?'

'Steady on, DCI Cole. I need to examine the body in situ. And I'm sure my scientific colleagues would like to assess the situation for themselves. I really can't permit you to remove it just yet. Judging by the state of,' he paused and scrutinised the corpse, 'her?' Stella nodded. 'Yes, well, judging by the advanced state of decomposition, I don't suppose a few more hours will make much difference.'

Stella had met Byatt before and considered him a competent but overly-fussy man, who tended to let his scientific curiosity obscure more operational priorities.

'Which I totally understand. But as SIO, the decision on when to move the body is mine. And she's going to Westminster as soon as you've pronounced her dead. Though I think we can all agree that's a formality at this stage.'

Byatt favoured her with a three-second glare, which she merely returned. Then he turned to the corpse and began the rudimentary checks for pulse and breathing before pronouncing her dead. Hamlyn winked at Stella. She had no trouble interpreting the signal. *Nice one!*

Ten minutes later, the corpse had been cut down from the bannisters, the CSIs being scrupulous about leaving the knots in the rope intact. Then toe-tagged, placed inside a black, leak-proof, plastic body bag and lifted onto a wheeled stretcher.

Alec Stringer, the CSM, had called a firm of private contractors who had transported the bagged and tagged body to Westminster Mortuary in a dark-grey Ford Transit marked, in discreet white capitals on each side, PRIVATE AMBULANCE.

Free of her protective clothing, which she'd stuffed into a black bin liner and handed over to a CSI taking a water break by the van, Stella pulled out a digital recorder and made a series of short notes that she'd get her PA to type up for the policy book.

'My first decision was to request the body be moved to the Westminster Mortuary. My rationale is that the continuing high outside temperature, plus the fact the central heating had been turned up to max, meant the body was decaying rapidly and I considered there to be a risk that further decomposition could hinder our attempts to gather useful evidence.'

'Nice arse-covering, boss,' Camille said, her rough-edged South

London accent a welcome relief after the hushed tones inside the house.

'Yeah, don't I know it? I wonder how many combined hours SIOs spend recording this sort of crap just on the outside chance there's an inquiry or a retrial and the defence want to crawl over our files looking for evidence of misconduct.'

'What next, then?'

'D'you speak to the neighbours?'

'Yep. Deceased was Sarah Sharpe. Sixty this year. The lady on that side,' Camille pointed to the house on the right of Sarah Sharpe's, 'said she was sure because she remembered the victim had a birthday party in June.'

Noting these scant details, Stella looked up, smiling to soften the impact of her words.

'Let's stick to Sarah, please, Cam. You know I don't like calling them victims. Not if we can avoid it. She had a name in life, so we continue using it in death too.'

'Sorry, boss. Sarah had a sixtieth birthday party in June. Might be worth trying to get a list of the guests, you think?'

'Yes. Good thinking. Take that action, would you? I'll write it up later and give you the top sheet. What else did you find out?'

'The bloke on the other side's a journalist. BBC, I think. He said Sarah was a journalist, too.'

'Papers or telly?'

'Papers. *The Church Times*.'

Stella's mind jumped back to Niamh Connolly, the woman she was already thinking of as his *first* kill. Yes, he wouldn't officially be a serial until number three, but she knew, deep down, what she and her team were up against.

Like Cam had said at the morning briefing, Niamh had been a vocal and prominent Christian. Now here was a second prominent Christian woman, killed within a week of the first murder.

Sure, the MO was different in places. The tortures were different for a start. And Sarah Sharpe had been left suspended from her own staircase naked, where Niamh had been partially clothed and seated. But the signature? Maybe the PM would reveal it.

'Can you get on to the offices of the *Church Times* first thing in the morning? Ask if she had a work diary on her computer. I want to know whether she'd been in the media recently. I wonder if that's how he's selecting them.'

Cam nodded.

'What about the geography, boss? Niamh lived in Wimbledon, Sarah here. It's, what eight miles between them? Maybe he lives in between.'

'I'm going to talk to Callie. If we've got the budget I think we should get a geographic profiler on standby. Nothing much they can do with two scenes but if he does it again, we'll likely have a triangle.'

'Something else, boss.'

'What is it?'

'Isaac Holt. Looks like he was in custody when Sarah Sharpe was murdered.'

'Yeah, worse luck. I'll tell Roisin when we get back to the station.'

37

TUESDAY 21ˢᵗ AUGUST 8.30 P.M.

The killer leaned forward, closer to the TV screen. One hand gripped a freshly cut half-orange, the other a grapefruit knife: the curved, serrated blade working back and forth in a steady rhythm, separating the flesh from the cup of peel. The BBC continuity announcer informed all those watching that,

'Despite the troubles at the food bank, Sister Moira Lowney still finds time to comfort a new novice. Tilly is worried that convent life is not for her after all, in the latest episode of *Habits of a Lifetime.*'

Sister Moira appeared, walking along a gravel path beside rectangular vegetable beds with a woman in her mid-twenties. Their heads were bent in towards each other.

Apple-cheeked and comically short beside the tall, willowy novice, the sister laid a reassuring hand on her young charge's forearm as they walked, her pale-blue eyes magnified by frameless glasses.

Juice spurted as the knife freed another segment.

38

Thirty minutes later, Stella and Cam were both back at Paddington Green, standing by the whiteboard in the SIU incident room, updating it with Sarah Sharpe's details.

Roisin and Def arrived within minutes of each other. Stella looked over her shoulder.

'Rosh, can I have a word?'

'Sure, boss. Here?'

'My desk.'

Keeping her voice low, Stella filled Roisin in on the situation at Finstock Road before showing her the photos Alec Stringer had taken.

'Where did Holt go after we turned him loose last week?'

Roisin's face spoke volumes. Stella knew it wouldn't be good news.

'He went to his mum's. She lives in Colchester. I had Will follow him up there. I mean, he might have come back and done Sarah Sharpe, but I'm not hopeful. Should we pull him in again?'

Stella didn't have to think for very long.

'Look, I know you thought you had him locked down for Niamh's murder, but there were already a shit-ton of holes in your hypothesis. Sarah Sharpe was nothing to do with the abortion debate as far as I can tell. Not a Catholic. No reference to her in any of Holt's literary outpourings in that sewer of a notebook. Look, keep him on the burner behind the back burner, but I want you to start looking at Sarah Sharpe's background. I don't think this is a personal thing, like a vendetta or something. And the victim selection isn't opportunistic either.'

'What is it, then?'

'I think it's about the Church, not about the women. Or, not that exactly, I mean it's clearly about the women, but it's their faith that's stoking his anger. Holt's a pathetic, nasty piece of work, but he's a fantasist. And his fantasies, sick as they are, don't match the reality of what we're seeing. Remember, Rosh, for him, it's all about sex. These killings, they're not.'

———

By 10.05 p.m. the rest of the team had arrived. Stella looked around at them, assessing who had had enough for the day. Their faces hadn't yet taken on the grey, stressed-out immobility that came with a case that refused to break. But she didn't want them working unnecessarily long hours. She filled them in on what they'd discovered inside 63 Finstock Road and then gave them the permission she knew they'd all need before clocking off.

'Look, guys,' she said. 'There's nothing you can do tonight that won't wait until morning. You've done some great work today, and with what Cam and I saw over at Ladbroke Grove earlier, it looks like he's targeting prominent Christian women. That's a step closer to catching him.'

'You going to issue a public safety warning, boss?' Garry asked from his position sitting on the corner of a desk.

'It might scare him off,' Baz said.

'Yeah, but it might save lives,' Roisin countered.

Stella let the discussion play out. It was one of the ways the team worked best, seemingly arguing about a decision or a piece of evidence, but really just digging down to the truth. She waited for a gap, then spoke.

'OK, look, officially it's not a serial killer yet. But I think we all know in our gut that it is. But for now, we'll go with a general warning to women, especially if they live alone, to be careful. Not to accept invitations to meet strangers at their homes, for example. That should buy us some time without letting him know we're onto him.'

'Boss?' Becky called out.

'Yes, Becks?'

'Should we compile a list of women who match the two existing victims? Like, Christian women with media profiles?'

'That's an excellent idea. OK, get onto that, please.'

Once they'd all left and the office was quiet, Stella sat back down at her desk. Callie's office was dark, which was a shame, as she'd have liked to bounce a couple of ideas off her. *That'll also have to wait till morning*, she thought.

She steepled her fingers under her nose and closed her eyes.

What's going on in that messed-up head of yours, eh? The Church Times *is C of E, so that chucks cold water on Cam's Catholic paedo-revenge angle. Holt was probably having a wank in his mum's guest bedroom, so he's out. Do you just hate religion in general? Or is it women you hate?*

The image of Niamh Connolly's mutilated torso swam into her inner vision where it took turns with Sarah Sharpe's bloated, arrow-ridden body. She frowned. There it was again: that insight she felt would open things up, swimming, like the last time, just beyond her grasp.

Not an insight, Stel, a memory. That's what it felt like. Something she was remembering from her own past, instead of connecting the dots between the two dead women. Her dad was saying something. And she, Stella, was rolling her eyes. Bored and making sure he knew it. So, that meant she was deep in the teenage tunnel. Half raging sex hormones, half withdrawn sullenness, and one hundred per cent gold-plated hostility to her parents. How they'd put up with her for those three or so years, she had no idea. *What were you saying, Dad? And why was I so hell-bent on showing how tedious it all was?*

'Praying for a breakthrough?'

Callie's question startled Stella. She jerked back in her chair, eyes wide.

'Please don't creep up on me like that! You nearly gave me a heart attack.'

'Sorry about that. What were you thinking about?'

Stella rubbed her eyes, which felt gritty with tiredness. She hoped her own face still had a little colour in it after sending her team home to catch up on their beauty sleep.

'Something I can't quite put my finger on. A memory. It feels important. It's to do with the bodies.'

Callie sat on the hard chair to the side of Stella's desk, face tightening.

'Bodies? As in plural.'

Stella nodded.

'As in a second murdered woman.'

'Shit! I've been in meetings all afternoon and then a dinner with the DAC and a few of her political buddies. I've not heard. Who?'

Stella sketched in the details of Sarah Sharpe's murder. When she finished with the description of the wounds, Callie blew her cheeks out.

'What do you need?' she asked.

'I want to talk to Jamie Hooke. Urgently. And I want a geographic profiler on standby. I'd also like to send the DNA samples Lucian found to an external lab. One-day turnaround. If it helps, I know a pawnbroker in Kilburn who'll give you a good price on your dress uniform.'

Callie's eyes flashbulbed.

'Oh, ye cheeky wee thing! Look, no promises, OK? But I'll try and rejig a couple of operations and free up some cash. Because mucking about with spreadsheets is my number one favourite late-night activity.'

Stella grinned.

'Would a drink help?'

'Aye. A bloody big one. But I drank the last of my Glenlivet yesterday. I haven't had a moment to get to Tesco.'

Stella leaned over and opened her murder bag, which sat discreetly on the other side of her desk from Callie. From an internal zipped pocket she pulled out a brand-new bottle of the malt whisky she knew was Callie's favourite.

'Ta-daa!'

'You sweet girl. Come on then.'

The two women, bound by friendship and some very dark times indeed, retreated to Callie's office. With a generous measure of the whisky in a tumbler at her elbow, Callie started giving her budget a massage and Stella opened her laptop and began writing up her policy book.

39

After a luxurious four hours of sleep, and a snatched breakfast of coffee and toast, Stella was at her desk and reading through the previous day's reports by 8.00 a.m. One by one, the other members of the team walked into the incident room, in varying states of alertness. Some were larks, but most were owls, preferring to stay late rather than get in early. However, by 8.30 a.m. everyone had arrived. Time for the briefing.

'Morning, everyone. First of all, thanks for your work yesterday. We do have one strong lead now, which is the DNA samples Lucian retrieved from the rope, which was made of flax, with embedded fibres of wool. Well done, Rosh, for sorting that out with the POLSA. We also know, again thanks to our colleagues in Forensics, that the weapon, well, two really, he used to remove Niamh's breasts was a pair of vintage sheep shears. Trouble is they'd have been bought in a junk shop or at a car boot or maybe eBay so our chances of tracking him down that way are slim to anorexic. As you all know, we now have a second murdered woman. So this guy looks like he's just getting started.'

'When do we get the DNA profiles from Niamh Connolly's place back, boss?' Def asked.

'We found some cash down the back of the sofa so it's out with an external lab. They promised me the result by seven tonight. There was blood and also skin cells, so with a bit of luck we'll have Niamh's and the killer's DNA right next to each other. Not quite his fingerprint in her blood, but close. Jumper? How are you and Def getting on with the opponents of LoveLife? I know Holt turned out to be a bust, but is there anyone else in the frame?'

Arran hurriedly swallowed the mouthful of toast he was eating and consulted his notebook. He had a scrim of grey stubble on his cheeks and the bleary look of a man who'd been awake half the night. Maybe one of his boys had been ill. Stella made a mental note to ask him later.

'We've been running through the people in what Niamh called the "crazies". I'd say you could write off ninety-nine per cent of them as trolls. Never going to do anything more than send abusive messages. But there are three people we want to talk to.'

People. Not men. That's interesting.

'Go on.'

Arran started to speak then stopped abruptly and started coughing.

'Sorry,' he choked out. 'Crumb…wrong way.'

Def rolled her eyes and picked up when Arran had left off.

'Alfie Brown, Josef Kulik, Yukiko Watanabe. The last one's a woman, before anyone asks.'

'Bit of a longshot, isn't it, Def?' Will asked. 'Research says serial killers are almost always male.'

She nodded.

'On the basis of the data, yes. But then, what about Beverley Allitt and Rose West? Or Myra Hindley? They do exist. Between them they killed at least fifteen people, mostly kids.'

'Tell us about them, Def,' Stella said.

Def nodded and smiled briefly.

'Alfie Brown, twenty-year-old white male, lives in Milton Keynes with his mother. Unemployed. Sent Niamh seventeen abusive emails and Facebook messages. Threatened to come to Wimbledon, which is interesting in itself because, as Jerry Connolly told us, the house was in his name, and, I quote, "teach you a lesson about the true meaning of cruelty".

'Josef Kulik, forty. Polish. He lives in Roehampton with his wife and three kids. That's only a couple of miles from the Connollys' house. Seven or eight minutes by car, thirty-five if he walked. There's even a convenient bus, the 493.'

'That'd be great, wouldn't it?' Baz called out. 'If we could nick him 'cos he was caught on the bus's CCTV.'

Def waited for the laughter to subside, then continued.

'Kulik wrote Niamh a single letter. Very graphic, wasn't it, Jumper?'

Arran, who had now recovered from his coughing fit, though it had left his eyes watering and his stubbled cheeks pink, nodded.

'He described in some detail what he'd like to do to Niamh. It included a threat to tie her up and cut her breasts off and make her eat them while he watched her.'

'Bloody hell!' Garry said, shaking his head. 'Where do they get it from, all that shit?'

'I'm going to see a psychiatrist tomorrow who might just explain it to me,' Stella said.

'You want to watch it, guv,' Cam chipped in. 'He might start poking about in *your* head while he's explaining the mind of a serial killer.'

More laughter.

If only you knew, Stella thought. *I'm only one off Allitt, West and Hindley's total combined.*

'Yeah, well, I don't think he'd find much in there. Just a ton of paperwork and a bunch of alcohol-damaged brain cells.'

Only Garry didn't join in the laughter. Stella hadn't told him the details of her lost two years after Richard and Lola had been murdered, but he knew enough about her history to know how much the banter sometimes cost her. Def battled on again.

'And finally, our *statistically unlikely* person of interest,' she winked at Will. 'Yukiko Watanabe. Thirty-three. Female. Single.

Lives in a shared flat in Finchley with three other Japanese women.'

'Why her?' Stella asked.

'Two reasons. One, she attacked Niamh on Twitter over a period of three months last year before going silent. Her last dozen tweets were really unhinged. I'm surprised Twitter didn't take them down. I mean, totally bizarro shit about mutilating Niamh and slicing her up.'

'OK, but so did hundreds of people, thousands, probably.'

'Second,' Def said, flipping a page in her notebook with a magician's flourish, 'Yukiko Watanabe's job.' She paused. 'She's a sushi chef.'

The room fell silent for a second as everyone digested the import of Def's last sentence.

'Good work, Jumper, Def, thanks. So you're following them up, are you? Need any support?'

'That would be great, boss,' Arran said.

Stella opened her mouth to start assigning jobs when the door to the incident room swung inwards. All eyes turned to see who had invaded their space.

Stella's pulse jerked up and she felt a wave of anger crash over her. Standing in the doorway was Craig Morgan. Without waiting to be invited, he strode in and perched on the corner of a desk, beside Garry.

'Good morning, Mr Deputy Mayor,' Stella said, managing to utter the pleasantry without adding, *and what the hell are you doing in my incident room?*

'Don't mind me, DCI Cole. I wanted to check in on the progress of your investigation.'

Knowing when she was beaten, Stella forced a smile that felt as if her face was audibly creaking. She nodded.

'OK. Baz, Becky, Roisin and Will, can you work with Jumper and Def on the two IC1 males and the IC5 female threatening Niamh, please? Take a person each. The usual. Interviews, financials, work history, and especially anything weird on the psychological front. Apart from the obvious.'

'We'd need warrants to get medical records, wouldn't we, boss?' Cam asked.

'Yes. But I'm thinking of a lower-key approach.'

'It's like Will and I worked it at Holt's,' Roisin said. 'Ask to use the loo and have a poke around in the medicine cabinet. You see tranquilisers, anti-depressants, anti-psychotics, any shit like that, it's a fair bet someone has the odd bad day.'

Cam nodded her thanks.

'That leaves me, Garry and Cam. Right, Cam, can you run point here for today, please? I want you to talk to Lucian about the rope. It looks as though that's the murder weapon. I want to know what kind of rope it is, who makes it, if there's anything unusual about it. If you can put a list of UK suppliers together, we can start looking at potential CCTV, customer lists, that sort of thing.'

'Yes, boss.'

'Garry? I need to set up a press conference for later with Callie. We've also got Sarah Sharpe's post mortem scheduled for 2.00 p.m., which should be fun given the state the body was in. Until then, can you help Cam, please?'

'Sure, boss.'

'OK, everyone. Thank you.'

The detectives, uniforms and police staff stood up to return to their desks. Morgan's voice sailed above the shuffling and chat.

'One last thing before you disperse, please.' He caught Stella's eye. 'If I may, DCI Cole?'

Not trusting herself to speak, Stella waved her hand, palm upwards, as if beckoning a guest. *Come on then. Get on and get it over with.*

'Ladies and gentlemen, I just want you all to know that as Deputy Mayor for Policing and Crime, I am hugely supportive of your work. I know this is a big case for you and I want to pledge, here and now, to give you all the support I can.' He turned to Stella and smiled, though she thought it looked as genuine as one of the fake Rolexes in the exhibits room. 'That was all.'

Garry continued chatting to Baz, but he watched as his boss slumped at her desk. *She looks done in*, he thought.

Morgan was peering at the whiteboards displaying the crime scene photographs. Then he sauntered over to Garry and Baz.

He held his hand out to Garry, who shook it reflexively. Baz did the same. Morgan smiled.

'It's DS Haynes, isn't it?' he asked, then turned to Baz. 'And DS Khan?'

'Yes, sir,' they chorused.

Morgan laughed, though it came off as a fake to Garry.

'Oh, no need for that, lads. Just call me Craig. So, listen, I just want to say, I'm massively proud to see that two BAME officers are working at the heart of one of the biggest murder cases London's seen in recent years.'

'Sorry,' Garry said, his pulse quickening. 'BAME?'

In fact, he knew perfectly well what the acronym stood for, but he didn't particularly like it, or Morgan's patronising attitude.

'Black, Asian and Minority Ethnic,' Morgan said, apparently oblivious to Garry's disbelieving expression.

'I'm not a BAME officer, I'm a detective,' Baz said, straight-faced.

'Yeah, and I'm Jamaican,' Garry added.

Morgan blushed. He touched his flaming cheek with the fingers of his right hand.

'Of course. Sorry. Political correctness gone mad.' He rolled his eyes. Another bogus move, in Garry's opinion. 'So, I just wanted to check, are you getting enough time off?'

'Well, it's a big case, Craig,' Garry said. 'You do the hours, don't you?'

'Of course, of course. But I want to make sure you're being treated fairly by DCI Cole.'

'What do you mean?' Baz asked, raising his voice. 'The boss is literally the hardest-working officer in this station and she treats us like family.'

Morgan held up placating hands.

'I don't doubt it. And your loyalty is commendable. But

sometimes senior officers forget what it's like for those lower down the ladder. Has she offered you access to counselling, for example?'

'What?' Garry asked.

'Counselling? It's in your contract and you're entitled.'

'Look, it's fine. Really.' He turned to Baz. 'Nothing we haven't seen before, is it, Baz? Remember the Soup Dragon?'

He winked with the eye turned away from Morgan.

'Tell Craig,' Baz said.

'OK, so there was this one case last year, Craig. We called the killer "The Soup Dragon". You see, what he did was, he murdered his victims, blokes about your age, funnily enough, and he cut them up with a cordless chainsaw in his bath. Then he poured lye all over them. You know what lye is?'

'No.' Morgan's face had lost the pink tinge of the blush, and he was looking pale.

'It's basically a solution of sodium or potassium hydroxide. Extremely caustic and perfect for digesting animal tissue. You know, flesh?'

Morgan nodded again.

'Mm, hmm.'

'Yeah, so he topped up the bath with lye, like I said, and then left it to get to work. It's supposed to dissolve the flesh until all that's left are these really powdery bones in a sort of brownish liquid. Looks like coffee. Then he would've pulled the plug out and let the, you know, stuff, run out before he crushed the bones. But the neighbours complained about the stink and called the police, didn't they, Baz?'

Tag-team, his eyes said to Baz, who picked up the story.

'We got the call about midday on a Sunday. I was just about to sit down to my Sunday lunch. Roast lamb, roast potatoes, Yorkshires, gravy, the works. Anyway, the lye had sort of half-worked. The bath was full of this, kind of, what would you call it, Garry? Gloop?'

Gary waggled his head from side to side.

'Nah, mate. Not gloop. He wasn't called the Gloop Dragon, was he? It was soup! You know, Craig, like one of those hearty soups with lumps in. Only the meaty bits were rotten and the carrots were body parts or whatever. Yeah. A really lumpy, stinky soup. I tell you what, though.'

'What?' Morgan said, his cheeks and forehead waxy, beads of sweat appearing on his top lip.

Garry tried to get his timing right.

'If you'd have eaten a spoonful, you'd never have touched Heinz Big Soup again.'

Morgan smiled wanly, then turned and fled.

The two detectives burst out laughing at the retreating Armani-clad form.

Stella came over, a smile on her face.

'What was that all about?'

Baz looked at Garry and rolled his eyes, then answered Stella's question.

'The twat wanted to know if we were getting enough time off. Had we been offered counselling?'

Stella's eyes widened.

Garry continued.

'He told me and Baz it was great to see two BAME officers at the centre of such an important investigation. Can you believe it? He actually called us BAME! Not that the alternative would've been any better.' A beat. 'Prick.'

'How did you get rid of him? He practically sprinted out of here.'

Gary and Baz took turns to retell the story of their invented serial killer case.

With their combined laughter causing other officers to look round, Stella shook her head, smiling, and returned to her desk.

———

Once the room had quietened down, she wandered over to Arran, who was on the phone. The call finished, he turned to her.

'Yes, boss?'

'You all right?' she asked.

'Yeah, of course. Why?'

Stella shrugged her shoulders.

'Nothing. Thought you looked a little, you know, extra-tired at the briefing.'

He rolled his eyes.

'Fergus had a night terror. Hasn't had one since he was five. Poor little sod was wandering about downstairs with his arms in the air asking where the bad men were.' He swiped a palm across his face. 'Bit like us, really. Anyway, took me and Kath half an hour to calm him down, then I couldn't get back to sleep.'

Stella patted him on the shoulder.

'Take it easy, OK? If you get a breathing space, go home and get an hour's kip. That's an order.'

He smiled, tiredly.

'OK, thanks. You ought to get some rest yourself, boss. Or at least a change of scene. You look a little, you know——'

'Rough?'

He shook his head hurriedly.

'No! No, boss. I just meant——'

She smiled.

'It's OK. I looked in the mirror this morning and thought it was another one of his victims.'

She realised that since her last day off had been cancelled by Niamh Connolly's murder, she'd not stopped working except for a few hours to sleep. She scanned the incident room. Every member of the inner team, and all the supporting detectives and staff were actively pursuing leads, chasing down information and combing through the various Home Office and police database. *Maybe I could afford to take a few hours off,* she thought.

She made a call.

40

Cam was perching on the edge of Lucian's desk.

'So, the boss said it was flax with wool fibres stuck in it,' she said.

'Yup.'

Cam frowned.

'And flax would be …?'

Lucian smiled.

'Flax would be fibres of the plant *Linum usitatissimum*. AKA, before your eyebrows go into orbit, the common flax or linseed plant. It's what linen is made of.'

Cam rolled her eyes. Not everyone at Paddington Green shared Lucian Young's obvious relish for finery, and as a proud Brixton girl, she maintained a strict no-contact relationship with the countryside.

'I'm more of a denim and leather girl, myself,' she said.

'Each to their own. Anyway, it's a natural fibre and it's used for making certain kinds of rope. But the interesting thing about our sample is its diameter. There aren't too many applications that call for it. Most natural ropes are used in commercial cargo applications or shipping, and they're a lot thicker. But I did find one hit that looks very interesting.'

'Go on then, spill.'

'Bell ropes.'

Still thinking about commercial shipping, Cam leaped towards the water.

'What, you mean like ships' bells?'

Lucian nodded.

'Yes. But also church bells. Campanology.'

'Bell ringing. And yes, before you say anything, Mister Clever-clogs, I'm not a total South London thicko. I do read the odd book.'

Lucian placed fanned fingers on his chest.

'My sincere apologies. And there was I thinking you were all about drug slang and gangstas.'

Then he winked, earning himself a playful slap on the arm from Cam.

'Yeah, well, you'd be surprised how many dickheads there are in this station who hear my accent and start mansplaining how the coffee machines work. So that's great. I don't suppose you can tell me how many suppliers of flax bell rope there are in the UK?'

He shook his head.

'Can't start doing detective work, Cam. I'd have your Fed rep down on me like the heavy mob.'

———

Back at her desk, Cam heaved a sigh. So much of her job seemed to involve dicking around on the Internet, as she saw it, when she'd much prefer to be out knocking on doors, interviewing people, tracking down witnesses – anything that involved contact with a human rather than a mouse.

Dutifully she switched applications to a web browser and typed in her initial best guess at a search term that wouldn't throw out thousands of irrelevant hits.

UK supplier flax bell rope

In a little under half a second, she was looking at a page of results, and smiling broadly. *I don't believe it!*

The information straining her credulity was simple. Clicking through the first few pages revealed that there were precisely five suppliers of flax bell rope in the UK. Five! Normally, she'd run a search and get the depressing news that there were hundreds, or thousands of web pages that might, but most likely might not, yield anything useful.

She made a list of the names and numbers of the five companies, then picked up her desk phone and called the first company, Searcy & Able. The semi-robotic voice of a BT message cut in almost immediately, telling her that the number was no longer active.

Must've gone out of business, she thought, running a line through the company name on her list. Her next call was more fruitful. The phone was answered on the third ring.

'Sherborne Ropes. How can I help?' a man asked in a soft Yorkshire accent.

'Hi. This is Detective Constable Camille Wilde of the Metropolitan Police. Can I talk to someone about flax bell rope, please?'

'Aye, lass. You can talk to me. I'm Arthur Sherborne. It's my company.'

'Oh, OK, thanks. So, Mr Sherborne—'

'Call me Arthur.'

'Thanks. So, Arthur, we're investigating a murder and I need to track down the supplier of some rope we believe to be bell rope. It's made of flax and it had some wool fibres embedded in it.'

'Murder, eh? You get plenty of those down in London, I'll bet.'

'We get our fair share.'

'Terrorists, too, I shouldn't wonder.'

'Yep. Some of those, too. It's not as bad as they make it look on the telly.'

Sherborne snorted.

'Telly? Nay, lass, you won't catch me watching telly. Too bloody depressing.'

Fighting back the urge to chivvy him along, Cam bided her time. She'd sat in on interviews with Def and watched the way the DS seemed to do almost nothing while hardened criminals unravelled in front of her.

'I know what you mean. I like a good book, myself.'

'Oh, aye, reading's good for the soul. That's what me old ma used to say. Now, about this rope of yours. What can you tell me about it?'

Congratulating herself inwardly for her patience, Cam seized her chance.

'Well, it's made of flax, as I said. And it's 12mm in diameter. Very clean, apart from, you know, a couple of stains. And, like I said, it has wool fibres mixed in or, not exactly mixed in, more like caught.'

'I see. Well, the thing is, Camille. May I call you Camille?'

You can call me Tinker-bloody-bell if it'll help you get to the point!

'Please,' she said.

'So, Camille. There's still a few of us making flax rope, so the question is, how are we going to identify which firm made it?'

'Yeah. I'm hoping you're going to be able to help me with that.'

'What colour?'

'Kind of off-white? Creamy, maybe?'

'Not the rope, the fibres!'

'Black and gold.'

'Aha! Now, you see, they've probably come from the sally.'

'Sorry, Arthur. The sally? What's that?'

'It's the fluffy tail at the end of the rope. Folk think it's the bit you pull, but it's not. It's more what you might call, ornamental. Now, we do ten colours. And two of them are black and gold.'

Cam's spirits, which had been dipping and swooping like summer swallows, rose in anticipation.

'So does that mean you supplied it?'

Sherborne laughed.

'Not so fast. You see, we all use the same ten colours. It's by way of being traditional.'

'Oh. OK. So, what, you're telling me it could be anyone?'

'Happen it could, happen it couldn't. But that's a rare colour combination. Most folk prefer to stay with the traditional red, white and blue.'

'Do you keep records of what colour sally people buy with their ropes?'

'Yes.'

Now we're getting somewhere.

'OK, look, if I came up to see you, do you think you could let have a look on your computer at your sales records?'

And please don't ask if I need a warrant. Be one of the helpful ones.

'Oh, aye. You can go through our records, but tha'll not find them on a computer. I'm afraid we're a bit behind the times on the sales side. It's all on paper. But, like I said, you're welcome to come up and look.'

Knowing in her detective's soul what the answer to her next question would be, Cam asked it anyway.

'I don't suppose you have CCTV, do you?'

'You'd be thinking us Yorkshire folk with our old-fashioned paper systems wouldn't have it, right?'

She thought she could hear the gentle sound of Arthur's mockery under his words.

'No! Nothing like that. But I—'

'Yes.'

'Pardon?'

'Yes, we have CCTV. Got a problem with thieving up here. Folk say it's the pikies, but who cares who does it?'

Spirits truly on the wing again after Arthur's cheerful admission that any search for the killer's order would mean hours sifting through paper invoices or receipts, Cam asked one final question.

'How long do you keep your footage before reusing the tapes?'

'Oh, a month or two? It's my son, David, who handles all that. Tell me, who else have you got on your list?'

Cam consulted her notes.

'Burslem Street Ropeworks in Whitechapel, the Grantham Bell Foundry, and Strutt and Nightingale.'

'Aye, that's all of us. Searcy & Able went bust turn of the year.'

Feeling that she'd got all she needed, Cam ended the call with a promise to visit within forty-eight hours.

———

She called the other three suppliers, all of whom confirmed that they supplied black and gold sallies when required and that she was welcome to inspect their order books, which, thankfully, were computerised.

Ending the final call she looked at her notebook and sighed.

Baz called over.

'Any joy?'

'Four suppliers of flax bell rope in the UK. All possibles. Halifax, Grantham, Cambridge and Whitechapel.'

Baz rolled his eyes.

'Someone's got a road trip coming up.'

Cam nodded. She was happy. A road trip. Digging. Interviewing. Investigating. *This* was what she'd joined for.

41

The ride from Paddington Green to Jason and Elle Drinkwater's house in East Sheen took thirty minutes. Stella pulled up outside a pair of electronically controlled gates punctuating a tall laurel hedge just as nearby church bells were striking eleven.

Fife Road was, she felt sure, the sort of address estate agents like her brother-in-law described as 'desirable'. No, scrub that. 'Prestigious!' She didn't begrudge them their wealth. Elle had explained once that she had inherited family money. One of her grandmothers had made a fortune in the cosmetics business. And Jason ran his own estate agency, so presumably worked hard for every penny.

The heat was stifling inside her leather bike jacket, but even though she envied those bikers she saw in T-shirts and shorts, the thought of what even a slow-speed slide along Tarmac could do to skin and muscles made her stick to her protective gear.

She flipped up the visor on her helmet, press the button on the intercom and waited. Her sister-in-law answered.

'That you, Stella?'

'Yep. Please let me in before I melt. It's boiling out here!'

Elle's tinny laugh was drowned out by the clack of the latch, then the gates moved inwards on silent hinges.

Stella gentled the bike through the gap and pulled up on the gravel circle that fronted the Victorian rectory the Drinkwaters had made their home. She leaned it over onto the side-stand then pulled off her helmet and stuffed her gloves inside. Yanking the zip down on her jacket, she crunched over the gravel, past Elle's sunflower-yellow Audi TT convertible.

The front door opened as she stepped into the porch, which was shaded by a swag of heavily perfumed pink roses. And there stood two young girls, one only a head shorter than she was, the other coming up to her ribs.

'Auntie Stella!' they screamed in unison, before throwing their skinny little arms around her and squeezing tightly.

'Oh, my goodness, look at you two young ladies!' she managed to gasp out, stroking the tops of their heads. 'Have you been taking special growing medicine?'

Polly, the older girl, had unwittingly saved Stella's life six years earlier, finding her with her back to the old oak tree on the lawn early one morning and about to blow her own brains out with a stolen Glock pistol.

The younger of the sisters was Georgie, just a babe in arms then but an intense little girl of six now, with dark-brown hair braided into plaits. In place of the pigtails Polly had been wearing the last time Stella had seen her, she sported a sharp little bob.

'I love your new haircut, Polly,' Stella said. 'It's very grown-up.'

'Thank you. I'm going to big school next month and this will be so much easier to look after.'

Stella smiled at her niece's oddly mature turn of phrase. Then the girls dragged her, one hand apiece, down the hallway, which was tiled in an intricate pattern of sky-blue, burgundy and white, and into the kitchen. Elle was filling the kettle, her rounded figure visible beneath a thin cotton sundress in a bright, tropical print.

'Mummy, Mummy! It's Auntie Stella. She came on her motorbike,' Georgie shouted. 'When I am old enough I am absolutely going to have a motorbike like Auntie Stella's. Only mine will be pink!'

Smiling, Elle came to Stella and the two women hugged.

'How are you? Is the case getting to you? We saw you on telly the other night,' Elle said, holding Stella at arm's length and looking deep into her eyes.

Stella smiled and felt some of the tension ease out of her shoulders. She had always loved the colour of her sister-in-law's eyes, a vivid, almost surrealistically bright green.

'Honestly? I'm knackered, but—'

Georgie gasped.

'You said,' then she giggled, covering her mouth with her hand. She split her fingers apart and whispered between them, 'a naughty word.'

'Oh, Georgie,' Polly said, rolling her eyes. 'Auntie Stella is a grown-up and a police officer. They can say anything they like.' She turned her face to Stella. 'That's true, isn't it? You could say,' she dropped her voice to a conspiratorial tone, 'the F-word, if you liked.'

'Well, I absolutely would not use that word,' Stella said, glancing over Polly's head at Elle, who was trying not to laugh, 'but sometimes, when I am at work, and I arrest a bad man or lady, some of them say all sorts of naughty words.'

Grinning, Polly asked the obvious question.

'Which ones?'

Stella shrugged her shoulders and raised her eyebrows.

'Oh, you know,' she said in a breezy tone, 'the usual ones.'

'But what, Auntie Stella? What ones?' Georgie asked.

Stella leaned closer.

'Bum.'

The girls giggled.

'Farty.'

The giggles turned to laughter.

'Last week, one even said...'

She looked over her shoulder then back at the two spellbound children.

'Willy-head!'

They squealed, delighted at her transgression.

Elle put her arms around the girls' shoulders and ushered them towards the French doors.

'Right, you two. Go and play in the treehouse for a while and let me and Auntie Stella have a chat.'

'Oh, chat!' Georgie said, pouting. 'That's just grownups doing talking for ages and ages about really boring things.'

'Come on, Georgie,' Polly said, taking her younger sister's hand. 'Let's leave them together for a while.' She turned to her aunt and mother. 'I'm sure you two have lots to catch up on.'

The two women sat at one end of the long refectory table. Elle poured tea and pushed a plate of homemade chocolate cookies at Stella, who took one and ate half in a single bite.

'Mmf. Ruvry,' she said as the cookie flooded her system with feel-good chemicals.

'Thanks, Polly helped me make them.'

'Who's turned into a very proper young lady since I last saw her. It can't have been more than a month ago.'

Elle grinned.

'I know, right? We got back from Spain last week, don't know why we bothered, given how hot it's been here, but anyway, it happened sometime on the return flight. At Malaga airport, she was like a bigger version of Georgie, and by the time we landed at Heathrow she was all, "Come on, Georgie, don't dawdle". Jason and I had kittens. It was so funny.'

Stella finished her cookie and, despite a pang of guilt, reached for a second.

'How is Jason?'

Elle passed a hand over her forehead.

'Oh, you know, busy. He's thinking of opening a second office, talking to the bank and lawyers, all that. But we don't see so much of him. He's always working, even when he's at home he's up in his office or out meeting clients for dinner. At least that's what he *says* he's doing.'

Stella had no need for her SIU 'spider-sense'. Her female intuition was enough. She sipped her tea and looked at Elle over the rim of the cup, seeing if she wanted to continue, be prompted or move away from the topic of Jason. Elle returned her stare.

'And when you say, that's what he *says* he's doing…'

Giving her sister-in-law, her friend, an opening.

'I don't know, Stella. I mean, I'm probably just being paranoid but I've just started to wonder recently whether he's, you know, seeing someone.'

'Why? Have you found long blonde hairs on his collar? That aren't yours, I mean?' she said, smiling in an attempt to keep it light.

Elle shook her head. Her own lips stayed resolutely downturned.

'No, nothing like that. He just seems a bit secretive. A couple of times recently, I've asked him where he was going and he just said, "client dinner", like that. Or, "bank meeting". He's normally so happy to tell me every little detail of what's going on, I've started to worry.'

Stella reached across the space that separated them and placed a hand over Elle's, feeling its coolness despite the warmth of the day.

'Look, whenever I see you two you seem like the perfect couple. He looks at you like he just met you. Maybe it's just a business thing he wants to keep close to his chest until he can do the big reveal. You know what men are like.'

Elle managed a small smile, which Stella could tell took some effort.

'You're right. I should trust him. It's just not like him, that's all.'

'Do you want me to interrogate him for you? I'm really good at it. I could sweat him for a few hours at Paddington Green. He'd crack in the end.'

Elle laughed properly. A loud, joyous sound in the bright kitchen.

'Oh, God, you crack me up. Listen, never mind my marital troubles. Or not,' she added quickly, 'tell me about your love life. Any handsome, intelligent men in the picture?'

Stella snorted.

'Sadly not, at this point. I've had a few online dates but, let's just say, I'm still sleeping spread out in the middle of my bed.'

'That bad, eh?'

'Oh, God, Elle, you have no idea! This one guy, right? We agreed to meet at the Royal Festival Hall. And I thought, well, this can't be bad. He's obviously cultured. He'd said in his email he was a distinctive dresser. So, you know, I'm picturing a handsome bloke in a nice suit or maybe jacket and jeans or something. Only thing is, when he turned up, he was dressed in this sort of scraggy, off-white linen robe belted at the waist, baggy trousers and long boots.'

Elle was grinning as Stella told her story, perhaps sensing where it was going.

'I couldn't not say anything so I said, you know, something like, "I like your outfit. Pretty bold". And he said, I'm not joking.' She started laughing herself. 'He said, "As a Jedi knight, I have to be ready at all times." And then,' she wheezed, 'and then he, he sort of flipped his *dress* to one side and he whips out this *thing*. I thought it was this monster vibrator and I said, "Easy, tiger, it's our first date," and he said, "This is a lightsaber. You're safe with me." Oh Jesus, Elle, I nearly peed myself.'

Unable to continue, Stella howled with laughter, Elle joining her, tears running down her cheeks, until the two girls stomped back into the kitchen and stood in matching poses, fists on hips.

'Auntie Stella, what are you talking about?' Georgie asked, wide-eyed. 'What's a vibrator?'

Unable to get any sense from the two shrieking grownups, Georgie and Polly looked at each other and rolled their eyes, then left mother and aunt to it.

Finally, dabbing her eyes, Stella heaved a great breath and shook her head.

'Oh, that was priceless. You're so lucky to have them.'

Elle smiled back.

'I am. I know that. And they're lucky to have their Auntie Stella, too. Sometimes I think I'm seriously lacking in the cool department.

Georgie is obsessed with your bike and Polly still talks about your police gun.'

A silence blossomed in the space left by Elle's last remark. Both women were thinking back to the day when Stella had left the house in Callie's company, destined for a private psychiatric institution and months of intensive psychotherapy. Only one of them knew how close Stella had come to being taken to a different kind of facility altogether.

The talk moved to other, easier subjects for a while.

'How is work?' Elle asked eventually, getting up to make more tea.

'It's a bastard of a case. This guy, I don't know how much you've seen on the news, but he's a bad 'un.'

Looking over her shoulder at Stella, Elle frowned.

'Do I have to be worried? About the girls? Or me?'

'No. Absolutely not. The girls are certainly not at risk. He's killed two adult females and that's enough to tell me he doesn't look at children as potential victims. And as for you, you should take all the usual precautions, but only the ones any woman living in the city takes. It looks as though he's going after women with well-known Christian beliefs. Ones who've been in the media.'

'Yes, I saw that Niamh Connolly had been murdered. It was in the English papers in Spain. Can't say I'm sorry.'

'Wow, OK, that's a bit harsh.'

Stella was genuinely shocked at her sister-in-law's remark, but she tried to soften her words with a smile.

'Oh no, I didn't, I mean, nobody deserves to get murdered but, you have to admit, the woman had the fire and brimstone look about her.'

'I know. But the way I see it, it's like those stupid old farts on the bench who say if a girl wearing a mini skirt and a tight top gets raped, it was because she was dressing provocatively. Maybe Niamh did rub people up the wrong way, but she was entitled to go about her business without being sliced up for her beliefs.'

'I suppose so. You're so annoyingly right sometimes, Stella, d'you know that?'

'I'll take that as a compliment. Listen,' she checked her watch, 'I'm going to have to head back, but it's been lovely to tune out of the case even for an hour or so. Can we get together again soon? All of us?'

'I'd love that. Just let me know when would be a good time. I'm guessing it won't be until after you catch this murderer.'

'Probably that's best.'

Unless Callie was right and this one's a runner.

———

The direct route back to Paddington Green would have taken Stella northwest, crossing the Thames at Chiswick Bridge and then through Hammersmith, Shepherd's Bush and up onto the Westway. Instead, she rode southeast, entering Richmond Park, its normally lush grass burnt an even brown, and pootling along in a queue of cars through the landscaped parkland. She had time to see a herd of deer lying in the shade of a stand of trees before leaving the Park and making her way to Putney Vale Cemetery.

She knelt in front of the two simple stones set beside each other.

Richard Gregory Drinkwater
18 October 1974 - 6 March 2009
Devoted son, husband, father.

Lola Meredith Drinkwater
2 October 2008 - 6 March 2009
A precious blossom, picked too soon.

She caressed the top of Lola's marker, then let her hands rest in her lap. With her eyes closed, she sat for a few minutes, listening to birdsong and inhaling the smell of flowers from the nearby graves. *I miss you both so much. But at least you're together. Take care of each other, won't you? I love you very much.*

Slowly, she rose to her feet and wandered back to her bike, nodding as an elderly woman carrying a bunch of pink carnations came towards her and offered her a sympathetic smile.

42

Stella snatched a hurried lunch in The Green Man, wolfing down a cheddar and pickle sandwich with a coffee, before rushing back for Sarah Sharpe's post mortem.

The procedure was the same as for Niamh Connolly's PM, except that Sarah Sharpe's body was far further along on its journey back to the elements from which it had been created. The PM suite at the mortuary stank of putrefaction and the oil of camphor was hopelessly outgunned in the battle to overpower everyone's sense of smell.

Having greeted Dr Craven, Stella, Garry, Lucian and Alec gratefully withdrew to the CCTV viewing room.

As Craven withdrew the arrows from the body, Stella spoke, without taking her eyes off the screen.

'Surely someone must have seen a bloke taking a bloody great bow and arrows into her house?'

Garry shook his head. He also kept his gaze fixed on the

televised dissection of the bloated corpse that had so recently been a committed Christian, a journalist and a badminton-playing best friend.

'I think they're from a crossbow, boss. The ends – the non-pointy ends, I mean – don't have the grooves cut in them for the bow string. I thought it was odd when I saw the crime scene photos so I looked it up. Crossbow bolts, or quarrels, if you prefer, have blunt ends, like that one,' he said, pointing at the screen, where Dr Craven's assistant was withdrawing one of the lethal-looking black shafts from Sarah Sharpe's abdomen.

'OK, but they're still pretty bulky, aren't they? Or do you get, what, compact models? Foldaways?'

'Point for the detective in the front row,' Garry said. 'I looked them up. You get the ones that look like they came from the War of the Roses or whatever, but nowadays you can get these really high-tech ones, look like something out of *Blade Runner*. And there are collapsible ones I reckon you could stash under a coat or a jacket.'

Stella furrowed her brow, momentarily distracted from the cutting, ladling and weighing happening on screen.

'Even then, with the weather as hot as it's been, maybe someone noticed a bloke in a coat or a bulky jacket, right? I mean most blokes I see are down to a polo shirt and a pair of shorts. There was even a bloke walking down the Edgware Road yesterday with no shirt on at all. I mean, this isn't Torremolinos, is it?'

Garry laughed, filling the small viewing room with his rich baritone.

'Standards are slipping, boss. You're lucky he wasn't wearing Speedos.'

Stella shuddered. Then she started half out of her chair.

'Oh, Jesus, look at that! She's coming apart at the seams.'

On the screen, Dr Craven's assistant had just removed a large, purplish-black organ – *the liver, maybe*, Stella wondered, when the torso seemed to split apart, and a couple of dozen feet of blackish-purple intestines squirmed from the body cavity onto the floor, amid a stream of viscous body fluids.

'Shit! I was going to have spaghetti Bolognese tonight, but that's put me right off,' Garry deadpanned.

Stella thumped him on the shoulder.

———

At four that afternoon, Stella updated Callie on the investigation, concluding with the observation that even though they were mercifully one short of the 'serial trigger', she felt it was time to issue a warning to the general public.

'The media are making a big deal out of it already, even without us confirming it's a serial. If we hold back completely, they'll accuse us of dragging our feet. And if, God forbid, he does it again, we'll be screwed seven ways from Sunday.'

Callie nodded her head, her lips a thin line. Wordlessly, she pushed that morning's copy of the *Sun* across her desk to Stella, who picked up the tabloid and unfolded it.

Beside a picture of Sarah Sharpe, a studio shot by the look of it, the headline, set in white type out of a black panel, screamed out at the reader.

TWISTED KILLER
SLAYS SECOND
'GOOD WOMAN'

As she read the two brief paragraphs beneath the headline, Stella could feel anger boiling up inside her.

The sick killer of anti-abortion campaigner Niamh Connolly has struck again. Yesterday evening, Sarah Sharpe, 60, the editor of The Church Times, was found dead at her London home.

A source close to the investigation told the Sun, 'These were good women. They've been butchered like animals.' The

Sun has seen photos of the victims' injuries, but as a family newspaper we can't print them as they are too distressing.

Stella flung the paper down. She looked at Callie.

'Some bastard's leaked the crime scene photos.'

Callie nodded.

'Aye, that would be my conclusion. Any point my asking how you're going to shut them down?'

Callie's meaning was clear enough. There were far too many people who had access to the photos. And in the age of digital imaging, finding, copying and sharing them was, literally, child's play. To track down the leaker would devour resources Stella simply didn't have to spare. They'd just have to live with it. She'd impressed on her team the need for total confidentiality. It couldn't have been one of them, could it?

A thought flitted across her brain. Morgan had been examining them after the morning briefing.

'You know as well as I do. We'd be chasing our tails when we should be chasing the killer. But I'll have a word in a few ears. See if anyone's been flashing the cash around all of a sudden. Buying themselves a new watch or paying off a car loan.'

'It's going to make today's press conference interesting,' Callie said, a wry smile twisting her lips. 'The beasts will be baying for blood.'

'Yeah, ours,' Stella said, still feeling like she wanted to hit somebody very hard. 'I don't suppose we can keep that prick Morgan out of it, can we?'

Callie shuddered. Then she shook her head.

''Fraid not, Stel. He has a right to be there and as he pays the commissioner's wages there's no way I can get support from higher up. I tell you, if anyone ever offers you a chief super's position, point over their shoulder and when they turn round to look, run for the hills.'

Stella stopped off at Becky's desk on her way to her own.

'Hi, Becks. How's that list coming on?'

Becky smiled. She never seemed to get tired. Stella envied her for it and supposed it must be something to do with being in your twenties and not racing up to the big four-oh.

'It's coming, but it's also growing. I'm up to seventy-nine, so far. All women who have been on radio or TV, or in YouTube videos, or written articles for the press, or spoken at conferences or workshops. Plus visitors from overseas. Did you know that there are over two thousand female televangelists in the USA, boss?'

'No, Becks, I did not,' Stella said, smiling.

Becky shook her head. 'I've watched some of their YouTube videos. They scare me!'

'Maybe that's why he's killing them. Maybe he's scared.'

'I tell you, boss, if you saw the hairstyles, *you'd* be scared!'

Stella laid a hand on the young DC's shoulder.

'This is excellent, Becks. And great idea of yours in the first place. Keep going.'

———

At 5.30 p.m., Stella sat beside Callie, staring out at the assembled journalists. After the *Sun*'s scoop, the number of replies to the standard release inviting the media to a briefing had almost doubled.

Tim Llewelyn had booked them into a room normally used for conferences at New Scotland Yard. It held a hundred seated. Today, that number had swelled by half again. TV reporters, photographers, camera crews, print journalists, bloggers: it seemed anyone with a press pass or National Union of Journalists card or Fisher Price 'My First Reporter's Kit' had blagged themselves a seat. Or, failing that, a couple of square feet on the carpeted steps leading up the sides of the raked auditorium.

To Callie's right, a frown etched into his features, sat Craig Morgan.

43

WEDNESDAY 22ND AUGUST 5.30 P.M.

Stella looked across at Morgan. In profile, his nose looked undersized for his face, a snub triangle where something more substantial was needed. He swept the room with his eyes before his gaze fell on Stella. He nodded, lips unsmiling. She felt obliged to return the brief, professional gesture, though internally she was anxious he was about to pull another stunt like the last time.

'I'll now ask DCI Cole to update you on the progress of the investigations into the murders of Niamh Connolly and Sarah Sharpe,' Tim said. 'Please save your questions for the end.'

Before he'd found his way to the side of the stage, a young woman sporting a shock of turquoise hair tied up in little plaits yelled out, an iPhone held above her head.

'Is this Jack the Second, DCI Cole?'

Stella ignored the question and was pleased to see a few of the older hacks shaking their heads and smirking. She read the prepared statement she and Callie had drafted with Tim's help.

'On Tuesday the twenty-first of August, the body of Sarah

Sharpe, sixty, was discovered by a member of the public at her house in Ladbroke Grove.

'At the moment we are working hard to identify the time of death but I can say that Sarah was murdered some time in the past few days. On behalf of the Metropolitan Police Service, I want to extend my sincere condolences to Ms Sharpe's family and say that we will be devoting all the resources at our disposal to catching her killer. At this point we have a number of promising leads and my team are working round the clock to follow these up.

'My first duty is to the public, and specifically to their safety. For that reason I would like to ask women to be careful about agreeing to meet people they don't know, especially if meeting at their own home is proposed. We do know that Niamh Connolly's killer used a false identity to persuade her to agree to the meeting. We are trying to ascertain whether the same approach was used on Sarah Sharpe.

'This man is extremely dangerous and we advise members of the public who believe they see anything or anyone suspicious to call the police immediately using nine nine nine. On no account should they approach them directly.'

Stella turned at nodded at Tim as the cameras flashed and buzzed. He stood and spoke into a handheld mic.

'Thank you, DCI Cole. Questions?'

The room erupted. Shouted questions collided in mid-air and rained down on the two senior detectives and the deputy mayor like spears hurled by hostile forces. Stella saw Vicky, hand aloft, and pointed at her. She raised her voice and injected a little steel into it.

'Yes, Vicky.'

'Do you believe the two murders were committed by the same person?'

'At this point we can't rule it out. There were similarities between the two murders, but without firm evidence linking them to the same perpetrator, we can't exclude the possibility that we're actually looking for two separate killers.'

Vicky smiled encouragingly at Stella as she wrote down the answer in her notebook. Stella had no time to acknowledge the gesture before a deep male voice bellowed out a question.

'Andy Robbins. The *Sun*. Do you deny that women in London are under threat from a serial killer?'

He'd thrown her a hospital pass of a question. 'Yes, I deny it,' could come back to haunt her if the killer went for his third. 'No, I don't,' would cause panic. But Stella hadn't got to be an SIO by buckling under incoming fire.

'Two murders, as yet unconnected, do not constitute multiple linked offences. As such, it is premature to use labels that would only lead to public anxiety.'

'Yeah, but a third one would do it, wouldn't it?'

Feeling she was being backed into a corner, Stella tried to deflect Robbins.

'As you know, three serious crimes committed by a single person is the criterion for considering them the work of a serial offender.' *Good, so far, Stel. You haven't said 'serial killer' out loud so they can't quote you. And the formal language won't sell papers.* She looked away from Robbins and pointed at the BBC's crime correspondent.

'Yes, Harry.'

'Both victims were prominent Christians. What do you make of that?'

Stella preferred the longer, rambling style of questions often asked by inexperienced journalists. While they were enjoying the sound of their own voice, she had plenty of time to prepare an answer. This was short and sharp. No thinking time. No hesitating allowed, either, it made you look weak and indecisive at best and a liar at worst.

'It's obviously a factor we are investigating. So far we've discovered nothing –' *Shit! Just said we've discovered nothing. Too late. Move on.* '– to indicate that the killer or killers had a religious motive.'

Stella was sweating under the combined heat of the bright TV lights and the blood rushing round her system like it was late for a wedding. Her pulse was thudding inside her ribcage, in her ears and her throat.

'Connor Davis, Buzzfeed News. Were they sexually assaulted?' a young guy shouted.

Christ! Stella thought, *he looks like he hasn't left school. But at least that was more of an underarm toss than the last one.*

'Niamh Connolly was not sexually assaulted. We are still waiting for the results of the post mortem on Sarah Sharpe so I can't give you an answer on her.'

She looked round at the forest of hands. Tried to block out the noise of the dozens of journalists shouting at her. Spotted a woman she'd had a couple of reasonably helpful exchanges with in the past.

'Liz?'

'Liz Valentine, *Guardian*. Thank you, DCI Cole,' she said, smiling. But it was a smile with a sting. The eyes betrayed her. 'Are you going to use a profiler?'

Frustrated that her contact had apparently decided to throw a spear instead of a beanbag, Stella opened her mouth to answer. And once again heard Morgan's voice emerging.

'Yes, we are looking at all avenues and certainly a profiler is in the mix.'

Stella whirled to her right to see Callie doing exactly the same. Even without seeing her boss's expression, she knew Callie would be struggling to maintain her composure. 'Every wee bastard that's ever watched telly thinks all you need's a bloody profiler to catch serial killers,' she'd said the previous night over the second or third single malt.

Callie faced front again.

'As DCI Cole said in response to an earlier question, at this point we are unable to confirm or deny that these two appalling crimes are the work of a single perpetrator. Therefore, whilst we do keep all our options open, there are no grounds as yet for thinking we are looking at a serial offender.'

Thanks, Callie. You took my head off the block and replaced it with your own.

But Morgan clearly hadn't finished grandstanding.

'Detective Chief Superintendent McDonald is right, of course. Nevertheless, I can confirm, as Deputy Mayor for Policing and Crime, that we are in the process of engaging the services of an experienced offender profiler. I intend to leave no stone unturned in bringing this man to justice.'

Stella was exerting herself so hard to prevent the stream of expletives in her head from bursting free that she missed Tim bringing the press conference to an end.

———

When the room had emptied out, Stella turned to Morgan.

'What the f—, what the hell did you say that for?'

Morgan smiled and wrinkled his forehead as if baffled.

'Say what, DCI Cole?'

'About bringing in a profiler?'

'Have you considered it?'

'Not as yet. Profilers are expensive and often a waste of time.'

'That's not what I've heard. But are you saying your budget won't stretch to an external profiler?'

Grateful for the get-out, Stella agreed. Too readily, as it turned out.

'Yes. You must know that we're under financial pressure. You're the one with his hands on the purse strings, after all.'

'That's true. Although the Mayor is the woman you should really be directing your anger at. I am only her deputy, after all. But here's the thing. I have a contact at Westminster University. He's a lecturer in Abnormal Psychology. And a Home Office-registered forensic psychologist. He's been doing a lot of good work on serial killers. I think I could secure his services at, what shall we say, a significant discount.'

Stella opened her mouth to protest that the last thing she needed was an academic looking to burnish his credentials by spouting off to the media about how the killer might, or might not be, a manual worker with mummy issues, when Callie laid a hand on her shoulder.

'If you think your,' she paused, 'contact would be amenable, deputy mayor, then please, send us his contact details.'

Morgan smiled at Callie. Then shook his head.

'I wouldn't want to put you or your officers to any trouble, Callie. I'll give Ade a call and get him to come in and meet you.'

With his words hanging between them, he left, shouting to an aide who was hanging about at the back of the auditorium.

Stella turned to Callie.

'He planted that question on Valentine.'

'Maybe he did and maybe he didn't.'

'But, Callie, we don't need a profiler. Jamie Hooke could actually give us something concrete, but you know what those profilers are like. A white male between eighteen and thirty-five who has poor social skills. That's basically the entire IT department of the Met!'

Callie smiled.

'You're not wrong. But Morgan's a powerful man. I heard he's going to be Labour's mayoral candidate next time. It pays to keep him onside.'

Raging internally at Morgan, and at Callie, Stella tried to hold back. And failed.

'You've drunk the political Kool-Aid. I thought you'd stand up for me.'

As soon as the words were out of her mouth, Stella knew she'd made a mistake. But there they were, hanging in the charged air between them. She looked down, ashamed to have insulted her friend. Callie's reply made it worse.

'I'm trying, Stel, believe me. But behind the scenes you have to pick your battles. Going head to head with that wee prick isn't the right one. So he gets in a profiler. It's like a bloody tick box nowadays. The media expect it, the brass, too. So we listen to whatever rubbish he comes up with and I'll try and make sure it doesn't come out of our budget, OK?'

'OK. Look, I'm sorry for what I just said. It's just, I really hate the way he's barging into my investigation to score political points. I want to say it's so unfair, but that makes me feel about fifteen.'

Callie laughed, a sound full of warmth and genuine good humour.

'Aye, well, how does that prayer go, "God, grant me the serenity to accept the things I cannot change, courage to change the things I can, and wisdom to know when the only thing that'll hit the spot is a bloody big drink"?'

Now it was Stella's turn to laugh.

'Come on, then. How about a swifty at the Chandos? It's only up the road.'

44

The pub sat at the southern end of St Martin's Lane, a stone's throw from Trafalgar Square. Tourists vied for space with office workers having a quick drink before fighting their way onto the overheated tube.

With two pints of lager in her hands and a bag of cheese and onion crisps dangling from her teeth, Callie cut an unlikely figure in her splendid dress uniform. Spotting her looking for a table, a couple of youngish guys, mid-twenties, Stella estimated, jumped up from the little round table they'd snagged by a coatrack.

'Hey, er, excuse me?' the nearest guy said. 'Would you like our table?'

'That is extremely kind of you,' Callie said through clenched teeth.

He shrugged.

'What you lot do to keep us safe, you know, I mean, thank you.'

Callie and Stella sat, thanking the two guys who moved a few feet away and found a shelf to sit their pints on.

'There's a surprise,' Callie said. 'I think the last time a man gave up his seat for me I was pregnant with Louisa.'

Stella sipped her lager.

'How is she?'

'Och, you know. Sixteen years old and thinks she knows it all. Plus having a mum who's a copper, well, it's not exactly, like, cool, is it?'

Hearing Callie doing a fair imitation of her teenaged daughter's lingo, but in a prim, Miss Jean Brodie accent, was too much for Stella. She snorted, ejected a spray of lager onto the table.

'Oh, God, sorry!' she said, swiping at the sticky liquid with an inadequate paper tissue.

'Not a problem. Good to see you laughing. Now, about the media.'

'Please say you're taking me off the board,' Stella said.

'I am. We've got, or we're about to get, to the point where some smart-bloody-arse journalist is going to figure something out, or our leaker's just going to sell it, and then I don't want you having to "confirm or deny" anything. As your PIP 4, I'll do it.'

Callie was proposing a course of action they'd worked between them many times. PIP stood for the College of Policing's Professionalising Investigation Programme. Stella, as an SIO, was qualified to PIP 3 – Major Investigations. Callie had reached the next level, which covered strategic management of highly complex investigations.

While Stella was responsible for managing the investigation itself, Callie had five jobs to do that would, hopefully, help Stella do hers. Provide overall command and leadership. Set up and manage any partnerships the investigation might need, other government agencies being the usual angle. Manage staffing, budgets and other resources. Handle top-level management of information and intelligence. And maintain public confidence.

Callie was looking ahead to the last two of these jobs. The media were savvier than they used to be. She blamed the Freedom of Information Act, among other things.

The beasts knew that Stella knew everything about her

investigation. A well-phrased question, 'Is the killer using dressmaking scissors?', 'do you have a suspect in custody?', 'are you interviewing Eastern European lorry drivers?' would leave Stella with nowhere to go but the truth. She'd have to give them a straight 'yes' or 'no' answer. Whereas Callie could parry the incoming shots with, 'I am not aware that is the case,' and they wouldn't be able to pin her down in a lie.

Stella finished her pint and wiped her top lip. The heat in the pub was almost as bad as that outside.

'Thanks, boss,' she said, feelingly. 'You want another?'

'Aye, go on then. Seeing as we've established ourselves a wee little *cordon sanitaire*, it'd be a shame to give up the table.'

Stella grinned. Callie was right. The presence of a sharp-featured woman in the full black-and-silver regalia of a chief superintendent seemed to be acting as a forcefield around the tiny circular table.

She returned five minutes later with two tall glasses of lager, their sides already sweating.

'That was quick!' Callie said, before taking a pull on her drink.

'They asked if I was with you and then pretty much shoved me to the front.'

Callie smiled.

'Nice to know there are still a few folk who respect the uniform. So, listen, as I *am* your PIP 4, how are you doing? In yourself, I mean. Getting enough sleep? Eating?'

Since Stella's return to active duty, Callie and she had met regularly for drinks or dinner to talk. As Callie had said a few years earlier, when one of your most senior officers has killed more people than ninety-nine per cent of the people she's trying to catch, it gives you an added incentive to make sure she's on an even keel.

Stella nodded.

'I'm fine. Probably drinking too much coffee, but then, I'm probably drinking too much alcohol, so they balance each other out. As for sleep, what do you think?'

Sleep. Every copper's drug of choice. Except, unlike cigarettes, alcohol and whatever else they might find to help them take the edge off, sleep was always in short supply. Worse than that, no amount of money, threats or pleading with your GP or the Force Medical officer would get you any more than you were prepared to give yourself.

Once you hit inspector, you were freed from the tyranny of shift work and, in theory, you kept office hours. But Stella reckoned there weren't many quality control managers, HR assistants or marketing managers who worked in offices where a 7.00 a.m. start might lead to an 11.00 p.m. finish plus a few hours at your kitchen table at home in the small hours when a child murderer, serial rapist or basher-over-the-head of old ladies wouldn't let you cash in your chitty for a few hours of blissful unconsciousness.

Perhaps sensing Stella's inner monologue, Callie rolled her eyes.

'OK, stupid question. But take it easy, d'ye hear? I know you like to look after your team and make sure they're not burning out, but so do I. And you're part of *my* team. Where are you going from here?'

'Actually, I thought I might go home. To be honest, I'm shattered. I want to watch Netflix and order a pizza and chill out for a few hours. Then I want to go to bed and sleep for eight hours straight, wake up feeling calm and refreshed, have croissants and freshly squeezed orange juice and then walk to work whistling the theme from *Hill Street Blues*.'

Stella held Callie's gaze for a few seconds. Then both women burst out laughing.

'Aye, and have a wee bit of hochmagandy with Ewan McGregor while you're about it, eh?' Callie asked, when she'd caught her breath.

'Nah. Tom Hardy, though. I wouldn't kick him out of bed for eating crackers.'

Trading their 'hot picks', Stella and Callie finished their drinks and left the pub.

The heat of the day was still radiating off the pavements, but a breeze had sprung up, blowing up Whitehall and across Trafalgar Square. Callie turned to Stella. 'Want a lift home? I'll give Bash a call.'

Kamal 'Bash' Bashir was Callie's driver. He'd been driving her around for four years now. His fanatical loyalty to his boss was the stuff of legend at Paddington Green. He'd once floored three Occupy protesters who were converging on Callie after she'd attended a meeting with bankers in Canary Wharf.

'Yes, please. I'll leave my bike at the station tonight.'

———

Stella offered Callie an ironic salute from the pavement, then turned and let herself into her building. She paused at the mailboxes and opened her own. It contained a voter registration card from the London Assembly and a piece of junk mail advertising gold coins.

Inside her flat, she dumped her murder bag in the hall and went through to the kitchen, opening a beer from the fridge and fishing out a takeaway menu from the sheaf tucked in amongst her cookbooks.

One of the books leaned out as she extracted the glossy, brightly coloured menus. *A Taste of Sicily*. She and Richard had bought it the week after they'd returned from their holiday on the roasting hot island.

She smiled at the memory of their attempts to recreate the local dishes they'd gorged themselves on during their two weeks in Taormina. They'd come to grief with a spectacularly fiery chilli and lemon pasta with baby octopus that had them both weeping with pain from the unfamiliar little chillies they'd found in a deli in Soho.

Still smiling, she put the menus back and reached for a butcher-striped apron hanging on a hook screwed to the back of the kitchen door.

Ten minutes later, she was stirring a chopped onion, a mashed up clove of garlic and a finely-shredded red chilli in some butter, white wine and olive oil, while spaghetti rolled and tumbled in a pan of salted water.

She sat down at the kitchen table to eat with a second beer, this time poured into a glass. The flavours of the spaghetti dish sent her mind spiralling back to the early years of her marriage to Richard, and then the arrival of Lola, their beautiful baby. So instead of reading reports or reviewing evidence, she stared at the collage of photos she'd made a few years earlier, then framed and hung on the wall to the left of the window.

In the photos, Lola was never older than five months. Dressed in outfits that indicated the two seasons she'd enjoyed, winter and spring, Lola beamed out of the pictures, or stared with that wide-eyed, bewildered, slightly alien look they'd called her 'why is this happening?' expression.

Stella sighed. She had managed, with a great deal of violent retribution and an equally substantial amount of professional help, to grow a protective membrane around her memories of Lola and Richard, and her life before the evil that was Pro Patria Mori tore her family apart. But still, it hurt.

Then her force-issued phone rang. She glanced at the caller ID. NDNAD. Her stomach fizzed with anticipation. This was the call she'd been waiting for: the National DNA Database, more properly known as the UK National Criminal Intelligence DNA Database.

'Stella Cole.'

'Evening, DCI Cole. Prue Brundage here, NDNAD. I've got the results of your samples here. You sent three, yes?'

'Yes.'

'The sample from the blood on the rope matched that from the victim's blood supplied by the pathologist. Niamh Connolly. The epithelial sample is unidentified, I'm afraid.'

'Male or female?'

'According to the standard amelogenin test, your unsub is a male.'

'And the third?'

'From the semen on the bed linen and pyjama trousers. They matched the sample provided by the victim's husband, Jerry Connolly.'

'OK, thanks. Email me the report as normal, please.'

Having ended the call, Stella sat back in her chair. Knowing the killer was a male hardly advanced the investigation. But it was better than nothing.

Then she slammed her palm down on the table. No! It wasn't better than nothing. It *was* nothing. All the second sample proved was that a man had handled the rope. But that could just as easily have meant a sales assistant at Sherborne Ropes was the killer. Hell, it could have been Arthur Sherborne himself.

45

Cam looked down at her laptop. She'd entered the addresses of all four rope suppliers into Google Maps and was staring disconsolately at the calculated journey time for the four hundred and thirty two-mile round trip. She called Stella.

'Morning, Cam, what's up?'

'Morning, boss. It's my ropey road trip. Is there any money for an overnight? Only there's nearly nine hours' driving just to get to each rope supplier.'

She heard the answer before Stella gave it. Didn't blame the boss. God knew, she was under the cosh already.

'I'd love to say yes, Cam, but the truth is every penny I spend on this investigation is being scrutinised by the bean counters like it was a drug dealer's deposit account. I'm putting in so many requests to Callie for experts, forensics, well, you know what it's like. Look, just, see how you go. If you get up to Halifax and you're too knackered to feel safe driving back, give me a call. I'll try to sort something out for you.'

'OK, no problem. Thanks, boss. I'm going to leave now. I'll call in if I get anything worth telling you before tomorrow's briefing.'

The call ended, Cam plugged the route into her phone. Brixton to Whitechapel, to Cambridge, to Grantham, to Halifax, then back home. Slurping down the rest of her mug of coffee and carrying her second slice of toast in her mouth, she grabbed her car keys and headed out.

———

Thirty minutes later, she pulled up outside Burslem Street Ropeworks in Whitechapel. Her Honda Civic Type R was perfect for zipping through urban traffic and Cam wasn't shy about using the throttle and the horn to get where she wanted to. Noticing that the green space facing the loading bay door was called Rope Walk Gardens, she stepped through the wicket and into the yard.

The visit yielded nothing useful – they had only ever sold one set of ropes with black and gold sallies, and that was to an African evangelical church in 2002. The sales manager produced all the shipping documents to prove conclusively that the rope had left the UK. Although he did explain that the park opposite had got its name from the trade his firm still practised.

'They used to braid the ropes by walking them out with a machine that twisted the strands together,' he told her, in the sort of voice she'd always associated with teachers.

46

THURSDAY 23RD AUGUST 8.30 A.M.
BROCKWELL PARK, SOUTHEAST LONDON

Habits of a Lifetime had catapulted its star, Sister Moira Lowney, from obscurity to the glare of the spotlights, as the British public took her to their hearts.

After the reality show's first few episodes had aired, the invitations to speak at public events and appear on chat shows and televised debates had started, first as a trickle, then a flood. The show's producer professed himself baffled, but delighted, that a programme about an order of nuns could have become the surprise hit of the summer season.

A self-described 'progressive', Sister Moira espoused liberal views on many of the moral issues of the day that infuriated those within the Church who cleaved to a more conservative line.

She also practised as a psychotherapist, offering succour to those whose suffering she felt she could relieve through a personal blend of Christian teaching, Jungian psychoanalysis and female mysticism.

The Carmelite Order of the Unified Spirit, over which Moira presided as Mother Superior, owned an acre of land on the outskirts of Brockwell Park, a southeast London suburb. In the eighteenth century a silk merchant had left the land to the nuns in his will. It offered plenty of places to film and a diverse cast of nuns, staff and patients, who were free to come and go as they chose.

The film crew had just left her first-floor office to film elsewhere in the community. Moira consulted her desk diary. Just one morning appointment and then nothing until lunch at 1.00 p.m., after which she was due to be filmed travelling to the food bank.

MJ Fox. 9.00 a.m.

'Excellent!' she said aloud. 'I can finish my article in peace.' She looked up at the ornately plastered ceiling rose, mouthing 'thank-you' and smiling.

MJ had called her a week earlier claiming, like many of her newer clients, to be a fan of the show. Sister Moira didn't mind that her fame – or 'notoriety' as she would jokingly refer to her raised profile – drew in those needing her help. She saw the TV show as a conduit. As something ordained. Other therapists advertised on the internet, or linked up with GPs' surgeries. She had *Habits of a Lifetime*. What mattered was that she could help.

Bending her head and closing her eyes, she placed the palms of her hands together and prayed.

'Dear God. Please move through me, your humble servant, to help MJ. Amen.'

She left her eyes closed a while, stilling her mind and allowing God to enter into the space she hoped she had created for Him.

After a while, she opened them again, placed her palms down on the desk blotter in front of her and waited for her client to arrive. Outside her window, a blue tit fluttered, trying to find a perch beneath the eaves. She watched the little bird struggle against gravity, fatigue and the geometry of the building before finding rest.

Ten minutes later, a tentative knock – two quiet taps, a gap, then one more – made her smile. Sometimes it seemed as if her clients had barely enough self-confidence to interact with an inanimate piece of wood, let alone a therapist.

She rose from her chair, rounded her desk, crossed the room and admitted MJ to her *sanctum sanctorium*.

'Please make yourself comfortable, MJ,' she said, gesturing at a low armchair upholstered in red brocade before taking a second chair on the other side of the fireplace.

'Thank you.'

Between them, on a coffee table fashioned from a slice cut from one of the felled trees in the gardens, a box of tissues stood ready.

Sister Moira didn't believe in pussyfooting around. She liked to get straight to the heart of the matter. Occasionally, clients found her directness off-putting, but for the most part her approach yielded results. She spoke again.

'What brought you to my door, MJ?'

A sigh. A hand drawn down over the face. Slumped shoulders. Lack of eye contact. Sister Moira had seen them all before. A troubled soul, inching towards salvation but fearful of taking that first, vital step. She waited.

'I feel so alone. As if I'm the only person who understands the world the way I do.'

'Tell me, how *do* you understand the world?'

'Oh. Well, I suppose I understand that cruelty is everywhere. That people torture each other while pretending to be kind. And that those who claim to hold the moral high ground are no better than the lowest, most-degraded forms of life.'

'And when you say those who claim to hold the moral high ground, who are you thinking of?'

'You know, the God Squad. Bible bashers. Tub-thumpers.'

MJ's voice had taken on a nasty edge and Sister Moira felt her pulse flicker.

'Yet you chose me as your therapist?'

'I chose you. Just not as my therapist.'

Realisation. The female police officer she'd seen on the TV news. The warning. She'd felt safe in ignoring it. Surely nobody would want to harm the star of *Habits of a Lifetime*?

Oh, Moira. The sin of pride.

At forty-seven, Moira was still physically fit. She was quick.

But her killer was quicker.

Sister Moira sprang out of her armchair. The killer followed her, arm swinging in, syringe plunging towards the gap between the nun's white coif and the high collar of her grey tunic.

47

You're must be feeling quite the fool, lying there? Maybe you're not as clever as you think you are, eh? Don't worry, the others were all pretty clever and look where it got them.

Now, where was I? Oh, yes. The nun. In some ways, she didn't deserve to die. I mean, she was pretty right-on in her attitudes. And she was working as a therapist. I bet half her clients had been abused by priests, so she was at least trying to restore some semblance of order. But still, a nun! I mean, if you get married to Jesus, I guess you have to expect a fair degree of pain in your life. Which, I have to say, she did get. Right at the end.

After killing Niamh Connolly and Sarah Sharpe, I think it's fair to say I had grown more confident in my abilities. You'd probably agree with me. So I gave her my speech before I drugged her. Yes, it was a risk, but I like to think it was a calculated one. I let her know who I was before I gave her the old chemical cosh. And I have to say, it was worth it to see the clear light of understanding dawn in her eyes.

Ha! Which was, obviously, the last light of any kind that dawned in them. So, once she was pliable, I moved behind her, out of her eyeline, and I held her head tight against my hips. I took out the grapefruit knife, which, by the way, is such a useful tool. You never see them nowadays, do you? Maybe people don't eat grapefruit anymore. Could that be it? It was a bit tricky, because I had to hold her head still and prise her eyelids apart with my left hand. But we got there in the end.

48

THURSDAY 23RD AUGUST 11.00 A.M.
BROCKWELL PARK

Sister Rose Macauley, Moira Lowney's deputy, was talking to one of the novices when someone coughed politely beside her. She turned. It was the producer of the show, a young man called, fittingly she thought, John.

'Yes, John?'

'Excuse me, Rose, I'm sorry to interrupt. Would it be possible to ask Moira if we could bring the food bank segment forward?'

'When to, John?' she asked with a smile. *Such kind eyes.*

'Well, sort of, now, if possible. I know it's short notice, but it would really help with this afternoon's filming schedule. I'm really sorry.'

She shook her head.

'No need to apologise. I expect she's in her office. She has an article I know she's desperate to finish. It's for *The Times*! I'll go and find her for you. I'm sure she'll be happy to come now.'

Arriving outside Moira's office door, Rose paused to steady her breathing. Inside her habit she was dripping with perspiration and she could feel the heat as a physical presence. Lately, they'd been discussing their garb, wondering whether they perhaps could adopt a more contemporary style of habit as worn by some of their sisters in the US. She'd bring it up with Moira that evening.

She knocked firmly, then twisted the knob and entered the office, ready with an apology for interrupting Moira's writing.

The sight that confronted her made so little sense that, as a reflex, she pulled the door to with a sharp little tug.

Sister Moira's eyes were bleeding.

She didn't understand.

Shaking her head, but already feeling a swell of revulsion flooding her chest, she opened the door again.

Then she did understand.

Sister Moira's eye *sockets* were bleeding. The eyes themselves, glistening in some sort of clear fluid streaked with pink, regarded her from a plate set in front of her on the desk.

As Sister Rose's screaming subsided, replaced by a coughing fit so violent she retched, half a dozen nuns, plus John and a sound woman, still carrying the long boom mike with its fluffy grey cover, raced up the stairs behind her and piled to a stop in the narrow hallway outside the office.

Clambering to her feet and supporting herself against the wall, she turned her tear-streaked face to the group.

'Call the police. Sister Moira's been murdered.'

49

THURSDAY 23RD AUGUST 11.20 A.M.
CROWTHORNE, BERKSHIRE

Stella knew that although most of the men living within its towering red-brick perimeter walls had been referred by the criminal justice system, Broadmoor was a hospital. That meant its residents were called 'patients' and not 'prisoners'.

As she dismounted her bike and removed the helmet at the main gate, she felt the oppressive nature of the place, as forbidding as any high-security prison and full of some of the most dangerous men in the UK.

Although the Yorkshire Ripper, Peter Sutcliffe, had been transferred years earlier, there were enough serial killers, murderers, violent rapists and arsonists to keep the staff busy at every hour of the day and night, 365 days a year.

She showed the guard her warrant card, waited while he photographed her and printed a visitor pass, and then still more while he checked with Jamie Hooke's secretary that the psychiatrist was expecting the visitor standing before him. He managed to make 'Detective Chief Inspector' sound like 'Hells Angels Full Patch' but

Stella wasn't surprised. She knew her unorthodox mode of personal transport didn't fit with the preconceptions of officialdom, especially the jobsworths who comprised its lower echelons.

Finally, the uniformed guard hung up.

'Know your way, do you?' he asked, his pallid features impassive.

'Has Mr Hooke changed offices in the last two years?'

'Not as far as I'm aware.'

'Then, yes, thanks, I do.'

She remounted the bike, stuck her helmet back on and trundled around the inner ring road to the main building housing the clinical and administrative staff.

After a second wait, this time in a clean, bright reception area furnished with nubbly woollen sofas and a wide-screen TV showing Sky News with the sound turned low, she heard her own name called.

'Stella! How nice to see you again.'

She stood, and turned to see Jamie Hooke striding across the polished floor tiles towards her. The forty-year-old psychiatrist moved like a dancer, she thought, light on his feet, balanced and graceful.

He wore a brown leather jacket, the shoulders and elbows smooth and shiny, over a soft, white, open-necked shirt. His jeans were faded into pale stars at the sides of his knees and a similarly pale patch on the right front pocket indicated the presence of keys and coins. Brown lace-up boots completed the outfit that said, 'I am a friend. Not a doctor. Not a threat. And definitely not a warder.'

She held out her hand but he ignored the gesture and held her lightly by the shoulders, kissing her on both cheeks. She could smell his aftershave, a light, woody aroma, and the underlying maleness she remembered from their last meeting. Then, he had helped her put a serial killer behind bars, not here at Broadmoor but at Frankland, a Category A prison in County Durham. Roger Cates had stabbed five young men to death and attempted to cook and eat their bodies.

He released her as swiftly as he had embraced her. He had a boyish smile that made her want to tousle his dark-brown curly hair.

'Too much?'

Stella grinned.

'Not at all. I enjoyed it. How have you been?'

'Come along to my office, I'll give you the quick version while we walk.'

Jamie's office, a large white-painted room, looked out over a tarmac courtyard where men were playing an energetic game of football despite the ferocious heat. On the short journey there, Stella had learned that his marriage had ended, amicably, six months after their previous meeting. He still saw his daughter regularly. And he had just been invited to give a speech at the American Academic of Forensic Sciences' annual convention the following February.

'And it's going to be in New Orleans,' he finished, his wet-slate eyes wide. 'How about that? I'll probably be late for my own session because I'm checking out some new blues bar.'

His combination of modesty and enthusiasm had attracted Stella the first time they'd met, and over the ensuing four years, nothing he'd done or said had diminished the feeling.

'I doubt that, but congratulations anyway. Do they get many overseas speakers?'

'Not sure. I wouldn't imagine so but, anyway, enough about me, as they say. How are you?'

'I'm good, thanks. Yes, really good.'

'Are you still keeping up your journal? You told me last time it had really helped you get over losing Richard and Lola.'

'Yup. Still do it every night. Just a few lines sometimes, especially when we're on a tough one, but yes, and it still helps.'

He smiled, ushering her to one of a pair of armchairs flanking a coffee table.

'Good. Coffee? Doctors and cops run on it and I just bought a new bag. It's a new company I discovered in Mozambique. A workers' cooperative. Fairtrade, the works. It even tastes good!' he added, eyes crinkling as he grinned at her.

'Sounds good, yes please.'

'Biscuits?'

'If you've got them. What are they, organic cranberry and Fairtrade macadamia nut cookies?'

He shook his head.

'Chocolate Hob Nobs.'

Stella laughed.

'Perfect! A copper's breakfast.'

While Jamie busied himself making the coffee and sticking an opened packet of the chocolate biscuits in front of Stella, she looked around the office. The usual array of framed diplomas and certificates occupied much of one wall, and the one facing it held hundreds of books: textbooks and reference works, mainly. One title in particular caught her eye.

'*Silence of the Lambs?* What's that, a teaching aid?'

He laughed without turning away from the coffee-making.

'You'd be surprised. Most of our patients, well, the literate ones anyway, they've all read it. Sometimes more often than is good for them. It provides a useful frame of reference when I'm discussing their condition with them. Now, try this,' he finished, turning with two mugs of coffee in his hands and handing one to Stella.

She sniffed experimentally. And smiled.

'Mmm, that's so good.' She blew across the surface then took a sip. 'I'm getting cigars, dried fruit and saddle leather.'

Jamie laughed.

'That's very good. Here, have a Hob Nob. I think you'll find you're getting milk chocolate, rolled oats and sugar.'

Stella hesitated.

'Please tell me you're not watching your figure?' he said.

Stella smiled.

'No!'

But being with you has made me think about it differently for the first time in a long time.

She took a biscuit, dunked it in her coffee and bit off half.

'And just a hint of lecithin and palm oil.'

Jamie folded his six-foot frame into the armchair opposite, placed his mug on a magazine on the table and spread his hands.

'So, tell me. What's got you eating a copper's breakfast with me on this fine August morning? Oh, and thanks for making the journey. Like I said, my schedule is particularly hectic at the moment.'

'Thank you for seeing me at such short notice.'

Jamie waved her remark away.

'If I can help you prevent someone from causing harm, it's never a problem, you know that.'

'OK. Thanks. Here it is.'

Stella told Jamie the story from the discovery of Niamh Connolly's body to that of Sarah Sharpe. She included details of the physical evidence, the mutilations, and of Isaac Holt's arrest and subsequent release. Throughout, Jamie sat still, his left ankle crossed over his right knee, sipping his coffee from time to time and munching his way through half a dozen of the biscuits.

When Stella finished – 'And I need to get inside his head, I need to figure out what motivates him, where he's going to go next' – Jamie rubbed his chin, his eyes staring at a point on the ceiling halfway between them.

He huffed out a sigh and lowered his gaze until he was looking directly at Stella.

'You know it's about religion, right?'

'Yes. Religious women, at that.'

'This is a man who is motivated by an intense hatred towards a certain kind of woman. I know at the beginning it's going to sound like I'm stating the bleeding obvious but bear with me. Let's feel our way into this. So, a very public opponent of abortion, a Catholic. Then a leading light in the Church of England. The editor of its house journal, no less. Despite its occasional handwringing over sexual politics, the Church of England tends not to excite people's passions. They'd rather resolve things over a cup of tea and some home-made cake. Mrs Connolly was fifty-two and married, Ms Sharpe, sixty and single. Apart from their gender, their faith and their public profiles, they seem to have nothing in common. So I think we can conclude that all three need to be present for our killer to consider them a target.'

'That's pretty much where we'd got to. What about the mutilations, the removal of their pubic hair?'

Jamie narrowed his eyes.

'It's not unusual for a sexual sadist to mutilate his victims' breasts, or their genitals, usually by cutting or biting. But you said the second victim, Sarah Sharpe, wasn't mutilated.'

'Not unless you count being shot full of arrows.'

'Which I don't, not really. And even though he removed her pubic hair, that doesn't sound like a sexual psychopath either. Given unfettered access to a woman's genitals, a psychopath into mutilation would take his time and, well, you know what they're capable of.'

'Oh, yes.' Then, prompted by Jamie's input, a thought struck her. 'What if he doesn't think of what he's doing as mutilating them? What if he thinks of it as torture? That would account for the different MO.'

Jamie nodded enthusiastically.

'It would, absolutely. Tell me, does he have a signature?'

Yes, or more than one. Possibly you'd call them components. Firstly, there's the cause of death. He strangles them with bell rope. And there's the missing pubic hair. He seems to shave them post mortem. That would work as a signature, right?'

Jamie nodded again, then finished his coffee.

'Yes. Yes it would. Have you found the hair or does he take it with him?'

'No, we haven't found it. We can work on the assumption that he takes it away, but that's all it is, an assumption. For all we know he could be flushing it down the toilet, or chucking it over the back fence.'

'In my experience, that would be unusual.'

Stella couldn't help herself. A grin spread across her face.

'You mean compared to all the crazy shit you deal with day in, day out, a serial killer who doesn't keep a dead woman's pubic hair on his person is unusual?'

Jamie returned the grin.

'OK, fair enough. But you know what I mean.'

'Yeah, yeah, sorry.' She spread her hands. 'That's what we've got, anyway. Pretty much the whole story. Can you tell me what's going on in his head, doc?'

'Here's what I think. Your killer is motivated by overwhelmingly powerful feelings of vengefulness. I would suggest that someone, almost certainly his mother, a female teacher or perhaps a family friend, humiliated him in some way when he was a child or possibly a teenager. Given the religious angle, I feel confident that this humiliation would also have been within a religious, specifically a Christian, context. Although it might sound contradictory I wouldn't rule out the idea that the humiliation was sexual in some way. You know, something to do with his being sinful.' Jamie paused. 'I don't think he's going to stop. And I think he's going to escalate.'

Feeling dread gathering inside her like black thunderheads boiling up over a landscape already riven with storms, Stella asked a question she only half-wanted him to answer.

'How do you escalate from torturing women, strangling them to death and displaying their corpses in their own homes?'

Jamie shrugged.

'I can think of lots of ways. He could take them somewhere only he knows about, and spend more time with them. He could increase the violence of the tortures. He could film himself with them. He could make family members watch. He could—'

Stella held her hand up.

'OK, OK, I get the picture. He's sick in the head and he's only getting warmed up.'

Jamie flushed and looked down.

'Sorry. I know I get carried away sometimes. I guess you want something practical from me. Something to help you catch him?'

'That would be nice. You know, his home address, or his National Insurance number?'

Jamie smiled grimly.

'No can do, I'm afraid. But how about this? I think he believes he's making some kind of statement. A public statement. Killers driven by religion tend to fall into one of two camps. Either they believe they're doing God's work, or they believe they're ridding the world of hypocrites. To me, it feels like your killer thinks he belongs in the second group. In his shoes I would be thinking in terms of higher-profile victims, the better to make my case. I am saying, "Hey, world! Wake up! These women are saying one thing and doing another. They preach faith and forgiveness but they're just torturers. I am just giving them a taste of their own medicine."'

Stella noticed the change in tense, from 'I would' to 'I am' and marvelled at Jamie's ability, no, his *willingness*, to adopt the persona of a serial killer.

'So we should try and think ahead, get to his next victim before he does.'

'That would be a good idea, obviously. Failing that you could announce at a press conference that women who fit the victim profile should take extra care.'

Stella heard shouting from beyond Jamie's office window. Male voices. She jumped to her feet and crossed to the window, heart racing. She had time to notice that Jamie was watching her from his chair, smiling. She looked down at the courtyard. Then she understood.

Half a dozen of the men playing football were jumping up and down, hugging each other. The opposing goalkeeper was bending to retrieve the ball from the back of his net.

She turned away and sat down again, feeling mildly shamefaced.

'Does it make you wonder how a bunch of violent rapists, serial killers and cannibals, after all the heinous crimes they've committed, can just play footie and give each other man-hugs when one of them scores a goal?' Jamie asked her.

She shrugged, not wanting to reveal how precisely he'd read her mind.

'Surprise me.'

He took a sip of his coffee before answering.

'Context. The men we treat here are almost constantly on guard in the outside world, often against the voices or inner demons that, as they see it, control their actions. Believe it or not, they feel safe in here. They can afford to drop their guard. We impose a strict routine, which many serial offenders feel comfortable inhabiting, given their own fondness for ritual. And although some of them selected male victims, the absence of women here lowers tension between them and with the staff. Finally, because we're a hospital, not a prison, they see themselves as people in need of help, not punishment, which allows them to reach some sort of accommodation with what they've done.'

'But even if you cure them,' Stella said, unable to resist hinting at her true feelings by pushing the word "cure", 'they're only going to be transferred to a Cat A prison.'

'True. But while they're here, we focus on treating their afflictions. The criminal justice system will pick them up again when – *if* – we feel they're sane enough to be discharged and a life behind bars awaits.'

'Why are you telling me this?'

Jamie smiled.

'You're an intelligent woman, Stella. Why don't you tell me?'

'Well, that's not even slightly infuriating! OK, context. I see the killer as a criminal. You see him, probably –?' she raised her eyebrows, and Jamie nodded, 'as a sufferer. People who are suffering want to be cured. And people who believe, however misguidedly, that they are righting wrongs also have a need to be understood. And they—'

An unwanted memory surged into Stella's consciousness. What would Jamie think if he knew just how many people she had killed to right the greatest wrong of all, robbing a mother of her child? She pushed it down.

Jamie nodded in agreement. If he'd noticed anything strange about the way she'd tailed off, he said nothing about it.

'And before you say anything, I believe your first duty is to catch him before he kills again. Arrest him, charge him and then hand him over to the courts, see him convicted. Job done. If he ends up here, well, that's another story.'

Stella paused, digesting Jamie's words. Context. Suffering. Understanding. It was her job to figure out a way to turn those insights into action. Then she spoke.

'We must stop him.'

Jamie nodded.

'Yes, you must. As I said, he's learning and he's growing more confident. Even though there doesn't appear to be a sexual motive, he's almost certainly getting a thrill from killing. He's learning how to do it and he's enjoying the feeling of control, of power that he gets from, as he almost certainly sees it, defeating the enemy and avenging whatever humiliation he feels was inflicted on him. He's enjoying making his victims suffer for their faith, but what he's really all about is paying back the original woman for whom Niamh Connolly and Sarah Sharpe were substitutes.'

Stella sat back in her chair and rubbed her hand over her face.

'Great. No pressure there, then.'

'There's something else I'd like to offer you that might help a little.'

'Yes?'

'Let me take you to lunch. There's a lovely little country pub about a mile from the front gate. They do a cracking steak and kidney pie.'

'In this weather? You have to be joking.'

'They do salads, too.'

'Actually, I could do with something substantial to eat. I've been mostly living off M&S sandwiches and takeaways for the last few days.'

'Is that a yes?'

Stella nodded.

'Come on, doc. You've pulled.'

50

THURSDAY 23RD AUGUST 12.25 P.M.

Stella felt the heat burning through her reinforced jeans and leather jacket and shucked off the latter as soon as she dismounted from the Triumph. Behind her, Jamie climbed off and handed back the spare helmet she routinely kept in the top box.

'That was fun,' he said, grinning. 'I'm guessing you were taking it easy.'

Stella unfastened her ponytail and ran her fingers through her hair before refastening it.

'I may have eased off the throttle on a couple of the straights,' she replied. 'Come on then, let's order some food. I'm starving!'

The bar of The Bull's Head was busy with punters from the nearby business park. Plenty of management types in clothes Stella supposed were 'business casual': the men in shirtsleeves and chinos, the women in cotton dresses.

The seemingly never-ending heatwave had driven even the most conservative firms to relax their dress codes, Stella had noticed each time she'd had to interview people at their workplaces. At the headquarters of an American bank based at Canary Wharf she'd been startled to see one man sitting at a desk wearing what appeared to be tailored shorts.

They ordered the same: steak and kidney pie and chips, plus pints of lager shandy. The barman handed Stella a flowerpot containing plastic flowers and a wooden spoon with a 17 painted on the bowl.

'The garden's nice, if we can find a shady spot,' Jamie said.

They were lucky. A trio of glamorous thirtysomething women – new and wealthy mums to judge from the hi-tech buggies parked beside the table – were getting up as Stella and Jamie arrived in the garden. Their table occupied a prime spot beneath the spreading branches of a copper beech tree with a gnarled trunk at least four feet across.

As they settled their babies down, a toddler ran out from behind a huge flowering shrub. He was clad only in a pair of lime-green shorts and old-fashioned buckled sandals. His face was flushed and his brown hair spiked with sweat.

'Tobias, come and get dressed, we're going now,' one of the mums said.

'I don't *want* to!' he shouted, folding his pudgy arms across his mud-streaked chest.

'We're going to play at Elsie's. You like Elsie.'

'I *hate* Elsie! I wish Elsie was *dead*!'

'It's "I wish Elsie *were* dead," Tobias, and no, you don't. You like Elsie.'

With much apologising to her friends and cajoling of the recalcitrant Tobias, the boy's mother wrestled him into a T-shirt and led him, protesting volubly, to the car park. Sitting in one of the vacated chairs, Jamie tipped his head fractionally in the direction of the departing yummy mummies and rolled his eyes.

Stella grinned at him, stifling a sudden urge to giggle.

Cooling down in the shade of the tree's broad canopy, she relaxed, and raised her pint glass.

'Cheers!'

'Cheers!'

The lager shandy was cold. The sugar in the lemonade gave a quick top-up to her fading energy reserves as the alcohol unwound a tight little knot in her stomach. She looked around the garden. In patches of shade, or sitting out in the full glare of the sun, groups of drinkers were laughing, chatting animatedly and eating: sandwiches, steaks, burgers and vast golden slabs of battered fish.

Normality, Stel. Looks nice, doesn't it?

Jamie was looking at her, his lips kinked up on the left side in a half-smile.

'Penny for them,' he said.

'I was just thinking about that old line, I don't even know if it's true or not, that no Londoner is ever more than ten feet from a rat. Sometimes I feel it's the same story with the people I hunt down and you treat. Statistically, how many of the people in this garden are psychopaths, would you say?'

Jamie laughed. He turned round in his chair and made a show of scanning the garden, which held about thirty or forty people. He'd hung his jacket over the back off his chair and she admired the way his shoulders stretched his shirt tight, revealing rounded deltoids and nice biceps. Not bodybuilder muscles, maybe Mother Nature plus a few hours in a gym from time to time. Or a few games of tennis here and there.

He turned back to face her.

'Statistically? None. Generally, we go with a figure of one per cent of the general population, though that jumps to twenty-five per cent in the male prison population. If you go to a high-secure unit or a hospital like mine, well, maybe fifty to seventy-five per cent. But if you want to include people with a personality disorder, there are probably three or four people here who qualify.'

'Hmm. Maybe it just feels like more.'

'Goes with the job, I'm afraid. If you didn't want to meet psychopaths you should probably have gone into, huh, well, I was about to say nursery nursing, but having just witnessed the antics of young Tobias I'm not so sure.'

Stella laughed. This felt good. Sitting in a pub garden with an attractive man, poking gentle fun at the idle rich and, for a few minutes at least, not worrying about stopping nutters from carving up innocent people for kicks. Reality asserted itself soon enough.

To her left a group of young guys in sharp suits, foreheads red and shiny with sweat, were arguing about football. Judging from their flushed faces, their half-drunk pints didn't appear to be their first.

The volume increased to the point a few of the other diners were looking round anxiously. Then the swearing began. Nothing too outrageous at first, but the temperature rose fast when one of the men hurled a c-bomb.

'You're such a cunt, Sol!' he shouted, then he jabbed an index finger into his friend's chest.

'Me? Fuck off! If anyone's a cunt round here, it's you.'

The other two men had backed away a pace or so, and now Stella could see real fear begin to steal across the faces of the punters sitting at the closest tables.

She put her pint down and smiled at Jamie.

'Better go and get them to cool off before someone starts throwing punches,' she whispered with a smile.

The she strode over to the group, who were swearing more freely now, the finger jabbing escalating to pushing.

'Hey!' she shouted, barging her way into the centre of the group. 'Quieten down, you're frightening people.'

They stared at her, this diminutive woman at least ten years older than they were. Their mouths hung open. Then the original shouter recovered his bravado.

'Fuck off back to your husband, darling. This ain't nothing to do with you, all right? We were just having a laugh.'

Stella turned round and stood absolutely square on to him. She looked up into his eyes, which were the same blue as the sky. The sweet smell of alcohol rolled off him like a warm breeze. He smelled to her like he'd been on the sauce since opening time. In a quiet voice, she spoke.

'He's not my husband. And I'm a police officer. What I'm

suggesting, is that you and your friends finish your drinks quietly, then leave. Let's keep this low key, all right? People have come out for a nice quiet lunch. They don't need you lot spoiling it.'

One of the other two men patted him on the shoulder.

'Come on, mate. Let it go. Let's do what she says.'

'No way! Why should we?' He turned back to Stella. 'Where's your ID, then?' he asked belligerently, thrusting his chin at her and hitting her with another gust of fumy breath.

Stella sighed. She produced her warrant card and opened it. He stared at it, then at her.

'Fine. We're just having a laugh. No need to get all high and mighty.' Then he turned and walked off a couple of paces. Stella breathed out. *Idiot.* Then the man spoke. A single, percussive word.

She closed the gap between them.

'I beg your pardon?'

'I didn't say nothing.'

A young girl in a floral shift dress and black Dr. Martens, maybe eighteen or nineteen, chirped up from a table to the man's left.

'Yes he did. He called you a cunt.'

Shit! Now I'll have to do something. Maybe a chat in the car park'll calm him down.

She stepped closer to the belligerent young man and placed her right hand on his right shoulder.

'OK, you, come with me.'

What happened next, took Stella by surprise.

He whirled round and threw the remains of his drink in her face. She staggered back, swiping at the beer that was stinging her eyes. Opening them, she found he was bearing down on her, teeth bared in a feral snarl.

And then he was on the ground.

Behind him, Jamie was standing, arms loose at his sides, one foot held firm in the centre of the drunk's back.

'You OK?' he asked.

'Yeah, yeah, I'm fine. Silly little sod just caught me by surprise.'

'You want to arrest him?'

'God, no! I wouldn't be out of your local nick before teatime by the time I'd done all the paperwork and been interviewed.'

Jamie nodded.

'I understand.'

Then he reached down and pulled the man's left arm behind his back and folded it so the hand was almost behind his head, eliciting a yelp of pain.

'On your feet!'

He pulled on the twisted-back arm, leading the man to scramble to his feet. His three friends had melted away as soon as he'd thrown his drink over Stella.

'You can't do this to me!' the man said, his voice a whine. 'I run my own company. I know my rights.'

'I bet you do. But you need to listen to me.' Jamie bent closer to the man's ear, so only he, and Stella, could hear. 'I am a psychiatrist at Broadmoor. You know, the special hospital up the road?' Wide-eyed, the man nodded. Jamie had his attention now. 'This lady isn't a police officer at all. She's actually a patient of mine. We're trying a little social experiment, giving her some accompanied time on the outside. See how she reacts to stressful situations. She made that ID in our workshop.'

The man's eyes swivelled to Stella, who smiled at him.

'Wha— What did she do, then?' he asked Jamie in a terrified whisper.

'I'm not really supposed to talk about it, but let's just say there are nine young businessmen in the Reading area who will never be able to father children. So, you know, if you could just apologise, it'll calm her down and then it's probably best if you leave.'

The man nodded, his head bobbing up and down rapidly. He turned to face Stella.

'Look. I'm sorry, yeah. Really sorry. I never meant to, you know, we were just, oh Jesus! Please, just leave me alone!'

Jamie released him and he took off for the car park.

'Don't drink and drive!' Jamie yelled after him.

A couple applauded, and soon the whole beer garden was clapping. Jamie made a low bow and led Stella inside.

'Thanks, Jamie,' she said. 'But didn't you just break about a million ethics codes?'

Jamie smiled.

'He was too drunk. I doubt he'll remember anything I said. And throwing beer over people is the sort of thing that makes you stay quiet once you sober up. Plus nobody heard except the three of us. I won't tell if you won't. Now, let's get you cleaned up.' He leaned over the bar and called through to a young woman ringing up a round of drinks.

'Excuse me? When you've got a moment, my friend has had beer thrown over her by one of your customers. She's a police officer. Can you help?'

The young woman took in Stella's beer-stained shirt and rushed over.

'Yeah, of course. Come with me. We've got a separate room to change in, with sinks and whatnot.'

Stella gratefully accepted the offer of help and when she emerged into the sunlit garden ten minutes later, wearing a spare staff shirt the woman had given her, Jamie pointed at the two plates piled high with pie and chips.

'Perfect timing. It arrived a minute ago. Compliments of the house. And I ordered you another pint. I like the new look. Very you.'

Stella looked down. The black uniform shirt was a size too small for her and had stretched tight over her chest.

'Another ethics violation, doctor?'

'Strictly speaking, as an NHS consultant, I'm a mister. And no, you're not a patient of mine. I'm free and clear.'

'Hmm,' Stella said giving him a hard stare, before slicing off a chunk of the steak and kidney pie, which was aromatic, perfectly seasoned and deeply satisfying.

They ate in companionable silence for a few minutes.

'Are you OK?' Jamie asked.

'What, because of that knob-end, you mean?'

'Yes.'

She smiled at Jamie and shook her head.

'He was nothing. Compared to some of the people I've fought off in recent years, he didn't even register. I was just pissed off because he got the jump on me.'

Jamie frowned.

'What is it?' Stella asked.

'When you say, "fought off ", what do you mean?'

'Just a figure of speech. You know what coppers are like. Turning every arrest into *Terminator* versus *Alien*.'

Jamie stared at her for a moment. She could tell he wasn't convinced. He was a shrink, after all.

He smiled.

'How's the pie?

'Great. Really good.' She wanted, needed, to distract Jamie. 'So listen, about my serial killer?'

'Yes?'

'Any more thoughts about how we could flush him out?'

Jamie took a pull on his drink then set the sweating glass down on the slatted picnic table. He sighed.

'Well, men like this, they're not exactly what you'd call susceptible to reason. In their minds, everything they're doing is perfectly logical, even if they're raping children or killing their entire family with a shotgun. But if I'm right, and he is driven by rage against the Christian faith and, specifically, its female adherents, maybe you could find a way to reach him by letting him know you understand how he feels.'

'What do you mean?' Stella asked, forking a couple of the golden chips into her mouth and chewing as she waited for Jamie to answer.

'I'm sort of thinking aloud, so forgive me, but I guess what I'm driving at is you could maybe draw him out into the open by seeming to agree with him and, oh, I don't know, offering to meet him. To listen to his side of the story, maybe help him bring his concerns to a wider audience. Actually, that sounds incredibly facile now I can hear it out loud. Sorry.'

Stella shook her head.

'No. It doesn't sound facile at all. To be honest, though, I don't think it would work. For a start, my boss would have kittens if I suggested putting out a public appeal where I said, "You're right, these Christian bitches deserve everything you give them. Let's go and have a latte in Starbucks and talk it all out". I mean, can you imagine it? The *Daily Mail* would go into orbit!'

They both laughed as the image of the outrage such a stratagem would provoke in the media sank in. Then Stella's smile slide off her face. She pursed her lips.

'On the other hand…'

'What?'

'What if I went to the other extreme? What if I said something like, you know, "As a committed Christian I truly believe I can bring this monster to justice", something like that. I bet he'd get revved up by that.'

Jamie shook his head violently.

'That's a really bad idea, Stella. Really bad. You'd be staking yourself out as the scapegoat, waiting for the man-eater to come prowling round, licking its lips.'

She pressed a splayed hand to her chest.

'Bloody hell, Jamie! That was a bit poetic. You been reading all those big books in your study or something?'

He smiled, but there was very little humour in it.

'Seriously, please don't even *think* of trying that. In all likelihood you are dealing with a violent psychopath, possibly with some kind of religious mania or delusion. Not only are men like that not susceptible to external reason or moral precepts, but they don't really see other human beings as people at all. They're just objects to be played with, rearranged and discarded once they bore their captor. You'd be putting yourself in grave danger.'

Stella nodded, placing her knife and fork together on the plate, which was still loaded with chips and a quarter of the steak and kidney pie.

'You're probably right. And I don't think my boss would be any more impressed with that idea than yours.'

A wasp, drunk on spilled beer and sunshine, flew around Stella's head and hovered a foot or so in front of her face. Lightning fast, she clapped her hands and snapped them open again. The wasp dropped dead onto her plate.

———

Stella dropped Jamie off at Broadmoor with a promise to keep in touch, then rode back to Paddington Green, the two conflicting ideas about how to tempt a killer out into the open swirling through her brain. And overlaying both of them, a third. That Jamie Hooke was the first man since Richard she'd properly fancied.

She arrived to find two emails from Dr Craven waiting for her. The first revealed that he'd completed the toxicology report in Niamh Connolly. One line stood out:

Presence of Temazepam and Ketamine detected in victim's liver.

So you drug them first, then you torture them, you sick bastard.

She opened the second email. A brief message from Craven informed her that his report on Sarah Sharpe's post mortem was attached. She opened the report, scanned the first few lines then pressed the print icon.

51

THURSDAY 23RD AUGUST 3.05 P.M.

Stella took notes as she read the post mortem report on Sarah Sharpe. The similarities between this death and that of Niamh Connolly were overwhelming. Even without a third victim, Stella knew in her gut that she was dealing with a serial killer. When she'd finished reading the report, and entering her conclusions in her policy book, she reviewed the points of similarity.

Niamh Connolly + Sarah Sharpe:
Strangled. NC definitely by rope, SS in all probability.
Tortured *ante mortem*: NC breasts removed, SS, shot with crossbow bolts.
Pubic hair crudely shaved.
No rape or sexual assault*.
Injected in neck: tranquiliser.

* Removal of NC's breasts. If non-sexual, then what?

Then there was the victimology. Two prominent Christian

women. Vocal in their beliefs, though from her background reading Stella knew they sat on opposite sides of the abortion debate. One happily married, one apparently happily single.

Despite the mutilation of Niamh Connolly's breasts, Stella wasn't picking up anything overtly sexual about the killer. Her mind was leading her away from sex and towards religion. But what about the big question, the question that could lead her closer to the killer if she found the right answer?

Is he picking them because of who they are or because of what they represent?

She needed to know if they were connected by anything other than the manner of their deaths.

She'd had the results back from forensic examination of their phones. Both women had appointments with someone calling themselves 'MJ Fox' on the days of their murders.

Stella wrote her points of similarity on the main whiteboard for the investigation – the 'murder wall' – and cleared a space in the centre, where she scrawled, 'MJ Fox = Killer's alias?'

Then she returned to her desk and called Jerry Connolly. The phone went to voicemail. Sighing, Stella delivered the message she'd composed, fearing that this would happen.

'Hello, Jerry, it's Stella Cole. I need to ask you a few questions about Niamh's network. People she may have known through the charity or socially. Please could you call me as soon as you get this?'

Stella's phone rang fifteen minutes later.

'Stella, it's Jerry Connolly. You said you needed to ask me about Niamh's contacts?'

'Yes. You may have seen or heard that we are now investigating a second murder, of a lady named Sarah Sharpe.'

'Yes, I did wonder whether the two were linked.'

'I can't be certain at this point, but what I did want to do was find out whether Niamh and Sarah knew each other.'

'Niamh kept her contacts in her phone, which you have,' he

said, not brusquely, but with the resigned tone of a man who sees little point in dressing up simple truths.

'Yes, and I've been through them all while I was waiting for you to call. I can't see Sarah Sharpe in Niamh's contacts. Look, thanks for your help, Jerry, and I promise you I will let you know the moment we have something concrete to go on. Oh, and one last question. Did Niamh ever mention a MJ Fox to you?'

'No. Why?'

'We found that name in her phone.'

'Sorry. Means nothing.'

He ended the call.

52

THURSDAY 23ᴿᴰ AUGUST 3.45 P.M.
HALIFAX

Cam had arrived at the offices of Sherborne Ropes in Halifax at 3.45 p.m. in a black mood. The managing director of The Grantham Bell Foundry Ltd had been almost desperate to help but had drawn a blank.

Derby had been a bust, too. Strutt and Nightingale had only ever sold one set of ropes with black and gold sallies, but those had been polypropylene.

Climbing out of the Honda's driving seat, she cursed the sporty little car for having such unforgiving suspension and such a noisy exhaust. It might have given her the edge negotiating the traffic between Brixton and Paddington Green, but after more than five hours behind the wheel on motorways and fast A-roads, her kidneys felt as though they'd been through a NutriBullet and her ears were ringing.

Arthur Sherborne, in whose office she now sat, looked exactly the way she'd imagined him from his voice. Age, early seventies. Eyes twinkling with good humour. Hair, mostly gone, what was left, silver.

His large-boned hand had almost crushed hers when they shook, though she suspected this was not some attempt to intimidate so much as a lifetime's manual work, bending, twisting and coiling ropes in directions they didn't naturally want to go.

'Now, then, Camille,' he said once they were seated in his office. 'Have you had owt to eat since breakfast?'

'I had two gingerbread men in Grantham,' she answered, warming to this grandfatherly man with his no-nonsense attitude and old-fashioned manners.

His wiry white eyebrows rose in surprise.

'That's not going to keep the wolf from the door, is it? Come on. There's a decent cafe down the road where I get my lunch. Let's see if Jane can rustle you up something to eat. Gingerbread men!' he repeated, derisively.

'I'd love to, Arthur. But I'm kind of on a tight schedule. I need to be back in London tonight.'

'Tonight?' he said, in a tone of outrage. 'That's a two-hundred-mile drive down the M1 and tha'll hit the rush hour, too. What time did you set off this morning?'

Smiling despite herself, Cam answered truthfully.

'Half past seven.'

He shook his head.

'So that's what, seven and a bit hours to get here, plus another five or six to get back again? If you were one of my lads you'd be breaking EU rules doing that much driving.'

'Yeah, well, we won't have to worry about them much longer, will we?'

'Happen we won't, but you should still take a proper rest. Can't the Metropolitan Police,' he pronounced every syllable as if it tasted bad, 'afford to put you up in a hotel overnight?'

'Budgets, Arthur. Austerity. I'm lucky my boss didn't make me hitch.'

He shook his head.

'Aye, well, let's have a think about that later. I expect you'll be wanting to get on and see our records, then?'

'Yes please.'

'I did a bit of digging myself. It would've taken you ages.' He pushed a sage-green folder across the desk towards her. 'It's all in there. Copies of the original invoice, customer's details, everything. It may not be computerised, but I like to think we're meticulous nonetheless.'

Cam spun the folder round and opened it.

Customer name: MJ Fox.
Address: 20 Dean's Yard, London SW1P 3PA.
Purchase: thirty (30) metres flax bell rope, black and gold sally.
Date & time of purchase: Thursday 28th June 2018, 4.02 p.m.
Payment: £130 (cash).

She looked up and smiled at Arthur.

'Thank you. That's brilliant. Now, what about the CCTV?'

Ten minutes later, alone in a tiny windowless room, Cam was speeding through surprisingly high-quality colour footage from the company's CCTV camera for the 28th June. As the time-stamp hit 4.07 p.m. she let out a shout of triumph.

'Yes! There you are!'

A baseball cap pulled low over the eyes and the camera-aware villain's downwards glance meant she couldn't see Fox's face. Despite the heat, he was wearing a baggy green parka, over the right shoulder of which was slung a coil of rope with a fluffy black and gold tail. Better still, she could see the car and its number plate: a dark-blue Ford Focus, registration AG54 LKF.

She printed out a copy of the screen, sending it to a printer in the main office as Arthur had instructed her, then went to meet it.

. . .

Back in Arthur's office, she thanked him and stood to go.

'Hold your horses, Camille,' he said with a smile, rising as she did. 'About that rest.'

She grinned.

'I can't, Arthur. I said, no budget for hotels.'

'Aye, well, as it happens, the vicar at Halifax minster's a personal friend of mine. We supplied their bell ropes, naturally, and she's a grand lass. I called Liz and she said she'd be happy to put you up for the night at the canonry.'

Cam was torn. Sit in rush-hour traffic on the M1 as part of a gruelling six-hour drive in the Civic but sleep in her own bed, or call it a day up here and set off for home refreshed in the morning? Then she thought of the two murdered women and what connected them and made her decision.

'That would be lovely and it was very kind of you.'

53

THURSDAY 23RD AUGUST 5.00 P.M.
PADDINGTON GREEN

The team were assembled. Their afternoon briefings had become an embedded part of everyone's day and they were all present. As was the deputy mayor, who had also cottoned on to the fact that this was an ideal time to update himself on what was happening in what he had begun calling, 'the case that all of London is watching'.

Stella had learned to contain her feelings, which were mostly directed towards dreaming up gruesome ways of despatching Craig Morgan into the afterlife. He sat on the corner of Garry's desk, favouring her DS with smiles of complicity Stella imagined as saying, *'She's up there giving out the orders, but we know who's doing the real work, don't we?'*

Garry remained stony-faced, refusing to make eye contact with Morgan.

Stella began by filling the team in on Jamie Hooke's ideas. As she spoke, she surveyed each face. She was looking for telltale signs of that grey, dispiriting mood that afflicts coppers working round the clock without making progress.

They live on caffeine, alcohol, nicotine, adrenaline and junk food: none of them decent substitutes for a decent home-cooked meal and a good night's sleep, and none of them able to restore the sense of purpose that solid leads provide. Morgan was busy on his phone, listening with half an ear, she supposed.

'You're not serious about playing the "God's Copper" card, are you, boss?' Arran asked. 'Sticking yourself out there as bait is a terrible idea.'

A chorus of agreement rippled through the incident room.

Stella shook her head.

'That's what Jamie said. On the plus side, it would certainly get the killer's attention if I claimed to be doing God's work. But on the minus side—'

'You might end up with your tits on a dinner plate,' Def interrupted.

'Exactly. Which would, I think it's fair to say, be career-limiting at best.'

'Sorry to interrupt, Stella,' Morgan said. 'God's work?'

Stella sighed. So he hadn't even been listening with half an ear.

'We discussed ways of drawing our boy out into the open. Jamie's idea was to suggest I empathised with him. Say I understood how he felt about the Church. I said why not go further? Say I knew that God was working through me to bring him to justice? Jamie felt that would be far too risky and, on balance, I agree. We were just brainstorming.'

Morgan nodded, and made a note on his phone.

54

THURSDAY 23RD AUGUST 5.15 P.M.
HALIFAX

Liz Stephenson turned out to be a vivacious forty-year-old with an athlete's figure and a thousand-watt smile that made Cam feel she'd been reunited with a best friend she'd never realised she had. Liz batted away Cam's thanks for the room, saying, 'It's the least I could do and Arthur's such a sweetheart, isn't he?'

Settled in one of the canonry's huge bedrooms, with a view over Halifax's rooftops and the forbidding blackish-brown stonework of the minster itself, Cam logged in remotely to the PNC. She entered the index number for the blue Focus. It came back as scrapped. A dead end. She was just about to start searching for the address when her phone rang. It was Stella.

'Hi, boss.'

'How's the road trip?' Stella asked. 'I was just briefing the team. I'm putting you on speaker.'

'Good. Really good. Hi, everyone. I think I've found the supplier of the rope he's using. It's a company in Yorkshire called Sherborne Rope. The MD's a lovely guy. He sold a thirty-metre bell rope with a black and gold sally, that's the fluffy bit at the end, on Thursday 28th of June. I've got the customer's name and address. Probably fake but you never know, he could be one of the stupid ones.'

'Please tell me someone remembered serving him,' Stella said.

'Sorry, boss. They had a temp in that day. I contacted the agency who supplied him, but they haven't come back to me yet. But Sherborne Rope do have CCTV and guess what? I got a shot of the buyer and his car.'

'Brilliant work, Cam. What are we looking for?'

'Blue Ford Focus. Index number Alpha Golf Two Four Lima Kilo Foxtrot. Only trouble is, I just ran it through the PNC, and that's when I hit a snag. That index number was last used on a white Nissan Micra, which was scrapped on July sixth, 2016.'

'OK, that's not so good, but it's more than we've got on him so far. It's still great work, Cam.'

'Thanks, boss. I thought, maybe Lucian could do something with the photo of the buyer.'

'If anyone can, he can. So what name did he give?'

'MJ Fox.'

'Shit! It's him! Niamh and Sarah both had appointments in their phones on the days they were murdered with an MJ Fox. What was the address?'

'Twenty Dean's Yard, London. In SW1. Hang on, I'll put you on speaker then I'll Google it.'

Cam's fingers flashed over the keyboard then she hit return and waited.

'OK, he's not one of the stupids.'

'Fake?'

'No, it's real enough. It's Westminster bloody Abbey!'

'Fits with the two victims, that's something. So, where are you? You going to be all right driving back tonight?'

Cam smiled.

'You won't believe this, boss. I'm staying the night with the vicar of Halifax minster.'

'Bloody hell, what did you do to swing that one?'

'Nothing. It was the MD at Sherborne Ropes. He pulled strings, well, ropes, really. He and the vicar are friends.'

'Ha! Only you, Cam. OK, look, get a good night's sleep and we'll see you tomorrow.'

———

Stella ended the call and turned back to the team. Morgan had left, she noticed.

'OK, so our killer's being clever. No doubt the deputy mayor's tame profiler will wow us all with some fresh angle.'

A barely suppressed laugh from Arran set the whole team off and Stella waited out the hilarity.

'We could track down the breaker's yard that scrapped the Nissan, boss,' Def said. 'Maybe they have a record of who brought it in.'

'Or maybe they're the ones who transferred the reg to the Focus,' Arran volunteered.

'Good, good, this is all good,' Stella said. 'OK, Arran, can you and Def get onto that, please. I did some research on geographical profiling. I know we only have two murders so far, but it seems that our killer probably lives with a fifteen-mile radius of the centre point of a line connecting Niamh Connolly's and Sarah Sharpe's houses. So I want you to work that area first. Because that's my feeling. We're looking for a Londoner.'

A female PC in uniform burst into the incident room, causing everyone to turn round.

'Ma'am?' she said, coming straight over to Stella.

'Yes, what is it?'

'There's been another one. Brockwell Park. A DI Patel from one of the South Division MITs just referred it to you, ma'am.'

55

THURSDAY 23ᴿᴰ AUGUST 6.00 P.M.
BROCKWELL PARK, SOUTHEAST LONDON

Stella nodded to the forensic officer charged with taking the crime scene photographs. The photographer's eyes, visible between the white face mask and the elasticated edge of his hood, were unblinking. A steady stare that she could read only too well. *Who could do such a thing to another human being?* And, for once, as she confronted evil in another of its many guises, Stella felt completely certain that if she were asked directly, she could answer, 'Not me'.

Standing shoulder to shoulder with Garry, overheated in her forensic suit, mask and booties, she surveyed the interior of the office, beginning with the ghastly tableau at the desk.

The dead woman's eyelids were – Stella searched for the right word – *draped* closed. And they were concave. Entirely understandable given that the dead woman's eyeballs, plus scraps of muscle and connective tissue, were sitting on the desk on a white plate with a gold-painted rim.

Stella knew she should leave and let the CSIs get on with their work without the SIO looking, literally, over their shoulders. But something about the picture in front of her was pinging an alarm bell deep in her brain.

'I've seen that before,' she said.

'I hope to God you haven't.'

'No, I mean it. It's just, I can't think straight with that,' she said, pointing at the body, 'in my face.'

Her day took a further nosedive when Lucian called her as she and Garry were pulling into the car park at Paddington Green.

'Hey, Lucian, what's up?'

'It's what's down that's the problem. Our oven packed up last night. We can't get it fixed until next week. I'm afraid Saturday's dinner is off. And Stefan's stuck his tools in a suitcase and flown up to Scotland to do a big landscaping job that just came in. I'm really sorry, Stella.'

Rather than feeling sad at the news, Stella felt a sudden flicker of nerves in her belly.

'Look, let's not let the evening go to waste. Why don't I book a table in town instead? We can eat out. I haven't seen Gareth for ages.'

Lucian sounded doubtful.

'Sure, that's a lovely idea. As long as you don't mind playing gooseberry.'

———

Back at her desk, Stella updated her policy book, then phoned a dim sum restaurant in Soho where she knew the owner, an elderly Chinese man.

'Mrs Stella! So good to hear from you,' he said. 'You want table, yes? For tonight?'

'For Saturday, Mister Yun. I know it's short notice but can you squeeze us in at nine?'

'For you, I find table any time. How many people?'

Crossing her fingers under her desk, she answered.

'Four, please.'

'No problem. We see you on Saturday at nine. I tell chef prepare special pork buns.'

———

In Halifax, Cam was sitting at a long, dark kitchen table, scarred and polished from many decades of use. Liz had just placed a plate in front of her, heaped with lamb chops, French beans and mustard mash. As they ate, the conversation turned to the case.

'So, is he using bell rope to strangle them?' Liz asked, her brows knitted.

Cam shook her head as she swallowed a mouthful of succulent, pink-tinged lamb.

'I'm afraid I can't say. I know, I mean, but we can't discuss details.'

Liz nodded.

'Of course, I understand. Sorry. More wine?'

'Yes, please.'

Liz poured two more glasses of the excellent rioja she'd served with the lamb.

'I just wish there was something I could do to help.'

'Maybe there is. You see, both women were prominent Christians. One a Catholic, one C of E.'

'Yes, I heard about poor Sarah through the Church grapevine.'

'So, while it doesn't look like Anglicanism is the link, Christianity almost certainly is. By the way, this is confidential, right?'

Liz laughed.

'It's not the confessional, not that we do that here, but yes. My lips are sealed.'

'Thanks. The man I'm looking at gave his address as 20 Dean's Yard in London. You know what that is, right?'

Liz nodded.

'It seems he's definitely trying to make a point, doesn't it?'

'Mm, hmm. What do you think could be going on in his head?

323

Like, what's his motive? Again, I can't give you details, but he did torture them before he killed them.'

Liz actually shuddered, her shoulders, upper arms, neck and head taking it turns to vibrate, like a dog shaking.

'How awful for them. It's weird, actually, because although I didn't really know either woman – although I knew *of* them – obviously, I heard them both on Radio 4 a few months ago.'

Cam sat bolt upright, almost knocking her wine over.

'Really? What programme?'

'They called it *Women of Faith*, I think. Some dreadfully worthy name, anyway. It was a sort of panel discussion.'

'Was it just the two of them? Apart from the interviewer or whoever, I mean?'

Liz took a sip of her wine then shook her head.

'No. There was a third guest. A nun. Rather progressive. Her name was, oh, let me think. Moira Lowney, that was it!'

Feeling a buzz of adrenaline in her system that totally overcame the effects of the wine, Cam fished her notebook out and made a note.

'Where was she from? Moira, I mean. What convent?'

Liz frowned.

'It was somewhere in London. Forgive me, I do know it, I can hear her saying it.' She closed her eyes and began humming tunelessly. Then her eyes popped open. 'Brockwell Park! I think she said they were a Carmelite order.'

Cam was already pulling her phone out.

'Sorry, Liz, but I have to phone my guvnor right away. I think Moira is in serious danger.'

———

Stella hung up, smiling at the thought of a night off, some excellent dim sum, and Jamie's company. Her phone immediately rang. She checked the screen.

'Cam. What's up?'

'Boss, there's no time to lose. You have to get over to a convent in Brockwell Park. Carmelite nuns, I think. There's a nun there called—'

'Moira Lowney. Sorry, Cam, you're too late. She's dead.'

'Shit! Same MO?'

'Yep. How did you know she was in trouble?'

'They were on a radio show together. Radio 4. Her, Sarah Sharpe and Niamh Connolly. Liz, she's the vicar I'm staying with, she heard it.'

Stella sighed.

'Well at least we know how he chose his first three victims,' Stella said. 'I just hope that means he's finished.'

———

Later that evening, having clocked up another five miles running round the streets of Northwest London, Stella sat out on her balcony, a glass of chilled Gavi in her hand, sipping the fruity Italian wine and waiting for her call to be answered.

'Hello, Stella. I was just thinking about you.'

'Oh, yes. Nothing bad, I hope.'

'On the contrary. I was mulling over the name your killer uses to fix his appointments.'

'What, MJ?'

'Well, partly that. It's androgynous, for one thing.'

'Perhaps he thinks it makes him sound less threatening. It is kind of cute. Sort of Millennial, if you know what I mean.'

'Agreed. But it's the surname I'm looking at. Fox. It *could* be his real name. Ted Bundy, Jeffrey Dahmer, Dennis Nielsen: none of them used pseudonyms. But this feels like part of his act. What does it say to you?'

'Wily? Cunning? Fox in a henhouse? It certainly fits his MO. He's enjoying himself.'

'That's what I thought. I think it means you're looking for an intelligent killer. We all talk about organised and disorganised serial killers. The former tend to be high intelligence, the latter, low. They're all dangerous, but the organised ones are harder to get.

They're often forensically aware and take great care to avoid being caught.'

'Which is just the sort of cheery news I need on the day I've looked into the sightless eyes of a dead nun,' Stella said, before taking a gulp of her wine. 'He's done number three. Officially a serial killer.'

'Oh, God, I'm sorry.'

'I know, but I'm kind of a bit battle-weary at the moment. I can't really deal with it. Listen, Jamie, I know this is a bit, um, sudden, and I'm sure you're busy, but, I mean, you're not free for dinner on Saturday night, are you? Only I'm meeting some friends and I'd love to bring you along. To meet them. They're gay. Not that that matters. You can just tell me—'

'Yes,' he said, laughing. 'I'd love to. Where and when?'

'Oh. Great. Sorry for gabbling. Nervous, I guess. Comes from talking to a psychiatrist. Dumpling Palace on Gerrard Street in Soho. Nine o'clock. That should give you time to get in from, where is it you live, Reading?'

'I used to. I moved last year. I'm in Kew now, just on the other side of the river from Chiswick. The commute's not too bad and I no longer have to live in Reading.'

Stella's stomach did another little backflip.

'Excellent. See you on Saturday, then.'

'See you, Stella.'

56

FRIDAY 24TH AUGUST 9.00 A.M.
PADDINGTON GREEN

Stella answered her phone.

'Ah, Stella. Craig Morgan here. The profiler I mentioned, Dr Adrian Trimmets? I've asked him to meet me at Paddington Green this afternoon at eleven. I hope you can be there to brief him.'

Stella had allocated the whole morning to meeting her team individually or in small groups to catch up. She sighed.

'Yes, OK, that's fine. I'll see you both at eleven.'

———

At five minutes to eleven, as Stella was finishing updating her Policy Book, a cough behind her made her look up and around. Craig Morgan stood there, in yet another expensive-looking suit, smiling down at her. Wanting to reassert some semblance of a balance of power, she stood and took a half-step towards him, forcing him to take a step back or be standing uncomfortably close to her.

To Morgan's left stood a short, round man dressed in a suit as badly fitting as Morgan's was tailored to his frame.

No taller than Stella and with a shaved head revealing male-pattern baldness. He also sported a meagre moustache and scrubby beard that gave him the appearance of one of the old Victorian drawings her dad used to delight in showing her, where the drawing could be viewed upside down to create a different face.

Resisting the urge to twist her head to see if it worked on Morgan's profiler, she held her hand out instead.

'You must be Dr Trimmets,' she said, recoiling inwardly from the hot, sweaty grip of his enthusiastic handshake.

He laughed, an oddly loud croak, too loud for the distance that separated them. His brown eyes bulged behind comically oversized black glasses.

'Ha! Please call me Ade. Even my students don't call me doctor.'

Stella pasted a smile onto her face.

'Ade,' she said. 'I've borrowed my guvnor's office, if you'll both follow me.'

Ensconced behind the desk and reflecting that she clearly had a way to travel in the hierarchy before she qualified for a chair as comfortable as Callie's, Stella looked at both men in turn. She saw the same emotion in both faces. Ambition. Morgan's for the mayoralty. Trimmets's for media attention and well-paid gigs for the Home Office.

Feeling like a recalcitrant teenager but unable to wriggle out of the situation she found herself in, she spoke now, hoping to maintain her slender advantage over the two men she'd mentally christened Stan and Ollie.

'Thank you for agreeing to provide a profile, Ade. And thank you, deputy mayor, for securing Ade's services for us at no charge.'

The profiler's eyes widened and he glanced leftwards at Morgan. *Oops! Did Stan not mention that part to you, Ollie?*

'We'll discuss Ade's fees separately,' Morgan said, smoothly. 'The main thing, the *important* thing, is that he gets to work as soon as possible to draw up the profile that will help you catch this killer.'

'Absolutely,' Stella said, mustering as much enthusiasm as she could. Which wasn't much.

Trimmets fixed her with a magnified gaze.

'First of all, DCI Cole, I need to offer my thanks to you. I know that we profilers aren't always held in high regard by working coppers and I can understand that. So many profiles are just statements of the bleeding obvious blended with enough caveats as to be almost worthless. I assure you that I will try my hardest to give you something actionable.'

It wasn't the speech Stella had been expecting. She'd checked out the man's website and Googled him. His pronouncements in other cases and the text on his site had led her to believe he was just another Cracker-wannabe, boosting his career prospects and income while doing nothing of any real value for the police forces paying his fees.

OK. So maybe I was wrong about you, Ade.

'Which is pretty honest of you,' she replied. 'Thanks. So, I've put a pack of information together for you, including copies of crime scene and post mortem photographs, interview reports with previous suspects and the victimology. Is there anything else you need?'

Trimmets steepled his fingers under his chin and looked up before staring at her.

'No. I think that's all. You clearly know how we work. You'd be surprised how many detectives think we can give them the name, address and shoe size of the killer just from a one-page evidence summary and a handful of photos.'

Actually, I wouldn't because no cop would do that, but if it makes you happy to say that, fine.

'Good. We'll give it to you on the way out. I'll just need your signature on this document.' She pushed a single sheet of paper across the desk towards Trimmets.

'What is that?'

'It's what we call a Short-form OSA. You know, Official Secrets Act. Basically it says that you are bound by a duty of confidentiality to the Crown. I know you would never *deliberately* leak any of this,' she smiled sweetly at Trimmets, 'but, you know, some people can be a little careless in their document storage. This says you promise to keep secure the information I provide you.'

Trimmets offered a nervous smile.

'What if something went missing?'

'Then I and a few of my colleagues would come to your place of work or your home, Taser you, then arrest you.'

Trimmets eyebrows shot up, and Morgan interrupted.

'Now, surely, Stella, that is ridiculously heavy-handed? Dr Tr—'

'Joke!' Stella said. 'Cop humour. No Tasers, I promise.' She paused, enjoying herself. 'Just the usual penalties for breaching the Act. Up to two years in prison and a fine. Or both. As I said, it's just a formality. Would you like to borrow a pen?'

———

At just after 2.00 p.m., Cam arrived in the incident room. She went straight over to Stella's desk.

'Boss! I'm just, you know, I want to say I'm gutted about Moira Lowney. If I'd just—'

Stella motioned for her to take a seat. Then she laid a hand on Cam's shoulder.

'Stop! If, nothing. That was really good work from you yesterday, OK? I know you're upset because you were too late to save Moira, but it's a solid lead. I've got Lucian doing his magic with the CCTV photo and another team looking at the Focus.'

Cam wrinkled her nose and smiled.

'Thanks, boss. So, I had another idea on the drive down. I want to contact the BBC. The producer of the show. See if I can get a list of all the women who've appeared. Maybe we can at least try to get ahead of Lucifer.'

Stella nodded. She liked the way the young DC didn't wait to be given jobs to do. She could think for herself.

'Good idea. Let me know what you get as soon as you get it. If he's using the show's guests as his victim pool, we need to warn them.'

57

FRIDAY 24TH AUGUST 5.00 P.M.
NEW SCOTLAND YARD

As she had promised, Callie kept Stella away from the media for the third press conference. She intended to keep this one short. And sweet?

No. Given the subject matter, and the announcement she had spent three hours drafting with Tim Llewelyn's help, bitter, sour, or possibly putrid would be a better word. She took a deep breath and began.

'Good morning, ladies and gentlemen. Yesterday, the twenty-third of August, some time between 10.30 a.m. and 3.00 p.m., the body of a woman was found in her office at the Carmelite Order of the Unified Spirit, a convent in Brockwell Park, Southeast London.'

Callie could see the frowns and pursed lips and the way one or two of the assembled journalists were leaning their heads together and whispering. And she could translate the body language.

Shit! This is it! A serial killer!

She continued before anyone could interrupt and disrupt the flow of her prepared statement.

'Sister Moira Lowney was forty-seven. She was strangled to death and her killer had mutilated her. We have very strong reasons for believing that Moira Lowney was murdered by the same person who murdered Niamh Connolly and Sarah Sharpe.' *OK, Callie, my girl, time to drop the S-bomb.* 'As such we are now treating the three murders as a series of multiple, linked offences.' *Wait for it, Callie, wait for it…*

As she'd agreed with Tim, she paused here and simply let the inevitable questions come in like a lobbed hand grenade.

'Ruth Kelly, *Evening Standard*,' shouted an attractive woman in her early fifties with a sharp bob of silver hair and vivid orange lipstick. 'Are you saying this is the work of a serial killer?'

As Kelly's final two words hung, suspended in the conference room, Callie felt utterly alone. She had a fantastic team, and people she could talk to, including her old boss at Lothian and Borders, Chief Constable Gordon Wade. But the responsibility for the next few seconds was hers and hers alone.

She knew that as soon as she gave her answer, this would explode from a London story to a global one, with all the attendant pressure, prurient interest, social media theorising and conspiracy theorist ranting that could add days if not weeks of unnecessary work.

She squared her shoulders and inhaled.

'Yes.'

———

Exactly ten miles south from Callie's padded chair in the New Scotland Yard media centre, the killer stared intently at the live broadcast, waiting to hear what the uniformed police officer said next. It was vital she told the media what connected the women. Then they would understand. And forever remember the name, Malachi Jeremiah Robey.

———

Callie waited for the hubbub to die down, signalling with her clamped red lips and thousand-yard stare that she had no intention of competing with the baying crowd of journalists.

'We believe that the killer of these three women has developed a grudge against the Christian religion. Niamh Connolly was a prominent Catholic. Sarah Sharpe was the editor of the *Church Times*. And his most recent victim, Moira Lowney, was the reluctant star of a TV reality show. We would reiterate our advice to the general public to be vigilant but, now, I must also add the advice that women with well-known religious beliefs, particularly if they have recently appeared in the media or in public forums, should be especially careful.'

Beside her, in his usual chair, Morgan answered the next question, which concerned, once again, the social class of the victims.

'Yes, they were respectable women, but that makes no difference in the London of which I am proud to serve as its Deputy Mayor for Policing and Crime.'

58

FRIDAY 24TH AUGUST 5.10 P.M.
STOKE NEWINGTON

Arianna and her flat-mate, Belle, real name Louisa Shepton-Grand, had the evening to themselves. Neither had any bookings, and the streets outside were still so hot that the Johns had all but disappeared.

Belle was massaging Arianna's shoulders, digging her strong brown fingers into the muscles each side of her friend's thin neck.

'Ah, that's good, mate,' Arianna groaned. 'But I really need a fix, you know? Why aren't there any blokes in Stokie who want a shag?'

'They're probably at home in front of the TV with a few cold beers. Maybe they're even doing their wives.'

Arianne laughed.

'Oh, yeah, well that's the end, then, innit? The day the Johns get it between their wives' legs, you and me babe? We really are fucked!'

Belle laughed.

'What about trying Islington? I bet there's a few rich bastards up there who're horny enough to do a bit of business.'

Arianna straightened and refastened her bra. She turned to Belle.

'That is actually not a bad idea. Come on, help me find something a bit more sophisticated.'

As they spread clothes out across the back of the sofa, Arianna turned and switched on the TV news. They gossiped about the other working girls they knew until a voice from behind them made Arianna turn round.

'Yes, they were respectable women, but that makes no difference in the London of which I am proud to serve as its Deputy Mayor for Policing and Crime.'

Sitting beside a uniformed female police officer, silver bling all over her jacket, was Tony. And he was speaking into the microphone, answering a question from a reporter. It seemed she wasn't the only one who'd decided to go upmarket. No hoodie and jeans this time. Tony was sitting there in a seriously high-end suit, probably Armani, or even Versace, she reckoned.

'Huh!' Belle said. 'He says that, but I bet they're having kittens 'cos it's not us toms getting sliced up for a change.'

Arianna's eyes were wide and her mouth had dropped open.

'Oh my God! That's Tony!' She stabbed a long bright-pink nail at the screen.

'What, the one who likes you to peg him with the dildo?'

'Yes! He's, like, the deputy mayor!'

'Are you sure, babe? Not being rude or nothing, but you're not always at your sharpest when you're working.'

'No, mate. I mean, yes! I'm totally sure. It's him. Look!' She pointed at a name card placed in front of her client. 'Craig Morgan, Deputy Mayor for Policing and Crime.'

Belle turned Arianna to face her, holding her thin shoulders and staring straight into her kohl-rimmed eyes.

'You could make some money out of him.'

'What, like put my prices up, you mean?'

Belle smiled and shook her head so that her long beaded braids swung and clicked.

'Sweet baby, you need to think big. Those politicians are always trying to keep their dirty laundry hidden away. He'll pay you big time not to go the papers.'

Now Arianna did get it. Her eyes widened. She had a flash of an image in her mind's eye. Her and Belle, cruising down Park Lane in a brand-new white Mercedes convertible.

'I think I might try that next time he comes over, but you better be there hiding in case he tries anything rough.'

'Don't worry. Let Belle sort out the details. He could be our meal ticket.'

Sadly for the girls, that was not to be.

59

Professor Peter Karlsson was ready for his ordeal by fire.

Standing off to one side of the stage, his publisher's PR manager was wearing black: a silk blouse, narrow-legged trousers that just skimmed the floor, and patent leather stilettos. Her blonde hair was swept back from a high forehead and held in place by a black velvet Alice band.

All in all, Karlsson thought, *quite the package*. The two of them were at the front of a packed room in the basement of a branch of Waterstone's a few hundred yards from Euston station. The low stage just had room for two armchairs and a black coffee table, on which rested a carafe of water, a single glass and a copy of the professor's new book.

In front of them, about forty invited guests sat on hard plastic chairs, fanning themselves with their stiff paper invitations, chatting and slugging back the wine – red or white, both the same temperature – that the publishers, Moathouse Press, had provided for the occasion.

Karlsson thought back to the day, several months earlier, when he'd received the invitation to the launch. He'd printed off the email and taken it from the immaculately ordered confines of his office to his secretary. She smiled as she saw him coming.

'Yes, Peter?' she asked. 'What can I do for you?'

'Could you check my diary then send a yes to this, please? If there's anything in there, cancel or move it.'

'Of course. Anything exciting?'

He grinned at her wolfishly.

'Yes, actually. My book launch.'

She smiled back.

'They won't know what's hit them.'

Back in his office, he resumed writing the proposal for an article to promote the book. He intended to take aim at a number of contemporary theologians and tear them apart.

He added a name to the list. Sarah Sharpe, the sanctimonious editor of *The Church Times*. Her recent hand-wringing editorials about human rights couldn't obscure the systematic abuses of those same rights inflicted on non-believers down the ages.

Yes. It'll be my pleasure. To destroy you all. A momentary flicker of anxiety crossed his mind as he thought of what his wife would say. He dismissed it. *Love is blind. It belongs in the compartment called, 'Things we never discuss'.*

———

The PR woman stood, jerking Karlsson out of his reverie. She stepped towards the mic stand and patted the air for silence. The hubbub died down as the chattering pairs and groups realised the show was about to start.

'Good evening, ladies and gentlemen,' the publicist said, beaming at the crowd. 'My name is Meriel Ottway and on behalf of Moathouse Press, it is my great pleasure to welcome you to the launch of Professor Peter Karlsson's latest book, um – ' she glanced at the card in her hand ' – *Unholy Pain: Martyrdom and the Cult of Cruelty in the Christian Church.*'

She paused, smiling, and the audience dutifully responded with a round of applause.

'I'm glad to see you've all got something to drink. I'm only sorry the fridge broke down so those of you on the white haven't quite got the temperature the winemakers envisaged.'

This little joke provoked a polite smattering of laughter. Karlsson could feel sweat trickling down his ribs inside his shirt and hoped it wouldn't start showing through his light-blue linen jacket. Meriel carried on with her speech.

'In a moment, I'll ask Professor Karlsson to share a few thoughts with you, then he'll read a short extract from his book. Then we'll open it up to questions from the floor. Before you leave, please buy a copy. Waterstones have kindly offered a ten per cent discount on all orders placed tonight, and I know Professor Karlsson will be delighted to sign any books you want to buy and take away. So—' She turned to Karlsson, catching him in the act of wiping a handkerchief across his hot and sweating forehead. 'Without further ado, here is the man you've all come to hear from. Professor Peter Karlsson.'

Once the applause had died down, Karlsson approached the mic. He stroked his neatly trimmed beard as he stared out at the dozens of people waiting for him to speak. He inhaled deeply, and spoke in the clear, sonorous voice he had perfected for holding lecture theatres spellbound.

'Picture a mortuary. Large enough to accommodate dozens of corpses. The victims have been subjected to the most hideous, disgusting, stomach-churning tortures imaginable. Mutilated. Burned. Crushed. Disembowelled. Scourged. Skinned alive. Gang-raped. Then, when their torturers grew bored, or had exhausted their appetite for violence against these particular victims, they killed them. By beheading… stoning… drowning… impalement… crucifixion.'

He paused to gauge the audience reaction. The indrawn breaths and winces told him he was on track. The slight push he gave to the phrase 'gang-raped' worked like a charm on the women in particular. Time to continue.

'The killers are known to the authorities. Because they *are* the authorities.

'Ladies and gentlemen, this is not the premise of a new series of *CSI*. Nor the imaginings of a pulp novelist. This is history. So who were the perpetrators of these egregious crimes against innocent people? The Nazis? Always a good bet, but no. Government torturers in Chile, Burma or Syria? Again, quite possible, but no. Serial killers, then? The modern age's favourite bogeymen. One last time, no.'

He spread his hands wide and took a few seconds to look around the audience. He caught the eye of a couple of his colleagues from the Philosophy faculty at University College London, who offered encouraging nods and smiles. They knew his schtick for what it was but were prepared to go along with it, needing to know Karlsson would return the favour when one of them had a new book out.

'No, ladies and gentlemen. The people who gleefully reduced men and women to mere cuts of meat, sometimes butchered or burnt beyond all recognition as human beings, were churchmen. And I use that word advisedly. Despite today's clamour for sexual equality, the tortures of which I speak were exclusively inflicted by men. In the name of God. The dictionary word for it is martyrdom. I prefer a simple word. Murder.'

He took a moment to wipe his brow, which was running so freely with sweat in the un-air conditioned basement room that salt was stinging his eyes.

He resumed speaking, now discussing the premise of his book. Despite the blood 'n' guts he'd opened with, his intention had always been to engage his audience with the serious point he was making. That the Christian church's foundations in wanton cruelty had infected its teachings through the ages.

It was a controversial viewpoint and had garnered him vociferous criticism in religious circles and their media outlets: *The Church Times* and the *Catholic Herald* in England, even *Il Osservatore*, the Vatican newspaper, which had weighed in with a full-page editorial excoriating *Il Professore Inglese che ha Dichiarato Guerra alla*

Chiesa – The English Professor Who Has Declared War on the Church.

After a short reading, Karlsson snapped the thick hardback shut and reversed until the soft edge of the armchair nudged against the back of his knees and he folded, gratefully, into its embrace.

Meriel was on her feet again, and Karlsson admired the perfect swell of her bottom in the tailored trousers.

'Thank you, Professor Karlsson,' she said to the audience, as if he were sitting somewhere in the middle of the fifth row instead of a few feet behind her. 'I'm sure lots of you have questions, but it's such a hot evening and I gather we've managed to get the fridge working so there are cold beers and wine available,' a small ironic cheer went up at this point, 'so perhaps we'll keep the Q&A short.'

A hand shot up immediately. It was connected by a pale, bare arm inked with a skull surrounded by roses, to a young man of maybe nineteen or twenty, long, dark hair like a girl's framing his angular face. A PR assistant hurried over with a wireless mic, which the young man took, mouthed a 'thank-you', then stood.

'Yes, hello, Professor Karlsson.'

Karlsson smiled, though inwardly he groaned. He knew his questioner. His name was Harry King, a PhD student in his department. He was Harry's advisor and, of late, he'd become acutely aware that Harry had developed a crush on him. *No!* he chided himself. *Crushes are harmless. This is something else.*

He'd checked with a colleague in the Psychology department. Professor Margie Sellars had been quite clear after he'd described Harry's behaviour. The 'chance' meetings in his street. The intimate photographs he'd emailed. The detailed and sexually explicit letters he'd handwritten and stuffed in Karlsson's pigeonhole at the university.

'Sounds like erotomania to me, Peter,' she'd said in her book-lined office. 'It's a rare form of paranoid delusion, also known as De Clerambault's syndrome. But Harry's showing the classic symptoms. You have higher social status than him. He believes you're in love with him.'

Karlsson had protested vigorously.

'But I've never shown him even the slightest encouragement! I've even met him privately to warn him off. I explained that I was straight, and happily – very happily – married.'

Margie had smiled.

'All of which he will have interpreted as signals, maybe even secret, coded messages, that you are in fact in love with him.'

'But what can I do?'

Margie shrugged.

'Erotomania is often linked to other underlying psychiatric disorders. He could be bipolar, or have some sort of schizo-affective disorder. I think your best first step is to try to get him to see one of the university GPs, if he doesn't have his own.'

That had been four weeks earlier, and Harry had smiled pityingly at him when he'd suggested, gently, that maybe, perhaps, he ought to check in with a GP, 'just to check everything's working the way it should, you know,' he'd said, pointing vaguely in the direction of his own skull, 'up there.'

'Oh, Peter,' he'd crooned, tapping him lightly, but disturbingly, on the tip of his nose, then stroking his index finger over Karlsson's moustache, 'you don't need to worry about me. I know how you feel about me. And once we've got rid of your wife, we can finally be together.'

———

And now, here he was, standing just ten feet away from him, a mic clutched in his long, pale fingers.

'My question is this. I know you have critics. Every genius does, of course. But don't you think that your work, your amazing work, I mean, would be more widely accepted if people were brought face to face with the realities of the cruelties you describe in your book.'

'I'm sorry, Harry. I don't think I understand what you mean.'

'Oh, sorry. I probably didn't explain it well. I'm a bit nervous. What I meant to say was, like, if people were being tortured and killed like that now, and it was, like, on social media and everything, well, there'd be an outcry, wouldn't there? Like with this serial killer on the TV?'

Karlsson smiled and shook his head. It was a good point. Just a pity it had to be Harry who was making it. He'd heard a few sniggers as he called him a genius.

'Well, yes. I'd have to agree with you. Some of the Renaissance paintings make the whole process look no more painful than having a tetanus shot. All those saints gazing wistfully into the middle distance while a couple of burly blokes in leather jerkins sawed them in half.'

Clearly satisfied, Harry handed the mic back to the hovering PR assistant and sat down, to begin making notes in a black Moleskine notebook perched on his lap.

Relieved that at least Harry hadn't proposed marriage, Karlsson relaxed. The next question was a lowball from one of his colleagues and he was off the hook. *Another few minutes and I get to the signing and then the pub*, he thought.

60

FRIDAY 24TH AUGUST 10.00 P.M.
ISLINGTON

At 10.00 p.m. Arianna emerged onto Stoke Newington High Street. Her usual outfit – spaghetti-strap vest, white PVC micro-mini and four-inch baby-pink stilettos was gone. In its place, a short-sleeved white top, still extremely low-cut but with sprigs of flowers across the upper half; a pair of white cotton shorts, as tight as a groper's fist but still decent; and a pair of white heels, half the height of her preferred footwear. Belle's verdict: 'if one of them bankers doesn't go for you in that getup, babe, they must be gay.'

She climbed into the sweltering interior of a 73 bus, touched her phone to the contactless pad and took a seat upstairs at the front, her favourite spot ever since she was a little girl going into London with her mum.

She alighted into the warm, humid air of Islington at the bus stop by Angel tube station. Unfamiliar with the neighbourhood, she headed north on Upper Street into the heart of the bourgeois North London district famous for its Labour Prime Ministers, looking for a pitch where the local girls wouldn't tear her a new one for crowding their patch.

A skinny white guy in a grey hoodie hissed at her from a shop doorway.

'Oi! You looking for gear?' he asked.

How come they always recognise us? she asked herself.

———

DS Tamsin Aldridge flicked on the indicator, ready to turn right off Upper Street into Liverpool Road and finish her extended shift. The station was a few minutes' drive away and she was looking forward to clocking off and meeting a few mates in The Craft Beer Co. Bar on White Lion Street.

Hands crossing on the wheel, she spotted a familiar face walking down from the Angel then stopping to talk to one of the street-level dealers on her list. The face belonged to Charlotte Evans, AKA Arianna. Tamsin made a split-second decision. She cancelled the turn and pulled over into the bus lane.

The pusher tugged his hood further forward and sauntered off. The tom turned, saw her, pasted a smile onto her skinny white face and leaned down into the passenger window, which Tamsin had just buzzed down.

'Hello, darlin'. Looking for business?' she asked, her bright lips curved upwards into a smile. Which slid off her face to be replaced with a scowl. 'Oh, shit!'

'Hello, Arianna. Jump in.'

Wearily, Arianna pulled open the passenger door and climbed in, slamming it behind her and folding her arms across her chest.

'Just my luck. I 'adn't even started yet!'

Tamsin smiled as she found a quiet spot to pull over.

'Well, then, there's nothing I can book you for, is there? So tell me. What's a nice girl from Stokie doing looking for trade in Islington?'

She watched as the downy hairs on Arianna's forearms erected in the air-conditioned atmosphere inside the car.

'Couldn't sleep, could I? I went for a walk.'

'Couldn't sleep?' Tamsin laughed. 'What's your bedtime, then, half-past nine?'

Arianna's voice took on a whiny tone.

'Look, DS Aldridge. Please don't take me in. Not tonight. I don't need it, awright?'

Tamsin smiled.

'I'm about to go off duty. The last thing I want to do is dive into a mountain of paperwork. So how about this? We're looking at a new crew shipping heroin into North London. You hear about new suppliers or you see new guys on the street, selling, you let me know, OK?'

Arianna shook her head.

'I can't! You know what they're like. They look down on us worse than your lot do. If I grass up a dealer you'll be pulling me out of a skip in tiny little pieces. I can't!'

Tamsin sighed.

'Oh well. I guess it's paperwork for me and a nice night in the cells for you, then, isn't it?'

'No, wait! I know something.'

Tamsin felt a little prickle of excitement in her stomach. *Probably nothing, but let's hear the girl out.*

'What kind of something?'

'You got to promise to let me out. And I want, like, immunity.'

Tamsin laughed again.

'Immunity from what? You're not exactly in the big leagues, Arianna.'

Arianna shook her head.

'OK, not immunity, then. I used the wrong word. I mean, I tell you what I know and you, like, put the word out to your mates to leave me alone for a while. And Belle,' she added quickly.

'I can't make that kind of promise, you know that. But let's hear it and if it's good, I tell you what. I'll put you down on the system as one of my informants. Then if you do get picked up, the arresting officer will refer it to me and I'll sort you out. Just as long as you stick to Stokie and soliciting and don't get involved in anything naughty. Deal?'

Arianna didn't even pause.

'Deal,' she said.

'Well come on, then. There's a nice bottle of prosecco with my name on it in a bar near here and I'm tired.'

Arianna took a deep breath and swivelled in her seat until she was facing Tamsin.

'You know that Craig Morgan? The assistant mayor or whatever he calls 'imself?'

Tamsin nodded. 'Yes.' The feeling was back, stronger than before.

'He's a client of mine. Likes me to do 'im up the arse with a dildo. A really massive one. God knows how he can bear it. Other stuff, too. Really kinky. S&M.'

The image was too much. Tamsin laughed so hard her stomach started cramping. When she'd managed to calm herself down and wiped her eyes with a tissue she turned to Arianna.

'That was epic, Arianna. Thanks. Look, I don't know if it'll be useful, although he is the Deputy Mayor for Policing and Crime, so who knows? But a deal's a deal. You're free and clear for two months, OK?'

Arianna nodded and smiled.

'Thanks, DS Aldridge. You take care.'

'Yeah, whatever. You, too, Arianna. Stay out of trouble.'

———

Arianna hadn't told Tamsin that the story about Morgan was a secret. There wouldn't have been much point, given the situation she found herself in. It was information, and information was there to be traded.

Tamsin traded it the moment she had the sweating pint glass in front of her. Knowing about the Deputy Mayor's sexual proclivities wouldn't help her clear a single case, but it would earn her major points in the gossip stakes.

From the table in The Craft Beer Co. Bar on White Lion Street, the information travelled into a number of homes, and the general CID office at Islington Police Station on Tolpuddle Street. One of the officers into whose ears the information was whispered was a female DI.

Greer Wallace had attended the same Edinburgh school as Callie McDonald. They were a few years apart but had reconnected in London through their membership of the school's alumni group on Facebook. And they were due to meet for a theatre trip the following Friday. She grinned. *I'll save it for the interval drinks*, she thought.

61

Stella stared at the whiteboard. Three murdered women looked back at her.

In their 'before' photos, each woman was smiling. Her hair was immaculate, her makeup in place, her posture confident yet relaxed. All were professionally shot pictures, from the media page on LoveLife's website, the About Us page on that of *The Church Times* and a publicity pack put together by the BBC press office to advertise *Habits of a Lifetime*.

In the 'after' photos, all traces of the women's dignity and poise had been cruelly stripped away. Stella clamped her lips together and vowed that she would see their killer behind bars whatever it took. *Whatever, Stel? Yes. That's what I said.*

She turned to face the team.

'Thanks for coming in today, guys. I know you've all got families and social lives. So, where are we? Arran, any joy from our three nutters who were threatening Niamh?'

He stood and cleared his throat. Stella was pleased to see he had

353

a bit more colour in his cheeks and he'd shaved properly. No blood-spotted scraps of tissue anywhere to be seen.

'Basically, they were all washouts as suspects. Although I have to say I wouldn't want to meet any of them down a dark alley. Especially Kulik. The guy's married with three lovely kids, all sweetness and light at his house, but when we had him in here it was like interviewing a completely different man. The stuff he came out with, it was really horrible wasn't it, Def?'

Def nodded.

'I hope to God his fantasy life stays that way but, if he ever decides to act out, we're going to look back on this case as the hazy, crazy days of summer. But his alibi was watertight. When Niamh was being butchered he was at work. He's a storeman at the Tesco superstore in Clapham. About thirty people can vouch for him and at least five we spoke to did.'

'Same with Alfie Brown,' Arran said, picking up the baton from Def. 'At the pictures with his dear old mum all of Monday afternoon at the Milton Keynes megaplex or whatever it's called. She keeps all her ticket stubs and pastes them into a scrapbook with a star rating. She showed me. *The Meg* got four, if you're interested. We checked the CCTV and you can clearly see young Alfie and his mum entering at 12.45 p.m. and leaving at 5.55 p.m. No way could he have got from Milton Keynes to Wimbledon, chopped Niamh's tits off, strangled her then driven back to Milton Keynes in that time.'

'Yukiko Watanabe's alibi was even better,' Def said. 'She was sectioned on March 15th. Paranoid schizophrenia. She's been in a secure psychiatric unit ever since.'

Stella watched the way the faces in the room reacted to each story, the uniform expression of depression, or maybe disgust, as each alibi was recounted. It couldn't be helped. But she needed something to gee them up.

'OK. So they're a bust, but we never really held out much hope, did we? Trolls are just that. Trolls. They stay in their caves and pour out their bile over the internet. The man we're looking for? He probably doesn't even have a Facebook account.'

She held up the CCTV photo Cam had found at Sherborne Ropes.

'I had Lucian go to work on this with his crew of geeks. Using an *algorithm*,' she made the word sound like 'magic wand', 'he calculated that the guy in the picture is five-eight. So a bit below average height. Which, I know, before anybody says anything, is about as much help as a chocolate truncheon, but there we are.'

62

SATURDAY 25TH AUGUST 8.35 P.M.
SOHO

Stella thanked her Uber driver and stepped out into the warm, humid Soho air. She inhaled the smells and tried to separate them as an exercise. Roast duck, coconut cakes, spilled beer on the pavement outside an Irish pub and, above it all, car exhaust fumes. She checked her watch for the tenth time and, realising she was early, headed away from Gerrard Street intending to walk for ten minutes and try to calm her jitters.

Reaching the junction of Wardour Street and Brewer Street, she looked right at the fenced-in churchyard of St Anne's. A few winos had created an encampment in one corner and they, together with a handful of assorted mutts, were basking in the late-evening sun.

To her right, a door marked BongoMedia.com burst open. A scrawny, bearded thirty-something man wearing a grey tweed cap staggered backwards into the street, crashing into her. He yelled into the slowly closing door.

'Ah'm the boss and if I want a topless model on the front cover then that's what we're doin', and nae wummun with Pee-Em-fuckin-Ess is gonnae tell me different!' he shouted in a broad Glaswegian accent. 'In fact, I'm comin' back in there and ah'll do it ma'sel.'

Then he pulled the door open and headed back into the dark stairwell beyond.

'Whoa there!' Stella shouted, stepping forward and gripping him by the upper arm, keen to avoid his assaulting whoever he'd been swearing at. 'You need to calm down.'

As the door closed behind Stella, he tore himself free, turned, stumbled and fell against her, throwing out a hand that ended up clutching her left breast.

'Get your hands off me!' she said, pushing him away.

'Ah, God, another fuckin' feminist. Whassa matter, darlin'? You on the rag an' all, are ye?'

She spun him around and slammed his face back into the wall so that his right cheek was jammed up against the grubby paintwork. Then she hissed into his left ear.

'I *am* a feminist, as it happens. I'm also a police officer. So unless you want me to arrest you and charge you with sexual assault, I suggest you just take yourself off somewhere quiet and get yourself straight, OK?'

She let him go and spun him round to face her. He was pale, and his red-rimmed eyes were having difficulty meeting hers.

'Copy that,' he said meekly, before sliding past her and pushing through the doors.

She let a minute or so pass, using the time to steady her breathing, then emerged into the sunlight and headed back towards Gerrard Street. *Next time you're early, sit at the bar*, she told herself.

————

She walked through the door of Dumpling Palace at nine on the dot. Mr Yun, bald head shining in the red lamplight, beamed when he saw her. His gold teeth competed with his hairless pate in an effort to dazzle Stella.

'Mrs Stella! You here at last! Your party upstairs already.'

He shouted in Cantonese at a passing waitress dressed in a scarlet silk dress. She stopped and came over to Stella.

'Come with me, please?'

Mr Yun had given Stella a corner table with a commanding view of the rest of the diners. Apparently deep in conversation were Lucian, Gareth and Jamie. Facing out, Jamie saw Stella first. He smiled and stood.

'Stella! We thought you'd got called in.'

She smiled, ignoring the flittering butterflies in her stomach, and went over to greet him. He kissed her on both cheeks, then let Lucian and Gareth do the same.

Once they were all seated again, and Stella had a glass of white wine in her hand, she looked over the table at Gareth. His unruly mop of black hair hung over his eyes, which were a deep, almost black-brown and crinkled with good humour. She'd met him a handful of times and didn't think she'd ever seen him without a smile on his face.

'How are you, Gareth?' she asked.

'I'm fine, Stella my girl,' he said in his soft Welsh accent. 'I just need to persuade Lucian to make an honest man out of me and I'll be set for life.'

Lucian grinned.

'Marriage is old-fashioned.'

'Not for us, boyo! It's the latest thing! You want to get in on the action before it's passé.'

As they bantered, their waitress arrived with a steaming plateful of translucent pastry buns with cinched tops tied off with bright-green chives.

'Chef make special pork bun for you. On the house. Mr Yun sends his compliments.'

Jamie raised his eyebrows at Stella.

'Come on then. What have you got on Mr Yun? Or are they protection buns?'

She took one and bit it in half, savouring the beautifully balanced flavours: the fragrant roast pork itself plus garlic, chilli, ginger and Chinese five-spice.

359

'It's nothing like that. I got a Triad gang off his back a few years ago. He took it as a debt of honour to keep me in dim sum till my dying day.'

———

An hour and several bottles of wine later, the quartet were laughing as Gareth told another of his 'Tales From Year One' as he called them.

'So you see, because it's so hot, I've gone in wearing Birkenstocks, haven't I? No socks, obviously. And this little girl in my class, she keeps putting her hand up while I'm telling them about sports day. They all do it, you see, trying it on so they can go and arse about in the cloakrooms. "Mr Hughes, I really need the toilet," she says. So in the end I give in and I say, "OK, then, Beulah, off you go, then." Anyway, she goes to squeeze past me to get to the door and she just lets go, doesn't she? All down her legs and all over my bloody Birkenstocks! Soaked, I was.'

Stella wiped her eyes and looked to her right at Jamie, who was wheezing with laughter. He turned and caught her glance and the laughter turned into a smile. A drunken smile, but a very nice one. He leaned a little closer. He smelled good.

'Your friends are lovely, DCI Cole,' he said.

'Yes, we are,' Gareth said. 'And we're very protective of our dear little fag-hag. So, Jamie. I think it's time you spilled the beans.'

'What about?'

'You and our lovely Stella here.'

'Gareth!' Stella said indignantly, eyes widening. 'Leave him alone.'

'No, Stella. I need to know. Jamie, what, exactly, are your intentions towards my soul sister here?'

Jamie grinned and straightened up.

'Strictly honourable.'

'Oh well, Stel,' Gareth said. 'Just another night in with your Rabbit, then.'

Her mouth dropped open as Gareth roared with laughter.

'I don't believe you, you Welsh knob!' she finally managed.

Lucian intervened. He had drunk less than Gareth and was clearly relishing the chance to play the diplomat.

'I think what Gareth *meant* to ask you, Jamie, was, what's it like, working at Broadmoor?'

Jamie's smile, so wide a moment earlier, disappeared. He rubbed a hand over his head and took a swig of wine.

'Well, that's a very good question. I suppose the answer is, never dull. I like to think I'm helping people, but obviously the people I'm helping have committed the worst crimes imaginable. So it can be,' he paused, and looked round at Stella, 'challenging. One thing I can tell you is they can appear to be extraordinarily normal men. Some of them, I mean. We've got the ones who howl at the moon and would eat the other patients given half a chance, but there are also, you know, blokes in there who if you met them in the street, you'd just nod and walk on.'

'You've got John Gaddowes in there, haven't you?' Lucian asked. Jamie nodded.

'Murdered seven prostitutes, sex workers, I should say, in Liverpool in 2004. All killed with repeated hammer blows to the face. Worst serial killer in Liverpool's history. They called him, with typical Liverpudlian wit, The Scallywhacker.'

'What's he like?' Gareth said.

'He's one of the *normal* ones,' Jamie said. 'In fact, I was having lunch with him last week. He started crying. I asked him what the matter was and do you know what he said? "I just watched a documentary about how they work donkeys to death in Spain. It was awful." And I'm thinking to myself, John, mate, you bludgeoned seven women to death with a ball-peen hammer and you're crying over donkeys?'

'What did you say?' Stella asked.

Jamie shrugged.

'I said it was awful, which is true. And I suggested he stick to less-upsetting programmes.'

At midnight, they left the restaurant. After exchanging goodnight kisses with Stella and Jamie, Gareth and Lucian wandered up towards Shaftesbury Avenue to look for a cab, leaving 'you two lovebirds', as Gareth had put it, on their own.

Gerrard Street was just as busy as it had been three hours earlier. Stella looked up at the red paper lanterns strung across the narrow pedestrianised street. It made her dizzy and she lurched sideways into Jamie, grabbing his arm to steady herself.

'You OK?' he asked her.

'Yeah. Fine. You?'

'Never better.'

'So.'

'So.'

'Doing anything tomorrow?'

'Nothing special. Thought I might catch up on some reading.'

'Aha. Uh, you know when Gareth asked you about your intentions towards me?'

'Yes.'

'You said they were strictly honourable.'

'They are.'

'That's a bit disappointing.'

'Why?'

'Because, *Mister* Jamie Hooke, I was going to invite you back to mine.'

Jamie smiled.

'I said they were strictly honourable. I didn't say they were chaste.'

Stella grinned.

'Well, in that case, would you like to *honourably* come back to Lisson Grove with me?'

He nodded.

'I rather think I would.'

63

SUNDAY 26TH AUGUST 9.15 A.M.
LISSON GROVE

Stella woke with a pounding headache, a dry mouth and her right arm flung out across Jamie's chest. Lying face-down, she raised her head off the pillow and turned to him. He was looking at her and smiling. *Nice eyes. Soft.*

'Morning,' she mumbled. 'What time is it?'

'Morning. Nine-fifteen.'

'How long have you been staring at me?'

'I wasn't staring, I was gazing.'

'With adoration, I hope.'

'Yes. I was also admiring your tattoo. What is that, a weasel?'

'A weasel? No! It's a mongoose. Her name is Mimi.'

'Very fitting. Brave. Takes on dangerous enemies. And an excellent hunter.'

'Exactly. Now, if you want to avoid Mimi's claws, please could you gaze into my medicine cabinet and bring me some paracetamol?'

'Of course, my lady! Your wish, et cetera.'

Jamie lifted her arm off and placed it beside her, then climbed out of bed.

'Nice arse!' she called after him as he left the bedroom.

'Sexist!' he called back, laughing.

Stella swallowed the painkillers, then lay back on the pillow and closed her eyes.

'I told you he's done it again, didn't I?' she asked.

'You did And it was on the news.'

'I didn't want to discuss it last night. I didn't want to spoil it.'

'Me neither, for the same reason. You want to talk about it now?'

Stella groaned.

'My head hurts too much!'

'Lie still then.'

Stella closed her eyes and snuggled closer to Jamie.

'There're some books on my bedside table if you want,' she said.

She felt his fingers running over the scar on her left shoulder.

'How did you get this? It looks messy.'

'That? A low-life shot me with a stolen pistol.'

'Ouch. I hope you shot him back.'

'Head hurts. Can't talk.'

She woke, unsure how long she'd been asleep. And she felt better. Her head had stopped throbbing. She lay still for a minute or so longer, listening to Jamie's breathing and the quiet whispers as he turned the pages of a book.

She slid her hand under the covers, down towards his groin.

'Oh, hello,' he said, turning to her with a smile. 'Someone's feeling better.'

'Yes, I am. And I'm very hungry.'

'You want to go out for breakfast?'

'Not that kind of hungry.'

Compared to the urgent, drunken sex of the night before, their lovemaking was slower, and much more pleasurable. They took their time to explore each other's bodies, finding out what each liked and where their magic places were.

Afterwards, Stella climbed out of bed and headed for the shower.

Towelling her hair dry, she looked in the mirror. She smiled at herself.

'*Now* let's go out for breakfast,' she said with a smile as she returned to the bedroom to get dressed.

Half an hour later they were sitting outside the Regent's Bar and Kitchen in the centre of Regent's Park.

'What can I get you?' a young waitress asked them in what Stella considered to be an indecently perky American accent.

'What do you recommend for a hangover?' Stella asked with a grin.

'Oh, definitely our Big Breakfast. You've got free-range eggs, scrambled, poached or fried, smoked streaky bacon, Cumberland sausage, chestnut mushrooms, black pudding – which, personally, I think is a tad weird, I mean *blood pudding*? – anyways, oregano-roasted tomato, baked beans and toasted sourdough.'

'Yes please. With fried eggs. And English Breakfast tea, please. Lots.'

'Two of those, please,' Jamie said.

'Sure! Coming right up.'

Rose bushes flanked the path leading from the Inner Circle road to the cafe. Their peach scent wafted across the terrace. Stella inhaled deeply and smiled at Jamie.

'Last night was lovely. Thank you.'

'You're welcome. I enjoyed myself too. Your friends are great. Especially Gareth.'

'I think he fancies you.'

'Ah. Sadly, he's going to be disappointed.'

'Can we talk shop?'

Jamie shook his head then pushed his fingers through his hair.

'Sure. I don't think either of us has the sort of job where we can just switch off at the weekend anyway. Fire away. Just promise me we can go to the zoo afterwards.'

Their waitress reappeared with two pots of tea, set two white china mugs down alongside a jug of milk, beamed at them, and was gone. Stella spoke.

'Moira Lowney was enucleated. You know what that means, right?'

'Eyes removed. One of my patients did it to himself a year or so ago. He used a teaspoon. It's surprisingly common.'

'Yeah? Well it's also surprisingly horrible to look at. He's officially classified as a serial killer now. Which you would think means I get a blank cheque from Callie but it's not like that. Austerity is the worst swear word in the job at the moment.'

'OK, but thinking's free. Let's do some of that. What do we know about him at this point? Go back to the basics.'

'He's a psychopath. He selects high-profile Christian women living in London as his targets. We think he had a deeply religious, possibly abusive childhood, with a domineering mother. He is drugging women, torturing them, then strangling them.'

'What sort of a feeling do you have for him? What's he like?'

'You said you thought this guy is intelligent. An organised killer. That fits with what we know of his MO. And he is definitely forensically aware. We've not pulled a single print, a single DNA sample, a hair, a clothing fibre. Nothing. There was a small trace of talc in Sister Moira's office, on the back of her chair, so we think he's gloving up before he goes to work on them.'

'Don't they say it's impossible for a criminal not to leave something behind, and the scene not to leave something on the criminal?'

'Locard's Exchange Principle, yes. But just because it's there doesn't mean you're going to find it. And with the budget cuts we've had imposed on us over the last few years, everything's been slashed to the bone. CSIs, equipment, external consultants,' she said, pointing at Jamie's chest. 'Lucian told me he even had to pay for some evidence bags out of his own pocket. They'd literally used up their budget and he couldn't get any until next month.'

At that moment, their waitress placed two enormous plates of food in front of them. Stella inhaled deeply. The mingled smells of meat, eggs, mushrooms and beans made her groan in anticipation. She reckoned the food in front of her was enough for at least a full day.

'Oh, God, that smells good. Forgive me, but I'm going to do some serious eating for a bit.'

They ate in silence for a while until, with only half her plate cleared, Stella leaned back and took a swig of tea. She stroked her belly, which felt as though it might burst.

'Need a rest,' she said.

'Me, too. Have you ever eaten one of these to the end?'

She shook her head.

'I normally have the Eggs Benedict.'

Jamie frowned. He looked down at his fork, on which a slice of sausage was currently impaled.

'There's something bugging me about the torture. It's ringing a bell.'

Stella nodded.

'I had a feeling when I saw Sister Moira's body. Like I'd seen it before. But it wasn't on another case.'

'Where then?' Jamie asked, popping the piece of sausage into his mouth.

'Not sure, that's the trouble. And there's a memory I have of arguing with my dad that seems to be really important. Let me think for a minute.'

Stella closed her eyes, feeling the sun warm her lids and letting the splodges of orange dance across her inner vision. The chatter of their fellow diners faded as Stella tried to go inside her own mind, searching for the memory.

Whether it was the lingering effects of the previous night's alcohol consumption, or being out for breakfast with Jamie, she didn't know, but she suddenly realised what her half-remembered argument with her father had been about. He and Stella's mum had taken the sixteen-year-old Stella to the National Gallery, and she'd complained, at length, about their choice of outing. But one painting had captivated Stella. And she was standing in front of it now.

A woman held out a gold plate on which a pair of eyes looked dolefully up at the ceiling. And there had been another in the same exhibition. A pale-skinned, muscular man, naked except for a loin cloth, hung by his wrists from a tree. His torso and limbs were pierced by arrows: through his left forearm, left pectoral muscle, almost over the nipple, lower belly and right thigh.

What was the show called, Stel? Come on, think!

Her eyes seemed to snap open of their own accord.

'Martyrs!' she said loudly, drawing a few curious stares. Then, in a quieter voice, so that Jamie had to lean towards her. 'He's martyring them. I went to an art exhibition when I was sixteen. It was called Sacred and Profane. One painting had a woman with her eyes on a plate, another this naked man with arrows sticking out of him like a hedgehog.'

Jamie nodded.

'I've seen those images, too,' he said. 'And if you don't mind, I've got a better idea than going to the zoo.'

———

An hour later, Stella and Jamie entered the National Gallery's foyer. The architect had obviously had a thing for marble. Huge rust-red columns of the stuff towered above them, topped with intricately carved capitals. The floor dazzled the eye with an intricate pattern of tiles in shades ranging from silvery-white to gold.

The place was packed. Throngs of foreign tourists. Art students carrying unwieldy wooden easels and oversized pads of paper. And, she supposed, a few Londoners drawn into this palace of high culture as a respite from the searing heat of Trafalgar Square, visible beyond the plate-glass doors.

Jamie extended his right arm, elbow crooked. She threaded her arm through his and walked beside him, sensing what he wanted to show her but content to be led.

She had to walk fast to keep up with his long-legged stride. At one point, an oncoming gaggle of young Japanese women in matching navy blazers, tartan kilts, long white socks and black patent leather loafers split them up. As Stella wove around them she found the time to admire Jamie's backside in the faded jeans she'd come to think of as his trademark.

Back alongside him, she asked him where they were going.

'Room 24. It's just along here.'

He led her into a large, rectangular gallery filled with gigantic paintings, mostly depicting religious scenes. As he pointed to a painting at the far end, Stella gasped.

There it was. The second painting she remembered seeing, or another treatment of the same subject. They stood before it, looking up at the artwork.

He was naked, except for a flimsy wrap of pale fabric at his groin, and he was beautiful. That was Stella's first thought. A man Gareth would probably nod towards and utter some Welsh phrase meaning 'I'd give him one'. And he seemed unconcerned at the arrows that an unseen archer had shot into his chest, side and calf.

'Saint Sebastian,' they said together.

'And Sarah Sharpe,' Jamie added. 'There's more, come on.'

They walked fast through the dawdling tourists and art lovers until Jamie brought her to a stop by laying a hand on her arm. He pointed at a painting that had Stella inhaling sharply.

The Renaissance painting hanging on the plum-coloured wall in front of her was titled 'Saint Agatha'.

The artist, Lorenzo Lippi, had depicted the saint as a large-eyed young woman in the fashionable dress of the times: rich velvets in deep blue and gold, with white linen cuffs, a double strand of pearls at her throat and her chestnut hair swept up from her neck apart from a few loose strands.

In her hands she held a pair of shears, but what held Stella's attention was the silver salver in front of her, on which, displayed as if they were sweetmeats, were a pair of milk-white breasts.

Jamie peered at the plaque screwed to the wall beside the painting.

'Saint Agatha was fifteen when the Roman prefect Quintianus

tried to force himself upon her. She'd vowed to remain a virgin and rejected his advances. He had her tortured, which included having her breasts cut off with pincers.'

'Like Niamh Connolly.'

'Like Niamh Connolly,' he agreed.

Stella looked at Jamie, who was looking at her intently.

'He's copying Old Masters.'

'Not just old,' Jamie said. 'Look.'

He pointed at the plaque. Beneath the text explaining the meaning of the painting, the gallery curator had added a reproduction of a second painting depicting Saint Agatha, this one by a young female American artist, a contemporary of Stella's.

The depiction of the mutilations was almost clinical in its accuracy, the fatty and glandular tissues inside the breast, and the supporting pectoral muscle and ribs inside that clearly visible. The saint held a plate on which the severed breasts had been placed like fruit.

Stella's heart was bumping in her chest. Sister Moira's eyes were pleading with her to make a connection. She looked up at Jamie.

'You know I told you about the third victim? Sister Moira Lowney?'

'Yes.'

'He gouged her eyes out and put them on a plate. Is that a saint, too?'

'I'm not sure. We could try the bookshop. No, wait! I've got a better idea. I know the perfect man to ask. He's a friend and he's just published a book about martyrs. He's the Professor of Moral Philosophy at University College London.'

They found a quiet corner and Jamie made a call. Stella took the opportunity to observe him as his eyes roved across the walls and ceiling while he waited for his friend to pick up. This close she could see the fine creases fanning out from the corners of his eyes. She thought they suited him. His eyes locked onto hers and he smiled. Then he spoke.

'Peter? Hi. It's Jamie. Listen, I'm going to have to keep this brief but I'm helping the police with this serial killer case.' He laughed.

'No, not from a cell. We're in the National Gallery.' A pause as he listened. 'Me and the SIO on the case. A DCI Stella Cole.' His eyes dropped to Stella's again and he grinned. 'Yes, she is. Very. So, here's the question. Was there a martyr, or a Christian saint, who had her eyes gouged out?'

He listened for a minute or so, nodding a couple of times.

'OK, thanks, Peter. I'm going to introduce you by email to DCI Cole. I have a feeling she's going to want to talk to you in more depth. Yeah, OK. Bye.'

He ended the call.

'And?' Stella asked, feeling sure it would be good news.

'Saint Lucy,' Jamie said. 'AKA Lucia of Syracuse. The stories vary but, according to Peter, she is famous for having her eyes gouged out by Paschasius, the Governor of Syracuse, because she wouldn't make a pagan sacrifice. She is often depicted in art with her eyes resting on a gold plate.'

Stella ran a hand over the top of her head and then grabbed her ponytail, tugging it through her fist as she tried to tame her racing thoughts.

'Renaissance art. Christian martyrs. Do they sound like the interests of a man of low-to-average intelligence, possibly with learning difficulties?' she asked.

'No. They sound like the interests of the complete opposite type of man.'

'Shit! I hate dealing with intelligent murderers.'

64

MONDAY 27TH AUGUST 8.55 A.M.
WAPPING, EAST LONDON

Andy Robbins had served as the *Sun*'s news editor for three years. Before that, he'd spent over thirty years working as a tabloid journalist in the UK, Australia and the US. And in that time, he'd grown a very sensitive pair of antennae or, as he liked to put it, 'bullshit detectors'.

His detectors were able to tell him reliably whether a lead was going to be gold or dross. He reserved his deepest contempt for the people who called, or increasingly emailed, him to confess to murders, especially murders of children.

'Another fucking slug-fucker,' was his melodious catchphrase on slamming the phone down on one more of the 'I did it' brigade.

So the hand-addressed letter sitting on top of his in-tray this Monday morning did not fill him with hope. He picked it up and slit it open anyway. *Never let your prejudices get in the way of a good story* was one of his many mottoes and he muttered it now. Because you never knew.

As he read, his mouth dropped open. This was it. The real deal. The twenty-first century's 'From Hell' letter.

Dear Mr Robbins,

You will know of Niamh Connolly, Sarah Sharpe, and Moira Lowney. They died by my hand.

These women deserved to die. For hypocritical adherence to a cult of cruelty. They called themselves Christians. I, call them MALADJUSTED TORTURERS.

The police will say, I am a monster. You may be tempted to follow their lead. But that is a CHIMAERA! Yes, monsters exist in this world of ours, but, I am not one of them. No! The true MONSTERS are those who corrupt the minds and morals of children, who maim them and ROB them of their innocence.

Please understand, I, do not derive SEXUAL pleasure from what I do – I am not a pervert – but only satisfaction, that, finally, the world will wake up to what is being done to children in the name of religion.

Do you think, I, am a crank? Then I will prove you wrong! I cut Niamh Connolly's BREASTS from her living body. I punctured Sarah Sharpe's pretensions with arrows. Check with the police. And Moira Lowney, another hypocrite, I enucleated. Her EYES bear witness to the truth of my message.

Print this, and help me bring my message, to those who claim the MORAL HIGH GROUND, but who, actually, wallow in the very depths of DEPRAVITY AND CORRUPTION.

The FIRES OF HELL await you! The Devil LIVES on in me!

I am, your obedient servant,

THE FOURTH HORSEMAN

PS I, am not done with them yet. You, have been warned.

Robbins wiped his top lip free of sweat, which had gathered there as he was reading. His heart was racing. He jumped up from his desk and poked his head out of the doorway of his office.

'Jodi!' he shouted across the newsroom, beckoning a leggy blonde reporter who had a mobile clamped between her cheek and her shoulder. 'Get your arse in here, pronto!'

As he watched her end her call, Robbins was already working on the angles. *The Fourth Horseman was Death. Too literary. Nobody will get it. He's killing high-profile Christian women. We need a better name.*

'Yes, boss, what is it?' Jodi asked, perching on the edge of a chair.

'Get onto one of your contacts in the Met and find out whether Niamh Connolly's murderer cut her tits off. Whether Sarah Sharpe's shot her with arrows. And finally, what the fuck does "enucleated" mean? Because, according to her killer, that's what he did to her.'

Jodi grinned at him.

'It means to have your eyes removed. You've got a story, haven't you?'

'Depends. If your tame plod confirms it, we're gonna scoop the rest of the bastards big time.'

65

TUESDAY 28TH AUGUST 8.00 A.M.

Stella was sitting at her desk, phone clamped to her ear, deep in conversation with an intelligence officer from the National Crime Agency when Garry hurried across the incident room with a copy of that day's *Sun* folded in his hand.

He opened out the tabloid and pointed at the headline, a screamer in hundred-and-eight-point type that took up over half the available real estate on the front page.

SERIAL KILLER
'LUCIFER' TELLS
THE *SUN* 'I'LL
KILL AGAIN'!

Most of the rest was devoted to a facsimile of a typed letter, with certain words and phrases blacked out.

'I'll call you back. We've got a shit-hits-fan situation. Thanks, John.'

She ended the call and grabbed the paper from Garry's hand.

'He's written a letter, boss,' Garry said.

'Yeah, yeah, I can see that.' She swiped a palm across her face. 'Sorry, Garry. Didn't mean to be sharp. For God's sake, what's his game?'

'I think you know, boss. He's taunting us, isn't he? Reckons he's invulnerable. Classic psychopathic trait. Egotistical narcissist.'

'Wow! Did you go to bed with the dictionary under your pillow last night or something?'

Garry grinned.

'I bin readin' under dem covers, baas, lernin' me ABC when me shoulda bin sleepin',' he said in a burlesque West Indian accent.

Stella's eyes widened and her smile, though shocked, was genuine.

'Could you just shut up, please, DS Haynes, before one or both of us gets hauled up for about eighty-five infringements of the Met's Diversity and Inclusion Policy?'

'Sorry,' he said, his voice returned to normal. 'What do you think, though?'

'Get onto the *Sun* and get that letter. I want the original, too. They'll probably be lawyered up to their eyeballs so find someone from the CPS who owes us a favour. Oh, and Garry?' she shouted at his retreating back.

'Yes?'

'If it's a fake, it means someone leaked the details of the mutilations. No point looking, this place makes the *Titanic* look watertight. But be on your guard, OK?'

Garry nodded, then left at a trot, weaving around huddles of detectives on his way to his desk.

———

Stella was deep into one of the SCAS reports piled up on her desk, when Garry reappeared in the doorway.

'Boss?'

'Blimey, that was quick!'

'No. It's the *Sun*. The news editor, I mean. He's here.'

He stood aside and Stella took in the sight of a burly man in his mid-fifties, pale complexion flushed with alcohol and a suit so rumpled even the old-school detectives in the room would have advised him to get it dry-cleaned.

Stella stood, trying to mask the anger she could feel like a cold weight in her chest. She spoke.

'DCI Cole. I'm the senior—'

'The SIO on the three murders, yeah, I know. We're covering them, remember? Andy Robbins.'

He held out his hand and, for a second or two, Stella considered scoring a cheap point by not taking it. But manners, and her sense that she might need an ally in the media, won out.

When they were both seated, with Garry leaning against the wall behind Robbins, Stella spoke.

'So, Mr Robbins. What can we do for you?'

'You saw the story we ran, right?'

Stella picked up that day's *Sun* and flipped it across the desk at him.

'It was hard to miss.'

'He wrote to us. A letter.'

'I know,' Stella said, feeling the exasperation growing uncontrollably. 'And you gave us a massive headache by publishing it. As you did by publishing leaked comments by someone involved in the investigation. In fact, DS Haynes here was on his way to see the CPS to get reinforcements before asking for it.'

Robbins smirked. Clearly enjoying himself.

'No need,' he said.

He reached into his inside pocket and pulled out a transparent plastic sleeve inside which she could see a cream envelope, with a handwritten address and a postage stamp. He held it out to her and she snatched it from his pudgy hand.

'That is today's biggest surprise, so far,' she managed to say.

He shrugged his beefy shoulders, straining the material of his suit.

'The *Sun* always likes to help the boys,' he paused, 'and girls, in blue. We kept a copy for our archives. That's the original. I'm guessing there'll be all kinds of clever stuff your techy people can do with it.'

'I'm sure there is. Tell me, who's handled this letter at your office?'

'The guys in the mailroom and me.'

'Good. Would you mind giving us a set of fingerprints so we can eliminate you when we test it? We'll have to send someone over to your offices later to get the rest.'

He shrugged.

'Not if it will help. But I want a promise they won't go onto any database.' He paused, and grinned. 'In writing. Please.'

Stella returned the smile.

'Of course. I'll type it up now. You can take it with you when you leave.' She turned in her chair. 'Garry, can you take Mr Robbins down to Forensics for elimination prints after this, please?'

'Sure, boss.'

She smiled at Robbins. A genuine expression this time. This was the best and biggest lead they'd pulled since the case had exploded into life with the murder of Niamh Connolly.

'Thank you,' she said.

He batted away the words as if they were flies bothering him.

'You're welcome. I just hope that if, sorry, when, you catch him, you'll look kindly on the paper that helped you. Maybe an exclusive with the killer, or a profile of you? And a few extra little titbits the rest of the pack don't get their hands on wouldn't go amiss, either.'

So that was it. A lead for a lead. Well, it wasn't such a bad bargain. And Stella knew she'd be able to keep the really important stuff back when she needed to.

She favoured Robbins with another smile.

'I'm sure we can find a path we're both happy to walk down.'

Stella watched as Garry led Robbins away. Then she saw something that brought her up short. Letting Garry get a few yards ahead of him, Robbins slowed briefly at Roisin's desk and turned to look at her. Stella could have sworn she saw him wink and mouth something.

Once Robbins had left with Garry, discussing football, Stella called Roisin over.

'What did Robbins say to you?' she asked, trying to keep her voice light, unconcerned.

'Huh! Prick asked if I'd ever considered modelling.'

'Arse!' Stella said.

Back at her desk, Stella pulled on a fresh pair of gloves from the box in her murder bag, which sat beneath her desk. She'd paid a struck-off plastic surgeon to remove her fingerprints with a process of his own invention a few years back, as a precaution when hunting down her family's killers. Ironically, this meant wearing gloves to handle evidence was more important than ever. Rather than muddying the waters with extraneous prints, she'd muddy them another way: if she were to be seen handling a knife, say, or, as in this case, a document, and didn't leave her prints, questions would be asked. Questions she would rather not answer. So. Gloves.

She cleared a space on her desk and removed the envelope from the plastic sleeve.

Lucifer had handwritten the address. No scratchy capitals in dried blood, instead, flowing, elegant script in what appeared to be blue fountain pen ink.

> Andrew Robbins, Esq.,
> News Editor,
> The Sun,
> 1, London Bridge Street,
> London,
> E1 9GF.

Stella thought her mum, an English teacher, dead some years now from bowel cancer, would have found the use of so many commas fussy and old-fashioned.

The frank cancelling the stamp had a generic LONDON mark so would be useless. And since stamps became self-adhesive in 1993,

DNA from the saliva of villains stupid enough to use their tongues instead of a swipe with a damp cloth had also disappeared. It didn't mean forensic examination of the envelope was a waste, though. It never was, Stella reflected, especially when the chief scientist examining the product was Lucian Young.

By a stroke of good fortune, Robbins had slit the envelope to open it, rather than unpeeling the flap, so that created a further potential area for investigation.

Stella turned the envelope over. The back was blank. *Oh well, I suppose a sender address would have been too much to hope for, eh, Stel?* She pulled the letter clear and unfolded it, laying it flat on top of the plastic folder.

She read slowly, paying attention to every single word, to the use of all capitals, to the punctuation, which was even more fussy than that on the envelope. And to the PS, which sent a sliver of cold fear through her. Because she knew what it felt like to be on a mission to kill. If Lucifer announced he hadn't finished, she knew that unless they closed it fast, there would be more horrors to come.

With the letter refolded and placed back inside the envelope and then the plastic sleeve, she called Roisin over.

'Yes, boss?'

'Rosh, can you take this down to Forensics, please? Usual tests, but also can you see if you can scare up a writing expert?'

'A graphologist, you mean?'

Stella shook her head.

'No. I don't buy all that bullshit about personality traits being revealed in people's handwriting. I mean someone who could look at the text and give us some idea about the person who wrote it based on the language. You know, is it likely they went to university? Are they using East End dialect?' She rapped her knuckles down on her desk in frustration. 'I don't know if that's even possible. But can you try?'

Roisin smiled and took the plastic folder.

'Of course. Leave it with me.'

Roisin took the stairs down to the forensics office, pausing on the way to extract the letter and read it.

You're a solid-gold fruitloop, aren't you? And I'm the DI who's going to put you behind bars. But not just yet. Let's give the boss some room to screw things up first, eh? Maybe they'll appoint a new CIO if a few more women get sliced and diced, then I should be in the frame.

She approached Lucian, who had his eye pressed against a microscope.

'Hi, Lucian,' she said.

He turned and smiled.

'Hi, Rosh. Haven't seen you down here for a while.' His eyes flicked down to the folder. 'What have you got for me?'

She held the folder out in front of her like a school prefect offering a present to the headteacher.

'Mr Top Science Bod, and officially the best-dressed man in Paddington Green, I give you the Lucifer letter. It's the original. The one the *Sun* published.'

Lucian took it from her.

'Wow! Who'd you threaten to get that?'

'Oh, you!' she said with a grin, pushing her flirtation engine to maximum power. She knew he was gay, but even gay men liked a bit of attention from an attractive women was her take on it. 'I didn't threaten anyone. As a matter of fact, the news editor just handed it in. So, what I'm wondering, and I know how busy you are, is whether you could let me know if there's any DNA on it, any prints, anything physical that might give us a lead. And also, I don't suppose you have some cool database of technical experts, do you?'

'I do, as a matter of fact, right there,' he pointed at his PC. 'Who do you need?'

'A textual analysis expert. I think it would be good to analyse the language of the letter, see what we can deduce about Lucifer. Whether he's a graduate or failed all his GCSEs, that kind of thing.'

Lucian smiled.

'OK, leave it with me. I know a couple of academics who'd be perfect. I can't promise when I can get it done, they all have their own schedules, obviously, and I—'

'That's fine, that's fine!' she interrupted, smiling so wide she thought her cheeks might crack. 'Whenever. And send the results straight to me, please. The boss looks like her poor brain is about to explode from data coming in from all over. The least I can do is work on this independently for a while. It'll probably come back clean after all. Isn't that what usually happens?'

Lucian sighed.

'Yup. I'm afraid so. Despite what the telly geeks seem able to do, we're really at the mercy of budgets as much as anything else. You know that. But yes, if I do get anything, I'll email it to you.'

'You're a sweetheart,' Roisin said, then turned and left the Lucifer letter behind her.

———

'Did she turn you then, Luce?' a red-haired blood-spatter analyst asked, grinning to reveal teeth adorned with jewelled braces.

'Nope.'

'Not for want of trying, though,' she said.

They both laughed. They'd seen all the many and varied ways detectives tried to get their pet projects pushed up the forensics department's to-do list, from cajolery to flirting, bluster to bribes of cream cakes. Roisin's efforts didn't even have the virtue of originality.

Donning gloves, Lucian put the transparent wallet to one side. It would need dusting for prints, which he felt sure would come back as belonging to Robbins.

He took the envelope to a spotless stainless-steel work table. Four high-intensity halogen spotlights glared down at carefully calculated angles so they rendered the large rectangle entirely shadow-free.

He removed the letter and spread it out beside the envelope. Next he placed a thin sheet of transparent, matte acetate over both, and smoothed it down with his palms, the nitrile gloves dragging over the surface of the protective cover.

Retrieving a high-end digital SLR camera from a workbench, he took a series of pictures, some with flash, some without, angling the camera so it cast no shadows over the two documents. Once he was satisfied, he laid the camera aside and removed the sheet of acetate.

'OK, then, Lucifer, let's see what you can tell us,' he said.

He pulled a swivel chair over and adjusted the height. Taking a magnifying glass from the pocket of his lab coat, he examined the front of the envelope.

And he smiled.

'Hey, Izzie, come and have a look at this,' he called to the blood-spatter analyst.

She got up from her desk and wandered over, standing beside him and leaning down. He offered her the magnifying glass.

'Huh,' she said, handing it back. 'No fool like a psychopathic fool.'

Stuck to the extreme righthand edge of the stamp, along the perforations, was a hair. Not a very long hair, perhaps an eighth of an inch; it was very fine and pale brown. Lucian peered closer and saw the waxy white root.

'What do you think? Eyelash?'

'Yeah, or maybe an eyebrow hair.'

'Can you get DNA from it?'

'It's got the root, so we might be able to get nuclear DNA,' he said. 'Given enough money and time. From that we could get an individual profile we could match against NDNAD. The shaft will only give us mitochondrial DNA.'

'Which would do what?'

'Which would only tell us whether they shared a mother with someone on the database.'

Lucian took a pair of fine-tipped tweezers from a black leather tool roll and teased the eyelash away from the stamp, before sealing it in a glassine sachet and placing that in a clear plastic evidence bag, which he labelled, dated and signed. Then he took out a scalpel from its elastic loop and worked the tip under one corner of the stamp.

Easing the blade deeper in with a series of tiny sawing motions, he took several minutes to lift it clear and place it, face-down, beside the envelope. The back of the stamp was clean. Not so much as a speck of dust marred the sticky surface, even though it might have been designed to collect it.

He spent the rest of the day examining the letter and envelope for physical evidence. After he'd run them under all his alternative light sources, from UV to different colour filters, he moved on to dusting the paper with fingerprint powder. And he drew a blank.

Last thing before leaving for the day, he called Roisin.

'We found what appears to be an eyelash stuck to the edge of the stamp. It's still got its root. The probability we can get a DNA profile is between sixty and seventy per cent, though. Hair's rubbish for DNA compared to body fluids or skin cells, I'm afraid. What do you want to do?'

'First, congratulate you for some excellent work. Second, I don't want to waste budget on something that, in all probability, won't even be the killer's DNA. It could be the postman's, somebody in the sorting office, even one of the journalists at the *Sun*.'

'Agreed. So no fast-track, then?'

'It'd cost too much money, and we're haemorrhaging it faster than Lucifer's vics, to be honest. Send it off, but tell them we're happy to wait in line.'

'You're the boss.'

———

And Roisin thought, as she ended the call, *Not yet*.

66

Five days after Stella had watched Adrian Trimmets leave with the case file, he emailed her his profile. Not 'preliminary', she noted. *Very confident.* Remembering his modest assertion that he would try to provide something genuinely useful, she double-clicked the icon and began reading.

> DISCLAIMER: this profile is based on available evidence and data as supplied by the Metropolitan Police Service. All conclusions, recommendations and analysis are given in good faith but are only guidelines. It is quite possible that the killer may exhibit all, some or none of the following characteristics. Dr Adrian Trimmets offers no warranty as to the accuracy, usefulness or effectiveness of this report and asserts that any and all responsibility for successfully apprehending the killer profiled in the following pages lies with the Senior Investigating Officer, DCI S. Cole, and her colleagues, and not with Dr Trimmets.

'Brilliant!' Stella said out loud, as she prepared to read on. 'The ultimate jobsworth. I bet you'll be all too keen to claim the credit when we do catch him, though, won't you?'

She clicked over to the first page. And sighed. He had apparently just copied and pasted from a textbook.

> Serial killers can be divided into two types: organised and disorganised...

She skipped ahead, looking for something original, her heart sinking with each fresh sentence.

> The killer is likely to be a white male, aged between seventeen and forty-five. Probably of lower-than-average intelligence, although he may exhibit certain high-functioning intellectual abilities.
>
> He will have poor social skills and will be either unemployed or employed in a low-skilled job. If he is employed in a high-skilled job, he will probably have received disciplinary warnings for poor performance. He will live alone or with a parent or parents. If he lives with a partner, he may be physically, verbally or sexually abusive.
>
> His choice of victims is significant. It suggests that he bears a grudge against Christian women. The torture indicates that he has a great deal of suppressed anger and further indicates that he probably exhibits poor impulse control in other areas of his life. He may, for example, be a compulsive eater or gambler and/or have problems with alcohol and/or drugs.
>
> The mutilations suggest that he has rudimentary knowledge of anatomy. However, his low IQ means that if he works in the medical profession, it will be on the periphery.

Potential employment could include mortuary assistant, hospital porter or even a printer at a firm of medical publishers.

The killer has grandiose opinions of himself as doing 'great work' to rid the world of religious hypocrisy. If caught, he will probably have a collection of religious books at his home.

He may well be a church-goer, attending so he can monitor the people he despises, although it is possible that his hatred for Christianity means he has adopted a different faith such as Islam, Judaism or Hinduism. He may also be a passionate and vocal atheist.

She'd had enough. Not bothering to print, she closed the document then shouted,

'What. A. Muppet!'

Everyone not on the phone turned to look at her.

Garry grinned.

'Not what you were hoping for, boss?'

'Oh God, you could say that. It's the usual garbage. He might be this, but he might that. He's anywhere from late teens to middle age. Blah blah blah. But the best bit, which I think might just unlock this bastard of a case for us…' She paused. 'In fact, listen up, everyone! I quote: "His choice of victims is significant. It suggests that he bears a grudge against Christian women."'

The laughter was loud. When it had died down, Roisin picked her moment.

'No shit.'

Cam brought a sheet of paper over.

'Boss?'

'Yes, Cam, what've you got? Is that the list of guests off the radio show?'

'Yes. I highlighted all the Christians. Yellow means they've already been on, pink that they've been invited. Apparently they do a mixture of shows, some on different religions, others focusing on just one. It's possible he could target a Jewish woman, or a Muslim, but I don't think he will.'

Stella shook her head.

'Me neither. Thanks, Cam.'

She skim-read the list. Picked out in yellow and pink were twenty-three women, with a brief note beside each name explaining why the producer had picked them for *Women of Faith*.

'What shall we do, boss?'

'I want you to call them. You're going to have to explain the basics, but keep it low-key. No mention of what he did to the first three. Advise them to be extra-cautious and to try and avoid being alone. Have you got their contact details?'

'No. The prick at the BBC gave the GDPR line. I swear to God, boss, it's like a magic amulet now. Everyone bleats out 'GDPR, GDPR!' as if that means they don't have to help us catch a serial killer!'

Stella grinned.

'All right, calm down. I don't want you having a heart attack. They're all reasonably well known, otherwise they wouldn't have been invited onto the show. See what you can dig up online first. If you get stuck, we'll have to have a nice chat to a magistrate about a warrant.'

Cam smiled and nodded.

'Thanks, boss.'

Stella watched her hurry back to her desk, approving of the way she did everything with determination. No slouch, no amble for Camille Wilde. *Good girl.*

67

In the play's interval, Greer set the two glasses of chilled white wine down on the table. She and Callie clinked glasses.

'What do you think so far?' Callie asked.

'I love it,' Greer replied. 'But before we discuss Anthony and Cleopatra, there's something I have to tell you.'

Then the information about Craig Morgan, somewhat evolved from its pure form when Arianna had passed it to Tamsin, leaped from Greer's brain to Callie's. Her eyes popped wide.

'No!' she whispered, her mouth already curving upwards.

'The bigger the better, apparently,' Greer said, maintaining a poker face and reaching for her glass.

'You have no idea how helpful that is,' Callie said.

'I've been watching your press conferences. I think I might have an inkling,' Greer said.

'Aye, well, hopefully I won't have to do any more except to announce we've got him. Either way, I've got that dirty wee clipe by the balls now.'

Greer threw her head back and laughed, drawing amused glances from their fellow patrons.

'You'll have to get wee Arianna to let go o' them first!'

68

TUESDAY 4TH SEPTEMBER 10.00 A.M.

Professor Karlsson had been surprisingly enthusiastic about meeting Stella. Perhaps the idea of discussing the link between Lucifer's MO and the tortures inflicted on Christian martyrs appealed to his academic brain.

'Can you come to my office?' he'd asked the previous day when she'd called. 'All my background research is here.'

She'd agreed and rode carefully through the morning traffic from Lisson Grove to Karlsson's office in Gordon Square. The UCL Philosophy department building was a five-storey Georgian house built of greyish stone. Parking her bike and shaking out her ponytail, she made her way inside and explained to the receptionist who she was and who she'd come to see.

Karlsson came down to collect her in person. Her mental image evaporated as he arrived in front of her, hand outstretched, smile playing on his lips. No shambling, slightly overweight bumbler in his fifties, wearing a tweedy jacket and bowtie. No shapeless corduroys, no erratic hairstyle. In their place, a trim man in his mid-thirties with a neat brown goatee seasoned with silver, and piercing, dark-brown eyes. He wore pinstriped suit trousers and a sharply ironed white shirt, open at the neck.

'DCI Cole, I presume,' he said.

'Stella, please.'

'Peter,' he said. 'Come this way. Did you have an easy drive over? The traffic on the Euston Road is murder, isn't it? No pun intended.'

'I rode over. I live on Lisson Grove, so it was a ten-minute journey.'

He looked her up and down.

'You must be very fit. You don't look out of breath at all.'

She smiled.

'My bike has an engine. I just sit there and twist the throttle when I want to go faster.'

He laughed.

'Ah. That'll teach me to make assumptions. A fatal error for a professor of Moral Philosophy.'

'And for a detective,' she couldn't resist adding as they reached the lifts.

Karlsson's office was a perfect match for his physical appearance, Stella decided, taking it in with a practised eye. No piles of paper or wobbling stacks of books to mess up the perfect proportions of the white-painted room. No half-dead pot plants or off-kilter posters taped to the walls. The two walls not interrupted by the door or the window were lined with shelves on which hundreds of books were arranged alphabetically by author.

A framed photograph of Karlsson shaking hands with the previous prime minister took pride of place on the wall behind the desk, itself a model of precision, and decluttered to the point it might have arrived that morning from a furniture store. The desk phone, closed laptop and lamp might almost have been supplied right along with it, under the heading, 'people who bought this desk also bought these'.

Karlsson gestured to the chair in front of the desk.

'Please.'

He eased his lanky frame into the padded executive number

facing Stella, pressed his fingers together under his chin and smiled, but kept his mouth shut.

Not in a hurry to get stuck in. I like that.

'Thank you for seeing me, Peter,' she said. 'And for your help yesterday. It was a very useful insight.'

He waved the compliment away.

'I've known Jamie for years. We like to help each other out whenever we can.'

'So, I don't know if you follow the news, but three women have been murdered in the last two weeks. I'm the senior investigating officer on all three murders, which we believe were committed by the same man.'

Karlsson spread his hands on the desk. Stella noticed a series of scars that ran across the fingers of his right hand.

'I know we academics have a reputation for being unworldly, especially philosophers, but I do try to keep up on what's going on in the real world. I read the *Guardian* from time to time. I saw one of their articles.'

He smiled as he said this. Stella interpreted the expression as a sign he could see how one who inhabited the ivory towers of academia might appear to a hard-working, real-world copper. He continued speaking.

'You're talking about Niamh Connolly, Sarah Sharpe and Moira Lowney.'

'Yes.'

'Jamie asked me about Saint Lucy. Are you saying one of the dead women had her eyes gouged out?'

'Yes, Moira Lowney. Though I'd ask you not to share that information.'

'Of course, understood. Copycats and so forth. Jamie asked me about martyrs. Is that the line you're pursuing?'

'At the moment, it looks promising, yes.'

'Bloody hell! Old Foxe would be delighted.'

Stella blinked.

'Sorry, Peter. What did you just say?'

He frowned.

'Oh. Nothing. Just that old Foxe would be jumping for joy if he knew.'

'Who was old Fox? A pet?'

'No, a writer. Foxe with an E. He was a sixteenth-century English historian. Best known for a work called *The Actes and Monuments*, but everyone calls it *Foxe's Book of Martyrs*. Why?'

'Again, confidentially, the killer is using the pseudonym MJ Fox when he contacts his victims. Jamie and I were talking about what its significance might be.'

Karlsson nodded.

'Makes sense. If he's obsessed with the pain and cruelty of martyrdom, Foxe gave some pretty graphic descriptions of the methods.'

Stella made a note in her book, while Karlsson asked another question.

'What did he do to the other two women?'

'Sarah Sharpe was shot full of crossbow bolts and Niamh Connolly's breasts were removed and placed on a dinner plate on the table in front of her.'

'Sebastian, Agatha, Lucy.'

'The saints, yes. We believe that the man the media have dubbed Lucifer is copying the methods used in their martyrdoms.'

'Oh no! I mean, yes. But it's more than that. In fact, it's worse than that. Shit!'

Surprised by the sudden expletive, and the academic's sudden pallor and stricken expression, Stella felt her interest quicken.

'What do you mean worse? I'm struggling to think of anything worse than having your eyes cut out while you were still breathing.'

'How about being skinned alive?'

'What?'

'Saint Bartholomew. Originally Bar Talmai, which means Son of Talmai in Aramaic. He was one of the twelve apostles, known as Nathaniel. The stories vary but, in the most popular version, Bartholomew was flayed alive after converting King Polymius, the King of Armenia, to Christianity. The king's brother, Astyages, ordered Bartholomew to be tortured and killed because he feared retribution by the Romans.'

Now it was Stella's turn to frown. What was he talking about? Why this particular saint?

'And you think Lucifer might do that next?'

'I don't *think* he will. I *know* he will.'

'How?'

'Because he's using my book as a guide.'

69

TUESDAY 4TH SEPTEMBER 10.15 A.M.

Karlsson swung round in his chair and grabbed a hardback off a shelf to his right and turned back to face Stella. He handed her the book then waited for her to open it.

She looked down at the book, which smelled faintly of ink. The glossy dust jacket was almost tacky to the touch. *New, then.* A reproduction of a mediaeval etching dominated the front cover. It depicted a woman hanging head down from a scaffold, while grinning yokels set about cutting down through her groin with a two-man saw. She read the title aloud.

'Unholy Pain: Martyrdom and the Cult of Cruelty in the Christian Church.' She looked up at Karlsson, whose eyes were tight with tension. 'Snappy,' she said.

'My publisher's idea. My working title was "Why is God Such a Sadist?"'

'Not a fan, then?'

'I think you could say not. In case you don't follow the *philosophical* news, I am known as Britain's foremost radical atheist.'

Stella nodded.

'Kudos,' she said drily. Then she remembered the final line she'd read of Trimmets's profile. *He may also be a passionate and vocal atheist.*

She opened the book to the dedication page.

'To Cee, for proving love is blind.'

'Who's Cee?'

'My wife.'

'How did she prove love is blind?'

'She's a Church of England vicar.'

Stella frowned.

'Must make for interesting dinner table conversations, then.'

Karlsson smiled.

'As I said, love is blind. We met at a debate organised by the university. On opposing sides, naturally. The teams went to the pub afterwards and by the time I'd presented all my arguments to Cee, I'd also fallen in love.'

Stella smiled, remembering her own courtship. How she, an ambitious cop, had engaged in a stand-up shouting match with Richard Drinkwater, a rising human rights lawyer, after a trial went the wrong way as far as she was concerned.

A year later they'd been smiling through clouds of confetti on the steps of the church in the Berkshire village where she'd grown up.

'Was it mutual?' she asked.

Karlsson waggled his head from side to side.

'In the end. I wore her down. But our dinner table conversations are about to get a whole lot more interesting.'

'Why's that?'

'Cee's about to be ordained as a bishop. Friday next, as a matter of fact. Up at York minster. It's quite the big circus. There'll be TV cameras, the works.'

Stella drew in a breath.

'What's Cee's full name?'

'Celia Thwaites. She's on what you might call the progressive wing of the Church. Uses her maiden name.'

Stella knew the name. Celia Thwaites was on Cam's list. But

was she in yellow, or pink? Stella cursed herself for not being able to remember.

'Peter, did you see my guvnor's press briefing the other day?'

'No, why?'

'Because we're working on the theory that he's targeting high-profile Christian women. Like Celia.'

Karlsson sat back in his chair. He ran a hand over his hair. Scratched at his beard. Looked behind him at the photographs. Then, finally, he looked at Stella.

He shook his head.

'Not possible,' he said.

'I'm sorry, what's not possible?'

'She's not high profile.'

'She will be after next Friday, won't she? Listen, this is very important. Has Celia had any approaches from someone calling themselves MJ Fox?'

Karlsson's eyes were wide and his face was drained of colour. Stella had seen it before; the look when a life lived in one world, an ordered, controlled, everyday world, collided with another. The world Stella and her colleagues dealt with all the time.

'I don't know. I don't think so.'

'Can you call her?' Stella asked.

'Yes. Yes. I can call her. Now, right? You mean call her now?'

'Yes, now. And tell her to make sure she stays with other people.'

Karlsson pulled out his phone.

Stella observed him closely as he spoke to his wife. *Are you the real thing, prof, or is this an act for my benefit?'*

'Hi, darling, it's me. Yeah, fine, look, I have to ask you something and it's incredibly important. What? No! Look, shut up a minute, will you? Has anyone calling themselves MJ Fox approached you recently?' Stella watched as he fell silent, listening, his brown eyes flicking round the room, unable to fix on any given point. 'You're sure?' he said. 'OK, great, great. No. It's fine. Just, if they do, don't do whatever they ask and call 999 instead. Yes. I think so. I've got a detective sitting in my office right now. Oh, and she says to stay with other people. What? Well, try. It's for your own protection. OK. Love you, too. Bye. Bye.'

He put the phone on the desk, then lined it up with the closed laptop.

'That was a no, then?' Stella asked.

Karlsson was breathing rapidly, his face still pale.

'Yes. Cee said she's been being careful after she saw the press briefing. But no MJ Fox. Do you think she's in danger?'

'Not while she's in public. There'll be far too many people watching and no doubt the minster people will have security in place. Probably the local cops, too. But I'll put in a call to the Head of Crime up there. Just so they know.'

'Thank you.'

'But, Peter, even if she isn't now, after Celia's ordained I'm afraid there's a strong possibility she'll be on the killer's radar. She'll fit his victim type.'

'So what do we do?' Karlsson asked. 'She'll be a Church of England bishop. We can't go into hiding!'

Stella blew her cheeks out. Thinking, *after looking at Cam's list, we'd blow the whole Met budget trying to protect everyone on it.*

'I know it's a cliché, but just be extra careful. Vigilant. It's still a very good way to protect yourselves.'

'But this is insane! You're telling me there's a religious nutjob killing women like Celia, and you can't do anything to keep her safe? I thought that was the whole point of the police!'

'It is. But we simply don't have the budget or the people. I'm sorry, Peter, really I am. Look, if it's any help, we think he's gaining his victims' confidence by using this alias, then charming or somehow insinuating himself into their homes. As long as Celia keeps her wits about her, I think she'll be fine.'

This seemed to reassure the panicky academic. *Maybe the detail and the reason worked where the advice to be vigilant seemed too flimsy,* Stella thought.

Karlsson's colour slowly returned. He even managed a half-smile.

'Thank you. I'm sorry for what I said just now. I was out of control.'

Reflecting that if Peter Karlsson's idea of losing control was raising his voice and asking perfectly reasonable questions, he obviously had never seen human beings *truly* lose it. She waved away the apology.

'It's fine, honestly. I'm just sorry we can't do more to help.'

By way of answer, Karlsson pointed at the book, lying forgotten on the desk between them.

'Look at the contents list.'

Stella turned a few more pages. Then nodded. Chapters one through three took as their subject matter the martyrdoms of Saints Sebastian, Lucy and Agatha. Chapter four focused on Saint Bartholomew.

She flicked through the pages until she found it. Beneath the chapter heading was a photograph of a sculpture. A man seemingly made of naked muscles holding his own peeled skin over an arm. The caption told the inquisitive reader that this was a work by a sculptor named Marco d'Agrate, completed in 1562 and available to view in Milan Cathedral: the *duomo*.

She looked up at Karlsson. 'Is the whole book like this?'

'No. The first section looks at the lives of five early Christian martyrs. They were all killed by the Romans. Then I move forwards through history, to the wave of Protestant and Catholic martyrdoms and on to modern times and the horrific crimes perpetrated in Africa, China and other places less tolerant than England.'

'Strange subject for an atheist, isn't it?'

He smiled.

'Not at all. I examine the history of martyrdom and the way the Christian church has venerated those who suffered while inflicting the most unimaginable sufferings on those who disagreed with whatever doctrine currently holds sway amongst the elite.' He paused, and a boyish grin offset the pompous tone of his remarks. 'Sorry, I'll just climb down off my soapbox, shall I?'

Stella shrugged.

'Up to you, prof. So what about chapter five?'

'Ah. Well, that would be Saint Lawrence. He was roasted alive, grilled, really.'

Stella closed her eyes and rubbed the lowered lids with thumb and forefinger as she tried to avoid visualising a man being burnt to death.

She failed, mainly because she had almost burnt a man to death herself. In the end, as Mister Justice Sir Leonard Ramage sat, bound, in his burning Bentley, Lola had appeared to her and said, 'The man is burning, Mummy, like I was.' Stella had run back to the car and shot Ramage between the eyes.

Now she felt her tiredness as a physical burden, a weight dragging her down. She yawned until her jaw popped. Opening her eyes again, she found Karlsson's gaze fixed on her. He was frowning.

'Are you all right?' he asked. 'Would you like a coffee? I'm sorry, I should have offered you a drink when you arrived but, to be honest, I don't get to talk to many detectives and I was distracted. Our restaurant does a perfectly acceptable cappuccino.'

'That sounds like a great idea. No sugar and an extra shot, please. Sorry, I'm not getting quite as much sleep as I would like at the moment.'

'I can understand why. With three murders to investigate, I imagine you must be surviving mainly on caffeine and adrenaline.'

She smiled and nodded.

'Something like that. Don't forget pizza and Chinese takeaways.'

'I won't be long, this time of day they're usually pretty quiet.'

With Karlsson, gone, Stella pulled out her phone and checked her emails. The team were sending her updates on their progress, but they were all pretty routine. Except for one. Cam had found Celia Thwaites on a YouTube compilation of inspirational female vicars.

She called her.

'Yes, boss?'

'Cam, can you look up Celia Thwaites on your BBC list for me, please? I need to know if she's a yellow or a pink.'

'Sure. Hold on.' Stella heard papers rustling. 'Here she is. Pink. Invited but not yet appeared.'

Stella realised she'd been holding her breath and let it out in a rush.

'Thanks, Cam. Gotta go.'

Ten minutes later, Karlsson returned with two corrugated brown cardboard takeaway cups topped with white plastic lids.

'Here you are,' he said, placing one of the cups in front of Stella. 'That'll put hairs on your chest.' Then he blushed. 'I mean, keep you awake. Sorry, forgive me, that was completely inappropriate.'

He looked genuinely upset, nervous even, and Stella felt some words of reassurance were needed.

'It's fine. Don't worry. Come down to Paddington Green and you'll hear a lot worse than that, I can promise you.'

'You're sure?'

'Yes! It's fine. Please, Peter, relax.'

He blew his cheeks out.

'You wouldn't believe the way things have changed in universities over the last few years. In the old days, you could make a comment like that to a student or a colleague and it wouldn't even be noticed. Now, you're likely to find yourself hauled in front of an ethics committee and ordered to take gender-awareness training. Not to mention the flaming you get on social media for committing a micro-aggression.'

Stella smiled and sipped her coffee.

'Mmm, that's good. Actually, I would believe it. The Met's going the same way. Admittedly we don't have DCs wanting trigger warnings. It wouldn't really work with investigating rapes and sexual assaults. But the climate's changing. I have to say, mostly for the better.'

Karlsson sighed. He drank from his own cup.

'I suppose you're right. But I tell you, sometimes I feel like the students wouldn't mind creating a few martyrs of their own.'

'On that subject, you said he was following the chapters of your book?'

'Yes.'

'When did it come out?'

'Friday the 24th of August. We had a launch at Waterstones in Gower Street that evening, why?' Then his eyes widened. 'Wait! That's too late, isn't it? When was the first woman murdered?'

'Niamh Connolly was killed on the 13th, Sarah Sharpe sometime between the 17th and the 21st and Sister Moira on the 23rd.'

'Oh my God! That means the murderer must have had access to the manuscript in advance.'

Stella nodded, reflecting that under pressure or shock even leading atheists reverted to invoking God.

'It looks like it. Who would have had access to your book before it was actually published?'

Karlsson's eyes went to the ceiling.

'Er, well, me, obviously. Cee reads all my stuff, too. Then there're the people at my publisher: my editor, the proofreader and indexer, the designer, production manager. Plus the typesetters and the printers. I suppose the distributor, too, though I think they only get their copies a couple of days before launch date.'

'I'll need a list of names,' Stella said, feeling simultaneously elated at the step closer to the killer she was taking, and also depressed at the thought of yet another list of people they'd need to check out.

'Of course,' Karlsson said. 'I'm afraid I don't know them all. I mainly deal with Kathy Marks. She's my editor at Moathouse Press. They're my publishers. I can give you her email and mobile number?'

'Yes please. We can follow up with her.'

Karlsson's face was still waxily pale, making his goatee look like a theatrical prop. He wiped a hand across his mouth.

'This is terrible. I feel responsible. If I hadn't written the book, those poor women wouldn't have been tortured so horribly.'

Stella shook her head.

'It doesn't work like that. These people, they're obsessed. The obsession comes first then they cast around for ways to make it real. If he hadn't got his hands on your manuscript, he would have just found another source. It's not as if information's in short supply these days, after all.'

Visibly relieved, Karlsson smiled thinly.

'I suppose not. But all the same. I don't think I'll ever be able to look at a copy without feeling guilty.'

Stella only vaguely heard Karlsson's last sentence. Her brain was engaged on a deeper process, tuning out from her immediate surroundings and focusing inwardly on something Karlsson had said just before leaving to fetch the coffees.

The insight, when it came, didn't flash or pulse, it didn't arrive with a fanfare or a beating drum. It was if she had been paddling on a beach and a wave had carried it in to shore and retreated, leaving the beautiful idea sparkling behind among the pebbles.

Her eyes came into focus on Karlsson's lips, which were moving.

' – anything else I can help you with?'

She nodded, hoping that her moment of inspiration had only taken a few milliseconds and that he hadn't noticed.

'Your book.'

'Yes?'

'The first five chapters go Sebastian, Lucy, Agatha, Bartholomew and Lawrence, right?'

'Yes.'

'Which would be arrows, eyes, breasts, skin, roasting?'

'Yes.'

Now she knew it. Her subconscious had come through.

70

TUESDAY 4TH SEPTEMBER 11.00 A.M.

Stella spoke, letting her insight out into the air between her and Karlsson.

'The murderer didn't follow that pattern. He's using your book as a guide. But the mutilations he inflicted were in the wrong order. Niamh Connolly corresponds to Saint Agatha. Sarah Sharpe to Saint Sebastian. Moira Lowney to Saint Lucy. Did you change the chapter order at any point?'

Karlsson drained his coffee, then nodded.

'There was an early draft where Agatha, Sebastian and Lucy were chapters one, two and three. But I decided to change it. I wanted to ramp up the horror as the reader progressed further into the book. I know it sounds weird, but I had to make decisions about which tortures were the least bad. It's an odd feeling, trying to decide whether gouging a woman's eyes out is more or less hideous than cutting off her breasts. In the end, I left it to the publishers.'

'So who had access to the early version?'

'Almost no-one. I discussed it with Cee, but only in outline. She never likes to read my early drafts. Says it takes up too much time when she knows I'll only ask her to read the final one as well. I worked on it here, but I always locked the latest printed copy of the manuscript away at the end of the day.'

Karlsson pointed over Stella's shoulder at a pair of black metal filing cabinets.

'All the various printed-out versions are in the bottom drawer, there, in the right-hand cabinet. Do you want to see them?'

Stella nodded and levered herself out of her chair, feeling dizzy for a moment, silvery-white sparks dancing in the periphery of her vision. She steadied herself with a hand on the back rest of the chair then walked to the cabinets. Karlsson followed her, crouched and pulled a keyring from his trouser pocket.

Thick wodges of A4 paper completely filled the drawer, sandwiched together in yellow suspension files. Karlsson pulled the mass of compressed paper towards him and tugged out the rearmost bundle. A thick red rubber band held the sheets together. He handed it to Stella, then closed the drawer and stood.

A small round table occupied a corner of the office and she put the manuscript down on its smooth white top. The first page bore a single line of type:

Why is God Such a Sadist?_PK_1

And a scribbled date in red pen: 31/1/18 with a cryptic 'FTD' beside the numbers.

Stella lifted it off and placed it, face-down, on the left of the pile. Just as Karlsson had said, the next page was titled:

Chapter One
Misogynistic Cruelty: Saint Agatha

Chapters two and three, on Saints Sebastian and Lucy, also confirmed what Karlsson had told her. Without sitting again, Stella asked Karlsson her next question.

'Did you ever leave this lying around where someone could have seen it?'

'Yes. It would have been on my desk, or on this table. I tried to remember to lock it away each time I left my office, but you know what it's like. You're late for a seminar, or a student's having some sort of existential crisis or the bloody dean wants you in her office. Well, you just go, don't you?'

Knowing the feeling only too well, Stella nodded sympathetically.

'Did you ever send this version in to your publishers?'

'No. They would have got what I considered at the time to be the final draft. This was the first.'

'OK, that's good in one way. It means we can discount that whole lot of people. No need for a list of them after all. On the downside, it means we need to build a new list of all the people who would have had access to your office while you were out and probably for long enough to photocopy at least the first five chapters.'

'Wow! OK. That could be quite a long list. The trouble is, if I wasn't here, it's hard to know who was, if you see what I mean. I think some of my colleagues in the Philosophy department could keep you occupied for several months just discussing the terms of reference for that kind of question. Which,' he said hurriedly, as Stella frowned, 'I know you don't have. Sorry, bad timing for a poor joke. But we do have a departmental secretary. She could help you, I'm sure. She's a little obsessive.'

'Obsessive?'

'Actually maybe over-protective is kinder. Anyway, she keeps a record of everyone who comes up asking to see any of us. If they came nosing around during office hours, one of the secretaries would have seen them. And, in fact, we only need to look at January.'

'Why?'

'That's when this draft was active. Look,' he said pointing at the annotation in the top-right corner of the title page. 'That's my code for "finished this draft". Come on, I'll introduce you. I think it's Mim in today. She and Anjali job-share. To be honest, I'm never quite sure which one of them will be in.'

.   .   .

The woman watering a houseplant on a high shelf looked over as Karlsson and Stella approached.

In her mid-thirties, she was solidly built though not fat, with pale, blotchy skin. Her lips, crested by a deep groove beneath her nose, moved up into a smile. She wore her pale-blonde hair long; it looked badly in need of a decent cut.

A real Plain Jane, Stella thought. Then reproached herself. *But your smile's nice.*

'Hello, Professor Karlsson. How can I help you?' she asked, putting her little plastic watering can on a nearby table.

'Mim, this is Detective Chief Inspector Cole. She's interested in who might have come up here looking for me when I was out. Say for,' he looked upwards, 'the month of January this year. Do you still have those notes you take?'

'Yes, professor. Give me a minute.'

The secretary sat down, clicked her mouse and tapped her keyboard, staring intently at the screen.

'Yes, here we are,' she said. 'Shall I print it out for you?'

'Please, Mim. Thanks.'

'Okey-dokey.'

Back in Karlsson's office, Stella glanced down at the list. It was, mercifully, not a long one. Just twelve names, eight of them female.

'Would you be able to put contact details against these?' she asked him.

'Can I see?' he replied, holding out his hand.

Stella handed him the sheet.

'Yeah, this'll be easy. They're all either faculty or students. Would it be OK if I sent it to you this afternoon?'

'Sure. That would be fine. Here's my card.'

He took her business card and then placed it beside his keyboard.

'Would you like a copy of my book, Stella?' he asked. 'You might need it for the case.'

'Yes please. I was going to ask, but thanks. And, um, I don't suppose you'd sign it for me, would you?' She felt a sudden blush heating her cheeks. *God, I haven't felt so embarrassed since I met Barney Riordan,* she thought, recalling a charity ball at the Savoy Grill where she'd been squired by the Premiership footballer. 'Sorry. I'm being silly. It's just, you know—'

Karlsson held up his hands, smiling.

'It's fine, really. Believe me, when your sales might go into the high hundreds if you're lucky, signing books is one of the few perks of the job. What shall I say?'

'Oh, I don't know. Er, could you, um, just put "To Stella". That would be great.'

Karlsson opened a drawer and retrieved a sleek black fountain pen, uncapped it, and wrote something on the book's flyleaf. He blew on the writing a few times to dry the blue ink and then swivelled it round so Stella could read the inscription.

To Stella Cole,
Remember, pain, our urgent master,
diminishes with time, but reason, sweet reason,
will, always, burn brightly.
With great respect, and affection,
Peter Karlsson.

'That's really lovely. Who said that?'
Karlsson grinned.
'I did. I hope you don't mind. It's one of the maxims I live by.'
She shook her head, feeling a lump in her throat.
'No, I don't mind at all. Thank you.'

———

Harry King walked into the Philosophy building and held the door open for a woman he hadn't seen before: she was talking on the phone. He heard a few words of her end of the conversation.

'I've just met Karlsson. Yeah. Nice guy. Helpful. But I'd hate to think what his search history must be like.'

Harry frowned. Changing his mind about heading for the library, he mounted the stairs and climbed up to the floor where Peter Karlsson had his office. He walked into the main office and approached the desk of the secretary.

'Er, hi. I need to see Professor Karlsson please?'

The secretary smiled.

'Of course. Do you have an appointment?'

'No. But something quite urgent has come up. I won't be long. I promise.'

Harry had met the woman before and knew how protective she was of Peter's privacy. Which was good. Geniuses needed their thinking time. It was one of the things he loved about him.

'He's just finished a meeting. He's in his office. You know the way, don't you? Harry, isn't it?' she asked.

'Yes,' he said, brushing a strand of hair away from his cheek. 'Thanks.'

He walked down the short length of grey-carpeted corridor to Professor Karlsson's office, knocked and went in.

Karlsson looked up. Harry noted the brief flash of irritation. He didn't mind. He knew Peter was good at hiding his true feelings.

'Hello, Harry. What can I do for you?' Peter said.

Harry sat before him, hands folded in his lap.

'I hope you don't mind my asking, professor, but I bumped into a woman downstairs and she was clearly discussing you. Who was she?'

Karlsson frowned for a second, then spread his hands wide and smiled. Harry loved him all the more for that smile. So open. So trusting. So intelligent.

'I suppose I can tell you. Stella, I mean DCI Cole, didn't swear me to secrecy or anything. Close the door, would you?'

Harry rose from his chair and turned away from Karlsson,

frowning. *Stella? That's rather intimate.* He closed the door firmly then returned to his chair, folding one leg over the other.

'You know the murders on the TV. The religious women. The ones they're calling the Lucifer Killings?'

Harry's hand flew to his mouth.

'Oh my god! You don't mean she's investigating those?'

He nodded.

'She came to see me because it would seem that the killer is following the chapters in my book. The first draft, I mean.'

Harry's eyes widened. It was a horrible thought.

'But that's terrible. When your book was supposed to warn people about the dangers of making a cult out of cruelty.'

'I know,' Karlsson said, scratching at the back of his head. 'She said not to, but I feel partly responsible.'

'Oh, Peter, no! You shouldn't think that way. It's not as if you're the one murdering those poor women, is it?'

He smiled.

'I suppose not. Thanks, Harry. Was there anything else? Only I have a stack of essays to read. Then I'm in faculty meetings all afternoon. God knows when I'm supposed to get any actual work done.'

Harry shook his head and smiled. Then he left. *Poor man*, he thought.

71

TUESDAY 4TH SEPTEMBER 8.05 P.M.
HAMPSTEAD

Peter Karlsson and Celia Thwaites lived in a striking modernist house on the northern edge of Hampstead Heath.

Her parents had bought The White House decades earlier, before the insane London property boom. On their deaths, it had passed to her.

The house sat in the centre of a half-acre of garden, hidden from the more traditionally-designed neighbouring houses by a screen of mature trees. Its white walls, large plate-glass windows and abundance of horizontal lines had led to many an architectural journalist and critic beating a path to the brushed-steel front door.

But on this particular evening, the couple's dinner was not being shared with a writer eager to discuss the influence of the Miami School or the difference between Bauhaus and Brutalism.

Just as well, really, as they were engaged in a flaming row.

The calves' liver, cooked to perfection just fifteen minutes earlier, now lay cold and pallid on their plates. The wine, on the other hand, was fast disappearing.

'Do you literally want to be tortured to death?' Karlsson shouted. 'Because, you know, please do tell me. It'll save me worrying about where you are.'

'Oh, for heaven's sake, stop being so melodramatic! The detective said I'd be safe as long as I stayed with other people, didn't she? Well, didn't she?'

Karlsson gulped some more wine.

'Yes, but in case I missed this part of the narrative out, I'm not one hundred per cent sure that Lucifer was there to agree with her.' He slapped his forehead, harder than he intended to, raising a red weal. 'Oh no, wait a minute! He wasn't! So, you see, that's kind of what I'm driving at. There's a serial killer picking off well-known female Christians and torturing them to death based on the first draft of my book, Cee. And I'm worried he's coming for you.'

Celia stood up, knocking the edge of the table so that her wine glass toppled over, releasing a flood of red onto the white tablecloth.

'Shit!' She refilled the glass and glared down at her husband. 'So, let me get this straight. I am about to be ordained as a bishop, which is the dream of so many women in the church, and beyond, I think it's fair to say, not to mention many of my own parishioners. And you, based on a, a, *hunch* of some detective, want me to call the Archbishop of Canterbury and tell him that, no thanks, Ewan, after all, you know what? I've decided not to become a bishop. Maybe you could find a man to ordain instead? Because, guess what? I'm not going to do it.'

Karlsson rubbed his hand over his moustache and beard, scrubbing furiously as if he might remove the wiry hairs by friction alone.

Part of his brain – the rational, professorial, intellectually rigorous, *atheistic* part – knew she was right. The probability of Cee's coming to harm was minimal. The most dangerous part of the whole trip to York was the car journey itself. She knew to avoid anyone calling himself MJ Fox. She knew to stay with other people, which would be hard not to, given the circumstances. And forewarned was forearmed.

But there was another part of his brain that was less amenable to sweet reason. A primitive, suspicious, terrified part, driven by primal emotions, fear uppermost. A part conditioned by millennia of evolution to believe, if not in God, then in the capricious nature of the Universe to inflict pain on good people and let bad people flourish. And that was the part in the ascendant now.

'Please, Cee,' he said now, unable to force his primitive self back into the dark cave from whence it had so recently burst. 'Please don't go. I'm frightened. I don't want to lose you.'

She smiled, and came round the table towards him, her arms wide. Ashamed of the tears, which had sprung unbidden from his eyes, he let her enfold him in an embrace so tender it unmanned him. He sobbed against her chest.

'Come on, darling,' she crooned into his ear. 'This isn't like you. What's got you so upset?'

'I don't know,' he said, his voice muffled. 'But I've spent the last five years writing about the most unimaginable tortures inflicted on women of the Church, and now I find I've written a manual for a serial killer. I'm so scared of losing you to him. And I don't even have anyone to pray to!'

He laughed as he said this, not because he found it funny, but because he realised, in a flash, just how fragile an edifice he'd built to house his beliefs.

'Oh, Pete,' she said, pushing him away a little and using her fingers to wipe his eyes. 'Do you want to pray with me now? Not to God. We can just use plain words and say what we want.'

He sniffed loudly.

'I think that could work.'

'OK,' she said with a smile. 'Come on. Let's go into the sitting room.'

They sat, side by side, on a sofa, knees touching, heads bowed, eyes closed.

'I don't know how to do this,' Karlsson said.

'There's nothing to it. Just say what's in your heart. I'll listen. Then I'll say what's in mine, and you listen.'

'OK.' He sighed. 'I want Celia to be safe when she goes up to York to be ordained. I love her so much and I'm frightened she's in danger. I want her to be protected. Bring her back to me safe and sound. Please. Thank you.'

Celia squeezed his knee, then she spoke.

'I want Peter to not be scared. I know he loves me and his love is so powerful that the thought of losing me is frightening him. I want him to feel that he can let me go to York to take the next step in my journey with Christ. Please reassure him I am safe and always with friends. Thank you.'

Karlsson waited a moment longer then opened his eyes. He turned his head and looked at his wife of ten years.

'I love you, Celia Thwaites.'

'And I love you, Peter Karlsson.'

———

Lucifer finished watching the woman's TED talk on YouTube. For the thirtieth time.

The Church of England vicar held her patronising smile as the video faded to black.

'I'm going to enjoy torturing you. You look so sure of yourself. So smug.'

Outside, the latest instrument of pain leaned against the wall. A six foot by three foot grille made of welded steel rods. All done by the book.

72

TUESDAY 4TH SEPTEMBER 8.30 P.M.
PADDINGTON

To celebrate wins, or forget about losses, Stella and her team installed themselves in The Green Man on the Edgware Road.

The place was always lively, and the other punters made enough noise that the cops could discuss cases without fear of anyone overhearing. Not just Stella's team, either.

On any given evening, a tourist wandering into its ornate black and gold Victorian interior would be hard put to find a table or few square feet of carpet that didn't contain at least three people based at Paddington Green nick.

Once a month, a smaller group of officers, all women, found their way to a private room in an Italian restaurant on a street behind Paddington Station. They called themselves 'Good Girls Drink Plonk', an ironic reference to the old slang word 'plonk' for a female officer, and met in Buccia di Limone to let off steam and share a few war stories.

Not one of them doubted her own ability to be as tough, as rigorous, or as blasé about the occasional horrors of the job as the lads; most knew they had to be more so. But there were some subjects the guys would always protest about, or turn into jokes, that they still wanted to talk about. Or turn into a different kind of joke.

The lingering misogyny in the Met. Childcare problems. Fitting a stab vest over a big bust. Changing your tampon on an eight-hour stakeout while sharing a Ford Mondeo with a male colleague. 'Good Girls' offered them an opportunity to kick back and relax fully, rank forgotten for the evening.

The humour in Buccia di Limone's private dining room could turn very dark indeed, and the targets would probably horrify the social media feminists, but there it was. If you were job, and a woman, you had a different outlook. And sometimes you wanted somewhere of your own to talk about it.

On this particular night, sitting around the long rectangular table covered in wine bottles, baskets of garlic bread, glasses and phones were twenty female officers, at every rank from constable to chief inspector.

Stella, Cam, Def, Becky and Roisin occupied one end of the table, bantering and laughing with colleagues from general CID and the counter terrorism command.

As she looked around the table, at the open, unguarded faces of her colleagues, Stella felt the tension that seemed to keep her muscles locked into a permanent state of extreme readiness begin to unwind.

She turned to her left, where Cam sat, glass in hand, regaling a counter-terror DS with the details of Isaac Holt's porn collection.

'Refill?' she asked.

'Yes, please. Thanks,' Cam said, smiling.

Stella leaned round her to introduce herself to the DS.

'Hi. Stella Cole. I'm in SIU.'

The DS, her chestnut-brown skin gleaming in the candlelight, beamed as she answered, her words tripping and tumbling over themselves.

'I know! I wanted to introduce myself but, you know, I mean, you're something of a legend to us. Oh god, I sound like such a fangirl! Sorry. I'm Alisha Rubens.'

'I don't know about being a legend, unless you mean because of my bike, which is, I have to say, legendary.'

'Yeah, the boss reckons cars are for idiots, don't you?' Cam said.

'I never said that!' Stella said in mock horror. 'All I said was, anyone who preferred sitting in traffic on four wheels when they could be flying down the outside on two was – OK, fine, I did say an idiot. But, ladies, you have to take my remarks in context.'

It was as if, in uttering that single, final word, she had performed some sort of magic trick.

The room, already dim apart from the pools of golden light thrown by the candles, darkened still further, until all that remained were the two faces looking at her, eyes sparkling, lips moving, though Stella couldn't hear them.

Instead, she was struggling to remember something Jamie Hooke had said in his office. She let her eyes become unfocused and stared at a wavering candle flame. *Here it comes. Please don't drift away before I've caught you. Here it is.*

She listened to Jamie's voice as he told her about the patients at Broadmoor and how they felt about being incarcerated.

'Stella, are you OK?' Alisha asked, her brows knitted together.

'What? Yes, fine! Sorry, I tuned out for a sec there.'

'Some case-breaking insight?'

'Do you know what? I think it might be, yes.'

'Bloody hell, boss,' Cam said, then took a quick sip from her glass. 'What was it?'

Stella gestured at the tableful of women, twirling spaghetti around forks, chewing pieces of steak, talking, smiling, pouring wine, laughing.

'Look at them and tell me what you see.'

Cam took her time. She worked her way round the table clockwise, pausing on each face. Facing Stella again, and with Alisha leaning closer, she answered.

'I see a bunch of women having a great time, relaxing, drinking, just being themselves.'

'Nobody looks stressed,' Alisha added. 'It's like, in the station you're always-on. Even at home, you're maybe dealing with kids or a broken-down boiler but, here, this is like our private place where we can just, you know, drop down a gear or two for a bit.'

Stella slapped her palm down on the wine-splotched tablecloth.

'Yes! Exactly! That's what the shrink I consulted said about the nutjobs they've got in Broadmoor. He said, "Believe it or not, they feel safe in here. They can afford to drop their guard."'

Cam took another sip from her glass of wine.

'What's the insight, then?'

'I think that's how Lucifer's getting past his victim's defences. He's getting them to drop their guard.'

'How?' Alisha asked.

'He's got a stooge. He's using a woman to make the appointments and then when they, the victims, I mean, when they open their front door and she's standing there, they relax. He probably comes in later or follows her in, I haven't thought it through. But what do you think? Is that plausible, or is it the chianti doing my thinking for me?'

Neither of the other two women spoke at first. Stella monitored their faces, desperate not to see lips pulled sceptically to one side. Cam broke the silence.

'I suppose it's possible. If I open the door at home and there's a woman standing there with a collecting tin or whatever, my first reaction is to fish around for a coin. But if it's a bloke, I'm more ready to give him the bum's rush. They're just always so ready to kick off if they don't get what they want, you know?'

'Can you really see it, though?' Alisha asked Cam. 'A woman helping a bloke to mutilate other women before strangling them?'

Cam nodded.

'I can, actually. I've got this girlfriend, right? Her ex-husband is a psychopath. I mean it! A real nutjob. You want to talk about control? He controlled every aspect of her life. She used to have a couple of cats, OK? So, after they got married, Johnno said he was allergic and she'd have to get rid of them. She actually agreed, which was bad enough, but when she said she'd take them to a shelter he said, no. She had to get them put down.'

'Please say she didn't,' Alisha said.

Cam shook her head.

'She tried. She took them down the vet's but the vet said they were fine and she wouldn't put down a healthy animal.'

Stella listened with a growing sense of foreboding. She reckoned she knew how the story would end.

'Thank God for that!' Alisha said. 'I hope that put him back in his box.'

Cam took a bigger swig of wine this time, then held her glass out to Stella for a refill. Stella poured then signalled a waitress for another bottle.

'No,' Cam said. 'It didn't. He was seriously rich and they lived in this converted watermill in Surrey. He said she had to do it herself. Drown them in the mill pond.'

Alisha covered her mouth with her hand. Stella could see that she, too, had tipped to the ending. Stella spoke.

'And she did it.'

'Yes, she did do it! I met her for a drink a week later. She was actually shaking with fear as she told me about him. I told her she had to get out.'

'And did she?' Alisha asked.

'Eventually. When he punched her in the face after she wouldn't wear a pair of earrings he bought her for some posh party or other. But it was messy. Restraining orders, injunctions, the works.'

'Look, I know that's awful and, believe me, I really feel sorry for your friend, but there's a big gap between drowning cats and carving up women, isn't there?'

'Yeah, but she ain't doing the carving up, is she? She's just emailing them or whatever and going, "Oh, hi, my name's MJ Fox and I want to give you a shitload of money for your charity." Then her husband, or whoever he is, does the dirty work. Maybe she just toddles off back home and does the school run, who knows?'

73

TUESDAY 4TH SEPTEMBER 11.45 P.M.

Roisin was sitting in front of her TV, with a beer at her elbow. Ignoring the flickering screen, she re-read the linguist's report, which she'd received after lunch.

At first glance, the letters appears to have been written by someone highly educated.

The following list of words from the text all score below 15% on the Latham-Schneider Frequency Scale. That means they are rarely or never used by 85% of the UK population.

Vocabulary
hypocritical
adherence
maladjusted
chimaera
enucleated
redemption

depravity

There are also a number of stylistic flourishes characteristic of writers who have achieved a certain confidence with the English language:

Archaic usage
by my hand
the very depths
your obedient servant

Alliteration
cult of cruelty
minds and morals
punctured…pretensions

Then there is the rather obvious use of religiose language:

adherence to a cult
moral high ground
depravity and corruption
bear witness
the fires of Hell
the Fourth Horseman
the Devil lives on in me

Finally, we have the capitalised words and phrases:

MALADJUSTED TORTURERS
CHIMAERA
MONSTERS
ROB
SEXUAL
BREASTS
EYES
MORAL HIGH GROUND

Let the Bones be Charred

DEPRAVITY AND CORRUPTION
THE FIRES OF HELL
LIVES
THE FOURTH HORSEMAN

For the most part, this list reads like an Old Testament game of Scrabble. Except for BREASTS and SEXUAL, which seem out of place. I am not qualified to advise definitively on the significance (if any) of this juxtaposition, but it seems to me that they relate, rather obviously, to pleasure, rather than pain.

I said at the beginning of this short report that the text appears to have been written by a highly educated person. The keyword is 'appears'. In my opinion, the opposite is true.

The long words are precisely the sort that can be gleaned from a few minutes' work with a thesaurus.

The almost poetic use of alliteration and other literary techniques would be familiar to a great many uneducated people, for example, those with a good knowledge of the Bible. Rote learning of Biblical passages would equip any literate individual with an awareness of the tools its translators employed.

But the main diagnostic tool I draw on in forming this conclusion is the use of punctuation. The writer has attempted a high-flown style, but his over-use of punctuation marks, especially commas, which are frequently misused, is the giveaway. It is a classic signal that linguists use to determine education levels.

Based on this, and other less easy-to-explain markers, I would be reasonably confident in asserting that the writer did not progress beyond GCSEs at school, or, if they did, they took relatively unacademic subjects at A-level, such as Photography, Business Studies or Art.

Dr Amanda Bassett, University of the West of England

Sighing, Roisin finished her beer and tossed the report to one side.

'Great!' she said to her empty front room. 'So we're looking for a bloke who thinks tits are sexy, scraped a few GCSEs and an art A-level, and who knows his Bible. Sounds like half the men I went out with in Ireland.'

———

Stella sat on her balcony, chin cupped in her hands, trying to think herself to the point where she could go to Callie with the hypothesis that Lucifer wasn't working alone. And, worse than that, he had a female accomplice.

At 1.45 a.m., she realised that what she needed wasn't more thinking, but less, and went to bed. She dreamed of kittens drowning in a sack, crying out in unison. 'Mummy, Mummy, please. It's so hot in here. Please save me.'

She woke at 6.15 a.m., bathed in sweat, her face wet with tears. Sniffing, she pulled on a sports bra, knickers, vest and shorts, donned her favourite Asics running shoes and was running towards the green oasis that was Regent's Park ten minutes later.

———

At 8.45 a.m., she was sitting across the desk from Callie, laying it out for her boss. When Stella finished talking, Callie looked up at the ceiling. She returned her gaze to Stella.

'It's not without precedent,' she said, finally. 'But I'm not sure it takes us much further forward in catching the bastard.'

'But you could hold a press briefing. Explain that we're looking at the possibility that a woman is acting in concert with Lucifer. Nobody should agree to any meeting organised by a woman they've never met before, however wonderful the prize being dangled in front of them is. That might slow him down or stop him altogether. Then at least we've bought ourselves some time to find him.'

Callie pressed her lips together. Stella watched her, waiting to see which way she'd jump.

'Let's hold off for now, eh? If you get him before he does it again, we'll be able to cut straight to the good news.'

'And if we don't?'

Callie sighed.

'Then I'll make the announcement and we'll have to deal with whatever the media throws back at us.'

Stella nodded her agreement and left to prepare for the morning briefing.

74

WEDNESDAY 5TH SEPTEMBER 10.00 A.M.
SHAFTESBURY

Amy Burnside enjoyed her work as the new Head of Philosophy and Ethics at Monksfield School, even if some of her colleagues had been muttering about her changing the title of the subject from the old Religious Education.

Ambitious? She supposed she was. But then, had Jesus merely sat in his father's carpentry workshop making milking stools, she didn't imagine he would have transformed the world as successfully as he had, in fact, done.

Her phone rang.

'Is this Amy Burnside?'

'Yes, who's calling please?'

'Hi, Amy. My name's MJ Fox. I'm afraid my name won't mean anything to you but I'm an Old Monksfieldian and I work for *The Times* now. I'm writing a piece about the changing face of Religious Education in Britain. How a new generation of more dynamic teachers are taking it in exciting and unexpected directions. Naturally I wanted to feature my alma mater if I could and, just between the two of us, I've heard you're doing some amazing work. Please say you'll let me interview you. I know it's the start of a new term but I hope you'll be able to squeeze me in among your many other responsibilities.'

How could she say no? And, more to the point, why would she *want* to? Her rebrand from the generations-old and, frankly, fusty 'RE' to 'Philosophy and Ethics' heralded a seismic shift in the subject.

More and more of her contemporaries were seeing the sense of broadening out the subject's appeal to a more issues-based curriculum. The children seemed to like it, too.

'Of course, MJ. I'd be delighted to be featured in your article. When were you thinking of doing the interview? I suppose it's all done by phone or Skype nowadays?' Secretly hoping that it was nothing of the sort.

'Oh, well, we could do it remotely if you'd prefer, but I was hoping to come to see you in person. I know it's a bit old school but I think one gets a much richer perspective on the person one's interviewing.'

Her heart leaped. Of course! And didn't she always tell her students that there was no better way to judge a person's sincerity in argument than to look them in the eye, whether they were professing their faith or their atheism, their belief in the death penalty or their espousal of patriotism?

'That would be perfect,' she said. 'I live in a small village just outside Shaftesbury.'

'I know, I checked out your LinkedIn profile. Look, Amy, please tell me if this is too soon, but I noticed on the school website that everyone has games on Wednesday afternoons. I don't suppose you could possibly squeeze me in for an hour or two later today, could you?'

Her heart stuttered in her chest. Today! Surely, this was a sign. Taking a steadying breath, she answered.

'Of course. What sort of time?'

They'd agreed a time and she'd suggested doing the interview at her house.

After she'd ended the call, she frowned for a moment as she added the appointment to the calendar on her phone. *How did* The Times *get my number?* she asked herself. Then she rolled her eyes. *They're journalists, dummy! It's what they do. Probably found it on my blog.*

She could see the headline now.

The New Apostles: Reinventing RE For The 21st Century

Smiling, she indulged herself with a daydream. A variation on the normal one, made all the more plausible by this delightful turn of events.

They'd be sitting at her kitchen table, journalist and subject, drinking her freshly brewed Fairtrade coffee and eating her homemade biscuits. Fresh lilies cut from the garden in a newly washed-out vase on the table scenting the air with their heady perfume.

She offered a small prayer of thanks that the council hadn't imposed a hosepipe ban and she'd been able to keep her prize blooms watered.

And then what? After the interview was published in *The Times*?

Other interviews, maybe in the specialist press. The *Times Educational Supplement* would be an obvious next step. And then one of the coveted two-minute 'Thought for the Day' spots on Radio 4's Today programme.

Bishops, radical theologians, religious writers: they all went on and gave the nation the benefit of their considered opinions on moral, ethical and religious issues. She'd soon be joining them and from there, who knew? She'd carry on at Monksfield, of course, well for a year or so. But the lecture invitations, the books she'd write…

A knock at the door interrupted her daydream, and her heart fluttered with anticipation.

75

Are those cable ties too tight?

[Muffled sound – attempt at speech?]

Shame. Still, they'll melt once we get you going. Anyway, where was I? Oh, yes. Amy Burnside. Well, the garden was a mess. I mean, not intentionally, and not from lack of attention. It was just the brutal summer weather. The lawn was burnt to an even beige. The grass actually crunched when I walked on it.

As I stood on the doorstep, waiting for Amy to answer the door, I imagined her jumping at the sound of my knuckles rapping on the wood. The journalist is here! She'd smooth down the front of her skirt and walk slowly to the door, wishing her fluttering stomach would calm down. Taking a deep breath, and smiling like her life coach had told her, she'd take a firm hold on the inner handle and open the door to her future.

'Amy?' I said.

'Yes,' she said.

I smiled and we shook hands.

'Come in!' she said, 'you must be boiling out there.'

I laughed. I said, 'Thanks. It is a bit on the warm side.'

She laughed too, perhaps relieved that I had a sense of humour. 'I thought perhaps we could talk in the kitchen,' she said. 'I've got some coffee made. And some biscuits as well. Home-made. I mean, I didn't make them just for you, I like to bake. Oh, god, that sounded rude. Why wouldn't I make biscuits specially?'

She was gabbling. Clearly nervous. I aimed for a reassuring smile. 'The kitchen would be perfect. And home-made biscuits sound lovely. I generally buy mine from Waitrose.'

She managed to lead me to the kitchen without committing another faux pas and poured us each a mug of the coffee from a cafetière she must have prepared five minutes before the time I'd said I'd arrive.

I placed my messenger bag on the floor under my chair, blew across the surface of my coffee then took a cautious sip. She waited, not breathing. I smiled. I could see her relax.

'That's really good coffee. May I?' I pointed to the plate of cookies.

'Oh, please, go ahead. They're cranberry, hazelnut and plain chocolate. The chocolate's melted a little. It's this heat. I'm so sorry. I hope you're not on a diet.'

'Why, do I look like I need to lose weight?' It was fun to mess her around like this.

'Oh no! You look great! I mean, fine. I'm sorry, I'm not used to being interviewed. I'm a bit nervous.'

I smiled and reached out to touch the back of her hand. Just briefly, a graze, nothing more. But I sensed her pulse quicken nonetheless. I spoke some more reassuring words.

'It's OK. But please, don't be nervous. We're just going to talk about your work and I'll record the whole thing so you won't see me scribbling notes the whole time.'

She smiled. Silly bitch.

'So, you said your article was about how Religious Education is making a comeback?'

'Absolutely,' I gushed. 'My editor is himself a practising Christian and he perceives a definite revival in what you might call the quest for the divine in modern society.'

She beamed and, for a moment, I felt like slapping her to wipe the expression off her over-made-up face. But I controlled myself. As always. I continued. Oh, and by the way? I'm going to give you the full conversation. You need to understand why I'm killing them.

I said, 'So, Amy, I'll start with a few easy questions, then we'll get into the real meat of the interview where I ask you about your new style of teaching. How does that sound to you?'

'That sounds fine. Whenever you're ready,' she said.

'So, you're a graduate, with a very impressive 2.1 in Philosophy from the University of Sussex and you did a one-year post-graduate teaching certificate?'

'Yes. I'd already made my mind up I wanted to teach as a career so it made sense to get started as soon as possible.'

'And what made you feel that the shaping of young minds was your vocation? Your calling, if you like?'

'Well, I suppose, partly my faith. You see, I always believed that Jesus' most important role was as a teacher. And what role is there, really, that's more important than helping young people grope their way towards the answers to the really important questions we all have to face?'

She blushed and touched her cheek. 'Oh dear, that sounded a bit pompous, didn't it? And I'm only twenty-eight, if you can believe it.'

I smiled. 'Not at all. I mean, it didn't sound pompous to me, not that I don't believe you're only twenty-eight.' Now it was her turn to laugh.

'Thanks.' She smiled, then cleared her throat. 'OK, next question.'

I looked down, then up at her again. Frowned and winced at the same time, which, by the way, took a lot of practice in my bathroom mirror. Delivered my prepared line.

'Uh, this is rather embarrassing, but I have a slight tummy upset.

I think it might be this weather. Do you think I could use your loo, please?'

She jumped to her feet, clearly only too pleased to help. 'Of course, you poor thing. It's upstairs, first door to your left.'

I made an apologetic gesture with my hands then left, at a walking pace. I went upstairs, more for form's sake, and was gratified that a couple of the steps creaked. I waited for a few minutes then descended.

The doorknob squeaked as I re-entered her kitchen. Amy looked round and smiled up at me. Then I hit her with the hypo. An easy stab into the soft flesh in her neck. Her eyes popped wide for a second then the old eyelids drooped as if she was drunk.

I changed my voice. No friendliness left in it at all. Not one drop.

'I have one final question for you, Amy,' I said. 'What gives you the right to poison children's minds with your obscene ruminations on right and wrong, good and evil?'

She tried to stand but I placed my hands on her shoulders and held her down. It wasn't hard. The drugs act very quickly.

'I don't—' she managed to say, as my hands left her.

'Yeah? Well, I do,' I said, which is a cool line, if you think about it.

Then I put my overalls on and started work. My goodness, there was a lot of blood! And I cut myself at one point. I know it was careless. But isn't that what they say about people like me? In the end our confidence lets us down?

76

THURSDAY 6TH SEPTEMBER 10.05 A.M.
SHAFTESBURY

Marcus Duckett was heading down the corridor that led from Monksfield's chemistry lab to the staffroom. He'd just finished teaching twenty Year Nines how to make bouncing custard and was looking forward to a coffee and a browse through the *New Scientist*.

Mid-morning sun streamed in through the windows that lined the east-facing wall, giving the corridor the feeling of an abbey cloister, albeit one with student artwork on the walls interspersed with posters advertising outward bound courses and sports fixtures.

He was sweating beneath his shirt and jacket and ran a finger round his collar. Why ties were mandatory he had no idea. Even at a school with a strong Christian foundation, *especially* at such a school, a little bit of compassion for the heat-intolerant wouldn't go amiss.

As he passed the door to D5, the classroom where Amy Burnside should be teaching her new Year Nines, he paused.

The noises coming from beyond the pale wooden door did not suggest that she had full control of her students. Which was odd, because she liked to boast of the way her 'acolytes' – as she called them – hung on her every word. He could hear the raucous, cracked laughter of adolescent boys and higher-pitched squeals of delight from the girls.

Duckett squared his shoulders, knocked twice, then twisted the door handle and strode into the classroom. Silence fell almost immediately. Students at Monksfield could be as rowdy as any others, but the school instilled a level of respect for teachers that produced the desired effect. But in D5, apart from himself, no teacher was present.

'Where is Miss Burnside?' he asked, scanning the room as he tried to dispel the absurd notion that the students had stuffed her under a desk or in a cupboard.

'Sorry, sir. We don't know. She hasn't shown up yet.'

This from a dark-skinned girl in the front row, her face now a mask of concern.

'What do you mean, she hasn't shown up yet? Has she gone home sick?'

'We don't know, sir,' said a boy with owlish glasses that gave him a passing resemblance to Harry Potter. 'She just isn't here. We didn't know what to do. Teachers are never late for lessons.'

Duckett recognised the boy. He'd come for hockey try-outs the previous Sunday.

'Archie, isn't it?'

'Yes, sir.'

'I want you to go the school secretaries' office. Tell them Miss Burnside hasn't arrived for your lesson yet. Say I told you to ask them to call her.'

The boy scraped his chair back and left smartly, closing the door quietly behind him. Duckett looked around with a sinking heart. *Bang goes my coffee break.*

'What is Miss Burnside teaching you at the moment?' he asked.

'We're discussing abortion, sir,' a blonde girl with braces on her teeth answered, brightly.

Oh, great.

'Fine. Well, I'm not sure I'm really qualified to teach you about… that… so instead maybe you could, uh—'

'We could organise a flash debate, sir,' the dark-skinned girl volunteered.

For a disconcerting moment, Duckett imagined she'd said 'masturbate' and then reality reasserted itself.

'Fine. Yes. You are?'

'Felicity, sir. Felicity Perry?'

'Good.' He looked at the nineteen expectant faces. 'Taking responsibility is part of what we like to instil in you at Monksfield. So I'm going to ask Felicity to organise the two teams. Your subject is…'

He paused, searching for something that might not be perceived as too safe, but without the risk of a student reporting back to Mummy and Daddy that they'd been discussing infidelity or underage sex or whatever Miss Burnside usually felt was appropriate.

Felicity saved him. He was beginning to like the girl.

'How about animal rights, sir?'

Relieved, he assented at once.

'Yes. Fine. Should animals have rights?'

———

While Duckett was supervising the setting up of the debate, Archie was delivering his message to the most senior school secretary.

Mrs Royal was known unofficially throughout the school as The Queen. Partly owing to her name, partly to her years, which, at sixty-one, put her well above the age of almost the entire complement of staff and ancillary workers such as groundskeepers, but mostly because of her regal and often imperious bearing. She listened as Archie breathlessly recited his message.

'– and he said to tell you,' he looked down, then back into her sharp eyes, 'I mean, *ask* you, if you could call her. Please.'

'Thank you, Archie,' she said, not unkindly, but with enough finality to let him know he was dismissed.

Children would do anything to skive off their lessons, even if their parents were paying five thousand pounds a term these days. She saw it as part of her duties to ensure that messengers didn't use their errand as an excuse to dawdle or waste time.

She called up the staff contacts pane on her database and searched 'Burnside'. She pursed her pale-pink-frosted lips as she saw the photo in the top-right corner of the record. Vain little thing. Teetering along on those absurdly high-heeled shoes.

Pushing away the thought that young women like Amy Burnside should put a few years in before 'reinventing' perfectly good subjects, Sylvia Royal picked up the receiver of her desk phone and dialled the mobile number beneath Miss Burnside's smiling face.

She tapped a newly sharpened pencil against a clean sheet of paper in her notebook as she listened to the phone ringing. Sighing with exasperation, she realised she would have to leave a message.

'Hello, Miss Burnside. This is Mrs Royal. You've been reported absent by your students and as I have not received notice of a holiday or sickness, I wonder whether you could call me at your earliest convenience. As I think you know, it's a school rule that staff are either present or accounted for,' she couldn't resist adding.

She clacked the receiver down and looked across at one of the other secretaries, who'd been listening with evident pleasure.

'They need to learn,' she said, tartly, before picking up the phone again and pressing the first speed-dial button: the headmaster.

77

James Haddingley, the headmaster of Monksfield, liked to spend ten minutes or so in the staffroom before school officially started. To chat to colleagues and hear the school gossip.

He was thinking about his new head of RE. *Philosophy and Ethics*, he mentally corrected himself. He liked Amy Burnside's approach. She'd brought a refreshingly dynamic presence to the school, which, he felt, had been coasting under its previous headteacher. But the school was strong on discipline, for staff as well as students.

He was waiting for Amy to put in an appearance, hopefully a shamefaced one, so that he could whisk her off to his 'eyrie', as he called his third-floor office overlooking the sports pitches, and give her a mild dressing-down. For appearances' sake.

A fleeting image of Amy Burnside sitting on his bed wearing nothing but a black lacy bra and matching knickers crossed his mind: he dismissed it.

When she hadn't arrived by 8.45 a.m., he left the convivial surroundings of the staffroom, with its brown-and-orange upholstered armchairs and coffee machine, and paid a visit to the secretaries' office. Sylvia Royal looked up as he entered, and leaped to her feet. It was a habit he'd been unable to break in her and it always embarrassed him.

'Please, Sylvia,' he tried again. 'There's really no need. I wonder, have you heard from Miss Burnside this morning?'

Running her hands under her thighs to straighten her tweed skirt as she sat, she answered his question.

'I'm afraid not, headmaster. I left her a message yesterday reminding her of our staff absence protocol, but apparently without effect.'

'Yes, well, I'd better go round and see if she's OK.'

'You have a meeting with the bursar at ten.'

He checked his watch and smiled.

'I'll be back in plenty of time. It's only a fifteen-minute drive to Amy's… I mean, Miss Burnside's house.'

The rush-hour traffic was against him, however, and it wasn't until 9.30 a.m. that he reached the brick-and-flint cottage where Amy lived.

Noticing that her iridescent-green VW Beetle occupied the single parking space, he parked in his usual spot: a layby a few yards beyond the turning that led to her back gate.

She never used the front door as it opened straight onto the road. He puffed out his cheeks as he left the Volvo's air-conditioned interior and the hot, humid air hit him.

He pressed the button to the left of the back door, and listened to the cheerful peal of church bells. Amy had told him proudly that she'd recorded them at Saint Martin's the first Sunday she'd moved in and downloaded them wirelessly onto her doorbell.

He smiled. He was only ten years older than her, but sometimes he felt like Rip Van Winkle.

When she didn't answer, he frowned. He wasn't given to anxiety, but something was telling him things weren't quite as they should be. Amy was a dutiful, conscientious young woman. If anything, he felt she could afford to let her stays out a few notches and still be among the top few members of staff for adherence to school policies.

He raised the wrought-iron knocker, hot to the touch, and brought the fat ring of black metal down against the matching stud in a loud rat-a-tat. Waited a few seconds. Straining to hear footsteps.

'Hmm,' he said to himself. 'Where are you, Amy?'

He was running through the possibilities as he walked around to the side of the house where the kitchen door opened out onto the garden.

Was she ill? In bed with summer flu? Or food poisoning? Had she had an accident? Reaching the kitchen, he pressed his face against the window, shading his eyes with his hand to block out the sun and get rid of his reflection in the glass. Where was she?

At first, he couldn't understand what he was seeing. Something was sitting at the kitchen table. But it couldn't be Amy, because this, *No, it isn't her*, this *thing* had no skin. *Oh god, no!*

The head was the worst, with those pale-blue eyes, *I loved your eyes, Amy*, streaked across with blood in a ravaged mask of muscle, the teeth bared in a white grin.

The horror battered at the gates of his consciousness, trumpeting its demands to be let in and given residence. And succeeded.

Haddingley screamed, and staggered away from the window. Not wanting to look again, or to leave her there alone any longer, he sat down heavily with his back to the rough flint wall and dug out his phone.

His index finger seemed to skitter over the virtual keypad and he had to try twice before finally hitting the 9 three times.

'It's Amy!' he said, answering the emergency operator in a hushed voice. 'She's dead.'

———

Things moved fast from that point. Stella's SCAS request meant every SIO in the country knew that a DCI Cole, Metropolitan

Police, was interested in any murders of prominent Christian women, especially if they involved mutilation and strangulation.

Stella got the news at 7.30 a.m. the following day. She called Garry, and he picked her up at 8.00 a.m. Using blues and twos as needed, he drove fast out of London towards the M3 that would take them southwest towards Shaftesbury.

They arrived in the pretty Dorset town at 11.15 a.m. As Garry drove through the town centre, Stella looked at the people filling the narrow pavements. Mostly white, mostly prosperous, to judge from their clothes, mostly middle-aged or older, though a few younger couples here and there were fighting gamely to bring the average age below fifty.

She talked Garry through the last few miles until they arrived at Amy Burnside's cottage, where they went through the usual procedure before being admitted by the loggist. Entering the kitchen, the coppers, thirty-odd years' experience between them, gasped at the scene before them.

78

SATURDAY 8TH SEPTEMBER 11.30 A.M.
SHAFTESBURY

The room stank.

Stella and Garry had wads of cotton soaked in oil of camphor clamped over their noses. But still, the cloying, soupy smell of putrefaction found a way past these flimsy barriers to coat the insides of their mouths and throats and fill their noses with its unholy stench.

Amy Burnside's pale-blue eyes stared out at Stella from lidless sockets in a striated mass of red, weeping muscles, woven over the skull in an intricate pattern of overlapping sheets.

Stella moved her gaze down over the skinned shoulders, breasts and torso, trying not to imagine Amy Burnside's last few minutes of consciousness, and praying that she would have passed out, or died from shock, before Lucifer had gone far.

Flies filled the room, and Stella had to swat a couple away from her face.

Amy's arms, now resembling an anatomical illustration, lay on the table, in a wide, shallow pool of blackened blood, around which flies were buzzing noisily.

Stella pointed to what, at first sight, appeared to be bunched, red fabric draped over Moira's left elbow.

'The sick bastard's getting more confident. This must've taken hours.'

'He must have left here looking like an abbatoir worker. Someone must have seen something,' Garry said.

'It's another martyrdom. Just like Peter Karlsson predicted. Which one was it again?'

Garry looked up at the blood-spattered ceiling then back at Stella.

'Saint Bartholomew,' he said. 'Chapter four. They skinned him alive. Karlsson had that picture of the statue in Milan, remember?'

'Agatha, Sebastian, Lucy, Bartholomew. He's following Karlsson's book, chapter by chapter. Oh, God, this is bad, Garry. Which saint is chapter five about? I can't remember.'

'Not sure, boss. I mean, not off the top of my head.'

'OK. Look, can you call them now and get somebody to look it up? I need to let Callie know she's got another meeting with the beasts to prepare for.'

Garry nodded and left the kitchen.

Finding a corner the spurting blood hadn't reached, Stella pressed her back into the comforting embrace of the right-angle between the walls and stared, hard, at the scene of almost unimaginable pain and degradation facing her.

What are you trying to tell me, Lucifer? You're going to reveal yourself soon, I know it. And when you do, I'll be there waiting for you. You hate them. But they're just stand-ins, aren't they? Is it your mother? Is she the one you're killing? Or did you already do her?

Garry returned a few minutes later, shaking his head.

'What is it?' Stella asked.

'I really hope we catch him before he does another one, boss.'

'Chapter five?'

He nodded.

'Saint Lawrence. Roasted alive over an open fire.'

'Shit!'
'Indeed.'

Once they'd finished at the crime scene, they drove into the centre of Shaftesbury to find a pub. Over pints and sandwiches – no lingering nausea for this pair of experienced murder detectives – Stella and Garry hashed out a series of actions.

POLSA: look for bell rope.
FORENSICS: blood/skin/hair/other phys. ev. NOT from Amy Burnside? Get phone unlocked ASAP.
WITNESSES: bloodied man leaving cottage?
FLO: check re relatives/friends. Did Amy have appt. with MJ Fox?
CCTV/ANPR: Look for dark-blue Ford Focus, registration AG54 LKF.

Stella called the school and left a message on the answering machine informing the listener that she wanted to interview the head. Next she called Callie.

'Hi, Stella, what can you tell me?'

'It's definitely him, boss. Amy Burnside was Head of RE at a local C of E boarding school. Now she's dead, with her own skin draped over her arm like a cape. Karlsson was right on the money. He predicted it. Just like Saint Bartholomew in his book. The only good news is Lucifer's getting careless, or cocky. He didn't bother taking the rope with him this time. I spoke to one of the CSIs. He reckons there's a good chance there'll be blood traces from Lucifer as well as Amy. You know, with all the cutting he did. We'll know for sure once we get Lucian's lab report.'

'Oh, that poor wee girl,' Callie said. 'OK, well, I'll do my duties at a press conference this evening. Anything you need?'

'Not at this point. The thing that's bugging me is: why her? I checked against Cam's list and she wasn't on it. I was sure that was how Lucifer was choosing his victims.'

'No possibility it's a copycat?'

'No. Even despite our Dear Deputy Leader's best efforts to leak every last detail of the case, we've managed to keep enough back that only Lucifer would be able to follow the pattern.'

'Then I'll have to leave it to you, Stel. Now, this will sound cold, but I have a meeting to go to. You coming back today, eh?'

'Yes, as soon as Garry and I have checked in with the locals.'

'Good. Take tomorrow off, d'ye hear? That's an order.'

Stella smiled.

'Yes, ma'am.'

'You cheeky mare! Away with you!'

79

Callie made her way to Scotland Yard, arriving at 5.10 p.m.

Knowing she had to announce that yet another woman had been murdered, in all probability by Lucifer, was playing havoc with her insides. She had twenty minutes spare and headed for the Ladies along the corridor from the media centre.

She emerged from the cubicle and stood in front of the mirror. Washing her hands, she glared at her reflection.

'Calpurnia Leonora McDonald, you need to get a grip, my girl. Now, get your face straight then go in there and do your job.' She smiled at herself. 'At least you'll be able to have some fun before it kicks off.'

She strode into the media centre with her spine straight and her shoulders back, looking first at the journalists slowly filling the seats, and then across at the podium and its sole occupant.

Yes, there you are, my slimy little friend. All ready for the ladies and gentlemen of the press to listen to your inane outpourings about how much you support the police. Well, my laddie, wouldn't they just love to hear what I found out about you, eh?

Morgan stood to greet her as she took her seat. He held out his hand.

'Callie. How goes the investigation?'

She gripped his hand and leaned towards him.

'Apart from the fact that some ambitious little shit's been leaking details to the press, you mean?' she said, masking her lips with a loose left fist as she'd grown used to seeing doubles tennis players do on court.

'What?' he hissed, though he was a practised enough operator to keep his PR smile glued to his face.

'You heard me. And that same ambitious little shit has been interfering with my officers and their murder investigation to further his political ambitions.'

'I don't know anything about a leak. But I'll have your badge for this, McDonald,' he murmured, still smiling.

'I rather think not,' she said. 'In fact, here's what I think. I think you're going to announce that you have total confidence in the police and their ability to close this case, and then you're going to plead Assembly business and leave. And not come back.'

'Oh, really? And what if I decide not to?'

Callie smiled sweetly, letting go of his hand and picking an imaginary speck of dust off his right shoulder. She dropped her voice still further.

'Then I will leak the fact that you, *Mister* Morgan, have been paying a seventeen-year-old prostitute in Stoke Newington named Arianna to bugger you with an oversized strap-on. After which I will send a team of officers to arrest you at City Hall in connection with a clean-up campaign in the area. I can't promise you there won't be a swarm of media people there to record the whole thing. After all, you know how leaky the Met is.'

Morgan's eyes bulged out of his head. He looked as if he were about to be sick. Callie moved back a few inches.

'She told me she was twenty,' he hissed.

'I don't care if she told you she was ninety,' she whispered back. 'You have your lines, now bloody deliver them.'

Then she sat down, looking out at the roomful of journalists, and nodded grimly. *Show time.*

After Tim Llewelyn had performed his customary emcee duties, Morgan, looking paler than usual, pulled his table mic a little closer.

'Ladies and gentlemen. Assembly business means I will have to leave before the briefing begins, but I want to reinforce my earlier comments that I have complete confidence in Detective Chief Superintendent McDonald and her team's ability to investigate this case and bring it to a successful conclusion.'

Then he simply stood, picked up his briefcase and left the stage, favouring Callie with a final, tight-lipped smile.

After reading out the agreed statement, outlining the depressing news of yet another woman's sadistic murder, Callie added a few extra words.

'We are working on the theory that the killer may have a female accomplice and that it is she who is arranging the meetings with his victims. We strongly advise women with well-known religious views not to agree to meet *anybody* they do not already know, *especially* if that stranger is a woman. Instead, they should call the police or the Crimestoppers number.'

———

From his home office later that evening, Morgan called the editor of the *Evening Standard*, proposing an exclusive: an interview on the Lucifer case.

Despite their coming from polar opposites on the political spectrum, the former cabinet minister agreed at once and, over dinner, Morgan outlined the story he hoped would put Remi Fewings on the back foot again. The editor said he would run the story on Monday across all editions.

80

Stella opened the door to her flat and there stood her best friend, Vicky Riley, a wrapped bottle in her right hand.

'Hi!' Stella said, stepping forward to hug Vicky. 'Come in. I've got some prosecco in an ice bucket on the balcony.'

They stopped in the kitchen, so Stella could take Vicky's bottle of Alvariñho, the spicy, fruity white they'd discovered on a holiday to Portugal together, and put it in the fridge.

Stella sized up her friend.

'Looking good,' she said.

Vicky was wearing a loose midnight-blue silk shirt, tight white jeans that showed off her bottom, a source of envy to Stella, and navy suede high heels. Her blonde hair was caught back in a clasp that revealed a long, elegant neck.

There had been a time when Stella had been mildly jealous of Vicky, and all the time Richard spent with her. She'd wondered whether Richard had had the hots for her, but it had all been their project, long-discarded, to investigate Pro Patria Mori.

457

'Thank you. So are you. Although,' she stretched out her hands and ran her thumbs under Stella's blue-green eyes, 'if these get any bigger you'll be able to carry your stuff in them!'

'Thanks, bestie! That makes me feel so much better.'

'Oh, you can take it. But seriously, Stella, you look like a week under the covers wouldn't be enough. With or without a man.'

Stella couldn't help the smile that stole across her face.

'Come on, let's go and get a drink.'

Vicky followed Stella through the flat and out onto the balcony.

'Sorry, did I just see you smirk back there?' Her hand went to her mouth and she widened her eyes theatrically. 'Ohhh. You've got a boyfriend, haven't you? I can see it in your eyes.'

Pouring the sparkling wine into tall glasses, Stella answered.

'What, despite the suitcases you mean?'

'Don't try to distract me. Cheers!' she said, clinking glasses with Stella then selecting an olive from a bowl on the glass-topped table between them. 'Tell me everything.'

Stella took a sip of her own wine and popped an olive into her mouth.

'His name is Jamie Hooke. With an "e".'

'Nice. Hooke. Stella Hooke. Mrs Stella Hooke. I like it.'

Stella grinned. One of the many things she liked about Vicky was her point-blank refusal either to ignore Richard's memory or to let it get in the way of the possibility that Stella still had a life worth living.

'Well, good. You can be my chief bridesmaid.'

She saw a flicker of a different sort of expression cross Vicky's face. Not the lightly mocking grin of a moment ago. Something different.

'So, what's he like?' Vicky asked. 'Obviously intelligent or you wouldn't be seeing him. Is he tall? Short? Divorced? What?'

'He's tall. He's got a nice bum. Not as nice as yours.'

'Obvs.'

'Obvs. And a good body.'

'Age?'

'He's forty. Divorced. Amicably. He has lots of curly brown hair.'

'That's a plus. Most blokes I know over thirty-five are either losing theirs or shave it all off to disguise the fact.'

'And he's really, really fun to be with. Great sense of humour and, yes, he is bright, but he's modest, too, you know? Doesn't ever assume I won't know what he's talking about, even when we're discussing his work.'

'Oh yes! And what line of work is the future Mr Stella Cole in? No. Let me guess.' Vicky put a finger to her chin and frowned. 'Hmm. Not a copper, I'd bet my house on that.' Stella shook her head. She snapped her fingers. 'No! I've got it!'

'What?' Stella said, enjoying having facts about Jamie winkled out of her.

'He's a medic. Everyone says cops and doctors go together. Irregular hours, though I can't see why that would work. I mean, you'd never see each other.'

'You're half-right,' Stella said, refilling their flutes. 'He's a psychiatrist. A forensic psychiatrist, as a matter of fact.'

'Wow! OK. So did you meet him on the Lucifer case?'

Stella shook her head.

'He's helped me out on a couple of cases but, this time, I don't know, something just clicked. We had a pub lunch, then I invited him out for a Chinese meal with Lucian and Gareth, then, one thing led to another and...'

Vicky placed her glass down on the table with a clink.

'Sooo?' she said, drawing out the single syllable.

Stella grinned.

'So, what?'

'What's he like?'

'I just told you!'

'In bed, minx. What's he like?'

Stella grinned.

'To be honest, we were both a bit pissed. The first time.'

'Oh, so he stayed the night! And in the morning?'

'It was very nice, actually. Yes. Very nice indeed.'

'And did you?'

'I did!' A beat. 'Twice.'

Vicky laughed.

'Oh, well, in that case you definitely have to keep him.'

Stella took a sip of her prosecco. Life, for the first time in a long while, felt as though someone, somewhere, had tilted the odds in her favour. A breeze had sprung up, rustling the leaves of the London planes in the street below, and dispelling some of the ferocious heat that had plagued the country for what felt like months.

She looked back at Vicky.

'You've got news, haven't you?'

Vicky's face split into a huge grin.

'Yes, I have.'

'I knew it! You smirked when I said you could be my chief bridesmaid. Oh my God! You're not?'

'I am! Damian asked me to marry him!'

Stella jumped to her feet, clonking her knee against the table and making the glasses wobble. She came round and embraced Vicky, hugging her tightly and kissing her on the cheek, hard.

'Vicky, that is such good news. Where did he propose?'

'Oh god, it was so embarrassing. We were at an awards dinner last night. I'd won one of the prizes and they'd roped Damian in to present it. So I went up onto the stage to collect it and he was holding the mic and he literally said, to the whole room, "And the winner of my heart is Vicky Riley. Will you marry me?" Then he went down on one knee and held out the box.'

Stella shook her head. Vicky and Damian Fairbrass had been going out for a few years, but she'd never suspected the *Guardian* journalist was the romantic kind. *You never know, Stel.*

'Where is it, then?'

'Too small. It's gone back to the jeweller.'

They carried on talking and drinking prosecco, only stopping at eleven to go out for some chips.

———

Much later, when they were sprawled on the couch, half-watching a film, Stella turned her head to Vicky.

'There's a mole inside the investigation. Some sod's been leaking details to the press.'

'Yeah. Some of the stuff the others've been reporting, I knew you would never have released it.'

'Have you heard anything?'

'Oh, you know that us journalists, no, wait, *we* journalists, never reveal our sources.'

'I know that. But, you know, have you heard if it's true? For sure, I mean?'

Vicky levered herself up on her elbows from her almost supine position and twisted round to look at Stella.

'Yes. I have. It is.'

'Good. Is it that twat Craig Morgan?'

'I just said, we never reveal our sources.'

'OK then, is it *not* that twat Craig Morgan?'

Vicky laughed.

'Nice try. No comment.'

Stella sat up straighter and finished her drink.

'If I say "It's Craig Morgan", and you just look back at the telly, and I take that to mean you're telling me it isn't him, you wouldn't be saying anything, would you?'

Vicky furrowed her brow.

'No,' she said, finally.

'Vicky?'

'Yes?'

'It's Craig Morgan, isn't it?'

Stella waited.

Vicky turned back to the TV and pointed.

'George Clooney's looking old, isn't he?'

81

Lucifer picked up a copy of the *Evening Standard* on the way out of the station. The morning edition of the paper carried the interview with Morgan on the front and third pages, accompanied by a library shot of Morgan looking every bit the serious mayor-in-waiting.

The thrust of his remarks was that the mayor had presided over a real-terms cut in the budget for the Met, resulting in falling numbers and morale among rank and file cops.

As Deputy Mayor for Policing and Crime, his hands were tied but the paper's readers should be in no doubt. Come the next mayoral election, should they elect him, he would fully address the Met's concerns over budgets in a way that would reveal his predecessor's contempt for the Service.

The quote from Morgan that Lucifer read with growing anger struck deep at the heart of the malevolent emotions that had led to the four murders so far.

'This sick killer has claimed to be setting the record straight about religion. I can tell him that, as a church-going man myself, I believe God wants me to see him brought to justice. And I will stop at nothing to achieve His wishes. We are working closely with a highly respected psychological profiler – Dr Adrian Trimmets of Westminster University – and I am confident we will bring the man calling himself "Lucifer" to justice.'

Lucifer scowled. *And I will stop at nothing to achieve* my *wishes. So you're not a woman. Who cares! Maybe it will throw the cops off my scent for a while.*

82

Stella and Garry pulled up in a visitor parking space outside the Elizabethan manor house that now served as the main building for Monksfield School, gravel popping and grinding under the car's fat tyres.

They emerged from the air-conditioned interior of the BMW into the scorch of yet another blazing day. Both detectives were wearing suits, Garry a navy two-piece, Stella, a steel-grey trouser suit. She rolled her neck and pulled the back of her jacket away from her shoulder blades, where it had stuck. Above them, a cloudless sky stretched away on all sides.

'Why can't detectives wear shorts and T-shirts?' she asked as they crunched across the gravel towards the front door.

'That would be an issue for Professional Standards and Competence, boss. Remember the bloke you saw without his shirt? That'd be us in weeks. It's a slippery slope.'

She grinned. She liked working with Garry. Built like an athlete

465

but with a decent brain inside the brawn, he was an excellent person to bounce ideas off, and he was pretty good with silly questions, too.

Around the mock-gothic front door, which was held open by a large stone doorstop on the tiled floor of the hall, deep-red roses hung in extravagant swags of blossom. Intertwined with them, an exotic creeper that Stella couldn't put a name to released an intense, sweet perfume. Overhead, bees hummed, a sound at once industrious and contented.

She looked up at an ornate, painted shield above the door. Mounted on a moulded wooden plaque, it was at least three feet from top to bottom. Stella didn't know the significance of the lions, knight's helmets and stripes, but one detail of the design leaped out at her. She nudged Garry.

'Look up there,' she said.

He followed her pointing finger.

'Very,' he paused, 'heraldic.'

'Look at the colours, Garry.'

'Bloody hell! Black and gold.'

They entered the cool of the lobby and turned right as the school secretary had instructed Stella when she'd rung to make the appointment. Down a short corridor lined with wide, whole-school photos stretching back over the years – the children in black blazers trimmed with gold – they found the school office. Stella knocked on the open door and entered.

Inside, three women were busy at computers. Two appeared to be in their mid-thirties, both blonde, both slim, both wearing glasses. They looked up and smiled at Stella and Garry. The third was cut from altogether different cloth. And wearing it, too.

Where the other secretaries had adapted their outfits to the heat, wearing cotton blouses and skirts or pale-coloured trousers, Mrs Royal, for this, surely, was the woman who had issued Stella with her instructions earlier, was resplendent in a fitted Chanel-style suit – a close-fitting boxy jacket and knee-length skirt in some sort of light pastel-pink tweed – and a white silk blouse.

'Of an age,' as Stella's mum would have said, a family phrase that meant anywhere north of sixty, Mrs Royal had ash-blonde hair cut in a short style, revealing a pair of delicate gold earrings. Her eyebrows had been pencilled and tweezed into an imperious arch that made her already forbidding features seem even haughtier.

She stood and rounded her desk, hand outstretched.

'You must be the detectives. I am Mrs Royal.'

Not Sylvia, then, Stella thought. *Too grand to be on first name terms with a couple of public servants? Or just too old-school?*

'Thank you for helping us out, Mrs Royal. I'm sure you must be a very busy woman,' Stella said.

'Yes, well,' she said, clearly mollified. 'After what happened to poor Miss Burnside, naturally, we are all shocked. I have arranged for you to interview the head at eleven forty-five. He has a very important meeting with the governors at one so please try not to delay him. After that, I thought you might want to interview Mr Duckett. He was the one who discovered that Miss Burnside was missing. And if there's anything else you need, please ask. There's a spare office down the corridor, the second door after this one. It's just a filing room, really. I've equipped it with a coffee machine and some pods and there's water and squash. Dial zero for an outside line if you use the phone.'

After this speech, Mrs Royal stood, waiting, her hands clasped in front of her, eyeing Stella and then Garry in turn.

Why do I feel like we're rabbits being looked at by a hawk? Stella thought.

'That is very kind and efficient of you, Mrs Royal. Thank you,' Stella said. 'As we've got fifteen minutes before our meeting with the head, we'll just have a wander round if that's all right with you. You know, to get a feel of the place.'

The older woman's eyes flashed behind her glasses but she didn't demur. Perhaps she respected another efficient, no-nonsense woman, Stella mused.

'Of course. The head's office is upstairs. Turn right at the top of the staircase and he occupies the room at the far end of the corridor.'

. . .

Stella led Gary back the way they'd come, out through the front door and back into the sunshine. She could hear shouts from a sports pitch beyond some hard tennis courts to the right of the visitor parking.

'Let's have a wander,' she said, heading in the direction of the shouting.

Pitchside, they watched as two mixed teams played an energetic game of football. The referee was a youngish guy with a heavy black beard, hipster-style. As he ran half the length of the pitch to keep up with a fleet-footed girl dribbling the ball towards her opponents' goal, he glanced over at Stella and Garry. Stella thought she saw a cloud flit across his face, but then it was gone.

A boy tackled the onrushing striker, and the ball emerged from the collision sailing high into the air towards the two plainclothes spectators.

Garry chested it down, backed up a pace then booted it back towards the nearest player, a gangling lad with a striking mop of ginger curls.

'Thanks, sir,' he called, as he turned and prepared for a throw-in.

'That was impressive,' Stella said. 'Still playing five-a-side, are you?'

Garry grinned ruefully.

'I try to keep it up, but you know what it's like in this job. Half the time I get down there and it's five of us in total.'

'So here's a thing,' she said, watching as the girl striker finally managed to put one past the opposing goalie. 'Serial killers are normally pretty conservative in their routines. Everything from MO and signature to victim selection. And that includes geography. I mean, Peter Sutcliffe wasn't called The Yorkshire and Hertfordshire Ripper, was he?'

'Nope. So are you still wondering why he came all the way out here to murder Amy Burnside?'

Stella nodded. She looked around, beyond the players racing

across the pitch, over their heads to the wooded hills beyond. She thought back to the rural landscape they'd travelled through on the drive down.

Hundreds of thousands of acres of pastoral land, like the Industrial Revolution had never happened. And then to the streets on which the first two victims had lived. One a long street of detached multi-million-pound houses facing Wimbledon Common, the other a more down-to-earth, though still expensive, Victorian terrace smack-dab in the heart of an urban neighbourhood.

She scratched her head, made itchy by the heat.

'Why would he move so far from London, Garry? And why here?'

'She was the Head of RE, so she fits the profile. Except, does she really? Do we know if she'd done any radio or telly? Was she a blogger? Without a public profile there's a big gap in the victimology.'

'That's where I am. So, if she wasn't a prominent Christian, then he must have known about her some other way.'

'A parent?'

Stella wrinkled her nose.

'Maybe. Although I hope to God you're wrong, because can you imagine having him as your dad? You'd be following in your old man's footsteps before your pubes had appeared.'

'What if he went here? You know, an Old Boy.'

'Yeah, that could work. Although Amy was only twenty-eight so he'd have to have been here quite recently. We need to ask the headmaster when she joined the staff.'

Garry checked his watch and nodded towards the main building.

'Come on then. Let's go and ask him.'

James Haddingley stood as Stella and Garry entered his office. Dark, widely-spaced eyes peered out from beneath neatly-cut hair of a uniform greyish-silver. A navy suit jacket hung on a hanger behind the door, and Stella noticed dark sweat patches under the arms of his sky-blue shirt. He was clearly still in shock.

As they shook hands, and he waved them to two seats facing him across the desk, Stella recognised the signs. A blankness in the gaze, slack muscle tone in the cheeks and jaw. That morning's shave had clearly been a slapdash affair: he had missed a whole section of his chin, where dark bristles clustered.

'I'm DCI Cole and this is DS Haynes,' Stella said. 'We are truly sorry for your loss.'

'Oh, thank you, but Amy wasn't family, Detective Chief Inspector.'

Stella smiled.

'I know that, but she was a member of your staff. Your website talks about how you view the school as a family. And please, call me Stella,' she added, turning to smile at her bagman.

'Garry,' he added, placing a large hand flat against his chest. 'Short for Garfield.'

'After the cricketer?' Haddingley asked. 'I'm a fan, by the way. That's why I asked.'

'On the button,' Garry said with a broad smile. 'My dad and granddad were massive fans of the West Indies. Sir Garfield Sobers was their hero. They were religious men, but I think given a choice between meeting Garry Sobers and God, they would have chosen Garry.'

'No need to die first,' Haddingley said. Then his face seemed to fold in on itself. A sob broke from his lips like a caged bird bursting from its prison.

He fished a paper tissue out of a box on the desk and blew his nose. He took another and wiped his eyes, then looked at Stella.

'I'm sorry,' he said. 'That keeps happening.'

'That's OK. Are you getting some help?'

'I've been too busy making sure the children are all right. Amy was a real favourite with them even though she was relatively new here.'

'How long had she been on the staff?'

'Two years. She joined us just in time for the Autumn term in 2016.'

'So that means two sets of leavers would have gone on from Monksfield during her time here, is that right?'

Haddingley appeared to be having trouble working back through the dates. He passed a hand across his face.

'Er, yes. I think so. Let me just…' He looked up at the ceiling for a second or two, then back at Stella who was waiting, patiently, for him to answer. 'Yes. The 2016/17 Year 13s and then the 2017/18s last June.'

'How many children would that have been? In total, I mean, across both school years?'

'Off the top of my head? I suppose about eighty? Seventy-five, maybe? Sylvia can give you precise numbers.'

Stella nodded and made a note. *I bet you're the only person here who she allows to use her Christian name*, she thought. *But that's a lot of checking we're going to be doing. Even if we only check the boys, it's still going to be forty-odd.*

'Yes please. And we'd like a list of their names and addresses, please.'

Haddingley seemed to wake from a half-sleep. He sat bolt upright in his padded chair and leaned across the desk towards them, eyes wide.

'You're not suggesting that one of the… No!' he said, raising his voice. 'That's impossible. I can't – this is a *Christian* school, DCI Cole. Our values are those taught by Jesus Christ.'

Stella smiled sympathetically.

'It's a line of enquiry, that's all. I'd be failing in my duty if I failed to consider every possibility.'

'But surely, you can't imagine for one moment that a, a child, could do… could …'

He faltered and looked away, through the window. Stella imagined he was clinging to a vision of a purer, more tranquil England, where RE teachers weren't skinned alive in their own kitchens and Metropolitan Police detectives didn't insinuate that one of your charges might be a sadistic killer.

She forbore from explaining to the reeling man behind the desk that, in her long experience, and that of her colleagues, children were capable of almost every crime imaginable, up to and including the sadistic murder of other children.

'As I said, at this stage it's just a matter of routine. So, the list?'

Haddingley shook his head violently.

'I can't. Hand their details over, I mean. There are privacy considerations. You've heard of GDPR, I'm sure.'

Stella groaned inwardly, remembering Cam's impassioned rant against the troublesome piece of legislation.

'Of course, and I am not asking you to breach anyone's privacy, James. But we are trying to track down and arrest a violent killer. A serial killer, in fact, who is preying on women who hold strong Christian views. Like Amy.'

'I'm afraid my hands are tied,' he said with an air of finality. 'All the parents have signed an agreement with the school. We are bound not to share their data or that of their children without their express permission.' He paused and, in an apologetic tone of voice, said, 'I suppose this is the bit where I tell you I'll need to see a warrant.'

Stella tried hard to accept that Haddingley was under stress and was struggling to stay afloat. But it was a complication she could have done without.

She turned to Garry.

'Make a note, please, Garry.'

'I'm sorry. You can see my position,' Haddingley said, looking as though he wasn't far from crying again.

'It's fine. It just means another delay, that's all. Let's move on. There are similarities between the way Amy was killed and the murders of three other women in London that we are investigating as a series. But when I trained as a detective, my inspector had this mantra when we were looking at a murder. "Let's clear the ground beneath our feet," he used to say.'

'What does that mean?'

'It means, let's not ignore the obvious while we going flying off into the wilds of speculation. Did Amy have any enemies, for example? Anyone on the staff, or in her personal life?'

Haddingley shook his head.

'No, not at all. Everyone loved Amy. She was young, she was open to new ideas, she was full of energy.'

The answer came too quickly. And Haddingley had smiled as soon as he started speaking about the dead RE teacher.

'But sometimes, especially I imagine, in a traditional school like yours, James, can't all that youthful enthusiasm rub people up the wrong way?'

Haddingley frowned and looked away.

'Look, Amy was going places, OK? She was ambitious. She wasn't content to just do things the way they'd always been done. But that was precisely why I hired her, don't you see? To shake things up. So yes, perhaps there are one or two of the old guard who saw her as a threat to the established order, but in our world that meant the odd waspish comment in a staff meeting, not killing her!'

'What about her personal life?' Garry asked.

'What about it?'

'She was single, right? Any ex-boyfriends – or girlfriends – who might have held a grudge?'

'Yes, Amy was single. And, as far as I'm aware, she preferred men. But we didn't really have the sort of relationship where she would have told me about a stalker.'

'No? What sort of relationship did you have, then?'

Haddingley's eyes locked onto Garry's.

'A purely professional one, I assure you. I thought you were here to investigate her murder, but all you seem to be doing is casting aspersions, first at my children, then at my staff, and now at me.'

83

MONDAY 10TH SEPTEMBER 11.45 A.M.
CITY HALL

Craig Morgan sat at his desk, staring out of the window at the river. He was thinking about power, and what a determined man with ambition could do with that accruing to the Mayor of London. The phone on his desk rang.

'Morgan.'

'Craig, it's Remi. I wonder, could you spare me a few minutes of your time?'

'Of course. Now?'

'Now would be good.'

Five minutes later he knocked on Remi's door and entered her palatial office. *When this is mine we'll be throwing out all these vile soft furnishings for a start*, he thought.

'You called?' he said with a smile.

'Have a seat.'

He plucked at the knees of his suit, then sat and crossed his legs.

'What's up, Remi?'

He watched her face, spattered with dark-brown freckles that contrasted oddly with her pale-caramel skin. Looking for any telltale sign that might indicate her mood.

'What's up? Oh, I don't know, maybe the fact that you know full well you voted the same way as I did on the cuts to the police budget in January. Only now you're sounding off in the *Evening Standard* about how I've, and I quote, "cut the Met off at the knees". And don't think I don't know what's going on. You're looking ahead, aren't you? To the election. You're trying to rebrand yourself as some sort of pro-police man of the people. Well, it won't work. And here's why. I'm going to—'

'Oh do shut up, Remi,' he said, enjoying the way her eyes flashbulbed and her mouth dropped open. 'You're not going to do anything. If you attack me in public, it'll confirm what I've been saying about you. A weird position for a Tory to adopt, going after somebody who's championing our dear little boys and girls in blue.'

Remi sat back in her chair, eyes blazing.

You're actually very attractive, he thought. *Shame you play for the opposition. I could imagine us together. I bet you like a bit of rough and tumble. You've got the look.*

Finally she spoke.

'I gave you the Policing and Crime portfolio. And I can take it away.'

He shook his head and grinned at her.

'Yeah, not so sure about that, actually. I've got some very, what shall we say, *influential* friends in the media. You try anything and I swear to God I'll bring you down. You'll fall so far and so fast you'll feel the wind whistling past your ears. Now, unless there was anything else, I have a meeting to discuss the rising tide of knife crime.'

Having delivered himself of what he considered an unbeatable parting shot, he got up and walked out, leaving her door wide open.

84

MONDAY 10TH SEPTEMBER 12.05 P.M.
SHAFTESBURY

Something in the vehemence of Haddingley's denial struck Stella. She decided to let Garry continue with his line of questions. She glanced at him for a second, then back at Haddingley. Garry picked up the subtle signal she'd sent him; one of the many pleasures of working with the same man for a few years was the almost telepathic rapport you built up.

'So you weren't her lover?' he asked.

'What? No! Of course I wasn't!'

'Why "of course"? I've seen a photo of Amy. She was an attractive young woman. Single, as you said. Full of,' Garry checked his notebook, 'energy.'

'I'm married, for one thing.'

Garry pursed his lips.

'I know you're a bit isolated out here, but even you must know, James, that married men have been known to play away from home.'

Garry had a certain way of speaking when he was sure of

something. Stella thought of it as his 'man-to-man voice'. Quiet, but assured, with just a hint of amusement, as if to say, 'come on, we both know what's going on here'.

Haddingley simply stared at Garry. Stella counted to five before he answered, in a low voice.

'This is a Christian school, as I told you before. The governors appointed me to maintain a very particular set of values. It would be… difficult, for me… professionally… if anything about my private life were to find its way to their ears.'

Stella pressed her right boot toe gently against Garry's left ankle, out of Haddingley's sight. She spoke.

'We're not in the business of stirring up gossip, or blighting people's careers, James. We simply need to get to the truth about the circumstances of Amy's death. So if there's anything you can tell us that will help us to do that, even perhaps something personal, now would be the time to speak up.'

Seemingly resigned to his fate, as he apparently imagined it, Haddingley inhaled, then spoke on the out breath.

'Amy and I were seeing each other. Sleeping together, to save you the trouble of asking. It started at the leavers' do just after the end of the summer term. At the end of the party, the school band always plays a slow dance and the children were egging the staff on, and we ended up together dancing to 'Whiter Shade of Pale'. We kissed, and, oh god, poor Amy!' he wailed, covering his face with both hands and slumping back in his chair.

Stella and Garry exchanged a look. Transmitted in the few, fleeting seconds of minutely varying facial expressions were a number of separate ideas.

I had to ask.

I know.

He didn't do it.

I know.

Let's leave the alibi question.

Sure.

'I'm sorry we have to ask these questions,' Stella said. 'And I assure you we will keep your private life private.' *Unless you're Lucifer, in which case I will personally expose you to the world for what you are.*

'Thank you. Is there anything else you want to ask me?'

'Yes. Can you tell us whether Amy had any sort of public profile? Outside school. Was she a blogger? Did she have a magazine article published, anything like that?'

Haddingley shook his head. He looked eager to help now that his secret was out.

'No, nothing like that. She had a Twitter account and she was on Facebook, like we all are, but it was just personal news and school stuff. You have to be so careful these days. The kids will pick up on anything and, before you know it, your drunken party antics are all over Whatsapp. Speaking metaphorically,' he added, quickly, glancing nervously at each detective in turn.

'OK, thanks. That's it for now. We'll contact you once we have the warrant for the leavers' data but, until then, we'll let you prepare for your meeting with the governors.'

'Thank you. Is Sylvia looking after you?'

'Yes, she's a star. We've even got a posh coffee machine, haven't we, Garry?'

'Better than anything at Paddington Green,' he lied, smiling.

'Good. Well, if you'll excuse me then,' he said, then stood and offered his hand again.

———

The meeting with Marcus Duckett was purely a housekeeping exercise and yielded nothing of any value, evidentiary or otherwise. He explained how he'd noticed the racket coming from Amy Burnside's classroom and gone in to investigate but could offer no new insights into her character, or her social or professional circles.

Stella and Garry slumped in two of the plastic, steel-framed chairs in the office Sylvia Royal had provided.

'These remind me of school,' Garry said, grinning. 'They were uncomfortable then and they're no better now. You'd think

Charlotte and Jonty would have their soft little bottoms cushioned a bit better than this, wouldn't you?'

Stella laughed.

'Maybe they do. Maybe the lovely Mrs Royal laid these on especially for us. And was that a little bit of chippiness from you, DS Haynes?'

'Me? Chippy? What, can't a black kid from Balham make a joke without being called a class warrior?'

'*I* didn't call you a class warrior. *I* just asked if you were a bit chippy. Now I think maybe you are after all, eh, Garry? Going to start throwing rocks through those lovely mullioned windows, are we?'

'I sincerely hope not,' a voice said from the doorway.

Stella and Garry looked round in perfect synchrony to see Sylvia Royal smiling archly at them.

'How long have you been standing there, Mrs Royal?' Stella asked.

'Let's just say the children's *little* bottoms,' she raised an eyebrow while looking at Garry, 'are cushioned by nothing more than their clothes.'

'Sorry, Mrs Royal,' Garry said.

Then she did something unexpected. She laughed. A full-throated sound that filled the small office.

'Oh, my goodness, DS Haynes, you sound exactly like a teenage boy who's been sent for chores.'

Seizing the opportunity, Stella spoke while the senior secretary was wiping her eyes with a lace-edged handkerchief.

'Mrs Royal, could we ask you a few questions about Amy Burnside?'

'Yes, of course,' she answered, all seriousness now. She pulled the door closed behind her and pulled up a third chair, forming a triangle with the two cops. 'What do you want to know?'

'We asked Mr Haddingley about whether Amy might have had any enemies here at Monksfield. He was very sure she hadn't. Would that be your view as well?'

Mrs Royal took her time answering. Stella sensed, not the

evasive pause of a suspect trying to construct a lie they could stick to, but something softer. As if she were weighing up how best to help the police without compromising the reputation of the school.

'I think James is, broadly, right. Amy had no enemies. Not as such. I think a couple of the older teachers, and myself, if I am being brutally honest, felt that she was a little too keen to shake things up before she'd fully worked out which bits of the jigsaw went where. But as the headmaster probably told you, disagreements in school life are generally fought on the battlefield of the staffroom carpet or the governors' meeting. You may have already deduced, if that is the right word, that I have been at Monksfield for a long time. A very long time, in fact. James is the fourth headteacher I have served. Not the best, I have to say, but certainly not the worst.'

'So you know how the jigsaw fits together,' Garry said.

'Indeed I do. Monksfield is a good school. And a peaceful one, by and large. It—'

'I'm sorry, Mrs Royal,' Stella interrupted, 'What do you mean, "by and large"?'

Mrs Royal looked away, then back at Stella.

'A figure of speech, that's all.'

'I know it's a figure of speech, but you strike me as a woman with a long and efficient memory, and a real sense of the school's history. So when you said it was a peaceful school, "by and large", I think you were thinking of something in particular that wasn't so peaceful, weren't you?'

Stella smiled as she added the final question but inside she had that indefinable feeling all good coppers get, that *something* is about to happen.

Sylvia Royal sighed. Then she patted her hair at the sides. She folded her hands in her lap and regarded Stella with that same, hawkish stare she'd used earlier.

'I suppose you'd only look it up anyway or go ferreting around in our bank accounts, wouldn't you?'

'For what?'

'Oh dear. We've kept it quiet for nineteen years, which isn't too bad considering what happened. I shan't bother asking you to keep it quiet any longer. James would. But I've been around a little longer than he has. I know how the world works.'

Her pulse racing, Stella willed herself to keep her voice level. But that feeling of *something* had just multiplied to a full-blown certainty.

'What are you talking about, Mrs Royal?'

'I think based on what I'm about to tell you, you should probably call me Sylvia.'

85

MONDAY 10TH SEPTEMBER 1.00 P.M.
SHAFTESBURY

Stella fished out her digital recorder from her bag and showed it to Sylvia.

'I have a feeling we're going to need a verbatim transcript of what you're about to tell us, Sylvia. Would you be OK with me recording our conversation?'

Sylvia nodded graciously.

Garry sat with his pen poised over his notebook. Belt and braces.

Checking the voice-activated recorder was working, Stella turned to Sylvia.

'What happened?' she asked.

'Let's start with when, shall we? It was the summer holiday in 1999, so July and August. As with most boarding schools, we have a few children who, for one reason or another, can't return home in the holidays. A few from military families, a few whose parents are overseas, diplomats, business executives and so on, you can imagine.

'One of our stayers-on was a girl, well, a young woman, really, named Lauren Bourne-Clarke. She was in the lower sixth, seventeen at the time and one of those girls you just know will go on to do great things. Lauren was what we still like to call an all-rounder. Good at sports, captain of several teams but also academically brilliant. She was also extraordinarily beautiful in that way only the very young seem able to achieve. Clear skin, even-featured and, oh, you know, that, that radiance.

'One of our other stayers-on was a boy named Malachi Robey. He was,' she paused and compressed her lips for a moment, 'troubled. I suppose that's the fashionable word for it. Omit the final letter and I think you'd be closer to the truth. He was obsessed by the more violent stories in the Bible. The gorier the better. Hardly surprising, given his name. I mean, what sort of parents name a boy Malachi Jeremiah in this day and age? He asked so many questions in RE that his teacher referred him to the local parish priest.

'He excelled in art, too, although there again, he was disciplined after creating these truly disgusting,' she wrinkled her nose, 'models, I suppose you'd call them. Miniature re-enactments of people being tortured. He made them in clay and painted them to look realistic. He called them his martyrs. His classmates complained about them. Said they made them feel sick.'

'You said he was trouble,' Garry said. 'Anything else you can tell us about him?'

'He used to absent himself from school to go hunting in the woods outside the school grounds. There,' she said, pointing to a distant splotch of dark green beyond fields golden with ripe cereal crops. 'Once he brought back a young doe he'd killed and asked the cook to roast it for dinner. He'd skinned it already, and cut out its eyes and its teats. He was covered in blood. The poor woman fainted.'

Stella could feel her copper's instincts firing like an electrical storm as she listened. Mutilating animals as a child was one of the cornerstones for the diagnosis of psychopathy.

'Go on,' she said.

'Well, to cut a long story short, Lauren presented herself at the office in a very sorry state, claiming that Malachi had raped her.'

'And then what?' Stella prompted.

'And then the whole thing was hushed up.'

'Hushed up, how? Didn't you call the police?'

Sylvia shook her head, making her delicate drop earrings shake a little.

'I wanted to, but the then headmaster, a Mr Alfreston, forbade me. He actually laid his hand on mine as I was reaching for the receiver. I can remember his words very clearly. He said, "Wait, Sylvia. Think of the school. Think of our reputation." I was thinking of the crying young woman in front of me and what would happen to *her* reputation, but he was a very domineering man. It was impossible to argue with him.'

'You could have, though, couldn't you?' Garry asked. 'You could have called the police and told Alfreston where to put the school's reputation.'

Sylvia sighed and Stella thought she saw the real woman behind the frosty facade. She had a narrow gold band on her ring finger and Stella wondered whether she had children of her own. And whether Alfreston had.

'Go on, Sylvia,' she said quietly.

'Yes, of course I could have done. I *should* have done. And my inaction on that day is something I have lived with and regretted every single day of my life since then. So, instead of calling the police, we called Lauren's parents. I say, "we", but it was me who had to do it. Alfreston's courage deserted him at that point. I told them that there had been an incident at the school involving Lauren and they needed to return to England to collect her urgently. They were film people, and at the time they were in Morocco, but I impressed upon them the seriousness of the situation, without giving the details, and two days later they arrived.'

'And how exactly did you, the school, I mean, hush it up?' Garry asked.

'Oh, the headmaster had consulted the governors by then. They'd approved an *ex gratia* payment from the school's contingency fund. One hundred thousand pounds. Malachi denied everything. He said she had seduced him. The difference in their ages made that a plausible story as far as the governors and Mr Alfreston were concerned.'

'How old was Malachi?' Stella asked.

Stella watched a flicker of anger cross the older woman's face. The cheeks lost their tinge of pink and her lips pulled back from her teeth, just for a microsecond, but Stella noticed it. A wild expression. A mother wolf protecting her cubs.

'Fourteen.'

'And they didn't pursue it through the courts?' she asked.

Sylvia shook her head.

'In the end they agreed it would be best all round if Lauren was spared that ordeal. It was only nineteen years ago but the legal culture towards rape victims was still rooted in suspicion of the accuser. Not like now with all that "Me Too" business. They took Lauren away that day and that was the last we heard of them. All parties signed a confidentiality agreement. I still have a copy in the school archive if you'd like to see it.'

'Yes please,' Stella said.

'I'll dig it out for you before you go.'

'So, what did you do with Malachi?' Garry asked. 'You must have been worried he'd do it again.'

Sylvia sniffed. Her eyes were glistening in the sunlight streaming in through the window.

'He was expelled the next day. The head called his father. Said if he didn't come and get his son immediately, he'd personally drive him to the station and put him on a train back to London.'

Inside, Stella was feeling cautiously optimistic. Admittedly, Malachi Robey had left years before Amy Burnside arrived, so he couldn't possibly have known her. But on the credit side of the balance sheet, they had a boy at a religious school who'd raped a girl three years older than him, then been expelled. He was never punished for his crime, which would have emboldened him still further. It wasn't the murderer's fingerprint in the victim's blood, but it was close. But there were other lines of enquiry emanating from the school that they still needed to follow up.

'Sylvia, you have been so helpful,' she said, a form of words she and Garry used to signal to the other that an interview was over. She heard him close his notebook. 'If you could dig out the confidentiality agreement and the record of Malachi's expulsion, that would be fantastic.'

Sylvia smiled thinly.

'Strictly speaking, I should remind you that you need a warrant for these documents, but…' she continued, holding up her hand to forestall Stella's next remark, 'that won't be necessary. I've had enough of the secrecy and the lies. My husband and I want to travel before we get too old. If the school wants to pursue me for breaching the rules, it'll have to deal with my newfound openness about what went on here in 1999.'

Stella nodded. She understood what was going on in Sylvia Royal's brain, or in her heart, perhaps. Once you decided enough was enough and that justice had to be done, nothing stood in your way. Certainly not a board of governors and the headmaster of a minor public school that had covered up the rape of one of its own students by another. She decided to try her luck just a little further.

'That's a very courageous decision. When we talked to Mr Haddingley, he said we *would* need a warrant for the records of your leavers from the last two years. I don't suppose…'

Sylvia's eyes flashed fiercely again. Clearly she'd reached some sort of crossroads in her moral life. She stood and turned to a filing cabinet and unlocked it with a key on a ring she brought out from a pocket in her jacket. Then she looked straight at Stella.

'I'm going to get Malachi's file and the confidentiality agreement, then take them into my office to make copies for you. Please don't look in the third drawer down, because that's where the hard copies of the leavers' records are filed and, as the head said, you need a warrant for those.'

Then she pulled out two apple-green cardboard folders from the drawer she was riffling through and left them alone.

Stella and Garry looked at each other. While he leaned his six-foot frame against the door, Stella pulled open the third filing cabinet drawer, located the folders she wanted, labelled, conveniently, 'Leavers 2017' and 'Leavers 2018' and photographed the pages with her phone.

Ten minutes later, Sylvia returned with the two apple-green folders and a plain white envelope, bulging with the copies. As she entered the room she glanced at the filing cabinet then back at Stella.

'Here you are,' she said. 'I don't know if it will be helpful, but I've put his last school photo in there. He was only fourteen, but perhaps your technical people can do something clever with it. If there's anything else you need, please don't hesitate to call me. I'll give you my mobile number. I may not be at the school very much longer.'

Stella noticed that Mrs Royal's lips were trembling. A fine sheen of sweat glistened on her top lip.

'Thanks. Here's my card. Call me if you think of anything else. It doesn't matter how trivial it feels. Any time of the day or night.'

Garry held out one of his cards, too.

'Just in case you can't get hold of the boss,' he said with a smile.

———

As they wove through the country roads, heading for the M3, Stella studied Malachi Robey's school photo. His deep-set brown eyes stared out at her from beneath a high, wide forehead, dotted with red pimples. He was smiling, but the expression hadn't really reached beyond the thin lips, which looked as though he had moved them into a curve by force of will. She'd seen the expression a couple of times before.

A face swam into view. It belonged to a sexual psychopath named Peter Moxey who the PPM conspirators had sent to kill her. Moxey's eyes had had the same bottomless-well look, right up to the point Stella had dug a broken bottle into them.

'Penny for them, boss?' Garry said.

Oh, you really don't want to spend your money on them, Garry.

'I was just thinking about Mrs Royal,' she answered.

He nodded.

'She really came through, didn't she? I thought she was going to be one of those ramrods who do everything by the book.'

'Me too. But then, I think she just saw the connection and it all fell apart. I've met people like Sylvia Royal before. Ex-soldiers, for example. They have a rigid code to live by and it gets them through the most incredible kinds of shit. But it's brittle. Once you get a crack in it, the whole thing shatters. I think that's what happened to her.'

'You think she's going to be all right? I thought she looked a bit off-colour when she came back in.'

'Probably just the relief at getting the whole thing into the open. Keeping those kinds of secrets eats away at people.'

As they passed Fleet services on the M3, Stella's phone rang.

'DCI Cole,' she said.

'Ah, yes, hello. It's Jerry Connolly here.'

'Hello, Jerry. What can I do for you?'

'It's Niamh's crucifix. I've had the rest of her jewellery back today from your forensic people. Her earrings and watch, wedding ring and so forth. But she always wore a gold crucifix on a thin chain and it's not here.'

As soon as he'd spoken, Stella's mind made the intuitive leap. *Trophy!*

'Can I ask you, Jerry, was Niamh definitely wearing it the day she was murdered?'

'Absolutely. She never took it off. Even in bed.'

'Did you see it on her, and I'm sorry to have to ask you this, when you discovered her?'

Connolly paused and Stella could only imagine the pain her question was causing him, as he'd be visualising his wife's mutilated body.

'Honestly? I can't remember. I think so, but I'm not one hundred per cent certain. The circumstances were,' he paused, 'extreme.'

'I totally understand. Look, we'll double-check and I'll get back to you if we find it. But there is another possibility, which is that the murderer took it with him.'

'Find it if you can, please. It means a lot to me.'

'Of course.'

'Wearing what?' Garry asked.

Stella was about to answer with the truth when a thought flashed across her brain. A thought to do with the mole in the investigation.

'An emerald ring. Can you follow up on the chain of custody for Niamh's personal effects when we get back, please?'

'Sure.'

'In fact, can you get me lists of personal effects for all four women, please?'

He nodded, and accelerated around a cluster of slow-moving traffic. Back to Paddington Green. Back to start looking for Malachi Robey.

While Garry started hunting down the lists of personal effects, Stella went to her office and closed the door.

She called Monksfield and asked to be put through to Haddingley. One of the younger secretaries answered and explained in what sounded like a tearful voice that he was still in his meeting with the governors.

'Could you tell him it's DCI Cole, please. I need to ask him a question urgently. And before you go, is everything OK? You sound upset.'

'It's Mrs Royal,' the young woman said. 'She, I don't know, fainted or something. We had to call her husband to take her home.'

'I'm so sorry to hear that. Perhaps it's the heat. She does like her tweed suits, doesn't she?' *Plus she just blew the whistle on a near-twenty-year rape cover-up.*

Stella listened to some Vivaldi on repeat for the five minutes it took for the secretary to locate Haddingley.

He came on the line, sounding stressed.

'DCI Cole. How can I help?'

'Did Amy wear a crucifix?'

'What?'

'Did Amy wear a crucifix? You know, maybe a little one on a chain?'

'Yes, she did. It was silver. Why?'

'It may be helpful to our enquiries. Thanks, James. Sorry to pull you out of your meeting.'

Calls to Sister Rose at the Brockwell Park community and the editorial offices at *The Church Times* revealed that both women wore gold crucifixes.

When Garry returned with the four lists, she thanked him and asked him to close the door on his way out. Ignoring his quizzical look, she started reading.

86

TUESDAY 11TH SEPTEMBER 8.00 A.M.
PADDINGTON GREEN

Standing in her usual place beside the whiteboard, Stella tried to strike an upbeat note. But the team of detectives and civilian staff in front of her looked weary. The faces of the four murdered women – apart from Niamh Connolly, horribly disfigured by blood, putrefaction or the absence of skin – stared out at them as if to say, *Why haven't you caught him yet? How many more of us must die?*

When everyone was settled, coffees and teas in hands, snack bars or chocolate substituting for breakfast, Stella smiled briefly and began.

'We have a new suspect.'

She turned and scrawled a name on the main whiteboard, underlining the first two initials in red.

MALACHI JEREMIAH ROBEY

Then she stuck his school photo on the board beneath his name.

'Who is he, boss?' Baz asked.

'He attended Monksfield between 1993 and 2001. While there, he raped, well, actually it was an allegation, but I'm inclined to believe it, a girl in the sixth form. Robey was fourteen at the time. His victim was seventeen. So we have a connection between a juvenile sex offender and the school where Amy Burnside worked.'

'Bit thin, isn't it?' Roisin asked. 'I mean, that's barely even circumstantial.'

'Hold on, Rosh,' Garry said. 'The boss hasn't even got started yet.'

Stella nodded to Garry. *Thanks.*

'Roisin's right. That is circumstantial. As is this. Robey was obsessed by torture and martyrdom. He made art models and apparently got sent off to see the local vicar because he had so many questions in RE. And, saving the best till last, he once brought back a deer he'd killed in the woods. He'd skinned it and cut out its eyes and teats. Which bears a direct correlation to the injuries inflicted on Niamh Connolly, Moira Lowney and Amy Burnside, three out of Lucifer's four victims. Circumstantial? Yes. But in my opinion enough to connect Malachi Robey to our murders and it explains why Amy Burnside was a geographical outlier. She represented the school that kicked him out.'

Becky spoke up.

'It would also give him a reason to kill her even though she didn't have a public profile.'

'Yes, you're right. So that's the two anomalies in Amy's case dealt with. Plus, and this is a lovely little detail, guess what the school colours are?'

Stella noticed Cam glance over at the whiteboard.

'Black and gold?'

'In one. So, here's where we are. I want everyone not engaged in something critical tracking down Robey. I read his school file on the way back from Monksfield. He grew up in Watford. From what the school secretary told us, my money is on him being a full-blown psychopath. That means he probably kept going. He may have been inside as a juvenile or an adult, probably for sexual offences, or

GBH, maybe arson. So let's look at that angle, too. I'll circulate his file so you've all got access. Rosh and Arran, can you sort out jobs for everyone, please? I'm going to talk to Jamie Hooke again. I need to get a handle on Robey's psychology. Hopefully so we can catch him before he kills anyone else but, at any rate, when we do get him, and we will, people, we will, it's going to be crucial to knowing how to interview him. Thanks, everybody.'

As the team dispersed, Stella sighed out a breath. She turned to Garry.

'Finally, it feels like we've got something concrete to go on.'

'You want me to start looking at the leavers' records? Just to be sure?'

'Not really. I'd much rather have you doing something on Robey. But yes please. We're under such a lot of scrutiny on this one we need to be watertight. Especially with that dickhead Craig Morgan hovering around.'

'No worries. There're roughly forty boys on the list who would have known Amy. I'll look for criminal records first, plus where they're living. Hopefully some have pissed off overseas. See how much I can narrow it down.'

'Take Becky and grab a handful of the CID imports. We need that list burning through as quick as possible.'

Ten minutes later, Stella walked into the forensics office at Paddington Green. A uniformed constable from Dorset had driven up late the previous day with all the physical evidence their CSIs had gathered from Amy Burnside's cottage and garden.

Lucian had laid all the items out on a table covered with clear plastic, taped around the edge.

In the centre, rolled into a coil, a metre of what Stella was sure was flax bell rope, supplied by Sherborne Ropes. A plaster cast of a shoe print, rough round the edges and with minimal definition. Several bloody fingerprints. And a great many blood samples.

Beneath each object lay its evidence bag, label signed and dated multiple times to preserve the chain of custody. Ranged along the back edge of the table, the crime scene photographs painted a grisly picture of the blood-spattered room. Stella experienced a sense-memory of the smell that momentarily nauseated her.

'The fingerprints are interesting,' Lucian said. 'They managed to get quite a few from the body itself. There were places where the fascia were stretched tight and the local CSIs did a brilliant job of lifting prints off them. If you look closely, you can see what appears to be the ragged edge of the glove he was wearing. I'm guessing it tore while he was skinning her, and he was too absorbed in his work to notice.'

'Can you get them sent to IDENT1? If it was Malachi Robey, I've got a strong suspicion he'll be on the fingerprint database.'

Lucian nodded.

'Already done. We should have the results back tomorrow.'

'What about the blood?'

'Well, that's the killer, no pun intended. I need to run some tests here to see if we can find any blood that didn't come from Amy Burnside. If we can find that, it's the killer's. Then we can fast-track it with NDNAD,' he said, then paused and raised his eyebrows. 'Budget permitting?'

'I'll have to clear it with Callie, but yes, I'm sure she'll OK the spend.'

'Good. Twenty-four hours after that, you'll have a profile and if his DNA's on NDNAD, you've got him: his blood in the victim's kitchen mixed up with hers. All you have to do then is find him.'

Stella nodded, her lips set in a grim smile.

'Piece of cake,' she said.

Lucian picked up the rope in his gloved hands.

'At first glance, it looks identical to the rope the POLSA found at the Niamh Connolly crime scene. We'll run the same tests. The footprint looks useless, I'm afraid. It came from the lawn, which was burnt to a crisp, apparently. We might be able to get an estimate of the size, but that's about all, I'm afraid.'

'No, it's fine. You've got plenty to be going on with. Let me know as you confirm things, OK?'

He nodded.

'Absolutely.'

'Great night, the other week, by the way,' she said.

She realised with a start that she wanted to talk about Jamie. Incongruously, given the charnel-house photos arrayed before her, but that was cop life.

'Yeah, Gareth and I had a really good time. And Jamie seems nice.'

She smiled.

'Nice? What, nice-but-boring nice? Nice-and-you'd-take-him-home-to-meet-your-mum nice? I need to know, Lucian.'

'Nice and I think he seemed struck on you. Nice and in your shoes I'd ask him out again. Nice and if you don't I will truly give up on your dating life. How's that?'

She grinned. Nudged him with her shoulder as she turned to leave him to his work.

'Nice,' she said over her shoulder.

Back at her desk, Stella called Jamie. She updated him on what she and Garry had discovered in Monksfield, thanks to Sylvia Royal's candour.

After listening silently, apart from a few muttered, 'Mm, hmm's, he spoke.

'It sounds like you have a classic psychopathic personality here. The parents come over on paper like religious obsessives. Had to be to pick those two names for their son. I wouldn't be surprised if it turns out the mother abused him sexually before he hit puberty. The rape sounds like an outpouring of anger and hatred against women. Based on the men I've treated here, I'd say he is totally confused about his sexuality. He's straight, but the incestuous childhood abuse will have left him, to use a technical term we like to employ in the psychiatry game, sexually fucked-up.'

'What are you saying? He's trying to kill his mother because she abused him sexually?'

'Yes, that's exactly what I'm saying.'

'What about the pubic hair? The absence of it?'

'I don't know. I'd hazard a guess and say he once saw her naked. Little boys are fascinated by female anatomy, and for most little boys their mother provides the first glimpse of an adult, that is to say, sexual, female body. If she shaved down there he would have keyed into that and he's recreating that experience in the women he's killing.'

'Any tips on catching him, doc? I'm asking more in hope than expectation, but if you don't ask…'

Jamie laughed and Stella let herself relax enough to enjoy the sound. Just for a few seconds.

'Way above my pay grade. All I can tell you is what you already know. Most serial killers, if they *are* caught, are caught by good old-fashioned coppering, or plain luck. Ted Bundy was finally caught because a cop stopped him for driving a stolen Beetle. Dennis Nilsen because neighbours complained about the smell coming from the drains. You're a good cop, Stella. And you've got a great team. Just keep at it. You'll get a break. I'm sure of it.'

'Thanks,' she said. 'I hope so. Do you know who's the hero of chapter five in Peter Karlsson's book?'

'Go on.'

'Saint Lawrence. They roasted him alive.'

'Then I'd better let you go. Oh, but one more thing.'

'Yes?'

'When this is all over, I don't suppose you'd like to come to dinner at mine? I cook a mean Thai fish curry.'

'I'd come to yours if you cooked me a fish finger sandwich. Thank you. I'd love that.'

Stella heard the pleasure in Jamie's voice as he answered.

'Good. Now, go and catch your serial killer.'

That afternoon, at 4.00 p.m., Baz approached Stella's desk, a wide smile on his face.

'Boss! We got lucky. Malachi Jeremiah Robey has a criminal record stretching back to 2001. Sexual offences mostly, including a conviction in 2009 for the rape of a fifteen-year-old girl. Apparently they suspected him of multiple murders of prostitutes, but the evidence for those was shaky, so the CPS went for the easy win and charged him with the rape.'

Stella's stomach lurched.

'Please tell me you're smiling because he was released before Lucifer started up.'

'He was. He served his full sentence, eight years. No parole on account of he was a naughty boy in Belmarsh. Didn't take the punishment beatings lying down. Left two guys in the hospital wing. One's in a wheelchair now, the other's blind. Robey gouged his eyes out with his thumbs and ate them.'

'When did he get out?'

'November last year.'

'Right. This is excellent work. We need to track him down. He is our prime suspect, OK? Prime. And I want him.'

Stella called everyone together and put the entire team on finding Malachi Robey.

'I want known associates, inside and outside prison. Arran, can you put a small team together and start hitting the databases, please?'

'Yes, boss,' he said, turning at once and tapping Will on the shoulder.

———

After the briefing, Roisin drove her own car eastwards, heading for Holborn, the long, wide street that ran east towards the City of London. At the far end, she turned left into Hatton Garden, the centre of London's jewellery quarter, and parked her car on a meter.

She retrieved her brown leather briefcase from the passenger seat and walked back ten yards or so, then turned left into a narrow archway between two jeweller's shops.

Thirty feet further down the alley, she emerged into a tiny

courtyard outside a pub named Ye Old Mitre. She politely excused herself as she squeezed through a knot of late-afternoon drinkers and entered the dark interior of the pub.

At the wooden bar stood Andy Robbins. She tapped him on the shoulder and he turned, smiling.

'Hello, Roisin. Red wine? Large one?'

'Yes, please.'

He turned back and when the barman approached ordered a glass of merlot for Roisin and a pint of Fuller's London Pride for himself. With the weather so warm, most of the patrons had opted to stand outside: the pub had no air conditioning. It meant they had no trouble finding a table, although the pub was stiflingly hot.

'Cheers,' Robbins said.

'Cheers.'

He took his jacket off and draped it over the third chair at the table. His pale-pink shirt had turned several shades darker under the arms and on the chest.

'I tell you what. If this heatwave doesn't end soon, we may have to start running stories about climate change.'

She snorted.

'In the *Sun*? Jesus! Bit highbrow for your readers, isn't it?'

'Don't be so sure. They're not all white van man and his missus. Anyway, let's talk about stories we're actually running. I assume you've got something new for me?'

'I have. The usual five hundred?'

'No problem.'

'Good. So, we're getting close. The prime suspect is a guy called Malachi Robey. He did eight years in Pentonville for rape. He's a psychopath. The public warning goes out tonight. You know the last victim, Burnside?'

'Yes. Not a Londoner though. You know why he killed her?'

'She was the Head of RE at his old school. He went to Monksfield until he was expelled for raping a sixth-former. And how about this, you know he's been strangling them with flax bell rope? Well, there are black and gold fibres in it. Guess what the school colours of Monksfield are?'

Robbins smiled and gulped down some more beer.

'Are they black and gold?'

'They are.'

'This is excellent stuff, Roisin. But I need a killer detail. Something nobody else'll have, even after the press conference. Even if they go down to the school.'

Roisin smiled.

'And you can have it. For another five hundred.'

Robbins didn't even hesitate.

'If it's as good as I think it's going to be, that won't be a problem. What have you got?'

Roisin sipped her wine.

'Money first. Then story.'

'Don't you trust me?'

Rosin smiled sweetly.

'About as far as I could throw you,' she said, poking a finger into his gut.

'Fine. Meet me here tomorrow, same time.'

———

While Roisin was meeting Robbins, Stella called in on Callie.

'I think we've got a name for Lucifer,' she said. 'A prime suspect. His real name's Malachi Robey.' She gave Callie a brief summary of what they'd discovered so far. 'Can you do a full-on public safety announcement? You know, the usual. "Extremely dangerous. Members of the public advised not to approach."'

'Sure. I'll get onto Tim. You OK, Stella? You're looking a bit grey round the edges.'

'Yeah, I'm fine. Just tired.'

'Aye, well, if ye'd take some time off like I keep telling you to, wee girl, maybe you'd be feeling a bit fresher. But,' Callie continued, before Stella could reply, 'I know that's not going to happen until you've closed this one. But remember what I said right at the beginning? I think I said something about having a feeling this one could be a runner. You know, if it is you're going to have to get some rest at some point. I don't want one of my best officers switching off permanently because she's too bloody stubborn to follow polite suggestions from her superior officer, eh?'

Stella smiled. Nodded.

'OK, boss,' she said. 'Message received and understood. I'll try.'

87

TUESDAY 11TH SEPTEMBER 11.30 A.M.
CITY HALL

'Hello, is that Craig Morgan?'

'Speaking.'

'Oh, great! Mr Morgan, my name is Lucy Sebastian. I'm a production assistant on *Newsnight*.'

Morgan sat straighter in his chair. *This is it!*

'How can I help you, Lucy?'

'We're planning tomorrow's show and, given your recent remarks in the *Standard* about the mayor's failure to resource the Metropolitan Police Service properly, and the Lucifer killings, of course, the producer asked me to invite you on as the main guest. In fact, we were really hoping you could persuade the psychologist to appear, too. Dr Trimmets, was it?'

Morgan pumped his fist, grinning. *Yes!* This would put Remi Fewings so far into the shadows she'd need a searchlight to find her way out again.

'I'd be delighted, Lucy, and I'm sure Dr Trimmets will need very little persuading by me, either. What time would you like us to arrive at the studios? I'm assuming it's your central London building, Broadcasting House?'

'Yes. We'd like you there for 10.00 p.m., if possible. So you have time for makeup and a relax in our green room, but please, let me send a car for you. Would 9.15 be OK for you?'

'Yes, fine. Thank you.'

Morgan gave the production assistant his address and then ended the call.

Look out, Remi. I'm coming for you.

He called Trimmets. Got voicemail. Spoke with a smile on his face.

'Ade, it's Craig. How do you fancy being on *Newsnight* tomorrow night? Be at my office at nine p.m.'

88

Once again, the *Sun* had printed details about Robey that went far, far beyond anything Callie had announced at the previous evening's press briefing.

In short, sharp sentences, it told its readers about Robey's history, his criminal record and a telling detail about his favoured murder weapon that only police officers and staff knew about.

Stella sat in her office, staring down at the blaring front-page headline. She could hear her back teeth grinding against each other.

**SERIAL KILLER
ROBEY IS SICK
SCHOOL RAPIST**

She re-read the article, wishing she still believed that Morgan was the leaker, then threw the paper across the room.

· · ·

'Arran, what have you got?' Stella asked at the afternoon briefing.

Arran slid forwards off his desk and cleared his throat, presumably not wanting a repeat of the toast-crumb incident. He pressed a button on a remote and projected a photo onto a newly cleaned whiteboard.

'Meet Malachi Robey, aged thirty-five. Weird-looking little sod, isn't he?'

The photo he was projecting had been created by a specialist graphics artist at Scotland Yard, using the school photo supplied by Sylvia Royal as a source. The artist had manipulated the original image using software designed to mimic the likely effects of aging given a standard set of factors, from diet to use of alcohol, tobacco and illegal drugs.

The face staring at them had an other-worldly quality. Photographic in quality but lacking any spark of humanity, which, Stella supposed, was hardly surprising given how little there had been to begin with.

The adult Malachi Robey had darker hair than the teenager, and a few faint lines across that unusually high and wide forehead. The jaw was heavier, and dark stubble across the upper lip, cheeks and chin emphasised the planes of his face.

The stare, so cold at fourteen, had, if anything emptied itself even further, so that Stella felt she was looking into a negative space where a person had been. What was that quote? Something about staring into an abyss? She made a mental note to look it up later.

'I've had it printed up and distributed throughout the Met's jurisdiction. If he turns up anywhere from Enfield to Croydon, Uxbridge to Upminster, someone'll spot him and call it in.'

'Thanks, Arran. Rosh, any news on that eyelash from the Lucifer letter? Or the text analysis? I thought we'd have had the results by now.'

Roisin looked down for a second, then back up at Stella.

'Still waiting. I'll get onto them after this.'

'OK, good. Baz, you're up.'

'Will and I have been through the leavers' lists from Monksfield and the list Professor Karlsson's secretary sent us. A complete bugger of a job, but nobody's a good fit for Lucifer. All alibied or basically just completely wrong for him.'

'Thanks, Baz, and the rest of you. It's a big box we can tick so nothing wasted there. Cam, how's it going with the list from the radio show?'

'Yeah, all done, basically. I spoke to each one in person.'

'How did they take it?'

'Actually, pretty well. I don't know if it's a God-thing, but they mostly seemed to feel that as long as they stayed with other people, He'd look after them.'

'Wow, OK, I was not expecting that. I guess there's something to be said for going to Church after all.'

Once the group had disbanded, Stella stood before the whiteboard.

First she looked at the dates of death. Dr Craven had sent her his estimate for Amy Burnside that morning.

Niamh Connolly: 13th August
Sarah Sharpe: 17th –18th August
Moira Lowney: 23rd August
Amy Burnside: 5th September

The list of similarities among the four murdered women was a long one.

Tortured according to chapter order of early draft of Prof Karlsson's book.
Strangled with flax bell rope supplied by Sherborne Ropes.
Pubic hair removed.
Drugged with Ketamine and Temazepam (injected in neck)
All Christians.
All except Amy Burnside = public profile.

'Everything all right, boss?' Garry said, coming to stand by her side.

'Yeah. I was just thinking about Amy Burnside. He did her last, but she looks like the lynchpin for the whole series. She represented the school that expelled him. The school where he committed his first rape.'

'That we know of.'

'OK, yeah, good point. That we know of. Why didn't he do her first?'

Garry shrugged.

'Honestly? I don't know. I mean, who knows how these nutters think? Maybe he wanted to get some practice in first. He certainly went to town on her more than the others. Maybe he woke up one morning going, "I know, I'll drive down to my school and butcher whoever's the current Head of RE." Maybe she was his grand finale?'

Stella shook her head, looking at the list of chapter titles from Karlsson's book. Someone had helpfully added colour photocopies of the illustrations of the martyred saints. She pointed to the illustration on the far right of the board.

'Look. Saint Lawrence. They roasted him alive. Apparently halfway through he said, "I'm done on this side, you can turn me over now."'

Garry nodded appreciatively.

'Good line. For a bloke being grilled alive. We'd better hope we find Robey before he turns some lady vicar into kebabs then, boss.'

———

Roisin re-read the email she'd received the previous day from the private forensics lab. In a few short sentences it informed her that they had been unable to extract enough DNA to build a profile. Dead end.

She went to tell Stella, wondering if she could find a way to lay the blame at Lucian's door. He'd been the first one to suggest not fast-tracking it, hadn't he? But the boss had left for the evening. So she parked it for another day.

She checked her watch. She had her meeting with Andy Robbins to look forward to.

———

The same drinks in front of them as the previous evening, Roisin and Robbins sat in a dimly lit corner.

'Have you got it?' she asked, without preamble.

Robbins nodded before opening his laptop bag for her to see the open-ended padded bag filled with banknotes.

'He's been taking their crucifixes as trophies. You know that's what serial killers do, don't you?'

Robbins smiled and nodded. He looked around, then took the fat envelope out of his bag and passed it under the table to Roisin, who slid it into her briefcase.

———

Later that evening, a glass of wine at her elbow and the day's reports in front of her, Stella looked up the quote she half-remembered. She read it aloud.

'"He who fights with monsters should look to it that he himself does not become a monster. And if you gaze long into an abyss, the abyss also gazes into you." Friedrich Wilhelm Nietzsche. Well, that's cheery.'

She finished her wine and went back to the details of the latest monster she was fighting.

Then she stopped.

'Our abyss is that letter,' she said aloud. 'And I want to gaze into it.'

She called Lucian and started speaking as soon as he answered.

'Hi, Lucian, sorry to call you at home.'

'Whoa there, boyo! It's Gareth. Lucian's cooking.'

Stella smiled.

'Oh sorry, Gareth. And could you not call me "boyo", please? I am a girl, you know.'

'And a very beautiful girl, you are, too, Stel. Just a term of endearment from the Valleys, nothing more.' Gareth had thickened his accent to almost music hall proportions, making Stella laugh.

'OK, fine. Well, boyo, do you think I could have a quick word with Lucian, please?'

'Fine. Always the bridesmaid, never the bride, that's me,' he said with an audible flounce in his voice. 'Luce, it's your girlfriend on the phone!'

Stella heard noises she imagined as a knife being placed on a chopping board and hands being wiped, then Lucian came on the line.

'Hola! What's up?'

'The Lucifer letter. Where is it?'

'The original's in my office and I sent a copy to a linguist I know. She said she'd prioritise it. She sent her report to Roisin last week, I think. Did Rosh not send it to you?'

Stella felt a cold fire ignite in her chest. Rosh was playing games. In the middle of a serial killer manhunt. She forced her voice to stay level.

'Oh, yeah. I think I saw it. Must have been a heavy email day. I'll go and recheck my inbox. Thanks, Lucian. What are you cooking?'

'It's a tagine of lamb with apricots, served with wild rice and bitter greens. Hungry? There's plenty to go round.'

'Oh, now you're making me sad! I'd love to, but…' She thought of Callie's parting shot. 'Actually, no. I mean, yes. Yes, please. Give me forty minutes.'

He laughed.

'Don't kill yourself on the bike – it'll be an hour at least.'

Before leaving, Stella called Roisin.

'Oh hi, boss. Still working?'

'Nope. Just heading out for dinner. One thing, Rosh.'

'Yes?'

'Did that forensic linguist send you her report on the Lucifer letter yet?'

Please, please don't say no, Rosh. Please don't lie to me.

89

WEDNESDAY 12TH SEPTEMBER 8.00 P.M.
LISSON GROVE

Stella listened to her heart beating, loud in her ears. She'd thought she could trust Roisin, thought her professionalism would overcome her jealousy. *But was I right, Rosh?*

'Yeah, she did. To be honest, it wasn't really any use. It was a box ticked, for sure, but no real insights, you know what I mean? More hedging than a maze.'

'Oh, OK. Shame. So, when did she send it to you?'

The hesitation lasted two full seconds. Stella counted.

'Uh, last week, I think. Let me check, I'll have to put you on speaker while I find the email. OK, here we are,' Roisin said, her voice tinny as it emerged from the phone's speaker. 'Yes, here we are. Tuesday the fourth.'

'Rosh, that was over a week ago. Why didn't you show me?'

'Like I said, it's pretty thin. Look, boss, we can all see how hard you're driving yourself. First in, last out most days. I can't remember the last time you took a day off. I just thought as it wasn't germane to the investigation, I'd—'

Stella had had enough.

'Not germane? The only direct link to Lucifer? Seriously, Rosh, that is complete bullshit and you know it. Why did you hold it back?'

Roisin raised her voice.

'I just said, I wasn't *holding it back*. In my judgement, it wasn't great product.'

Stella could hear the anger, but she knew the sound of a junior officer on the back foot as well. And that's where Roisin was now. She shook her head, fighting down an urge to start in on Roisin about loyalty and playing as a team, not as individuals.

'Well please would you email me a copy right now? You know, for a second opinion on the *product*.' Stella couldn't help the jab at Roisin's spy talk.

'Of course. It's on its way. Was there anything else, boss?'

'No thanks. I'll see you tomorrow. Have a good night.'

I hope you get nightmares.

Her phone pinged a few seconds later. She printed out the report, folded it in four and stuck it her pocket, then grabbed her jacket and helmet and her bike keys and headed out.

She rode fast. Thirty-eight minutes later, having only once resorted to her blue flashers, she was heeling out the Triumph's kickstand and leaning it over on the parking area beneath Lucian's Docklands apartment building.

Gareth opened the door and, after kissing her extravagantly on both cheeks, pushed a glass of red wine into her hand.

'Château Musar, Lebanon's finest and a fitting accompaniment to Lucian's latest culinary extravaganza,' he announced.

She took a sip of the deep-red wine.

'Mmm, lovely. Do you always speak like that, or do you put it on especially for me?'

He widened his eyes and placed a hand on his chest as if fainting.

'Stel! You wound me. It's just the poetry in my Welsh soul,' he moaned. 'A boy can't help his roots, can he?'

Lucian appeared, dressed in soft, grey trousers and a loose-fitting sea-green shirt.

'Stop bullshitting, Gar,' he said, smiling. He came over and kissed Stella. 'His parents have a house on Primrose Hill in Cowbridge. It's the most expensive place to live in Wales.'

Gareth looked offended. He pushed a hand through his hair and pouted.

'I can't help it if my *mam* and dad are minted, can I? I'm just a South Wales boy at heart. I reckon Barry's more my spiritual home than Cowbridge.'

'Of course it is. If by Barry you mean Manilow!' Lucian said.

Stella enjoyed listening to the two men banter. She could feel her shoulders unwinding after the ride, which had been fuelled by her anger at Roisin's duplicity as much as 95 RON petrol.

She sipped her wine and sat at the kitchen table. There, she pulled out the linguist's report and read it while Gareth and Lucian continued to bicker.

Something about the list of capitalised words was knocking at the doors of her consciousness, demanding admittance. But with the noise the boys were making she couldn't focus. She took the report out onto the balcony and slid the double-glazed doors closed behind her.

The apartment building faced the Thames and, apart from the occasional chug from one of the launches, the river was quiet. Holding the report in front of one of the lamps on the balcony, and trying to let her mind drift a little, Stella looked at the list.

MALADJUSTED TORTURERS
CHIMAERA
MONSTERS
ROB
SEXUAL
BREASTS
EYES

513

MORAL HIGH GROUND
DEPRAVITY AND CORRUPTION
THE FIRES OF HELL
LIVES
THE FOURTH HORSEMAN

And then she saw it. The hidden message in the text. She gasped.

'Shit!'

She went back inside, grabbed a pen off the countertop separating the kitchen from the dining area and started crossing out words and letters.

'What is it, dear girl?' Gareth asked. 'You look like you've seen a ghost.'

She shook her head as she finished scribbling.

'Not a ghost. A killer. Look.'

Stella had altered the list so that the visible parts read:

MAL~~ADJUSTED TORTURERS~~
~~CHIMAERA~~
~~MONSTERS~~
ROB
~~SEXUAL~~
~~BREASTS~~
EY~~ES~~
~~MORAL HIGH GROUND~~
~~DEPRAVITY AND CORRUPTION~~
~~THE FIRES OF HELL~~
LIVES
~~THE FOURTH HORSEMAN~~

Gareth scanned the list, frowning. Then he looked at her.

'Malachi Robey Lives,' he said. 'What does that mean?'

'They're words from the letter Lucifer wrote to the *Sun*.'

'Oh God, yes! I saw that. Dreadful stuff from start to finish.'

'And Malachi Robey is our prime suspect. He was telling us his name in the letter. Crowing over it.'

Then, feeling nauseous, she sat back and pulled her ponytail through her fist.

'Oh, shit! Roisin said she got this on the fourth. Amy Burnside was murdered on the fifth. We could have prevented it!'

Lucian came over and laid a comforting hand on Stella's shoulder.

'Are you sure? It would have been a long shot even then.'

'I don't know, Lucian,' she said, suddenly exhausted. 'Maybe we could have tracked him back to Monksfield in a day. Maybe not. Can I ask you two questions?'

'Go on.'

'Can I stay here tonight, please?'

'Of course!'

'Thanks. Then can I have some more wine, please?'

He poured her another glass.

———

Stella slept badly. She woke at six, left a thank-you note on the kitchen counter and slipped out, closing the door quietly behind her.

She rode home, enjoying the relative freedom of the near-empty streets, showered and changed and was at the station just after seven, breakfasting on a takeaway coffee and a croissant.

90

Stella sat at her desk, waiting, pain gnawing at her gut. In front of her lay that day's *Sun*. The headline told her all she needed – and didn't want – to know. And she'd been right to seed the emerald ring story with Garry – even though she regretted the lie, she'd never really suspected him .

The mole had taken the bait and stuck her head in the noose.

TWISTED KILLER
ROBEY TAKES
'TROPHY' FROM
EACH VICTIM

The tiny paragraph below the headline pulled the noose tight.

Police believe that Malachi Robey, the man wanted for the 'Lucifer' killings, is taking a crucifix 'trophy' from each of his victims, the *Sun* can reveal.

517

Beneath the newspaper lay the forensic linguist's report and, beside it, the list of capitalised words with her own crossings out. Beside that lay a crime scene photo of Amy Burnside's flayed body. She was staring at the dead young woman's naked, blood-streaked eyes wishing she could turn back time.

From across the incident room she heard Baz greeting Roisin, who'd just pushed through the double doors. She stood up and watched as Roisin made her way to her desk, which was about ten feet away from Stella's. Then she called her over.

'Rosh, have you got a minute, please? My office.'

At the final two words, Stella saw a black cloud flit across Roisin's usually untrammelled features. She also saw a couple of the other officers look up. Everybody knew Stella hardly ever used her office.

'Sure, boss. Everything all right?'

Stella didn't trust herself to answer, so she gathered the documents from her desk and preceded Roisin into the office, sitting down behind the desk and allowing the DI to come in, close the door and take a seat opposite her.

'Couple of things, Rosh,' she said, so angry that her voice was trembling.

'OK.'

'First, I want you to tell me the truth. Have you been leaking details of the investigation to the *Sun*?'

'What? No! I thought we all agreed it was Morgan.'

'Yeah, we did. But I haven't seen him around for the last few days and yet the *Sun* is still getting inside information.'

'It could be anyone. Someone in Forensics, the exhibits room… there must be dozens of people. Why are you picking on me?'

Roisin was doing a good job of looking indignant. It was time to pull the lever that would drop the trapdoor from under Roisin's feet. Stella picked up the *Sun* and pointed to the paragraph of text.

'See that?'

Roisin leaned forward and read the twenty-six incriminating words.

'That could have been anyone. You said yourself Garry knew, and you left a message with Forensics.'

'I lied.'

Roisin's pale-blue eyes widened. Stella watched the colour drain from her face.

'What?'

'I lied, Rosh. Nobody knows about the crucifixes except Robey, me, and you. So unless you want to suggest he's our mole,' she paused, 'or I am, then that leaves you. This is corruption, Rosh. You've been taking money from a journalist in return for confidential information. I could have you investigated by Professional Standards.'

Roisin wasn't done. Instead of admitting it, she seemed ready to brazen it out.

'The Ghost Squad? You've got nothing to give them and I resent the accusation! Maybe one of the victims' relatives mentioned it. You have no proof it was me. I've got a good mind to take this to my Fed rep.'

Roisin put her hands on the arms of her chair, beginning to push herself out of it. Stella sat back in her chair, pulse racing. She hadn't expected Rosh to go on the offensive. Time for the yank on the dangling legs before the hanged woman could climb back up through the trapdoor and escape.

'Wait!' she said, raising her voice. 'Sit down. I said there were a couple of things.'

Roisin subsided into the chair, which squeaked a tiny protest.

Slowly, as if displaying incriminating evidence before a suspect, which she supposed she was, in a way, Stella moved the paper to one side and placed two of the three documents in a row facing Roisin.

The report.

And the photo.

Roisin looked down reflexively, and Stella watched the way her eyes skittered past the picture of Amy Burnside's flayed corpse before returning to her own.

Breathing heavily, Roisin spoke.

'Sorry, am I supposed to be seeing a connection here?'

Stella placed the list of words on top of the other two documents. The version she'd amended at Lucian's the previous night.

'Read it for me, please, Rosh. Out loud.'

Roisin frowned, then she looked down.

'Mal,' she paused. Then, 'Oh, Christ! Malachi Robey lives.'

She looked at Stella.

'Look, I'm sorry, OK? I just didn't think it was relevant.'

'Yes,' Stella snapped. 'You already told me that. I think your exact words were it wasn't germane to the investigation.'

Roisin looked away and shifted in her chair. The body language wasn't hard to read. Nailed. But she still wasn't ready to stop fighting. She scratched at her ginger hair, held back today in a bun, and Stella noticed that her narrow nostrils were flaring.

'Look, first you accuse me of being the mole, now you're saying I, what, obstructed justice? Just tell me, am I in trouble, or not? You've had it in for me since the day you came back from the dead, so if you want to assert your authority, please,' she spread her hands, 'be my guest.'

Stella felt the power of speech momentarily desert her. Roisin was glaring at her, eyes narrowed, so that the shadows deepened their colour from pale blue to cobalt.

Stella breathed in through her nose and let it out slowly.

'You kept that report to yourself for over a week, which was bad enough. But here's the thing, *Detective Inspector Griffin*. If you had thought that maybe, just maybe, it *was* germane to the investigation, and shared it, then someone, maybe me, maybe one of the babies, maybe even you, I don't care, but someone might have joined the dots the way I did last night and decoded the message that Lucifer was Malachi Robey. And if we'd have done that, maybe we could have found out about him being at Monksfield, and gone down there and warned Amy Burnside, who therefore,' she snatched up the photo of the dead woman and brandished it like a weapon, 'might not have ended up with her skin draped over her arm like a fucking pashmina!'

Stella sat back in her chair, breathing heavily, feeling her pulse in her throat and not liking the sensation of something living trying to push its way out from the soft place beneath her jaw.

Suddenly, the fight seemed to go out of Roisin. Her eye muscles relaxed and she slumped back in her chair. Her eyes glistened and the tip of that long, narrow nose had reddened. She plucked at the sleeve of her shirt. She sniffed.

'What are you going to do?' she asked in a quiet voice.

'What would you do in my shoes, Rosh? What would *you* do?'

Roisin shrugged, then pulled a tissue from her jeans pocket and blew her nose.

'I don't know. File a disciplinary report on me? Demote me? Kick me out of SIU? Report me to the Ghost Squad?'

'Yeah? Well, maybe you would. Me? I'm a shit manager. I know that. The thought of taking this to Callie, or those numpties in HR, fills me with horror more than that does,' she said, pointing at the photo. 'So here's what I'm going to do. I'm going to ask you to stay. For now. Because, believe it or not, I actually think you're a good detective. A good detective with a thing for stabbing me in the back, but still. And I need you to help me catch Malachi Robey. But, just to be clear, I have never "had it in" for you. I know you thought the DCI's job was yours but, guess what? It wasn't! I earned it fair and square, more than you'll ever know. And it was six years ago. So leave it, Rosh. Just leave it. Work the case. Then, if you want a transfer, I won't stand in your way. But I need you to know something.'

She paused, forcing Roisin to ask the question.

'What?'

Stella lunged forwards, causing Roisin to rear back in surprise. She lowered her voice.

'Don't *ever* get on my wrong side again. You really wouldn't like the person you'd find there.'

Stella didn't bother with the old trick of looking down at paperwork. She just stared at Roisin until the DI got up and left.

She blew her cheeks out and looked at the ceiling, rolling her head on her neck and listening to the joints crackle.

91

THURSDAY 13TH SEPTEMBER 10.00 A.M.
LABOUR PARTY HEADQUARTERS

Roly Fletcher scowled. He checked his watch again. Morgan was forty-five minutes late for their meeting. He pressed the intercom button on the desk phone.

'Melissa, could you try Craig Morgan again, please?'

'Of course,' her buzzy voice answered.

A minute later she poked her head around his office door.

'Sorry, Roly. I tried his office number and his mobile. No answer. I left a message, but…'

Fletcher smiled.

'It's fine. Thanks.'

Once she'd disappeared and closed the door behind her, Fletcher called Kendra Fawcett.

'What's up?' she asked the moment she picked up. Ever efficient.

'Craig Morgan's up. Or rather, he isn't.'

'What do you mean?'

'He's not up here, in my office. He was due three-quarters of an hour ago to discuss talking points. And he's not picking up his phone.'

'OK, leave it with me. I'll make a few calls.'

She rang back ten minutes later.

'I spoke to Fiona. She's at a conference in Milan but she spoke to him yesterday morning. Apparently Craig was going to be on *Newsnight* last night as the main guest. But I watched it; he wasn't on. I called the BBC and they said they'd not invited him.'

Fletcher experienced a flash of anger. He'd suppressed his doubts about Morgan. The man's arrogance, his vanity, the odd questionable remark about women when the two of them were alone. He had drive, ambition and a true believer's fervour for Fletcher's political programme and that was what mattered.

'I hope we haven't backed the wrong horse, Kendra,' he said, finally. 'You need to find him and get him over here to explain himself.'

———

At Paddington Green, Stella was having a better day than Kendra Fawcett. Lucian had just been to see her with the news that he'd managed to isolate two separate blood samples from Amy Burnside's cottage. He'd driven them himself to the private forensics lab and they'd promised the results would be phoned through to Stella no later than nine the following morning.

'I spoke to Prue Brundage. She said you two had spoken before?'

'Yes. She called about the samples from the Connollys' house.'

———

Kendra failed in the task Fletcher had assigned to her. Morgan hadn't turned up to work. He hadn't returned home, either. When his wife got back from her conference late on the Thursday night and couldn't locate him, she called the police.

He was formally recorded as a missing person – a MisPer in police parlance – at 11.57 p.m. on September 13th.

92

FRIDAY 14TH SEPTEMBER 6.00 A.M.

Stella's phone rang. She was already up, sitting at her kitchen table, writing in her journal.

'DCI Cole?'

'Yes, who is this please?'

'It's Mim. Professor Karlsson's secretary?'

Mim's voice sounded tiny, shaky.

Stella pulse jumped. She breathed in and out slowly through her nose, willing herself to project calmness into the little mic by her mouth.

'Hello, Mim. What can I do for you?'

'I'm sorry for calling so early, but I couldn't sleep. I'm so frightened.'

'What are you frightened about?'

She could hear Mim's breathing. Shallow, fast breaths as if she were panicking. Finally, Mim spoke, almost inaudibly.

'I think my husband is Lucifer. I think he's the one who's been killing those poor women.'

Stella's heart was pounding. She forced herself to keep her voice steady.

'Why, Mim? Why do you think your husband is Lucifer?'

'I found him burning these bloody overalls in the incinerator in our back garden. And he came home the other day all covered in it. He said he'd got into a fight. But I don't think he had because he hadn't got any, you know, he hadn't got any wounds. No cuts or bruises. Not even a scratch. And he's been going on about the women when he sees the news. Calling them whores and all these horrible names. He said they deserved it because they were peddling lies. And, and...'

'What, Mim?'

'He's got a special room in the house. I'm not allowed in it. It's locked, but I know where he keeps the key. I went in it the other day when he was at work. Oh, it was so awful. Just all these gory pictures cut out of books of people being cut up and burned and tortured. The women's names, you know, the ones on the news? He'd written their names under the pictures.'

Stella's heart was racing.

'Where is he? You have to tell me so we can stop him before he kills any more people. He needs help. He's ill.'

'I'm frightened. They...' Her breath caught and Stella heard a cough, then what sounded like a sob. 'They raped me.'

'Who, Mim? Who raped you?'

'Malachi. And this woman who works for him. They've been doing it to me for years. She's got a knife. I'm so scared. You don't know what he's like!' she finished, her voice growing louder and more strident. 'He'll kill me! He'll kill you, too!'

'No he won't. Not if you let me help you. Where is he, Mim? Where's Malachi?'

'He left last night. He said he was going up to York. Apparently they're going to ordain a new woman bishop at the minster there today.'

Oh, shit! Celia Thwaites!

'OK, look, Mim. This is very important. What sort of car does Malachi drive?'

'Er, it's a van, really. A VW Transporter. It's white.'

'What's the registration? Do you know?'

'Yes. He makes me do all the paperwork for it. It's one of those personal ones, you know? R for Roger, then a zero, then B for Bertie, E for Egg, Y for Yellow.'

Stella shook her head as she saw what she'd written.

R0BEY

'Thanks. I need you to come to Paddington Green Police Station, Mim. We can protect you.'

'I'm too scared. Can't you come and get me in a police car or something?'

'That's what I meant. I'm going to go into the station and get a car myself. I'll drive straight over and collect you. What's your address?'

'It's not very glamorous, I'm afraid. It's 55 Gasworks Lane, Beckton.'

'OK, good. I'll put it into my satnav and it'll bring me right to your front door.'

'Oh, God, thank you. Please hurry.'

Stella gulped her coffee, then closed her journal and returned it to the drawer in the kitchen dresser. Before leaving, she called Garry.

'Morning, boss,' he said, his voice thickened and blurry with sleep.

'Garry, wake up. This is urgent. I just got off the phone with Karlsson's secretary. You're not going to believe this. Robey's her husband. He's driving up to York minster right now. They're ordaining Celia Thwaites there this morning as a bishop.'

'Shit! Karlsson's wife.'

'Yes. I think he's going to take her or kill her there, right in front of the TV cameras. Call the local CID. No! Get Callie to go in at the top level. Plus, I've got his vehicle.'

'Go on, I'm ready.'

'It's a white VW Transporter. Index number Romeo Zero Bravo Echo Yankee.'

'All right. I'll put it on the wire. We might strike lucky and get him on ANPR or with a traffic car. He'll be taking the M1 probably. I'll get the plate circulated. We're going to get him, boss.'

'I bloody well hope so. Listen, I'm driving over to Mim's place to fetch her back to the station. Once you've put wheels in motion to get Robey, can you sort out an interview room?'

'Sure.'

'Thanks. I've got to go. See you later.'

Fifteen minutes later, she was pulling out of the car park beneath Paddington Green in the dark-grey 5 series she and Garry had taken down to Monksfield.

Halfway to Beckton, lights flashing and siren wailing, she briefly wondered whether she should have delayed long enough to round up one of the babies to come with her. For the experience as much as anything else. Callie would need soothing for the breach of protocol but Stella could handle her. And she reckoned she could handle damaged goods like Mim Robey as well.

———

At 7.15 a.m., Stella pulled into the kerb outside 55 Gasworks Lane, Beckton. Built of sand-yellow brick, the house sat a quarter of the way down a long, curving street, bounded at one end by the derelict gas works that had given the road its name and at the other by an industrial estate.

She climbed out and stretched. Despite the early hour, the temperature was still above-average for the time of year. She'd jumped straight into the Beemer from her bike and she was hot inside her jacket.

The front door opened directly onto the pavement. She stretched out a finger and pressed the doorbell.

The woman Peter Karlsson had introduced as Mim, and whom she now knew to be Malachi Robey's raped wife, answered within a few seconds. A couple of inches taller than Stella, she was dressed in jeans and a plain black T-shirt. No makeup to disguise the redness around her eyes or the pink blotches on her cheeks.

'Come in,' she said quietly, then turned and hurried down a narrow hall.

Stella followed her into a spotless kitchen. Mim's movements were jerky, as if every step were a conscious effort. Fear could do that to a person, Stella knew only too well.

'Do you want some, tea, DCI Cole? I just made a pot.'

'Yes, please, that would be lovely. And please call me Stella.'

Mim touched her throat just at the notch between her collar bones. She smiled nervously.

'OK. Thank you. I'm sorry, I'm just, it's never what I wanted, you know. He's a very difficult person to disobey.'

'Don't worry. We've put out details of the van and called North Yorkshire Police. I'm sure they'll catch him before he can do any more harm. Listen, do you have a recent photo of Malachi? It would really help us.'

Miriam shook her head.

'I'm sorry. He doesn't like having his picture taken. I've only got an old school photo.'

Stella smiled.

'That's OK. We have one of those already. How's that tea doing?'

'Oh yes, of course. Sorry.'

Mim poured two mugs of tea and, after she'd made the usual offer of sugar or sweeteners, placed them on the small table that took up most of the kitchen.

She sat opposite Stella.

'Am I in trouble?' she asked, her lower lip trembling.

'No. You said Malachi has repeatedly raped you. He's a violent psychopath. Men like Malachi are very controlling. You are as much a victim as the women he killed. Do you know the name of the woman with him? The one who helped him rape you?'

Mim looked down at her hands.

'Lilith,' she said, in a voice so quiet Stella had to lean forwards to catch it. 'I know you say I'm a victim, Stella. But I should have seen him for what he was. I should have called you sooner. People will want to punish me, won't they? But they don't understand what he's like.'

Stella took a sip of the tea and looked out of the kitchen window. Beyond the sagging fence panels at the end of the tiny back garden, she could see stacks of wrecked and flattened cars and the huge jointed arm of a yellow crane, from which a black electro-magnet hung on its umbilical cord of cables and chains.

'It's ours,' Mim said.

'Pardon?'

Mim lifted her chin towards the crane.

'The scrapyard. Malachi was left it by the original owner. He worked for him after leaving Monksfield. Ten years he was there, and when he died, the owner, I mean, it turned out he'd left to Malachi. He said he was like a son to him.'

While Mim was spilling out the details of Malachi's life, Stella was recalling her conversation with Cam about the car they'd seen on the CCTV footage from Sherborne Ropes. And their conclusion that scrapyards were an obvious angle.

'Does Malachi have any other cars besides the Transporter?' she asked now.

Mim nodded.

'He takes cars from the yard sometimes. If they work, I mean.'

'Can you remember any in particular?'

'The last one I remember seeing him in was a blue Ford Focus. I think it's there now. I can take you to it, if you want?'

'Yes, please. Can we go now?'

'Mm-hmm. We can get into the yard through the back gate.'

Keeping level with Mim, just in case she decided to bolt, Stella took in the mountainous stacks of squashed cars and the huge pyramids of discarded domestic appliances.

The people who had once inhabited the house the Robeys shared would have marvelled that such luxuries were available to ordinary, working people like them. Then they would have blinked in shock as they saw how little needed to go wrong with one before they were thrown out and replaced.

In the centre of the yard, a Portakabin stood in a square of bare concrete, from which a narrow metalled road led away towards the derelict gas works.

Mim pointed.

'That was the office. Malachi uses it now but I don't know what for. I'm not allowed in there. Look,' she said, pointing. 'That's the Focus.'

Stella walked over to the car and took a photo of the number plate: AG54 LKF.

Keeping her fingers interlaced behind her back, she peered in at the driver's side window, careful not to let her nose touch the glass. The interior was tatty but clean. No lakes of dried blood or spattered upholstery. A few fast food wrappers and takeaway coffee cups in the passenger footwell. Her phone rang.

Still scrutinising the inside of the car, she pulled the phone from her jacket pocket. The Caller ID said NDNAD.

'DCI Cole.'

'Hi, it's Prue Brundage here. Sorry for the early call but I thought you'd want to know. We found a match from that last DNA sample you sent in. The second sample of blood from Amy Burnside's kitchen? There's no direct match to anyone on the NDNAD but we have found a familial match to one Malachi Jeremiah Robey. The sex is female. He must have a sister.'

'Thanks, Prue,' Stella said, distractedly. Her eyes had just fallen on a shimmering twist of transparent plastic decorated with pink chevrons. *What's a tampon wrapper doing in there?*

93

FRIDAY 14TH SEPTEMBER 7.30 A.M.
BECKTON, EAST LONDON

Stella heard the scrape of Mim's boots on the bare concrete. She spun round, only to meet the incoming hypodermic needle, which Mim, face impassive, drove deep into the side of Stella's neck.

Mim stepped back, smiling. Stella tried to kick out at her, leaning back slightly, but only succeeded in toppling herself to the ground as her balance went.

Mim came towards her and pulled her, firmly but not roughly to her feet.

'Up we get,' she said, as if speaking to a child. 'I'm afraid you've discovered my little secret, Stella. And I'm sorry, but I lied to you about Malachi. He's not in York. He's here. And he's not my husband. He's my brother. Come on, I'll take you to him. It'll be a nice surprise for both of you.'

Stella tried to speak as Mim led her by the elbow towards a long, low hut built of breeze blocks and roofed in what looked like white-painted asbestos sheets. Her tongue felt huge in her mouth and all she could manage was a mumbled, 'Nah'.

Her thoughts were sliding around in her head and she found it hard to organise them into a coherent pattern. All she knew was she was in mortal danger, and she cursed herself for coming alone.

Mim opened a steel door let into the side of the hut and pushed Stella inside. Stella stumbled over the lower edge of the door frame, which protruded up from the ground by a couple of inches.

'Whoopsie!' Mim said. 'We don't want to fall in, do we?'

She pointed to a low wall a few feet in front of them.

'Come and have a look. Malachi's in there.'

Stella kept her gaze fixed on the topmost course of bricks, struggling to stay focused despite the drugs flooding her system and rendering her as biddable as a well-trained dog.

She bumped into the wall and looked over the edge. About halfway down was a black mirror, from which her own pale face looked out at her.

'Whassat?' she slurred.

'That,' Mim said, 'is the pit. It's where we store all the old engine oil from the cars and trucks and whatever else people used to leave here for us to deal with. A few motorbikes but, as I say, mostly cars and trucks. Probably ten years' worth or more. It's lined with concrete. It's twenty feet long by ten across. Mal told me it's ten-feet deep as well. "Don't fall in, Mim," he said, "or you'll never see daylight again."

'I once amused myself by calculating its volume. Would you like to know how much pitch-black, stinking engine oil a pit measuring twenty by ten by ten feet can hold? Yes? OK. The answer is: fanfare, maestro, please, twelve thousand, four hundred and fifty-eight gallons. So now, three-quarter's full, it's, oh, about nine thousand gallons. In case you're wondering, when the pit was full up, and Jack – he was who Mal worked for – was in the right mood, he used to call some company who'd suck the oil out into tankers, pay him some piddling amount and then cart it all away to be recycled into tar or, I don't know, industrial lubricants or plastic breast pumps or whatever. Not my specialist subject, I'm afraid. Did you find out about Mal's prison sentence?'

Stella tried to make the muscles of her mouth and jaw work. Her tongue flopped uselessly from side to side.

'Ye-yeah. Waypiss.'

'That's right! He *was* a rapist. Not a killer, though. That was my job. I used to deal with the women after he'd finished with them. So you were right. He did have a female accomplice. Me! They were tarts, mostly. Until this one day, he picked up a teenaged runaway. He got careless and left his DNA all over her. She escaped and, to cut a long story short, no pun intended, they arrested him. He did eight years in Belmarsh. He served his entire sentence 'cos he kept getting into fights inside. The other prisoners didn't like him. I don't really understand why. She was fifteen which is, technically, under the age of consent, but it's not as if she was enjoying her life. Otherwise, why run away? And there wasn't exactly a shortage of supply was there?

'Anyway, at least it meant when he got out in November there was no tiresome probation officer trailing after him. He just came home and went back to work. But they wouldn't leave him alone, would they?'

'Who?' Stella mumbled.

'They called themselves Paedo Hunters. A mob, that's all. Local men who took it upon themselves to find out who was on the sex offenders' register and persecute them. They found out where we lived and on the last day of December, they came for him. They kicked him to death, just over there,' she said, jerking her thumb over her shoulder towards the concrete apron.

'So after they left, I took poor Mal and dropped him down there. It's where I'm going to put you, too, once I've finished with you. Now, come on. Let's get you somewhere a little more comfortable. Oh, and let's drop the "Mim", shall we? I think you should call me Miriam.'

94

FRIDAY 14TH SEPTEMBER 9.00 A.M.
PADDINGTON GREEN

Garry's phone rang. No caller ID.

He put his mug down and answered.

'Hello?'

'DS Haynes?'

'Yes, who is this, please?'

'It's Sylvia Royal.'

'Oh hello, Mrs Royal. What can I do for you?'

'Well, I feel awfully embarrassed about this. I tried to call DCI Cole but her phone went straight to voicemail, and you said to call you if I couldn't reach her. You see, after you left on Saturday and I told the headmaster of my decision to leave, well, I had a funny turn. They had to fetch an ambulance and I've been at home ever since. In bed. Derek's been keeping me comfortable but I've been taking sleeping pills and they've left me awfully muzzy and—'

'Sylvia, please, slow down. It's fine. What did you want to tell me?'

'Sorry. It's just, I don't know why on earth I didn't tell you this when you and DCI Cole came to Monksfield the other day, but I was so upset, what with poor Amy Burnside being murdered, and all that history I had to rummage through about that awful boy, and then I had my turn. The thing is, I completely forgot to tell you something that, I don't know, might be important? She was so quiet, you see. I think that's why I forgot about her.'

'Who was quiet, Sylvia?' Garry asked, patiently waiting for Sylvia Royal to stumble through her apology, using the time to pull his notebook towards him and click a ballpoint ready.

'His sister. They came here together, both in 1993. She was two years his senior, so ten when she arrived. She was a strange little thing. Wouldn't look at you. She'd sit so quietly in a room you wouldn't know she was there. She stayed on when he was expelled. Quiet as a mouse for the rest of her time here. I don't recall her getting so much as a single set of chores.'

Garry wrote: Sister. Two years older. Quiet. Then scribbled, Name?

'Sorry to interrupt. What was her name?'

'Oh. Of course. Yes. Miriam Judith. More Biblical names, you see. The parents must have been obsessed.'

Garry wrote the names down, thanked Sylvia and ended the call.

Something tweaked at his thoughts. He called out to the incident room in general.

'Hey! How do you make Miriam into a nickname?'

'Mim!' someone shouted back.

'Oh, shit!' he said. 'Karlsson's secretary.'

Garry walked over to the murder wall and looked at the dates when Robey had murdered his four victims.

Niamh Connolly: 13th August
Sarah Sharpe: 17th–18th August
Moira Lowney: 23rd August
Amy Burnside: 5th September

Then he called Peter Karlsson.

'Hello?'

'Professor Karlsson, it's DS Haynes. I need to ask you about Mim's working hours over the last couple of months.'

Karlsson sounded surprised.

'Oh. OK, what do you need to know?'

'I want to know if she was working on the following four dates. Got a pen?'

Garry heard Karlsson open a drawer. He remembered the immaculate desk.

'Go ahead,' Karlsson said, all business now.

'August thirteen, seventeen, eighteen, twenty-three. September fifth.'

'Right. I'll have to get onto HR about this. They'll probably take a few hours and then—'

'No!' Garry said, louder than he meant to. 'No. I need to know right now. I'll hold on. Tell them it's urgent police business.'

'Is everything all right? Where's Mim?'

'Just call HR for me, please.'

The clunk as Karlsson put his phone down was loud in Garry's ear. As he waited he tried Stella again. Voicemail. He didn't bother leaving a message. He had a bad feeling in his gut. He stared across the room at the murder wall. Tried to keep his mind free of the image that kept bullying and shoving its way in. A fifth woman's face on the board. Stella's face.

Karlsson's voice broke into his thoughts.

'Hello? Garry?'

'Yes, I'm here.'

'No.'

'No, what?'

'Sorry. No, Mim wasn't working on any of those days. It was always Anjali.'

'Thanks. Bye, Peter.'

'But what—'

Garry didn't give him time to finish his question. He walked the length of the incident room and knocked on Callie's door, then entered. She looked up.

'What is it, Garry? I'm drowning in paperwork here. Look,' she flapped a sheet of paper at him, 'I've got a bill from that idiot Trimmets that the other idiot, Morgan, somehow forgot to pay.'

'OK, you know we went to see Professor Karlsson? The martyrdom guy?'

'Yes. Robey's following his book.'

'Yeah, but the first draft. Which means he must have had access to it. So, the secretary at Monksfield called me a few minutes ago and told me Robey had a sister called Miriam. The same as Karlsson's secretary. I just spoke to the professor. She wasn't working on any of the days that the murders took place. She must be the accomplice. The boss was right.'

'That's excellent news. Well done. Who's going to arrest her?'

'That's the whole point, ma'am. It's the boss. She's gone over to Beckton to collect Miriam. She told her she was Robey's wife. Stella's walking into a trap.'

Callie's eyes flashed and her lips set in a determined line.

'Right. Find Miriam Robey's address and get over there pronto with a TSG team. Keep me posted.'

'Yes, ma'am.'

He nodded and left at the double, visualising the men and women of a Territorial Support Group team, in their all-black gear and assault rifles.

Back at his desk, he tried Stella's number.

'Hi. This is DCI Stella Cole. Please leave a message.'

'Boss, it's Garry. Mim isn't Robey's wife. She's his sister. Her name's Miriam Judith Robey. The initials: MJ? She would have had access to the early draft. It could all be coincidence, but I think she's been helping him all along. She's the one setting up the meetings with the victims. I'm coming over with a TSG team. Don't go into the house, boss.'

He texted her a shorter version of his message:

Mim = Robey's sister. Miriam Judith. MJ! Same initials as killer. She's helping him. Stay back. On way with TSG.

· · ·

'What's going on?' Def asked him.

He frowned and tightened his lips, then blew out the breath he realised he'd been holding.

'I think the boss is in trouble. OK, listen up!' he shouted. 'We need to find out where Miriam Judith Robey lives.'

Having set them to work, Garry ran for the door, heading for the TSG office.

It took fifteen minutes to sort out a TSG team, and get them on standby for the moment someone ran Miriam Robey to ground.

There are plenty of ways to find out someone's address. If the person looking has the right access. The DVLA has a database. So does the Land Registry. The Department of Work and Pensions. And HM Revenue and Customs.

Then there's the credit rating agencies like Equifax. Even pizza delivery companies have lists of customer names, addresses and mobile numbers. That's before you start hitting the PNC, HOMLES2, CRIMINT, and the databases maintained by the various intelligence agencies.

But sometimes the fastest way is the common sense way. So Garry simply called the HR department at UCL.

After a threat to arrest him for obstruction, the young guy who answered the phone decided that Miriam Robey's privacy wasn't his main concern and coughed up the address.

Ten minutes later a three-vehicle convoy tore out of the carpark beneath Paddington Green, blues and twos clearing a path through the morning traffic. Garry led, with Will beside him.

Cam was driving her own car with Arran beside her. The twelve-member method of entry team from the TSG plus their equipment were packed into a couple of Mercedes Sprinter vans.

Switching to the broadcast channel on his Airwave, Garry addressed the officers in the other vehicles.

'The address is 47 Charlotte Road, Watford, WP2 7YT. No sirens once we're within half a mile. Confirm?'

'TSG team confirms.'

'Team two confirms.'

This was Arran, riding shotgun with Cam behind the wheel.

It took the convoy a further twenty-nine minutes to reach Miriam Robey's address in Watford, having hit the M1 at ninety and accelerated from there.

Garry's heart was thumping as he slowed to a stop outside the house, a dismal-looking terrace with browning plants in green plastic troughs in the ground-floor bay window. Behind him, the other three vehicles drew up and disgorged their occupants.

Arran took charge.

'Garry, you and Will head round the back. Take half the TSG guys with you. I checked the street plan on the way. The house backs onto another street. They've got back-to-back gardens. I don't see her as a fence-jumper, but belt and braces, eh?'

Garry nodded to Will and they sprinted to the end of the road and disappeared around the corner.

'Cam. You wait with me. The TSG guys'll do their thing then we go in, yes?'

'Yes, boss.'

He turned to the sergeant in charge of the TSG team. He carried a red steel battering ram known officially as an Enforcer and by everyone who actually used it as the 'big red key'.

'Ready, sarge?'

The man nodded. Burly, shaved head, stab vest. No nonsense.

'Let's do this.'

Arran and Cam stood back as the method of entry team approached the front door. Behind the sergeant, five uniformed male and female officers stood ready to charge in and subdue anyone thinking of getting violent. The sergeant braced his legs and swung the ram. The door was cheap and splintered on the first impact.

The sergeant kicked it open and stood back long enough for his five colleagues to rush through, yelling at the tops of their voices, 'Armed police! Get down, get down!'

Arran and Cam went in after them.

95

Stella opened her eyes. She had a fearsome headache and her vision was blurred. Something foul-smelling was tied over her mouth. She sat perfectly still for fifteen minutes, as the pain at the back of her skull dissipated and the two of everything she was seeing resolved into unity.

The proportions of her surroundings told her she was inside the Portakabin. If it had ever really been an office, it wasn't one anymore. Bare of furniture, except for an empty steel rack in a corner and a single chair facing her across four feet of dusty floor, it had the flyblown look of the derelict houses she'd raided in her early years putting crack dealers away. She was lying on her side, hands tied behind her. She looked down. Her ankles were fastened with thick black cable ties. The room smelled of mildew.

Miriam appeared in the doorway. She strode into the centre of the floor and sat down on the side chair. She carried a black book in her right hand. Black with gold-blocked writing. Stella's vision blurred again as she squinted up at it. In her left, Miriam held a

547

sandwich. The smell of the bread and cheese made Stella's mouth water.

Miriam pooched out her lips in a little moue of shame.

'Now, where are my manners? Here I am eating, while you have nothing.'

She pulled the gag down over Stella's chin.

The sandwich, one perfectly semi-circular bite taken out of it, advanced towards Stella's mouth.

'Want a bite?'

The thought of placing her mouth on something those teeth had touched, that tongue had touched, brought back the nausea that had largely disappeared. She shook her head.

'No thanks. I'm good.'

'Well, I think we both know that's not true, but so be it. Now I can tell you what's been going on. Please try to pay attention.' Her eyes widened. 'By the way, did you get my little message in my letter to the *Sun*?'

'The capitalised words. Malachi Robey lives. Very clever.'

Miriam smiled.

'Oh, I was cleverer than that. I left the last three words uncapitalised. You should have realised I wouldn't spoon-feed you. The full message was "Malachi Robey lives on in me". D'you see? Because he does. And, as a nice little dig, it's sort of God-y in a way. I was rather pleased with it, to be honest.'

'Yeah? Well good for you, you sick bitch.'

'Stella! How rude! When I offered to share my sandwich with you, too. Anyway, I forgive you. Shall I tell you about Malachi?'

'Why not? I'm not going anywhere and I could do with a good laugh.'

Miriam frowned. But she stayed in her chair.

'Naughty girl, trying to provoke me. Are you hoping for a quick death? A painless one? I'm sorry to have to disappoint you but yours will be the worst so far. So, since you asked so nicely, from the moment of his birth, my sainted bitch of a mother began her crusade against him. Take his name, for instance. Malachi Jeremiah Robey.

'I'll say that again. Malachi. Jeremiah. Robey. Thanks, Mother! You named him after two Old Testament prophets. In Nineteen – Fucking – Eighty Five. To put all this into some sort of context, in his class at infant school, there were five Jacks, three Davids and two Jameses. Well, there were until James Davies fell under the wheels of the school bus on our trip to the Brecon Beacons, but, still.'

Stella heard the faint buzz of a phone's vibration alert.

Miriam looked down at her jeans and frowned. Then she simply resumed speaking.

'Mother. Where shall I start? How about this. She breastfed him until he was two and a half years old. He didn't want it: her fat dug shoved into his mouth. But she was a very religious woman, you see. She believed that we are born with original sin baked in. And she took it upon herself to see it was purged from his body and mind at every available opportunity.

'Solid food encouraged boys to grow and, according to Mother, that led to impure thoughts and deeds. Keeping him fastened to her tit would dilute the effects and weaken those desires to the point that prayer, and regular, vicious beatings, would triumph.

'She worked as an upholsterer at the Ford factory in Dagenham. Dad was a taxi driver. Owned his own cab. But Mother only worked for the nobility of it. That and the money Ford paid her, I mean. Her real occupation. Her real *passion*, was her church. And, no, before you ask me which church, that's not what I meant at all. I must practise being more precise so you don't misunderstand me as I tell you the story.

'She had anointed herself as a pastor and ran a church from the lounge, as she delighted in calling our front room. It was about the size of a rabbit hutch, and stuffed with pot plants and stupid statues of saints. She had about twelve congregants who used to shuffle into our terraced house on Sunday mornings and moan and mumble as Mother preached on the subject of sin and redemption.

'The beatings started the same day he had his first erection. He told me all about it afterwards. She pulled him out of the bath by his wrist and commenced to smack his wet behind until he screamed for mercy. "You dirty little boy!" she screamed. "You dirty little boy!"

'In the end Dad came in and told her to stop but she just carried on with the beating, and yelled at him. I heard every poisonous word. "You put your demon seed in me and your vileness is coming out in him now, can't you see?" she screamed into his face. "You slink about with that slut down the road, don't think I don't know. You fornicate with that whore and half the street knows it."

'Mother wasn't a large woman and, although he could have torn her head off her shoulders, Dad elected not to and left, shooting me a pitying glance. Like I said, the beatings started that night. And so did her constant attempts to undermine his self-confidence. Every chance the old sow got, she would belittle him.

'My father moved out nine months after the "bathtime incident", as I learned to think of it. Mother was right about one thing, though. Dad *was* screwing a woman down the road and they moved in together. "Shacked up in a house imbued with sin," was how Mother put it at the time, showing a fine disregard for staying within a single style of speech.

'As well as the beatings, Mal had to endure Mother's ravings about how he was the embodiment of original sin, the continuing stain on her character, a wretched boy just waiting to become a fornicator like his father.

'To be honest with you, looking back it's fairly clear to me that Mother was suffering from a severe form of mental illness. A borderline personality disorder in all probability, mixed with paranoid delusions and religious mania. At the time I just hated her.

'When he was eight, he told me he'd started experiencing feelings towards girls. Exactly the feelings Mother was so terrified of, in fact. He told me he wanted to rape a girl. OK, fine, as we're sharing all our secrets, he told me he wanted to rape a *lot* of girls. Possibly *every* girl. I reined him in, of course, I did. But what's bred in the bone, as they say.

'Anyway, killing. That was more my area than Mal's. Our neighbour, old man Garbutt, had a cat. He doted on it. He called it Greta, you know, after the actress. Greta Garbo? Her catchphrase was "I want to be alone." It sounds better if you do it in a cod-German accent. You know, "I *vant* to bee eh-*loan*."

'Old man Garbutt said the cat was like the actress. "Greta prefers her own company," he used to say. "Just as well given what horrible things human beings do to animals." Did I mention he was a vegetarian? He was a vegetarian.

'One day in the summer holidays, when our contemporaries – you remember them? The Jacks, Davids and Jameses. The Chloes, Emmas and Sarahs – were off on their bikes or hanging around the swings, we stole a sandwich bag full of Rich Tea biscuits and a bottle of made-up orange squash and set off to track Greta.

'I saw her first, outside Garbutt's front door. She was sunning herself on the porch. Licking her fur. No wonder they get those disgusting fur balls in their guts. All that coughing and retching they do. Well, I could have told her why. It's all that fur you ingest, you idiot cat! Why not, oh, I don't know, *stop licking your fur*!'

Miriam screamed these final four words. Stella flinched at the naked display of such animalistic rage. Miriam seemed calm again. She smiled down at Stella.

'Sorry, Stella, that was a bit OTT, wasn't it? Where was I? Oh, yes! Greta's belly sort of swung when she walked. I'd asked Mother about it and she said, and I quote, "There's another painted whore who opened her legs. Now she's carrying a brood in her belly like I was forced to." Which, with a little effort, I translated to mean Greta was going to have kittens.

'I walked up Garbutt's front path, past all his stupid chrysanthemums in those unrealistic sweetshop shades fanciers of that particular flower like to look at, can't think why but there you are, live and let live, I suppose – and I crouched down and stuck out my fingers. "Hey, Greta," I said softly. "Why don't you show us where you like to be alone and we can play together?"

'And Greta hissed at me and swiped a paw at my outstretched hand. Fascinating fact: cats' claws are retractable. Imagine that! Sharp little stilettos they can shoot out at will like miniature flick-knives. Now there's a great idea from Mother Nature.

'I sucked the blood out of the scratches and hissed back. Greta got to her feet, turning herself practically inside out as she arched her back at me and then stalked past me down the path. Which is *exactly* what I wanted! Dumb cat.

'Then it was a simple matter of dogging – Haha! Joke!– her footsteps as she tried her "I *vant* to be eh-*loan*" act on us. But, needless to say, it didn't work. With her belly full of kittens she wasn't really very fast and we were dedicated.

'So after about ten or maybe fifteen minutes – I'm not sure, so we'll call it fifteen to be on the safe side – she turned right and led us into the loading bay at the back of a shopping precinct near our house. She scooted in between two of the big old galvanised steel dustbins they used to have before everything went wheelie-bin and we followed her in. I was big for my age but I was good at squeezing into little tight spaces.

'We'd found her lair. A scratty old blanket some shop-owner must have tossed out. She'd nested in it. There were scraps of food all around and even the back half of a dead mouse, which I picked up and examined. Now she was on her own territory and not old man Garbutt's, she seemed to relax. She wasn't hissing anymore, which was a good thing. And those retractable claws were, as the name suggests, retracted.

'I'd stolen something else from home. I took it out of my pocket now. A tin of sardines in vegetable oil. I snapped off the key and pushed the little steel tab through the slot and started to twist the key over and over, rolling up the razor-sharp lid around it.

'I deliberately let some of the fishy oil dribble onto the blanket and when Greta smelled what it was she was in like Flynn! Licking, purring all at once. And eyeing me at the same time.

'The lid came free with a kind of grating tearing noise and I put the tin down in front of her. She looked, I can only say, genuinely grateful as she lowered her pink nose and sniffed the silvery-brown fish before dabbing her paw in and hooking out a mouthful.

'That's when I picked up a half-brick and brought it down smartly on Greta's skull. Well, she went down without a fight. I mean, it was a pretty good first attempt. Smack! went the half-brick. Crack! went Greta's skull. And that was that.

'I was thinking we should take her body somewhere quiet and see if we could find the kittens, but just then one of the shopkeepers, old Ali from the Paki shop, came round with a bin bag full of some stinking rubbish. He saw us crouching in there behind the bins and told us, rather rudely, by the way, even though we hadn't done anything to him, to get lost.

'I don't mind telling you, I found the whole experience rather liberating. I went home, did my chores, listened to another of Mother's sermons on sin and scuttled off to my bedroom just as soon as I could. We didn't have a telly in the house (now why aren't you surprised?) so I read.

'It was about a month after that when I killed Mother. I hated her so much for what she did to him, I guess I just snapped.'

96

FRIDAY 14TH SEPTEMBER 10.00 A.M.
WATFORD

The hall floor was littered with free newspapers, takeaway menus and junk mail. The house had a musty smell.

Arran yelled out.

'Miriam Robey! This is the police! Come out here now!'

Behind him, the uniformed sergeant and a couple of the TSG officers headed up the stairs, their boots clumping on each tread.

Arran ran through to the kitchen at the back of the house. It was spotless. Unused.

He turned to Cam.

'The other rooms.'

He ran back, with Cam behind him, throwing open doors to dining room and sitting room. They were empty. Not only of Miriam Robey but of furniture. One by one, the TSG officers shook their heads as they passed him, heading outside.

'Shit!' he said. 'She doesn't live here. She's just using it for legal purposes.'

'So what do we do now, boss?' Cam asked.

'We need to get back to Paddington Green. We have to find out if she's got another property. Fuck!' He slammed his hand, palm out, against the wall. 'We've been played.'

He called Garry.

'The place is empty. Get back to the station. I'll see you there.'

Back at Paddington Green, Arran convened the whole team, bringing in everyone from wherever they were and whatever they were doing. Callie was there, too. She spoke now.

'Stella's not at her place. She's not answering her phone. Her Airwave's dead, too. I'm assuming she's missing. We also need to track down Miriam Robey. I don't want to jump to conclusions, but if she's been helping her brother, they might have snatched Stella. So, everyone, I want you digging deep. Every source we have up to and including Special Branch, MI5 and MI6. Plus the internet. Surface and deep web. Go!'

The group scattered like rabbits before an oncoming greyhound. Callie returned to her office and called her own boss.

97

Miriam carried on talking. Stella listened with half an ear. She was remembering a conversation she'd had with a gangster named Freddie McTiernan, a fearsome East End character who'd ended up shot dead in his own front room by Adam Collier. She and Freddie had been discussing the difference between old-school villains and their newer counterparts.

'For instance,' Freddie said, 'in my day, you wanted to tie a bloke up, you used rope. A few decent boy scout knots and Bob's your uncle. Now it's all cable ties. Haven't they heard plastic's bad for the planet?'

'Yeah, but given time you can undo knots,' Stella had countered. 'Cable ties are impossible to get out of without a knife.'

'That what you think, is it, Stel? Come into the workshop with me. I want to show you something.'

So she'd followed the 'retired' gangster out into his spacious workshop and let him bind her wrists with a heavy-duty black plastic cable tie.

'Looks secure, doesn't it?' he asked her.

She twisted her wrists experimentally, succeeding only in digging the sharp edge into the soft flesh of her wrists.

'Yes. And it hurts.'

'Watch this,' he said, picking a nail out of a little yellow box on a shelf. He pushed the point into the little box that locked the plastic tape in. 'All right, now pull.'

She did as she was told, and gasped as the ridge tape slid free of the locking mechanism.

'See,' Freddie said. 'New ain't always better.'

She refocused on Miriam.

'Malachi had been off sick for two days with a cold. I deliberately stayed in bed, even though I knew I had to be washed and dressed and ready for school. So, in walks Mother at quarter past seven and sees yours truly snuggled under the covers.

'She goes into her routine, screaming about my blasphemous conduct, and how I was the embodiment of corruption and she pulled the blanket and the sheet off me. She turned away and flung her final threat over her shoulder. "If you're not downstairs, washed and dressed in five minutes, you'll go to school without any breakfast."

'I jumped out of bed the moment her back was turned. "Yes, Mother," I said. "I'm sorry." She walked out through my bedroom door and along the narrow upstairs hallway. I followed her on tiptoes. I don't know what demon or deity was howling into that empty space between her ears but he was doing a great job of drowning out any ambient noise from the real world.

'And then, when she reached the top of the stairs and put her right foot out, I charged at her and hit her amidships with both my outstretched palms.

'I still remember the feel on my hands of the Crimplene dress she was wearing. It was a sort of slippery, slidey sensation, but rough, as well. Not at all like you'd imagine a silk blouse would feel. The pattern was enough to give you a migraine! I mean, really, it was horrendous! Lime-green, peacock-blue and a sort of off-white, all in intersecting diamonds.

'Our stairs were straight, no half-landing. Thirteen in all, if you counted either the landing at the top as a step or the last step you took when you put your foot down onto the floor in the downstairs hall as a step – if you were going downstairs, obviously! Well, what I mean is, let's say you're standing with both feet on the ground in the downstairs hall and you say to yourself, well, I think I'm just going to go upstairs to bed or whatever, the toilet, maybe, and you start climbing. Well, if you counted "one" as your right foot hit the first stair and you stopped counting when your same foot or maybe the other one hit the top landing, you would just have said "thirteen" – unlucky for some, eh, Mother?

'So when I pushed Mother, she didn't scream. Instead she made kind of an "Ooh!" noise. Not as if she were surprised, like at the circus when an acrobat does some amazing trick. More like when her period pains were really bad and she'd get a cramp or whatever and, in a low way, she'd go "ooh!", you know? Anyway, that.

'Her arms went out in front of her and, for a moment, she looked as if she'd elected to do a forward pike with two and a half twists, degree of difficulty two-point-nine. Then she landed about halfway down, so, what, the sixth stair? Technically it should be the sixth-and-a-half but I don't think that's a thing. Call it the sixth from the top. It was not a great success.

'Her head went sideways and her neck snapped with a really quite loud crack. Over she went, skirt flying, showing her knickers, to land in a bit of a tangle at the bottom. Somewhere along the line one, or I think easily it could have been two, of her limbs broke or became dislocated. More popping than snapping noises, so maybe they were dislocated after all.

'And there she lay. Dear Ol' Muvver! Dead as a doornail. Looking, frankly, a bit of a mess. Blood leaking out of her nose and she must have caught her lip on something on the way down because it wasn't properly attached to her face anymore.

'Mal came out of his room, took one look at Mother, then went back into his room. I told him to come out when I said it was OK.

Then I went down the stairs, holding onto the bannister and stepped over her at the bottom.

'We used to have a phone in the kitchen. Dad screwed it to the wall. I wasn't allowed to use it to call my friends when Mother was alive but I felt even she would have allowed me to call the emergency services. Which I did now. "Hello?" I said, "My mummy just fell down the stairs." "Oh," the woman at the other end said. I suppose she could hear from my voice that I wasn't very old. "Is your mummy awake?" "No," I said. "She's asleep. Her eyes are closed and I think she's got a nosebleed." "OK. Is she breathing?" "Yes, she is." "Good. Listen, we need to get Mummy to a hospital. What's your name?" I told her.

'She asked me if I knew my address. I felt like saying "yes of course I know my address, you stupid cunt, I'm not a little child," but I didn't say that. "Yes," I said. "It's Martlebury, 47 Charlotte Road, Watford, WP2 7YT." "Good. I am going to send an ambulance for Mummy and I want you to wait with her. Will you be OK doing that?" I assured her I would and rang off.

'I had no idea how long the ambulance would take to arrive, not having any prior experience, so I went up to my room to fetch my book – *Treasure Island* by Robert Louis Stevenson. I think in my mind I was going to take it back downstairs to read sitting on the stairs but I had just got to a really good bit, so I sort of flopped onto my bed and read it there.

'Then I had another brilliant idea. I went into Mother's bedroom. She had a phone in there as well as the one in the kitchen. A Trimphone, I believe it was called. In a shade of green that was very fashionable in the late seventies: avocado. I tried to avoid looking at all her religious statues and called Dad instead. He'd made me memorise his home phone number before he left and I called it now.

'He answered. One of the joys of being self-employed was that Dad could set his own hours. Driving a London taxi was, he explained to me, "the best job in the world". You're your own boss, you make good money, decide on your own hours, whereabouts you want to ply your trade, – "ply" is such a good word, by the way, don't you agree? "Dad?" I said. "That you, Mim? What's up?" "It's Mum," I said. "She fell down the stairs."

'There was a pause. I mean a noticeable pause. Then Dad spoke. "She all right then, is she? Not hurt too badly?" Here's a quick translation of that for you. "Is she dead then? Did the twisted bitch finally get to meet her Maker?" "I don't know, Dad. I think she might be pretty badly hurt."

'I could hear the glee in his voice. "Right. Listen to me. Where are you and Mal?" I said, "I'm in Mum's room and Mal's in his." Dad said, "Go to your bedroom. And stay there. I'll be right round." Almost as an afterthought, he asked me, "Did you dial nine nine nine?" "Yes, Dad."

"Good. That was the right thing to do."

Miriam paused and looked down at Stella. As if seeing her for the first time, her eyes roved up and down her body before coming to rest on Stella's.

'I'm so sorry. You must be thirsty. Would you like a glass of water? '

Stella fought down the urge to swear and plead for her freedom. She coughed.

'No thanks. I'm good.'

Miriam shrugged.

'As I was saying, Dad arrived ten minutes after I'd called him. I'd say the ambulance crew turned up about three minutes after that. Maybe two. Dad had to ring the doorbell. Mother had changed the locks after he left. I got Mal then went down and let Dad in. He came in and bent down beside Mother. He actually put his face against her nose. Then he stood up and put his hand out. I took it and he led me and Mal into the kitchen.

"'She's dead," he said, when we were sitting opposite him at the breakfast bar. "I know, Dad," I said. "What's going to happen to me and Mal?" He smiled. "Don't worry. Everything'll be fine," he said. Which turned out to mean being packed off to boarding school.

'Apparently Carol, Dad's squeeze, was expecting, and they didn't have enough room as it was. His taxi business was thriving, he said. Got himself a second cab and a driver to go with it. He could afford the fees and tuckshop money besides. And that's when my life took another tottering step to what you could call "the Dark Side".

'Monksfield was co-educational so Dad sent us both there. Naturally, boys' and girls' dormitories were well separated and, as you can imagine, the penalties for transgressions were severe. For the first six years Mal managed not to stray. But soon after his fourteenth birthday, he told me he really felt that he *deserved* it. You know? I mean, he had been *so* patient.

'In the holidays, most of the children went home to Mummy and Daddy. Or their super-rich uncles or their fairy-fucking-godmothers for all I know. Naturally, that wouldn't work for us. No, my dear old dad made that perfectly clear. He and Carol were expecting again or so he said and it was best if we just stayed at school.

'So we were stuck in "ninety acres of beautiful rolling Dorset countryside", as the school brochure had it. I suppose he sent us all the way over there because he didn't want us anywhere close to his new family. Can't say I blame him. Not really. Not when you look at how we turned out.

'We weren't alone. There were a few other kids whose families were so dysfunctional they couldn't even have their offspring around for a couple of months in the summer. A couple of Army brats. A boy who *clearly* had mental health issues. And a couple of girls. One of them was a dull little bird. But the other one?

'Lauren Bourne-Clarke was a different kettle of fish altogether. She was in the sixth form, seventeen, and clearly destined to be a model or an actress. Her parents worked in the film industry, hence her name. Lauren. You know? Like Lauren Bacall, the actress? It doesn't matter. Anyway, they were on a shoot that was delayed because of a revolution in Angola or a tropical storm in Bangladesh or wherever the fuck they were.

'So she stayed on at school while all the other beautiful people – that's what we called them, her and her little coterie of followers, we being the great unwashed, the saddos, the losers – fucked off to Bali or New Zealand or wherever.

'Lauren was beautiful. She had proper tits, too. Mal was

obsessed with her. She played tennis, hockey, football and was superb in all of them. She fenced. She was clever, too. Captain of the Debating Society and widely predicted to go on to Oxford or Cambridge. Or possibly Princeton or Harvard. And, I'm sorry to say, a whore.

'Oh, she had lots of friends and she volunteered at the local children's hospice at the weekends, but *I* knew. I could see what lay behind that facade. Lauren Bourne-Clarke had the *look*. Lauren Bourne-Clarke would offer herself up to whichever randy sixth-former or pencil-dicked art teacher who so much as smiled in her direction. So Mal decided she might as well give herself up to him, too.

'He followed her one morning. And I followed him. She was heading off to the woods at the far end of the football pitches. "Pitches", plural. Did I mention what a very well-endowed school Monksfield was?

She had a notebook with her, so maybe she was going to write a nature poem. Or it could have been a journal. You know, "Dear Diary, today I masturbated until my fingers bled thinking about sucking off the headmaster."

'They left the manicured pitch with its pristine white lines and passed through the long grass to the woods. Then he tripped over a root and swore, and of course then Lauren did turn round and see him. She smiled at him. "Hi. You stuck here for the holidays, too?" she asked him.

'He nodded. Then he took a few steps closer. "I'm going for a walk. Want to join me?" Lauren said. "Yes, please," he said. "Come on, then," she said, and carried on walking as if this was the most natural thing in the world.

'We hadn't really figured out the practicalities, so when they came to another patch of long grass, he hit her as hard as he could on the side of the head with his open hand. He was big for his age.

'So when he clouted her, she went over sideways with a yelp like when you kick a dog in the ribs so hard you feel one of those thin little bones give beneath the toe of your boot. Then he fucked her.

Then he ran back to school. Like I say, he hadn't thought about the practicalities.

'The fallout was pretty much what you would imagine. Or would you? For a start, they didn't call the police. He was fourteen for one thing, so technically a minor. He could have said, "She wanted it. She made me." After all, she was whoring herself around all over the school.

'But, more to the point, think of what it would have done for the school's reputation. I mean, Monksfield was a nice enough place but it wasn't exactly Eton. Plenty of other private schools to suck up the droves of kids pulled out of "Three Grand a Term School For Sex Fiends" if they didn't squash it.

'What happened was they called in the parents when they got back from Mauritius or Zanzibar or wherever and explained that there had been an *incident*. Paid them off with a shit-ton of money. Persuaded them that it would be unlikely to even get to court, what with it being his word against hers and also he was fourteen, as I said. The Bourne-Clarkes took the money and ran.'

98

FRIDAY 14TH SEPTEMBER 11.11 A.M.
BECKTON, EAST LONDON

Swallowing hard, Stella spoke.

'That's quite a story. But I'm surprised you haven't cut and run. Half the Met will be out looking for me when I don't call in.'

Miriam shrugged her wide shoulders and checked her watch.

'I think I've got a while yet. And, don't forget, they're going to come looking for you at the house. Not in here.'

'So you killed them all because of what your mum did to your brother, is that it?'

'I loved Mal. He could have had a normal life. But she beat the normality out of him. Beat it out, and worse. Her and her freakish beliefs. I've shown the world that they can't be trusted.'

'How, though, Miriam? How have you shown the world? You didn't leave messages.'

Miriam's eyes widened.

'Didn't leave – oh, come on, Stella. You don't think my little displays might have been just a tiny little clue? Plus, the *Sun* was very helpful, publishing my letter. Though as you know, I signed it The

Fourth Horseman. "Lucifer" was all wrong. He was a fallen angel, after all. He'd sat at God's side. Whereas good old Death is a destroyer, pure and simple.

'Now, never mind all that, I suppose you're wondering how I wheedled my way into those women's confidence? It wasn't difficult.

'I just told them what they wanted to hear. In their own way, they were all too proud for their own good. Look at Niamh Connolly. She screamed when she turned round and found me inside her home. I thought she was going to faint. That or wet herself.

'Then I just dangled money in front of her and it all went away. Now, I don't want any more interruptions, so I'm just to going to refasten your gag and then I'll begin.'

After stooping to jam the gag back into Stella's mouth, Miriam Robey embarked on a lengthy explanation of the steps she'd taken to murder her victims. Hoping her digital recorder was picking up the confession, Stella continued to work away at the cable tie binding her ankles.

———

Finally, Miriam seemed to reach a conclusion to the grisly story she had spent the previous forty minutes telling her captive audience.

'Then I put my protective suit on and started work. My goodness there was a lot of blood! And I cut myself at one point. I know it was careless. But isn't that what they say about people like me? In the end our confidence lets us down? But before I do leave London for pastures new, I do have one, final message to send the world. And I'm going to use you to send it.'

She stood, and Stella shied away. But Miriam stepped away from the chair and towards the door. She smiled down at Stella.

'Oh, don't worry, I'm not going to kill you. Well, not yet, anyway. I wasn't completely lying about that bitch Celia Thwaites. I had planned to make her my next victim. Then you got too close to the truth and I had to change my plans.

'You remember chapter five of Peter's book? Saint Lawrence?

Mal taught me to weld before they killed him. I've made a grille. I was going to roast her alive, but you'll have to do. I'll go and get it. You'll want to see it, I'm sure. You know, before I strap you to it.'

She turned back to her chair and picked up the book, which she'd placed on the floor.

'Obviously I'm not a massive fan of the Bible, but I did want to read you one quote. It's from Ezekiel. It was one of Mother's favourites.'

She flipped the pages until she came to a scrap of green paper, which she crumpled and dropped to the floor. She cleared her throat and began reading.

'Woe to the city of bloodshed! I, too, will pile the wood high. So heap on the wood and kindle the fire. Cook the meat well, mixing in the spices; and let the bones be charred.' She looked down at Stella. 'The city of bloodshed was Jerusalem. Some scholars think the passage is a metaphor. But I prefer to take it more literally. I'm going to roast you until nothing's left but charred bones.'

Then she left, shutting and locking the door behind her.

Stella set to work immediately. Grunting with the effort, she finally managed to work her bleeding index finger under the ankle strap of her right boot.

Her leg was cramping agonisingly, and the cable tie cutting into her wrists amplified the pain. She ignored it and worked at the growing loop of leather until it came free of the buckle.

Crossing the index and middle fingers of her right hand, and squeezing them hard round the strap, she pulled it out of the buckle. With a hiss of triumph she took the freed prong between her fingertips and began to manoeuvre it towards the tab of the cable tie around her wrists.

Her head was twisted round so far she could feel the muscles, tendons and ligaments in her neck straining against each other. The pain was excruciating, but nothing compared to what was waiting for her. She tried to ignore it and thanked God once more that she was still flexible enough to perform these agonising contortions.

For what felt like minutes, but was probably only thirty seconds, she felt around with her fingertips, finding the tiny aperture and then losing it again.

Finally, she felt the prong slide home, between the tape and pawl, home into the heart of the locking mechanism. She took a deep breath through her nose and, as she let it out, pushed the prong.

Holding it against the pawl, she slowly began to pull her left wrist away from her right. *Oh God, it's coming!* she thought, almost weeping with relief.

The door banged open. Heart thumping, Stella forced herself to go limp. Ignoring the agony of her twisted muscles, she lay still.

99

FRIDAY 14TH SEPTEMBER 11.39 A.M.
BECKTON, EAST LONDON

Dangling a green plastic fuel can from the fingers of her right hand, and holding what looked to Stella like a makeup bag in her left, Miriam looked down at Stella and cocked her head to one side.

'I've piled the wood high. It's in a pit, so obviously it's not high as in above ground, but there's a lot of it. And it's so dry thanks to this weather we've been having. I wondered whether I really needed the petrol, but you can't be too careful, know what I mean?'

She came closer, bent and tugged the gag away. Stella coughed as she drew in a lungful of clean air.

'You comfortable down there, Stella?'

'More comfortable than your brother.'

Miriam pooched her lower lip out.

'Oh, that's not nice. I suppose you're trying to provoke me, is that it? Want me to kick you to death instead of burning you? I have to say, it does have its merits. I did it to one of Mal's girlfriends after she tried to run away. In fact, I almost broke my toe. She's in the oil pit, too.'

Her attention seemed to jump the tracks. She shook her head violently.

'Look!' she said brightly. 'I brought you something to drink.'

Stella watched, horrified, as Miriam unscrewed the black lid from the fuel can. As it came free, the room filled with the heady tang of petrol. She upended the can over Stella's head.

Gasping and spluttering, trying to avoid swallowing, Stella swore up at her tormentor.

'Fuck you, you crazy bitch!'

Miriam righted the can and screwed the lid back on. She shook her head.

'Nobody's going to get fucked here today, except you. Although it wasn't always a love-free zone. Mal and I, well, when I said he raped me, that wasn't precisely a lie. We were very close. Plenty of cosy little spots to choose from. We used to take turns. Choosing, I mean.

'You see, before he was old enough to fuck that little tart Lauren Bourne-Clark, I used to let him practise with me. Boys have so much energy, I knew if I didn't, he'd probably go off and do something silly with one of the neighbourhood girls, and I wasn't old enough to clear up after him yet. Oh, Stella, what a face. After all I've done, *that's* what's given you the heebie-jeebies?'

Knowing it was all but pointless, Stella tried one final time to reason with Miriam. Because she was beginning to realise that here was a specimen of evil beyond anything she'd encountered.

'Miriam. He abused you, can't you see that? He messed around in your head until you didn't know right from wrong. Let me go and I promise I will help you. You need treatment, not punishment. I know someone who could give you that help. Someone kind. He works in a hospital—'

'I don't care where he fucking works!' Miriam roared. Then she dropped her voice straight back into a conversational tone, which scared Stella more.

'And it wasn't poor Mal who abused me. That was Mother's sacred duty. Me and Mal both. I won't tell you what she required us to do but, believe me, when I tell you that if I ever did know the difference between right from wrong, Mother's little prayer meetings twisted it out of all recognition.

'I learned from her that right is whatever you want. Wrong is anything that gets in your way. And, right now, you're in *my* way.'

She pulled a translucent orange lighter from her pocket. She turned it in the sunlight streaming in from behind her.

'Pretty. Mal and I used to like making fires. In the garden, you know? We caught a pigeon once. I think it must have been a baby because it was just sort of flopping around on the ground and it didn't fly away when Mal grabbed it. I threw it on the fire.' Miriam smiled. 'It made such a stink! And this really funny noise. I'm not joking, it was hilarious. A sort of screech. More like a parrot than a pigeon.'

She flicked the wheel and Stella watched as a perfect tulip-shaped yellow flame danced above Miriam's thumb. It disappeared when Miriam released the valve. She flicked again, and again the flame danced.

Stella strained against the cable ties but only succeeded in cutting deeper into her wrists. If Miriam wanted to, she could turn Stella into a human bonfire right here in the cabin and there'd be no more worrying about freeing herself from the cable tie. No more journal. No more Jamie. No more anything.

Please, God. Give me a fighting chance. At least let me take her on before she kills me.

Miriam grinned down at Stella.

'All right, pigeon?' she asked, flicking the lighter over and over again. 'Shall we see what sort of a sound *you* make?'

Then Miriam frowned. She stared up at the ceiling and her lips moved silently. She seemed to reach a decision. She pocketed the lighter.

'No. A plan's a plan. Saint Lawrence it is. Now, you lie still. We have to make sure you look like Mother.'

Stella watched, horrified, as Miriam knelt astride her and placed the makeup bag by her left hip. Shuffling backwards so her weight was over Stella's knees, she undid her belt and the button at her waist and pulled down the zip of her jeans.

'What are you doing, you twisted bitch?' Stella yelled.

'Quiet,' Miriam said.

She yanked Stella's jeans and knickers down over her thighs and stared at her pubis.

'Hold still because this might sting a little.'

Then she unzipped the makeup bag and produced a cheap disposable razor.

'Right,' she said when she'd finished. 'That's better. Oh, I almost forgot!'

She leaned forwards and reached inside Stella's shirt front. Stella reared up and tried to fix her teeth into Miriam's wrist but received a hard shove that sent her head smacking painfully onto the hard wooden floor.

'Try that again and I'll cut you into pieces before I cook you. Now hold still.'

Again, Miriam reached inside Stella shirt. Stella felt nauseous as the younger woman's hand pawed around her throat. Then she withdrew it.

'Shame,' Miriam said. 'Nothing for my collection.'

'Fuck you!'

Miriam stroked her fingers over Stella's lips before she could squirm her head away. Then her eyes seemed to focus on something far beyond the confines of the Portakabin.

'You have such a foul mouth, Miriam,' she said in an oddly deep voice. 'Worse than your brother's. I know what you get up to. I know how you lie together. Filthy sinful children. We must burn it out of you.'

Her eyes zeroed back in on Stella's and she smiled.

'Right! I'll see you in a minute.' She adopted an Australian accent. 'I'm going out to light the barbie.'

Sloshing the petrol can against her thigh, Miriam left the cabin and closed the door behind her.

Stella tried to steady her breathing as she resumed her delicate work on the cable tie. Once again, she lined up the prong of her boot buckle and began the excruciating work of wiggling it into the locking mechanism and freeing the tape.

Eyes sore and weeping from the petrol fumes evaporating off her skin and clothes, she held herself rigid, so anxious was she not to dislodge the delicately balanced pieces of plastic and metal.

Once again, she pushed the locking tab out of the way. Now that the tape was clear of the pawl, she was able to draw it out, sensing each individual click as another plastic ridge bumped out from the tab.

All she wanted to do was yank the tape clear but she was terrified that the prong would slip and lock her back in again, so she continued with the snail's progress of the tie until, with a sudden release, it came free and her wrists flew apart.

Stella had to stifle a scream as blood, and feeling, flooded back into her cramping muscles.

She rubbed some feeling back into her wrists, ignoring the blood that had made them slippery, then hauled her knickers and jeans back up and refastened her belt. That left her ankles, which were still tied.

She rolled to the corner where the steel rack leaned drunkenly against the wall, pushed her ankles against the upright and began sawing the cable tie up and down against its sharp metal edge. The whole time she worked, she kept her eyes glued to the door, alert to the sound of Miriam's footsteps.

The cable tie gave with a snap. She rebuckled her boot, then scrambled to her feet and reached into her jeans pocket, but her phone was gone.

Of course it's gone! She thought. *She would have taken it the moment you were out. At least the mad bitch didn't find the recorder.*

She crossed the cabin and leaned back, readying herself to kick out at the flimsy-looking lock. Then the door opened. Miriam stood there, backlit by the sun. Her face flashed with anger, teeth baring, eyebrows drawing together.

'No!' she shouted. 'You are a very bad girl!'

Hands curving into claws, she lunged at Stella.

100

FRIDAY 14TH SEPTEMBER 12.15 P.M.
BECKTON, EAST LONDON

Stella dropped into a crouch, so that Miriam's outstretched fingers passed harmlessly over her head. Then she launched herself forward, butting Miriam in the midsection.

Powering up from her hips, she drove Miriam backwards into the wall beside the door, cracking her head against the particleboard.

But Miriam was strong, and she rolled sideways, out of Stella's way, before kicking her viciously in the left thigh.

Stella yelled with the pain and staggered back as her leg muscles temporarily shut down.

Miriam closed with her hands outstretched once more, reaching for Stella's eyes.

Stella had learned to fight with Sergeant Doug 'Rocky' Stevens, her unarmed defence tactics instructor in the Met. Twice. Once, on an official course and once, privately, when she'd asked him to teach her how to fight dirty. She drew on the second course now.

She jabbed a blade of stiffened fingers into Miriam's exposed throat. The effect was instantaneous. Her eyes bulged and her arms dropped as she scrabbled at her windpipe. Stella leaned away and kicked out at Miriam's right knee.

But Miriam anticipated the move. She sidestepped Stella's incoming boot and shoved her hard in the chest. Stella stumbled and fell heavily on her side, winded, able only to watch as Miriam turned and ran out of the door.

She pushed herself upright and ran after Miriam, who was on the far side of a firepit, from which bright yellow-orange flames roared several feet above its lip.

The green petrol can lay discarded near a six-foot by three-foot metal grid. It appeared to be made from the ribbed steel rods used to reinforce concrete. *The grille*, Stella thought.

Miriam disappeared behind a stack of burnt-out cars. The sound of a big diesel engine starting shattered the silence and from the other side of the abandoned consumer goods, Stella saw a gout of charcoal-coloured smoke jet up. It didn't sound like a truck. It was a deeper, bassier noise.

Rounding the corner of the stack of cars, Stella pulled up, heart pounding. A stitch in her side was stabbing her repeatedly with each rasping breath she dragged into her burning lungs. Miriam had disappeared.

In a half-crouch to ease the knifing pain in her ribs, Stella turned through a full circle. Nothing. To her left, the cars. To her right a mountain of discarded fridges, freezers, washing machines and dishwashers.

Then the entire pile of white domestic appliances fell forwards, the topmost machines freefalling towards her.

As she screamed and dived towards the base of the pile, she caught sight of a jointed yellow arm tipped with a clawed bucket.

Stella balled herself up, arms wrapped around her head, and squashed herself inside a fridge missing its door. The crashing began a second later as several tons of German, Dutch, Korean and Japanese white goods smashed into the ground inches from the toes of her boots.

She squeezed her eyes shut and thrust herself backwards,

praying that whoever had made the fridge had spent enough money on the chassis to protect her now.

Is this how skiers feel in an avalanche? she wondered, as the light dimmed to almost-blackness around her and the air vibrated with each percussive impact.

With a final, huge, crunching jolt that Stella felt through her hips, the avalanche ended.

She opened her eyes.

Beyond the aperture where the fridge door had once closed, a foot of clear ground lay between her boots and the rear of a washing machine, its blue and red water pipes and corrugated grey plastic drain hose tangled like guts.

Shimmying forwards on her back, and yelping with cramp, Stella looked up as she unfolded herself into the narrow space. It was roofed by a smooth, white-painted sheet of metal. She managed to twist herself round onto her belly. She looked over her shoulder. The way was blocked. Ahead, the sinuous aluminium cooling pipes of a second fridge.

She willed herself to breathe shallowly and strained to hear something from beyond her prison. And she did. The rumble of the backhoe's engine, clearly in gear and getting louder with each passing second.

The bang was deafening. Above her head, the appliance sealing her in thumped downwards by six inches. Panicking, she pulled herself forwards on her elbows and tried to push out at the back of the fridge. It might have been part of the bedrock beneath the yard.

Sparks danced in her vision.

She flinched as another grinding crash shook her prison cell, and from somewhere above, clangs and the screech of metal against metal told her the whole unstable tower was collapsing. Then the engine noise died. In the silence, Stella could hear a ringing in her ears. She knew she was hyperventilating, but was unable to slow her breathing down.

Miriam's mocking voice came to her.

'Cosy? You won't be soon. I'm going to dig you out and then I'm going to burn you alive. Do you know how painful that is, Stella? Do you? I'm going to roast you on my barbecue and, when you're done, I'm going to chop you into tiny little pieces and burn them until the bones are charred and nothing is left but ash.'

A few seconds passed, then the engine started up again. Stella looked over her shoulder again, then at the unyielding grid of metalwork in front of her.

She thought of Lola, dying of thermal burns in Richard's car. And of the years of therapy and sheer bloody hard work she'd endured to free herself of Other Stella: the demonic spirit of vengeance that had consumed and then inhabited her.

She thought of Polly, and how close the little girl had come to seeing her Auntie Stella with her brains blown out on her mummy and daddy's stripy lawn. She thought of Vicky, of Elle and Jason and Georgie, and of Jamie. And she realised how frightened she was of dying.

She filled her lungs with air and screamed.

'No!'

This is not my day to die. Not here. Not now. I'm not giving in to you.

101

FRIDAY 14TH SEPTEMBER 12.33 P.M.
BECKTON, EAST LONDON

Feeling as clearheaded as if she'd just woken from a long night of dream-free sleep, Stella shuffled backwards, letting her knees bend until they were touching both confining metal walls.

Your strength's in your legs. Push!

Stella pressed the soles of her boots against the sheet of metal hemming her in. Grunting with the effort, she exerted even more pressure, sweat stinging her eyes.

As the screech and grind of the shifting appliances above her continued, she shoved and kicked out in a series of draining moves.

Stella folded her knees up again, wriggled backwards another eight inches and resumed shoving and kicking at the appliance blocking her one and only way out. It shifted back in a sudden slide.

Pushing, wriggling, kicking, shoving, working her way back on her elbows and belly, Stella kept up her assault on what she could now see was some sort of commercial microwave oven.

With a cry of triumph, she booted it backwards. Over her shoulder, she saw light streaming down onto the ground. A black space beckoned. No pipework, no jagged sheets of steel, no lumps of concrete designed to stop washing machines doing the cha-cha across the kitchen floor.

She reversed out into the black cavern and sat up. In front of her, the narrow tunnel she'd just extricated herself from collapsed with a tearing bang as God knew how many tons of discarded steel crumpled it like an eggbox.

Slithering sideways, her face often less than an inch from the side of a cooker or tumble dryer, Stella pushed her way out of the place where she'd thought she was about to die. A narrow crevasse led all the way out onto the far side of the block of scrapped machines.

She looked around for a weapon. And she smiled, grimly.

As if placed there by a medieval armourer, spike-topped steel fence posts lay in a pile several feet tall beside a mangled silver Porsche. She ran over and picked up the nearest post. Six feet long from its squared-off base to its razor-sharp split tip, it was satisfyingly heavy in her hand.

She turned and strode back towards the sound of the backhoe. Stella yelled over the roar of the engine.

'Miriam Robey! Give yourself up! You need help!'

And she heard, from the place she didn't want to look at, her other voice. The voice she'd banished as a separate presence in her world, but which, from time to time, made its presence felt between her ears.

No she doesn't. She needs to be put down.

Climbing out of the cab, Miriam shouted back at her.

'No I don't! I need justice for Malachi!'

She jumped down from the big yellow earth-mover and ran.

102

FRIDAY 14TH SEPTEMBER 12.59 P.M.
BECKTON, EAST LONDON

Stella wasn't as fit as she had been in the year after Richard and Lola had been murdered by Ramage, when she'd run hundreds and hundreds of miles to keep her grief, and the truth, at bay. But she was still in good shape, unlike Miriam Robey, whose large-boned frame no athletics coach would have chosen for their runners.

Carrying the fence post like a spear, Stella rounded the rusted carcass of a truck cab in time to glimpse Miriam vanish behind more squashed cars.

She sprinted after her, almost losing her footing as she made the turn. Then, with a sudden sense of impending catastrophe, she ducked, fully expecting to meet a crowbar wielded by Miriam, coming in the opposite direction.

No incoming ironwork whistled above her head. Miriam was halfway towards the hut housing the oil pit. Stella yelled at her again but Miriam didn't waste any oxygen shouting back, closing in on the hut in an ungainly run.

Stella reached the door just a few seconds after Miriam. She hadn't closed it and Stella could see her inside the gloomy building, limping, and clutching her side, as she made her way round the pit.

Inside, Stella glanced to the far end of the hut, where a huge steel roller shutter presumably gave onto an access road for the tankers. It was closed now, though, so the only way out was through the narrow door at Stella's back. Her breath was coming in huge gasps and the stink of petrol on her skin was making her retch.

'Miriam! Stop!' she yelled, her voice echoing off the hard surfaces all around them.

Miriam stopped on the far side of the pit from Stella. Twenty feet of crow-black engine oil separated the two women. She turned to face Stella, arms hanging by her sides, her lower half obscured by the wall. Her chest was heaving and her face was scarlet, as if the blotches that usually flared on her cheeks had expanded to fill all the available space.

'It was Mother's fault,' she screamed. 'Mal was a good boy, but she tortured him. She deserved to die! She deserved it! And so did all the others!'

'Miriam Robey,' Stella called out across the black mirror, fighting to keep her breathing under control. 'I am arresting you for the murders of Niamh Connolly, Sarah Sharpe, Moira Lowney and Amy Burnside. You do not have to say anything, but it may harm your defence if you do not mention when questioned something which you later rely on in court. Anything you do say may be given in evidence. Now, come here. It's over.'

Miriam laughed.

'Beautifully delivered. Just like they do on the telly. All right, I'll come.'

She turned to her right and began walking round the pit, never taking her eyes off Stella, a lopsided grin seemingly painted in place. Stella reached behind her for her folding handcuffs then swore as she realised Miriam had taken these along with her phone and Airwave.

Miriam turned the second corner of the rectangular pit so that she was facing Stella. Stella shifted her grip on the fence post. Then Miriam spoke, and changed everything.

'I'm coming, Stella, like you asked. But not so you can arrest me. I'm not going to spend the rest of my days locked up with the likes of Rose West and those freaks. They're sadists, just like Mother. I was just avenging Mal.'

In her right hand she held a machete. She lifted it in front of her face and waggled the fearsome, foot-long blade from side to side.

'I was going to use this on you after I'd cooked you. To make it easier to char your bones. But before will do just as well.'

Then she shrieked, a discordant wail that had the short hairs on the back of Stella's neck standing up as it bounced off the hard walls. Baring her teeth, Miriam raised the machete above her head and charged at Stella. Stella turned sideways on to Miriam, bent her knees, then lunged forwards, gripping the fence post two-handed.

The bifurcated spike penetrated Miriam's chest, just to the right of her breastbone. She swung out with the machete and Stella screamed as the heavy blade chopped into her left arm. She looked down and saw blood flowing fast from a deep cut in her jacket. But then, Miriam's strength seemed to leave her abruptly. The machete fell from her open hand, clanging onto the concrete floor. Both arms hung limply at her sides.

Stella heard a roaring in her ears. Her vision telescoped down to a small circle surrounded by black, with Miriam's face filling it. She leaned forwards on the fence post, twisting and pushing it deeper into Miriam's chest.

Miriam staggered back, blood gushing from her open mouth. Stella let go of the fence post and watched as Miriam folded backwards over the wall, swinging the remaining five foot of fence post in an arc so that the blunt end pointed at the ceiling.

'Your fingerprints are all over it,' Miriam gurgled through a mouthful of frothy scarlet blood.

Stella shook her head.

'None left. A lovely Greek man called Yiannis made them go away. Now I'm going to make *you* go away. Because maybe your brother *was* a tortured soul. Maybe your mother, who sounds like a complete bitch by the way, *did* screw him up for life. But you? You're a cold-hearted killer. Pure and simple. The cat? The girls? I think you enjoyed it all. I think you got off on torturing those poor women to death. Revenge had nothing to do with it.'

Then she grabbed Miriam around the shins and lifted her over the wall and into the waiting oil. The drop to the surface was about five feet. Miriam entered the viscous black soup with a slimy, plopping splash. The oil sucked her down and as Stella looked over, the surface was already smoothing out, a gentle wave traversing towards the four walls.

Clutching her left bicep, and trying to ignore the blood flowing out between her clenched fingers, Stella returned to the house.

Letting go long enough to struggle out of the jacket, and crying out with the pain as the damaged muscles tried to help, she ripped her shirt sleeve off, spun it into a makeshift tourniquet then wrapped it round her arm above the deep cut Miriam's machete had opened.

Working one-handed, and using her teeth, she managed to tie it off tight enough to slow the blood to a trickle. She folded a tea towel into a dressing, pressed it over the wound with her free hand, then bandaged the whole thing up with a second tea towel.

Satisfied she wasn't going to bleed to death, she looked around for a phone.

She found a cordless phone in the sitting room. Stella sat heavily on a scuffed black vinyl sofa. She punched in Garry's mobile number from memory, one of two or three she had stored away.

'Boss! Oh, thank Christ! Where are you?'

'I'm at Miriam's house. It was her, Garry. She wasn't the accomplice. She was Lucifer. Malachi Robey was killed last year. Murdered by vigilantes. It was her all along.'

'Shitting hell, boss, are you OK? I sent you a text saying I thought she was MJ.'

'I'm fine. But she took my phone.'

'You're really all right?'

'Yeah, I'm fine. I'm fine.'

'You got her, yeah?'

Got? How d'you mean, Garry?

'She's dead. She attacked me with a machete, laid my arm open halfway to the bone. I fought back and she fell into an oil tank in the scrapyard behind the house. Look, come over, OK? Soon as you can. And bring some paracetamol. This arm hurts like a bastard.'

After she ended the call, Stella walked back into the scrapyard, holding her wounded arm above her head. She stopped at the pile of fence posts by the ruined Porsche and picked one up with her right hand. She walked with it to the hut containing the oil pit, and threw it in, near where she estimated Miriam would have landed. She repeated the process seven more times.

Garry arrived forty-five minutes later. Stella heard the sirens as the marked and unmarked cars and an ambulance roared down Gasworks Lane and screeched to a halt outside 55. She'd cleaned her wrists up under the tap while she was waiting.

She walked down the hallway and opened the front door. Garry was standing there, a look of concern on his face. He glanced at her blood-soaked arm, then back at her.

'Jesus, boss! You look a mess. And you stink of petrol!'

'Charmer.'

He led her to the waiting paramedics, who took one look at her improvised dressing and were all for whisking her straight to the nearest A&E department. She shook her head.

'Not yet. I want to look round the house. Just stand by, OK? Then I'll come with you. She didn't hit an artery or I'd have bled out by now.'

'At least let me elevate it for you,' one of them said.

A couple of minutes later, sporting a blue sling fastened with Velcro, Stella made her way back inside as uniformed officers began setting up the outer and inner cordons.

In a small back bedroom overlooking the scrapyard, Stella and Garry found Miriam's records of her crimes.

Photographs of her victims cut from newspapers and

magazines, or printed out from websites and social media profiles, and stuck to the wall with Blu-Tack. Below the row of women, their faces obscured by thick black crosses, Craig Morgan and Ade Trimmets smiled out at them, each man's features disfigured by a red X.

'She did Morgan and Trimmets as well,' Garry said. 'No wonder we haven't seen them hanging about at the station or muscling in on the guvnor's press conferences.'

Stella turned to a tatty, self-assembly wardrobe with a wonky door that had refused to close. With a gloved right hand, she pulled it open. She lifted clear a coil of flax bell rope with a black and gold sally and placed it on the narrow single bed's worn pink coverlet. She turned back to the wardrobe.

Resting on a shelf at waist height was a shoebox. Stella lifted it out, revealing a second, smaller, carton, which she also collected. She sat on the bed to open them. Garry looked down as she lifted the shoebox lid away to reveal syringes, plastic bottles of clear liquids labelled *Temaz.* and *Ket.* and a dozen or so pairs of nitrile gloves and the thin, blue nylon overshoes provided in public swimming pools. It also contained her phone and Airwave.

She opened the smaller carton. It contained five matchboxes. The boxes were marked in black pen: NC, SS, ML, AB, CT.

They looked at each other.

'Trophies?' Garry asked, voicing their shared thought.

'Let's find out, shall we?'

She picked up one of the little boxes and held it out to Garry.

'Do the honours,' she said.

Garry poked a gloved finger against the end of the drawer. In the silence the soft rasp as it emerged was clearly audible. Seeing what was inside, she nodded. Then she and Garry opened the other four matchboxes and Stella laid them in a row.

The box marked CT was empty. The boxes marked NC, SS, ML, AB each contained a small crucifix: three gold, one silver.

Each crucifix lay on a bed of tangled, curly hairs. Dark-brown. Black and grey. Tawny. Greyish-white.

103

FRIDAY 14TH SEPTEMBER 2.00 P.M.
NEWHAM, EAST LONDON

While the other units were cordoning off the house and the scrapyard behind it, Garry drove Stella to Newham University Hospital. Fifteen minutes later, she was sitting on a bed in the A&E department, watching as a junior doctor, young, male, stressed-looking, injected her with anaesthetic.

'That'll ease the pain. It's a nasty cut. What was it, a machete?'

'Yes. Get a lot of those down here?' she asked.

He smiled ruefully.

'Too many. It's too deep for me to do it here. There's some muscle damage. We've got a theatre waiting for you.'

Stella opted for sedation and local anaesthetic over a general. Ever since a schoolfriend's brother had died during a routine operation to repair a detached retina after a rugby game, she'd tried to avoid general anaesthesia.

As the anaesthetist injected a sedative dose of midazolam into a vein in her right arm, Stella smiled up at her and drifted away from the operating theatre.

She found herself in a church. Sunlight streamed in through the stained-glass windows, tinting everything in rainbow colours. She walked towards the altar, pausing to look at four tombs, on top of which statues of women, hands placed together in prayer, reclined. She recognised their faces. Niamh, Sarah, Moira and Amy. All smiling. All at peace.

A woman who looked like Stella approached her from the direction of the altar, a bottle of wine in one hand, two silver goblets encrusted with jewels dangling by their stems from the other.

She smiled at Stella and set the goblets down on the closest tomb before filling them with red wine until it brimmed over. Handing one to Stella, she spoke.

'Nice one, babe,' she said. Then she winked.

———

When Stella came round, it was to find Garry at her bedside, checking his phone.

'Hello, Garry,' she said.

He smiled down at her and took her hand.

'Hello, boss. How are you feeling?'

'Yeah. Pretty good. My arm's a bit numb.'

'Probably the anaesthetic. I checked with the surgeon. He said you had peripheral nerve damage. It'll take a couple of months to return to full sensation but, other than that, you're good to go.'

Stella looked down at her green and white hospital gown.

'Not quite. Give me a few minutes to get dressed.'

Once she'd completed the forms to discharge herself from the hospital, and they were driving back to Paddington Green, Stella spoke.

'How are *you* doing?'

'Me? Fine, now. I was scared we'd lost you.'

She grinned.

'Yeah, but you wouldn't have minded that much. No more teasing about your love life for one thing.'

He smiled back.

'True, true, I hadn't thought of that. And no more ranting about the coffee running out. Although I think there's one bloke who might have missed you.'

'Who's that?'

'Jamie Hooke. He called the station asking for you. I had to give him the gist of it. You know, what with you two…'

'Being an item?'

'Yeah.'

'What did he want?'

Garry shrugged.

'Nothing. I think it was just a social call. You should probably phone him.'

Stella nodded. She called Jamie.

He answered almost before the first ring had purred in Stella's ear.

'Oh my God, are you OK? Garry said you were missing.'

'Yeah, I'm fine, I'm fine. Robey had a sister. She called me pretending to be his wife. She was the killer.'

'Did she hurt you?'

'Yes. She got in a swipe with a machete. But don't worry,' she added hastily, hearing his indrawn breath. 'It's all patched up, good as new.'

'Wait a minute, "was" the killer?'

'She's dead. She attacked me. Self-defence. I can't say anymore, there'll be an internal inquiry.'

'Look, call me as soon as you can. I want to see you.'

'OK. Me, too. I'd better go.'

'He all right, then?' Garry asked.

'Yeah, fine. Just a little shaken. You know how overprotective men are.'

Garry laughed.

'Yeah, especially when the woman is a little shrinking violet like you, boss.'

Back at Paddington Green, Callie called Stella into her office the moment she appeared at the door of the SIU incident room. Having first checked Stella was OK, and offered her a drink – refused – she moved on to business.

'What happened?'

'I chased her into a kind of hut where they had an oil storage tank. I cautioned her and tried to arrest her. She ran at me with a machete.'

Stella lifted her left arm to show her boss the bandage. The painkillers the hospital doctor had given her were doing an adequate job but she still felt the underlying ache, and winced.

'Then what?'

'I tried to wrestle her off me and, in the struggle, she went into the oil. I couldn't risk going in after her. I thought I'd drown.'

'You know I'll have to call in Professional Standards.'

It was a statement not a question.

Stella nodded.

'Death of a suspect while being arrested. It's OK, boss. I've got nothing to hide.'

———

Two hundred miles to the north, the new Bishop of Whitby led the congregation at York minster in a special prayer. Celia Thwaites spoke with a clear, steady voice as she asked those gathered in the sight of God to remember Niamh Connolly, Sarah Sharpe, Moira Lowney and Amy Burnside.

———

It took the detectives three days to organise a couple of tanker trucks to drive to Beckton and pump out the oil pit. The fleet manager confirmed by text that the final volume, as measured by the trucks' gauges, was nine thousand, three hundred and forty-three gallons.

Preserved like ancient peat bog people in the anaerobic conditions of the oil-filled pit, and as slick and black as sea lions, were eighteen corpses, fourteen female and four male. Those at the bottom of the pile had been squashed and distorted by those above.

The topmost body, impaled on a fence post that the CSM concluded must have been one of those submerged in the oil, belonged to Miriam Robey. Below her were Craig Morgan and Ade Trimmets. The men's skulls were stoved in and they had been strangled, but not mutilated. Both were recognisable by their facial features alone, which were easy enough to clean up with detergent.

The scrapyard search took a full month, with a team of thirty CSIs, cadaver dog teams and specialist searchers from across the Met working full time. Burnt fragments of women's clothing, mainly cheap nylon underwear, vinyl miniskirts and stilettos, were discovered in a three-foot deep firepit.

Along with the homemade grille, the team recovered a battered, brass-banded wooden sea chest. It contained a pair of vintage Burgon & Ball sheep shears, a collapsible crossbow, a bone-handled antique grapefruit knife, and a skinning knife, all of which were spattered or stained with blood and tissue fragments that matched Miriam's four female victims. Fingerprints recovered from the tools and weapons matched Miriam's.

The rope Stella found in the wardrobe, when measured, was found to be twenty-five metres long. It matched exactly the composition of those manufactured by Sherborne Ropes. Miriam Robey's DNA was all over it.

The bodies from the oil pit were autopsied over a five-week period at Westminster Mortuary. Dr Craven was one of the team of forensic pathologists who carried out the post mortems.

Malachi Robey was identified by a DNA match to his record on NDNAD and a match to tattoos and prison dental work on his criminal record. Cause of death was given as massive internal injuries including a ruptured liver and spleen.

The final male corpse, which had been down in the oil for longer, judging by its position relative to the others, was identified as belonging to a Jack Haggerty, the original owner of the scrapyard. His skull was crushed. Haggerty's name was still on the title deed as the owner, so whatever sort of legacy he'd left Malachi Robey, it wasn't one recognised by the courts.

Eight of the female bodies were eventually identified through DNA and fingerprints as belonging to prostitutes who had been reported missing by their friends. All had been arrested at least once and were logged on NDNAD as well as IDENT1. The causes of death were varied, from blunt force trauma to the back of the head to manual strangulation.

The five remaining female corpses, all judged by the pathologists to have been aged between fourteen and sixteen, were never identified. They, too, had been bludgeoned or strangled to death. The best guess of the investigators was that they were runaways, possibly from the care system. Budgetary constraints and the sheer volume of new cases led to their cases being quietly sidelined.

All the identified bodies that could be were returned to relatives for burial or cremation. The five lost girls were taken to Kensal Green Crematorium in an unmarked private ambulance. Stella travelled with them and watched as their ashes were scattered, with due reverence, over a rosebed in the memorial garden.

The internal inquiry into the events at the scrapyard behind 55 Gasworks Lane took three weeks. The department's investigators seized the fence post on which Miriam Robey was impaled. They left it to drain for five full days and then examined it for fingerprints using every chemical, electronic and digital technique available to the Met, and some they had to buy in from an external forensics lab. It came back clean.

The inquiry determined that DCI Cole had used force proportionate to the perceived threat and had acted not only professionally but with personal courage in attempting to bring a known serial killer to justice. The formal conclusion was that DCI Cole had not been guilty of any form of professional misconduct.

Stella received a Commissioner's Commendation for her actions at the scrapyard.

104

NOON, SATURDAY 27TH OCTOBER
HYDE PARK

The bright autumn sun was warm, though the breeze blowing across the lake carried a promise of colder times to come.

The two couples in the rowing boat on the Serpentine were laughing. Jamie had just lost an oar overboard and he and Damian were engaged in a frantic effort to retrieve it. Sun glittered off the water, turning the spraying droplets into airborne diamonds.

'Come on, Jamie,' Stella said, almost helpless with laughter. 'Or do Vicky and I need to show you how it's done?'

'Oh, ha! Very funny!'

She looked over the side of the boat at her reflection. Just for the briefest moment, as a splash disturbed the smooth surface, the woman looking back at her appeared to wink.

Then the water smoothed out and it was just Stella again, smiling back.

The oar retrieved, the quartet resumed their leisurely progress around the lake.

The End

Read on for a BBC Radio 4 interview with Stella.

RADIO INTERVIEW WITH DCI STELLA COLE. PARTIAL TRANSCRIPT.

You're listening to BBC Radio 4. In the first in a new series of interviews with the people who keep us safe – soldiers, police officers, prison warders, paramedics – Vicky Riley interviews Detective Chief Inspector Stella Cole of the Metropolitan Police Service in *Our Lives, Their Hands*.

Vicky Riley:
    Let's get some of the basics out of the way first, DCI Cole. What made you decide to join the police force?

Stella Cole:
    [laughing] Well, the first thing we should do is drop the DCI bit. Just call me Stella. I won't arrest you! As to your question, I studied Psychology at university and I became fascinated by the question: why do some people do bad things? I wanted to understand it but I also wanted to be part of the fight to stop them. The police was the logical career choice.

VR:

So, Stella, you didn't think of following an academic path. Research and so on?

SC:

I could have done, I suppose. But I'd had enough of studying and research by that point. I guess I wanted to get my hands dirty. [Laughs] Probably not the best choice of words. Let's say I wanted to be hands-on.

VR:

And you certainly were. You were one of the youngest female officers ever to make detective inspector in the Metropolitan Police.

SC:

Yeah. The Met's come in for some stick over the years about equal opportunities, but my experience has been pretty positive.

VR:

So no sexism, then? No problems when your male colleagues saw you get promoted ahead of them?

SC:

Look, the Met isn't perfect, what organisation is? Certainly not the BBC. But there were plenty of female officers who watched me get promoted as well. Maybe they wanted it as much as the guys. Maybe they saw me as a role model. I don't know. But, right now, my boss is a woman and although her boss is a man, his boss is a woman. And, obviously, the commissioner is a woman, so I think it's a pretty safe assumption that the Met, whatever its past, promotes on talent not gender.

VR:

Let's turn to your work. Now, I know you can't discuss on-going cases, but can you give me a flavour of the type of case you get involved in? I believe you work in a specialist team that deals with a particular sort of crime?

SC:

That's right. It's called the Special Investigations Unit. We look at crimes that, by their nature, fall outside the normal run of things.

VR:

Such as?

SC:

I'm sure your listeners will be familiar with the most serious types of crimes from the news or TV dramas. Hopefully they don't have personal experience.

VR:

You mean murders, sexual offences, things like that?

SC:

Yes, plus arson, terrorist offences, obviously. Well, the Met had established teams who investigate those types of crimes, but there are times when things go beyond what you might call a simple murder, and yes, I know that murder is never simple. But if there are, for example, multiple victims, or aspects of the case that require a different style of investigation, that's where we get involved.

VR:

Let's call a spade a spade. Are you talking about serial killers?

SC:

We prefer not to use that term. We tend to talk about multiple linked offences. But yes, that could be an example, though I would stress that this sort of offender is incredibly rare in the UK. Despite what the telly would have us believe.

VR:

[laughing] Yes, if we believed everything we saw on TV we'd never get a wink of sleep, would we? Now, you've said you and your colleagues work on these sorts of very serious crimes, maybe a serial murderer or perhaps some sort of very dangerous terrorist. And I'm wondering what kind of a personal toll that sort of work takes on you and your colleagues?

SC:

[sighs] Obviously, we have to get involved in some fairly distressing situations. But we're working against the criminals. So when we solve a case, make an arrest, see a perpetrator found guilty in a court of law and sent to prison, that acts as a massive boost to our morale. I guess on a personal level, every police officer will tell you more or less the same thing. You develop coping mechanisms. Everyone knows about copper humour. It can be pretty dark at times, but it's really a safety valve.

VR:

You've looked people in the eye who have committed all sorts of the most horrendous crimes. Most recently, the serial killer Miriam Robey. Are they evil? Mad? What?

SC:

That's a very good question. Some of them are clearly insane, and when they get to court, that's what the process will determine. We have a specific verdict of not guilty by reason of insanity and in that case, although they don't go to prison, providing the evidence against them is strong enough to convict, they're sent to a secure psychiatric institution. As to evil, I'm not sure what that word means. It feels almost like a word for theologians to use, not police officers. It does get used, of course, and some of the criminals we've had in this country, well, I guess evil would definitely cover it. Personally, I'm less interested in labelling them except as innocent or guilty. I guess, deep down, I'm still just a girl in blue.

GLOSSARY

A* – top grade at A-level, equivalent to US A+

A-level – exam taken in a single subject e.g. biology at the end of British secondary school education at age 18

arsey – pugnacious, argumentative, especially with authority e.g. police

banging up – sending to prison

bobbies – British uniformed police officers

boffins – scientists, technical specialists

bollocks – literally, testicles; slang expression of disgust meaning, "Oh, shit!", "rubbish"

brief – British lawyer equivalent to a US attorney, especially a trial lawyer (barrister in British legal system)

cut-and-shut – illegal practice of making one car by welding together two undamaged halves of other cars

diddling – cheating (someone out of something)

dip – pickpocket

DC – detective constable (lowest rank of detective in British police forces)

DCI – detective chief inspector

DCS – detective chief superintendent

DI – detective inspector

DIY – do-it-yourself (in the UK reserved mainly for household jobs like putting up shelves, minor electrical or plumbing jobs)

dodgy – unreliable (of people or things), not completely legal

DS – detective sergeant

DVLA – Driver and Vehicle Licensing Agency

fag – cigarette

FATACC – FAtal Traffic ACCcident

fence – someone who buys and sells stolen goods, to perform that activity

filched – stole (sneakily rather than brazenly)

FLO – family liaison officer, police officer whose job it is to comfort families of victims of crime and keep them informed of developments in the case

FMO – force medical officer

GCSE – general certificate of education, single-subject exam taken at age 16 in British secondary schools

ghosted – moved from one prison to another with no notice

ghillie – (Scottish) man or boy who helps people on a hunting, fishing or deer stalking expedition

git – horrible person

Hendon – short for Hendon Police College, Metropolitan Police Service's main training centre

hob – cooktop or stovetop

holdall – carryall

home counties – the counties surrounding London: Surrey, Kent, Essex, Middlesex, Hertfordshire, Buckinghamshire, Berkshire, Sussex; as an adjective applied to accent, it means upscale/privileged

IPCC – Independent Police Complaints Commission, body responsible for overseeing the police complaints system in England and Wales

J20 – a fruit-flavoured, juice and water soft drink available in British pubs and bars

kit – equipment, to provide equipment e.g. "kit you out"

kosher – trustworthy

lairy – loud, aggressive, excitable

loadout – a soldier's personal array of weapons and equipment

M&S – Marks & Spencer, British department store

Met – The Metropolitan Police Service AKA "Scotland Yard"

muppet – stupid or dimwitted person

nicked – stolen

numpty – stupid or dimwitted person

occie health – Occupational Health, police department responsible for monitoring, protecting health of officers

PACE – Police and Criminal Evidence Act 1984, legislation governing conduct of police officers in England and Wales

pissed – drunk

plods – uniformed police officers

plonk – derogatory term for female police officer

Portakabins – brand name for portable or mobile buildings

posh – upscale (in case of newspapers, "serious" broadsheets as opposed to tabloids)

ructions – trouble, complaints, shit hitting fan

SC&O – Specialist Crime & Operations, unit within the Metropolitan Police Service responsible for dealing with all serious crime in London

SC&O19 – specialist firearms command

screw – prison officer

SIO – senior investigating officer

Special Brew – super-strength lager (9% alcohol by volume) brewed by Carlsberg, AKA "tramp juice"

tags – simple graffiti, usually a set of initials or a nickname

toe-rag – despicable or worthless person

topped – killed

tweaking – obsessive repetition of simple act like scratching face, common to methamphetamine addicts

UDT – unarmed defence (or defensive) tactics

villains – criminals

witness nobbling – threatening or blackmailing witnesses of crimes into not testifying

WPC – woman police constable

ACKNOWLEDGMENTS

Many people helped me make this book as good as I could manage. In the order they worked their magic, they are:

The serving and former coppers, Andy Booth, Ross Coombs, Jen Gibbons, Simon Harradine, Sean Memory, Trevor Morgan and Chris Saunby.

Andrew Cochrane of Ellis Ropes Ltd. for talking me through the intricacies of bell-rope manufacture.

Elle Graham-Dixon for allowing me to borrow (and mess around with) the name of her supper club, Good Girls Eat Dinner.

My first readers, Sandy Wallace, who often sees and explains to me things I was only dimly aware of doing, and Simon Alfonso, my sternest critic.

My "sniper spotters": OJ "Yard Boy" Audet, Ann Finn, Yvonne Henderson, Vanessa Knowles, Nina Rip and Bill Wilson. My cover designer, Nick Castle. My editor, Nicky Lovick. And my proofreader, Liz Ward.

I also want to thank my wife Jo and my sons, Rory and Jacob, who are supportive, patient and forgiving as I run gory criminal scenarios past them at the dinner table.

Andy Maslen, 2019

COPYRIGHT

ALSO BY ANDY MASLEN

The Gabriel Wolfe series

Trigger Point

Reversal of Fortune (short story)

Blind Impact

Condor

First Casualty

Fury

Rattlesnake

Minefield (novella)

No Further

Torpedo

Three Kingdoms (coming soon)

The DI Stella Cole series

Hit and Run

Hit Back Harder

Hit and Done

Other fiction

Blood Loss - a Vampire Story

Non-fiction

Persuasive Copywriting

Write to Sell

100 Great Copywriting Ideas

The Copywriting Sourcebook

Write Copy, Make Money

ABOUT THE AUTHOR

Andy Maslen was born in Nottingham, in the UK, home of legendary bowman Robin Hood. Andy once won a medal for archery, although he has never been locked up by the sheriff.

He has worked in a record shop, as a barman, as a door-to-door DIY products salesman and a cook in an Italian restaurant.

As well as the Stella Cole and Gabriel Wolfe thrillers, Andy has published five works of non-fiction, on copywriting and freelancing, with Marshall Cavendish and Kogan Page. They are all available online and in bookshops.

He lives in Wiltshire with his wife, two sons and a whippet named Merlin.

AFTERWORD

To keep up to date with news from Andy, join his Readers' Group at www.andymaslen.com.

Email Andy at andy@andymaslen.com.
   Join Andy's Facebook group, The Wolfe Pack.

43368080R00366

Printed in Poland
by Amazon Fulfillment
Poland Sp. z o.o., Wrocław